FREEHOLD: DEFIANCE

FREEHOLD: DEFIANCE

EDITED BY

MICHAEL Z. WILLIAMSON

BAEN

FREEHOLD: DEFIANCE

"A Broader Skillset," © 2021 by Jamie Ibson; "Health and Safety Enforcement," © 2021 by Jonathon D. Green; "Trouble in Paradise," © 2021 by Kevin J. Anderson and Kevin Ikenberry; "The Humans Call It Duty," © 2007 by Michael Z. Williamson (first appeared in *Future Weapons of War*, edited by Joe Haldeman and Martin H. Greenberg); "Solitude," © 2021 by Jessica Schlenker; "Province of Man," © 2021 by Jaime DiNote; "The Strongest Link," © 2021 by Jamie Ibson; "Bidding War," © 2021 by Michael Z. Williamson; "The Bugismen," © 2021 by William McCaskey; "They Also Serve...," © 2021 by Michael Z. Williamson; "Replacements," © 2021 by Justin Watson; "Semper Malevolem," © 2021 by J.F. Holmes and Jason Cordova; "Fire in the Deep, Angel on the Wind," © 2021 by Christopher DiNote and Philip Wohlrab; "The Price," © May 2010 by Michael Z. Williamson (appeared in *Tour of Duty*, 2013, by Michael Z. Williamson).

All other content © 2021 by Michael Z. Williamson.

A Baen Books Original

Baen Publishing Enterprises
P.O. Box 1403
Riverdale, NY 10471
www.baen.com

ISBN: 978-1-9821-2536-3

Cover art by Kurt Miller

First printing, May 2021

Distributed by Simon & Schuster
1230 Avenue of the Americas
New York, NY 10020

Library of Congress Cataloging-in-Publication Data

Names: Williamson, Michael Z., editor.
Title: Freehold: defiance / edited by Michael Z. Williamson.
Other titles: Defiance
Description: Riverdale, NY : Baen, [2021] | Series: Freehold ; 11
Identifiers: LCCN 2021005964 | ISBN 9781982125363 (trade paperback)
Subjects: GSAFD: Science fiction.
Classification: LCC PS3623.I573 F7415 2021 | DDC 813/.6—dc23
LC record available at https://lccn.loc.gov/2021005964

Pages by Joy Freeman (www.pagesbyjoy.com)
Printed in the United States of America
10 9 8 7 6 5 4 3 2 1

For our families, who don't always understand us,
but tolerate and support us.

Contents

1   A Broader Skillset
Jamie Ibson

29   Health and Safety Enforcement
Jonathon D. Green

47   Trouble in Paradise
Kevin J. Anderson and Kevin Ikenberry

71   The Humans Call It Duty
Michael Z. Williamson

85   Solitude
Jessica Schlenker

99   Province of Man
Jaime DiNote

127   The Strongest Link
Jamie Ibson

155   Bidding War
Michael Z. Williamson

173 The Bugismen
William McCaskey

191 They Also Serve...
Michael Z. Williamson

215 Replacements
Justin Watson

247 Semper Malevolem
J.F. Holmes and Jason Cordova

271 Fire in the Deep, Angel on the Wind
Christopher DiNote and Philip Wohlrab

309 The Price
Michael Z. Williamson

333 About the Authors and Editor

A Broader Skillset

Jamie Ibson

September 207, Freehold of Grainne

Cecil Tanaka grounded his aircar on the pad outside his home, and his daughter Keiko raced from around the side of the house. Her brothers, twins Donal and Faolain, toddled after her.

"Daddy!" she shouted, and as he knelt to her level, she wrapped her arms around his neck. In that instant, he knew he'd made the right decision.

"Hiya, sweetheart." He kissed her forehead and hugged his boys. "How was your day?"

"Was good. Mommy chopped another chicken an' I gots to help."

"Is that so?" Tanaka asked with a raised eyebrow. "What did you get to do?"

"I collected feathers," Keiko said proudly, "And I frew da guts in da compost."

"Well done," he said and opened the door for his brood to head inside. His wife, Aoife, stood near the kitchen sink, and indeed she was holding one of their chickens, skinned and dressed, under the running fresh water. He eased behind her, wrapped an arm around her waist, and kissed an ear.

"Can you grill this up?" she asked. "I was going to roast it but lost track of time. We can do veg if you'll handle the meat."

"Sure." He nodded and headed to the bedroom to change out of his utilities. Once back into his civilian clothes, he took the chicken, cutting board and a knife out into the yard, to watch the kids "help" as he made dinner. Aoife and the kids pulled carrots,

1

onions, and peppers from the garden, and washed them as he lit the grill and butchered the chicken into kebab-sized chunks.

"Everything alright?" she asked. "You look deep in thought."

"Conflicted," he acknowledged. "Something at work today. They had . . . I dunno, five platoons? Six? Pulled from all over. Legion, Blazers, Support, it was a pretty big mix of troops. We'd been hand-picked for some kind of op. Seemed like intense, hardcore shit, they couldn't even tell me what it was until I'd committed."

"When do you go?" Aoife asked. Her tone was conversational; she was utterly calm and knew that a Blazer could be summoned away at any time. That didn't settle the heart pounding in his own chest, though. He lay the chicken on the wire grill, inhaled the sweet mesquite smoke and just listened to dinner sizzle for a moment.

"I'm not," Tanaka said. "I turned it down."

"You what?" his wife asked. This time surprise betrayed her.

"I had no idea how long it would take," he said. "I couldn't just disappear. If they could commit to 'a month,' then I would have considered it, but when he waffled on it maybe being a year, maybe never, maybe forever? That was too much. The guy calling the shots had me rattled a bit, and if I'm reading between the lines, someone high up thinks there's a shitstorm coming. If there is, I want to be here."

December 209

Sergeant Cecil Tanaka's comm blared an alert, and he glanced at the screen. Around him, every other squad leader's comm chimed in too. They were perched on the cliffs above an "occupied town," in reality an urban assault training ground. First Squad had already tied onto their assault ropes and Second stood by, ready to follow them down. For the exercise, Lieutenant Chandra had been KIA, and Senior Sergeant Laughlin was away on leave, leaving Tanaka the senior "live" NCO in charge of the assault.

:: All units 3rd Blazers, ENDEX. Ready all weapons for live use, vertol transport inbound, ETA 17 segs. Rioting in downtown Jefferson, details to follow. ::

He processed the abrupt change in orders, took a deep breath, and bellowed "END EX!" at the top of his lungs. "Two Fox, end ex! Team leaders, verify all troops have removed all exercise gear and weapons are live. Masaro! Get down there and blow us an LZ, we've got a wing of Bisons incoming! Donahue! Once you're down, set up a checkpoint and verify everyone, OPFOR included, has dumped their training adaptors and secured all blank ammunition. Prepare for real-world ops. Move now!"

Sergeant Masaro, Platoon Two Fox's Third Squad leader, spent half a seg personally verifying that all his troops were ready for real-world ops again. Once satisfied, they bounded down the cliff face headfirst. Company CQ was parked half a klick up the road, and they'd have all the demo Masaro's squad would need to blow a hole in the surrounding forest big enough to support a full flight of Bison landers.

Lieutenant Chandra had been "recovering" from his "wounds" under a bluemaple, observing his NCO's performance. Any NCO in the Freehold Military Forces had to be ready to take over one, possibly two rungs up the chain of command. Tanaka offered a hand and hauled his platoon leader back to his feet. "Welcome back to the land of the living, sir."

"Much as I appreciate being a 'casualty' and watching you work, it's nice to be alive again." Chandra grinned. "I'm sure your assault would have been beauty in motion. Now let's get down there and sort the troops out, shall we?"

Five big bounds later, Tanaka rotated in place to land on his feet and Chandra helped him step clear of the lines.

"The Caledonian judge awards a solid eight-point-six," Corporal Donahue said approvingly. Tanaka and Chandra handed their own training adaptors over, and Donahue stashed them with the rest. "All training equipment accounted for, we are good to go. The 3rd Mob element are going to be joining us, even though they're in OPFOR uniforms. Any idea what's going on?"

"Comm said 'rioting,'" Tanaka replied. "Five gets you ten it's those fool malcontents the aardvarks foisted on us. Has there ever *been* a riot in Jefferson? I wish the council had just spaced the lot of them like Naumann wanted to."

"No bet," Chandra said. "Doesn't matter. Confirm just how many vertols they're sending and how big the LZ needs to be. Once Masaro's got the LZ blown, organize the troops into chalks and be ready to load the moment the Sixes touch down."

✧   ✧   ✧

The scene below them was chaos. Tanaka's HUD illuminated friendly Legion units below them, troopers on foot backed by GUVs and MPs, ready to take prisoners. Comms chatter on multiple freqs washed over him, adding to his overall understanding of the battlefield below. He noted which Legion units were holding which streets, and where hotspots had popped up. He spotted one intersection below them where someone was dragging a protestor up a flight of stone steps, face-down, outside the Civic Center, leaving a blood trail in their wake.

"Apartments on fire," their pilot commed, and highlighted the building in question. 3rd Legion was already in motion, and Tanaka saw a squad of troops escort a fire suppressant truck towards the vulnerable building. He heard a gunshot, the familiar staccato crack of an M-5. Tanaka scanned the crowd, and sure enough, some of the Legion troops were in close contact with rioters who were pelting them with bricks, stones, and other abuse. A few rioters were laid out prone, probably wounded or dead. The Legion troops were holding the line, backstopped by the GUVs and their heavy machine guns. Tanaka saw one Legion troop shoot a man who had been rushing the line armed with a club or pipe. The man collapsed and grabbed at the soldier's knee once he was down, which earned him a swift boot to his wounded leg. These rioters were *motivated*.

Tanaka's comm buzzed, and he checked his updated orders from his Platoon leader.

:: Platoon Two Fox rifle teams, drop on rooftops. Clear top to bottom, ID trespassers, handoff to MPs. Weapons teams three, six and nine, backstop Legion troops on the ground and assist MPs. Once clear, rifle teams will recycle to Bluebird to lift again and repeat as necessary. —Chandra ::

Bluebird was tagged on his comm's map function as the rooftop of the Civic Center. The "Mobsters" from 3rd Mobile Assault Regiment, who'd been the "enemy" on Tanaka's field exercise now held it against any hostiles, and it had become the operations command post for the riot. Tanaka's map populated with areas of responsibility, and he claimed a street as belonging to Platoon Two Foxtrot. The pilot brought the VC-6 in low, low enough that the troops could dismount without ropes, and Donahue led Fox Five's half-dozen Blazers out the crew door. Turbines screamed, and the vertol lifted again to deposit Tanaka and Fox Two on the next apartment building over.

The Blazers stacked on the roof access door. The residents of the apartment used the roof as a social gathering area, judging from the lounge chairs and garden boxes. The building access was open, and Specialist Davis took point.

On the top floor, they advanced down the hallways, hammering on unit doors. "THIRD BLAZERS, EVERYONE OUT!" they shouted. One door flew open, a naked angry man standing there with a pistol in hand, another naked man cowering behind. Three M-5s pointed directly at his face and chest, and he lowered the gun immediately.

"Downstairs, now," Private Flores barked.

"What's going on?" the second man asked, his voice timid. Taking pity on the couple, Flores lowered his rifle and lowered his tone.

"You haven't noticed the *riot* outside?" he asked in disbelief, and the man shook his head in the negative.

"We've been busy," he said defensively.

"I can see that. Given the circumstances, put on some pants and shoes and wait in the lobby. You have thirty seconds. If you insist on bringing that piece down with you, please do so in a holster." Leaving Flores for security, the rest of the team moved on. As they cleared the third floor, their comm buzzed again but it was voice this time.

"*Two Fox Five, Two Fox Two, we have a situation, over.*"

"Fox Two, go ahead."

"*Fox Five, hostages, second floor, the building opposite yours. Aardvark scum surprised a resident and holed up on the balcony. They're not going anywhere for now, over.*"

"Fox Two, roger. Masaro, can your marksman get eyes on?"

"*Fox Six, standby.*"

A moment passed as their weapons team leader directed his marksman, below in the street with the MPs, to scan the balconies for the situation. Then Masaro came back over the platoon net.

"*Negative, Fox Six doesn't have a clear shot. Target is facing into the apartment, with the hostage between him and us.*"

Tanaka dashed back up one floor to an already cleared unit with Davis and cautiously approached the balcony. He spotted the dogfucker at once—some purple-haired punk with a dual mohawk and sleeveless vest top. Reddish orange, glowing, bioluminescent tattoos covered both arms, poked out at his collar, and covered his scalp. His one visible ear had been clipped several times along the edge, giving it a jagged, sawtoothed appearance. He held his teenage hostage between him and Fox Five, in the other building's hallway.

"I have a shot," Tanaka said and placed his scope's crosshairs over the dead man's neck. His finger took up the slack in the trigger while he willed his pounding heart to slow down. He took several deep breaths to steady himself and when the man leaned out, shouting something at Fox Five across the street, his head cleared the hostage and Tanaka squeezed the trigger.

The target dropped, limp, as Tanaka's 4mm round smashed through his brainstem. The hostage screamed and jumped away, but the tango was down and she was unharmed. A second later, Greg waved a hand through his balcony doorway, then stepped out and put an entirely unnecessary insurance shot into the aardvark punk.

"Nice shooting, Fox Two," Greg said, leading the young woman back inside, away from the rapidly spreading pool of blood on her balcony. "We've got her now."

"Roger," Tanaka acknowledged. "Resuming clearance."

On the ground floor, Donahue's team had already linked up with the rest of the team. The building manager identified three trespassers, and Masaro's weapons team led them away in shackles. The Legion troops had advanced their line as well and were holding in place until more Blazers could cycle through the buildings ahead.

"Once more, Sarge?" Donahue asked.

"Lead the way, Greg," Tanaka nodded, and the two rifle teams broke into a fast lope back to the Civic Center, to board another Bison and do it all again. *Couldn't have waited until after year's end?* Tanaka cursed silently to himself. *Just three more weeks and I'm done with their bullshit.*

February 210

"How long have you been doing this?" Cecil asked the wrecker driver. The driver was...distinctive. He wore a homespun linen tunic, heavy leather utilikilt, neo-Norse braids, and a high-vis vest. He moved with the sure ease of a professional as he set up his equipment.

"Bout . . . three, three and a half years," he replied, and flashed Cecil a grin. He lifted the ruined nose of the Maruto passenger van off the ground and started attaching the secondary safety cables. "Ain't no shortage of work for crashes and the like. You?"

"Just got out of the Third Blazers a month ago."

"Nice. I was First Combat Rescue, myself. Fenris Einarssen, of Einarssen Towing."

"I'd have thought you'd join the City Safety EMTs, with a résumé like that," Cecil replied. "Combat Rescue's hardcore."

"I had my hands in enough guts to know I'd had enough," he admitted. "If the EMTs need a hand they know I know what I'm doing, but I'd rather just be cleaning up wrecked cars instead of ruined bodies."

"Fair," Cecil agreed. This ridgeline was a bitch—it looked out over much of Jefferson, and he could make out the Heilbrun airfac tower from here, several klicks away. The field was buzzing with activity, with whole squadrons of Hatchet, Bison and Hummingbird vertols lifting and winging away.

The steep approach and equally steep descent made it a dangerous, blind ridgeline and they frequently had wrecks as people crested it at speed and collided with oncoming traffic. But, given the Freehold's utter lack of traffic control and the absence of a grid, you drove your ground car as best you thought for the conditions and took your chances. Locals, sick of having to divert around crash after crash, had erected caution signs and approached the crest with trepidation and care. Anyone not from the area who didn't realize how treacherous the hill could be ignored the signage at their peril. Tanaka had only been with City Safety for seven weeks but he'd already responded to four collisions on this hill alone.

Einarssen tapped some commands on his pad, and the cables went taut, and the van scraped as it lifted off the ground. While he did that, Cecil sat in his response vehicle, finished his form-work and sent all the details for the wreck to HQ, so City Safety could bill the offending driver (or their insurance) for the labor. He waved farewell to Einarssen and signaled that he was about to pull into traffic, when an FMF GUV "Jeeves" blew past him at high speed.

There goes more business, he thought, and stomped on the brakes *again* as two armored cars followed the GUV in the direction of Heilbrun. His comm rang. The caller ID registered a name he hadn't seen in a month and a half; not since his last day with 3rd Mob.

"*Sergeant* Donahue, to what do I owe—"

"Where are you?" Greg interrupted, his voice urgent.

"Panorama Ridge, what's going on?"

"Seek shelter, do it *now*. The UN's hitting us hard. We lost signal to Ceileidh, Green Door and Breakout within a few divs of each other and light-speed lag meant the Fleets barely got word before they started eating shipkillers. Orbital cover is *gone*. Get home, bunker up, and I'll come to you if I can."

"Wait just a—"

"*Sarge, don't fucking argue and trust me on this, alright*? I wouldn't have called if this wasn't a goddess's honest threat. They're fucking *invading*, and I'm still twenty segs out from Heilbrun by air. More people to comm, gotta go."

And then he cut the link.

Tanaka held his comm in his hands, weighing it as though it held Donahue's words. Greg had filled Tanaka's spot when he'd mustered out, and he knew him to be a solid, dependable troop. Could Donahue be wrong? Of course, he could—anyone *could* be wrong. But what were the odds?

Another flight of Bison vertols ripped by overhead, turbines screaming like the pilots had them redlined.

Oh.

At that very moment, a tearing sound ripped by overhead like the boom of a suborbital ballistic flight. Fiery streaks like Odin's own tracer fire tore great holes in Grainne's atmosphere. They were already past him, clearly travelling many times the speed of sound, and the orbital KEWs converged on Heilbrun like a time-on-target artillery salvo. Cecil looked away just before the bright flash of impact.

With spots in front of his eyes, he looked back. A dust cloud obscured the base now, and rapidly transformed itself into a mushroom cloud. More thunderous kinetic rounds impacted, adding their energy to the destruction. Air cars were flung off course, buffeted by the explosion and he saw at least one Bison lifter lose control, smash into a NavAid tower, and explode into a fiery wreck. Incendiary fragments rained down on the streets far below, but then he couldn't see anything else because the blast front swallowed and obscured everything behind it. A swirling ripple of atmospheric chaos and destruction emanating from the impact site uprooted trees, knocked down fences and structures, overturned cars and smashed everything in its path.

Cecil's issued ground car was a light, fast response vehicle, with little more than an EMT kit and an auto-doc. *Einarssen's wrecker, on the other hand...*

Decision made, Tanaka bailed out of the driver's seat and raced for the passenger door of the heavy truck. Einarssen saw him coming, and to his credit, realized what was going on. Tanaka vaulted up into the cab and threw on his restraint belt just as the pressure wave hit.

This far from the impact zone, the effect was mitigated, somewhat. The glass on the windshield resisted the blast front, but Cecil opened his mouth and covered his ears nonetheless to minimize the effects. The air pressure was brutal, as if he'd dove too deep too quickly, and the heavy wrecker rocked on its suspension. The machine tipped up on three wheels, then crashed back down onto all six, but at least gravity was still where it was supposed to be. Cecil was knocked around the interior of the cab and despite the belt, slammed against the door next to him, stunning himself.

He wasn't sure how long he lay there afterward. Long enough for secondary pressure waves to wash over the truck, but none of them rivaled the first. Seconds stretched for what felt like divs until all was quiet. When he sat up, he could see well enough out the badly cracked windshield to know the worst was over. Groaning, he looked over at the driver's seat. Fenris's forehead bled from a superficial gash, but he otherwise appeared unharmed.

"What in Goddess's name..." Fenris cursed. Tanaka summarized his call from Donahue, and the two men stepped down out of the wrecker to better see the damage the orbital strike had wrought. The ringing in his ears left everything muffled, like they'd been after the last Cabhag concert. The circle of devastation surrounding Third Army's primary base was evident from his vantage. Fires burned and smoke drifted into the sky, only to dissipate as air currents flowed and the wind blew, severely disrupted by the concussive force of the kinetic weapons. Small black dots in the air resolved to be foreign, fixed-wing aircraft. They roared by overhead, low and fast, and Cecil's blood ran cold when he recognized the distinctive silhouettes of UN Avatars and Sentinels, their interceptors and air-superiority fighters.

He checked his comm to call Aoife, but it had no signal. Whether that was because of an EW attack, the signal towers were down, or the explosion had damaged his comm, he didn't know. A wing of fat UN Guardian vertols flew by overhead, and he jammed his comm back into a pocket. One flared hard and began descending, far below him, down the ridge. Its tail end was uphill and its nose faced downtown. The tail ramp was already down, and Cecil could make out the pointy white snout of a UN ILAWAV, their Infantry Light Armored Wheeled Assault Vehicle.

"*Dogfuckers*," Fenris snarled, then pulled a heavy rifle from behind the driver's seat and slung it over his back. Cecil dismounted, and Fenris threw a jump bag with mag pouches at him, and then he pulled a comm of his own. With one command, the cables connecting the wrecker truck to the van released, and with another, the driver wheeled the massive truck out onto the roadway. Once the Guardian was below ten meters, Fenris gave his wrecker the command to punch the throttle up to one hundred percent, and free of its burden, the heavy truck shot forward. It barreled down the face of the ridge, closing with the unsuspecting Guardian whose pilots were facing the other way. The rear ramp touched down, and Fenris snarled out a triumphant "HAH!" as the wrecker smashed into vulnerable vertol. The heavy truck snapped one of the ramp hydraulics, leaped upwards into the belly of the beast, smashed into and through a stationary ILAWAV, sending both vehicles through the Guardian's cargo hold like a pair of wrecking balls. The interior frame bent, the additional mass overloaded one side of the carrier, and the whole vertol twisted violently sideways until it tumbled further down the steep hillside.

"Alright, Combat Rescue, I'm impressed," Tanaka said, and jogged down the hill, following the path of destruction. Einarssen followed, and moments later they were picking their way past armor plates, parts and people spread along a broad trail of carnage. Something had ignited somewhere, and the largest chunks blazed away, spewing acrid smoke. Cecil recognized one twisted heap of metal as having been the door for the cab of the truck with "—RSSEN —OWING" still legible, but the majority of the wreckage was still fifty meters distant.

One soldier in a UN uniform had been thrown clear and struggled to get to his feet. He bled from a gash on his forehead and lacked a sky blue UNPF helmet, having lost it when he was thrown clear. Seeing Tanaka approach, he cast about and dove for his rifle. Cecil slowed, and drew his custom Merrill Peregrine pistol and trained the sights on the invading troop.

"UNPF..." The soldier gasped and coughed. He spat blood, and Cecil suspected a punctured lung. "Stand...down."

"Lower your weapon, soldier," Tanaka commanded. "Your rifle is unloaded."

The soldier's eyes widened in panic and he raised the barrel skyward as his support hand sought a magazine from the pouch on his chest.

"Last warning." Tanaka's command voice was loud and clear. "Don't do this."

The soldier finally got the magazine free of his chest rig, and as he went to load the rifle, Tanaka shot him once in the head.

"Idiot," Tanaka spat and scanned in both directions to ensure there weren't any other survivors trying to flank him. He was pleased to see Einarssen covering his flanks with his heavy battle rifle. His rifle had been in the trunk of the City Safety car, so he needed a replacement. Tanaka stripped the dead UN soldier of his kit, loaded the rifle, chambered a round, and made his way down to the wrecked Guardian where a crowd was forming. As they descended, Einarssen confirmed to Cecil that yes, the tow yard had many damaged-but-functional multiton vehicles they could similarly use as ground-based missiles against UN troops. Tanaka and Einarssen verified that no one had any serious injuries, on-site or at home, and Cecil stepped up on the bent remains of an ILAWAV turret to address the crowd.

"Ladies, men, obviously the UN is invading. You all know what they've done over the last year, trying to stir shit up, sending us their criminals, malcontents, and scum. Make no mistake, this is a no-shit invasion and the regular FMF just got pasted. It's up to us to fight back. If anyone lacks a gun or ammunition at home, scavenge what you can here, but get gone before reinforcements arrive. If any of you wish to join us, bring whatever weapons you can quickly access and meet us at—?"

"Five-four-two Crow Lane," Fenris supplied. "That's the city's wreck yard."

Another Guardian, supported by a pair of light gunbirds, arrived on station and the crowd hurriedly dispersed.

Isaac Chow, one of the civilians in the crowd, led Einarssen, Tanaka, and another volunteer away from the crash. Chow had classically Mandarin features, a shock of black-and-purple hair shaved on the sides, and when they piled into his ground car, he pulled a load-bearing harness and a 7mm Merrill Gyrfalcon PDW from the trunk. He threw the vest on over his polo and slung the boxy weapon across his chest. The tropically colored kilt he wore was patterned like one of those tacky shirts they sold in the archipelago, complete with Grainnean palm trees. It was completely incongruous with the rest of the look, which seemed more like standard issue Ripple Creek than anything else. Cecil eyed the Gyr with a raised eyebrow—the subguns were standard issue for Special Warfare troops. Chow caught him looking, and grinned.

"A friend of a friend was raving about how great these little beasts are. It's a tack driver out to two hundred meters and cuts through soft armor like it ain't even there. You ever shot one?"

"Once or twice," Tanaka allowed. "A friend of a friend had one on Mtali. We spent a lot of time on the range turning ammo into smoke and noise. Or, just smoke," he said, gesturing to the suppressor.

They reached Chow's ride, and Fenris and Cecil piled in the back bench, ready to engage any targets on their flanks. A fourth they didn't know rode up front, as Chow pulled away heading for the tow yard. Five segs and eight turns later, it was clear the UN already had troops on the ground and were occupying the city with more success than they'd seen at Panorama Ridge. They'd spied one Guardian unloading, and it was evident each of the fat-bodied vertols held a self-contained Vehicle CheckPoint team: one ILAWAV carrier with a basic anti-air rocket packet bolted onto the turret, a mechanized infantry squad riding inside, folding dragontooth barricades, and razorwire. In moments, the infantry had the dragontooth barricades erected and were spiking razorwire into place to prevent all foot traffic from passing by.

Chow detoured around two checkpoints, and then hauled the wheel over to the left.

"Hold on!" he warned and mounted the curb to drive through one of the city's many well-manicured parks between two VCPs.

One soldier noticed them and opened fire; both passengers returned it with enthusiasm. That sent the UN soldiers at the whole VCP scrambling for cover. The suppressed shots were still loud inside the vehicle, but nowhere near as deafening as the blast front had been. Tanaka bumped his head on the ceiling of the car as they erupted from the grassy area, over the curb, bounced once, and caromed around a corner to disappear down an alley.

"Is anyone's comm working?" the man up front asked, and the rear passengers checked theirs.

"Still nothing!" Cecil confirmed.

"Nope!" Fenris said and pointed out the windshield at the works yard. "Drop us by the northeast corner and stay close."

"Solid," Chow agreed, and after passing one more cross-street, he slammed on the brakes. His three passengers bailed out, and they slipped down a parallel alley and jogged towards the yard.

"Name?" Tanaka asked the man who had sat up front as they approached the yard. "Where'd you work?"

"Mikael Gatons," the man said. He was young, perhaps fourteen Freehold years. He had shaggy ginger hair and a well-manicured beard, a stylish green collared shirt with gold thread and designer jeans. "Second Mobile Legion, signals. Just one hitch, I got out last summer."

"Any relation to Bjorn?" Tanaka asked.

"He was my uncle."

"He was a good man, taught me everything I know about climbing. Alright. All the vehicles here in the yard are damaged, but functional. Look for any models that can be remotely operated by comm so that we can use them as thousand-kilo missiles."

After a few segs of scouring the yard, each of them had wheels that could be written off at a moment's notice. Einarssen used his comm to open the gate, and all three filed out. Chow's vehicle emerged from a side street, and they found a quiet spot to park and scheme a few blocks away.

"Suggestion," Chow said and laid out his plan. It was only a kilometer or so back to the park, and he used his superior knowledge of the area to best effect. Armed with only the fraggiest of frag orders and a hastily set h-hour, Chow, Tanaka and Einarssen parked their vehicles behind an alleyway south of the VCP, while Gatons carried on westward for a few blocks before doubling back. Chow knocked on the rear kitchen door to a

Filipino restaurant that faced the park. The proprietor cracked the door open a sliver, a chrome semiauto shotgun leading the way.

"We're closed," he growled.

"Friendlies," Chow replied. "*Teman*," he repeated in Indonesian. The owner opened the door a bit wider. He was a short, darkly tanned man with salt-and-pepper hair who looked fierce behind his trench sweeper.

"What do you want?"

"Access to your rooftop," Chow said. "Then we'll be on our way."

"You're not going to get me killed by one of those . . . tank things, are you?" The owner eyed the guns the men carried dubiously, but that he was carrying a beefy shotgun of his own suggested he at least understood the risk.

"Honest answer, war is a dangerous thing and you can't know how things are going to go," Chow replied. "We certainly don't plan to get killed in the first div of the war, but then again, the enemy gets a vote too."

The restauranteur gave that some thought, and nodded, opening his door to allow the three men to slip inside. He closed the door behind them and locked it. He guided them up the stairs, and out onto the third-story roof. They stayed low, below the parapet, and watched the segs count down until, on cue, the former signals operator opened fire on the UN's position.

The response was fast, and dramatic. These troops had clearly drilled in urban operations before their deployment, and the UNPF infantrymen took cover behind the ILAWAV, firing from the prone beneath and between its road wheels. Gatons's opening shot had struck the troop manning the heavy machine gun in the turret, and the spray left on the turret's glacis when the gunner dropped out of view suggested he was dead.

"Light these dogfuckers up," Chow whispered, and the trio rose to their knees and opened fire.

The flanking maneuver caught the UN troops in an enfilade and five of the UN troops suffered hits before the remaining pair identified the new source of fire. Tanaka had been aiming for their torsos, and the UN rifle proved more than adequate to the task. Tanaka noted that Chow was going strictly for *headshots*, despite the range. As promised, his Gyr subgun proved extremely accurate, able to penetrate the trooper's sky-blue helmets or even slip beneath them to hit an unprotected throat. The unwounded pair ran for the rear access hatch and disappeared inside. A few moments passed, and then the turret rotated in place to target the trio on the rooftop.

"Shit!" Chow cursed, and the three on the rooftop scattered, throwing themselves prone. Heavy machine-gun rounds chewed through the plascrete railing, sending fragments and dust into the air. On cue, Gatons's salvaged ground truck barreled out of the street and struck the ILAWAV amidships. Like the wrecker versus the Guardian, the inertia of the heavy truck at high speed was catastrophic. The ILAWAV skidded sideways, struts and tie rods folded under the impact. It crushed the wounded UNPF soldiers behind it.

Shattered plascrete dust on the rooftop settled, and Tanaka cautiously rose to one knee. From his vantage, he watched Gatons emerge from the side alley's mouth, put insurance shots into several crippled UNPF troops, and retreat back down the alley again. Tanaka heard a wet cough, and turned to see Chow still prone, covered in grey plascrete dust—except for the dark stain in the center of his chest that was spreading all too quickly.

Einarssen muttered something about having his hands in someone else's insides again and tore open his own kit to get out dressings, coagulagent and a nano. Tanaka put pressure on the wound, and his hands were immediately stained crimson, but the blood was frothy, indicating a lung shot. Fenris checked Chow's back and confirmed the heavy machine-gun round had punched completely through.

"Fuckin' aardvarks get a vote too..." Chow gasped. "Figures, Murphy getting me killed...in the first div...of the war..." he coughed out. Then he lay back and went still.

"Shit." Fenris shook his head, looking at the medipack which, given the through-and-through wound, would have been wholly inadequate regardless.

Tanaka checked Chow's pockets for ID, in case he got a chance to notify the Veteran's Association, but all he found was a single challenge coin that read "Scout Shuttle Door Gunner" and on the reverse, "FMS Zulu." That clinched it, in Tanaka's mind. The Zulu was a SpecWar stealth boat, and although little was known about the ships, they did not have door gunners.

A plaster-coated Einarssen and a bloody-handed Tanaka, now carrying Chow's GyrFalcon subgun as a backup, met Mikael

Gatons by the rear door to the restaurant. Nothing needed to be said—they simply remounted their vehicles and moved on.

Tanaka's comm buzzed and he was pleased to see signal had been restored. It buzzed for a solid twenty seconds as a dozen messages and updates dumped into the device all at once. Most of the messages were from Aoife or Greg Donahue. He punched in Donahue's number first, and his former subordinate and friend answered on the first ring.

"Goddess, Ceece, we've been worried sick. I told you to head home, but since you're not here, where the hell are you?"

"I'm trapped on the far side of town with a couple of vets and there are VCPs everywhere. We've bloodied their nose a bit, but our luck's going to run out sooner than later." He explained what they'd been doing and asked about his family.

"Everyone's fine, everyone's safe for now, but obviously I can't guess how long that'll last. Let's meet me at Phill's at oh-dark-thirty and bring any of the City Safety fellows you trust. The aardvarks' lifters have been dropping cans down on the coast off Commerce Boulevard. We're going to kettle them and put the pressure on."

"Phill's, after sundown, bring friendlies. Roger, see you there."

"Oh, and write down any really important numbers on your comm and start scrubbing the history any time you make a call. If the UN gets its grubby paws on our comms, it will compromise us."

"Good point, will do. My lady there?"

"Here."

Aoife's voice came on the line.

"Will you be coming home?"

"Not yet. We'll see what Greg's people have in mind, but I'm worried if I come home, I'll put you guys all in danger."

"I'll...I'll get on the nets and speak to a couple of colleagues, see if there's anything I can do for them."

"So long as you're not going to get identified, sweetheart."

"I know what I'm doing, Cecil Tanaka, just as you know what you're about. Let me pass the phone around so you can tell your kids you love them."

One by one, Keiko, Donal, and Faolain shared the comm and wished their father good luck.

"Help your mother out, and I'll be home once it's safe for me to come back. Don't none of you go looking for mischief, as bored as you'll be," he commanded. "Love you all."

Phill's Mediterranean Grill specialized in Greek, Italian, and Middle Eastern cooking. Unlike the one by Hawthorne Park, it was a known, favorite spot of many Special Warfare troops. Tanaka, Einarssen, and Gatons made their way in one by one, darting from shadow to shadow until they slipped in the side door, which Phill had kindly left unlocked. Tanaka was relieved to see half a dozen more of his fellow City Safety colleagues, some veterans, some not, and more he didn't recognize at all. Spying Donahue near the raised stage, Tanaka gave him a quick wave and found a seat. The light was turned way down, leaving everything in shadows.

Once the entire group had met and fed, Donahue took control of the meeting. He spread a tourist's map of Jefferson out on a table, one that focused on the downtown core.

"For those of you who don't know me, I'm Sergeant Greg Donahue of Third Blazers. No, it's not a cover for me being an operative, as my recently retired boss Cecil here can attest." He gestured to Tanaka, who nodded but didn't interrupt. "Commander's intent, buy time for civilians to evacuate the conflict area before this gets completely out of hand—"

One of the others, a young man about Gatons's age, interrupted. "I'd say it's already pretty fucking out of hand, Sergeant."

The woman seated next to him elbowed him in the ribs, and he quieted down.

"Yes, it is, but we have several things going for us. The UN thinks it's occupying Jefferson but consider how many veterans have made their homes here in the Capital Region District. I have already discussed this matter with retired Senior Sergeant Hamilton and retired Sergeant Tanaka. *They* are stuck in here with *us*. We're going to put the screws to them and make them engage in bloody war for every square meter of ground. I'm going to ask the majority of the City Safety staff to continue what Blazer Tanaka's team began." Donahue identified several key intersections on his map and circled the region where the UN had been landing their cargotainers to establish their base. "Start plugging streets and alleys with vehicle wrecks, here, here and here. Use tomorrow to move the vehicles nearby, but just park them innocently for the time being. If the UN is establishing stationary VCPs, we can smash them at will while avoiding them as required. For now, we're going to let them set up their checkpoints like a baseball on a T-stand. Save a couple of large trucks for bridges, tunnels, and choke points, I especially want Riversedge and the south branch of the Frigid Ditch an uncrossable heap of rubble and shattered crystal carbon.

"Tanaka, I've sourced some proper fabbers and material. How quickly can you mock up, say, a thousand bogus anti-vehicle mines?"

Cecil thought for a moment. "Depends on how detailed you want them. For a simple polymer casing, I can have all the basic FMF designs laid out in half a div. After that, the only question is how much raw material I have and the fabber's limitations."

"You'll have them. We have access to...caches, caches with weapons, equipment, several different kinds of mines." Donahue turned to the rest of the group. "Pull all the utility covers and get them to Tanaka, and he'll have all the raw material he could need. Any live mines, we equip them with anti-lift devices so the UN can't just bulldoze them out of the way. The UN won't be using det-cord stringers to blow them all, not inside a city, so their progress in vehicles will grind to a halt, everything will be airborne or on foot. Meghan, I'll need you and your engineers to come up with a distribution plan around the UN shoreside base."

Retired Senior Sergeant Meghan Hamilton, who had elbowed Loudmouth, nodded.

"Otherwise, I want ongoing harassment ops, sniper fire, and I want them lost and confused, I want rocks pitched from balconies and I want intel on their leadership. We are now in the very definition of a target-rich environment, but we can't let them attrit us. Think of every dirty trick you've ever read about in any guerilla resistance situation for the entirety of human history and pull out every stop. Death by a thousand cuts, soldiers and veterans."

"What do you need from me?" a rasping voice asked from the corner. Tanaka hadn't noticed him at first, so silent and still, he'd remained in the shadows of the darkened restaurant, and Cecil shivered. He'd met Handler Corporal Brad Ministrelli once before, and meeting one of the combat leopard handlers often left an impression not soon forgotten.

"Did Elvis or Betty...?"

"No."

The hardened expression on Brad's face, and the laconic answer made it clear that Ministrelli was keeping his emotions locked down in a pressure cooker. After an awkward pause, Donahue continued.

"You and I will be securing our...absent friends' apartments, condos, homes, as many as we can. They might be gone, but anyone single should have space we can use to hide people or kit. Then start working the wider region outside Jefferson itself."

"There's a handful of decent, if banged-up air trucks at the yard," Einarssen offered. "They're yours if you need them."

"Works." Brad nodded. "I know for a fact Team Two was in the field, on exercise. The lieutenant's team is going to go dark, disappear, and they'll start working the problem independently. If I can make contact I will, but our primary field gig is recon. There's a whole heap of equipment they'd want before hunting in an urban environment. They'll be hard to find."

"Even if we can make contact, support will be as it happens. For now, start with anyone you know personally, and start building a net. Get a list of needs and wants, capabilities, and skills. Medics, armorers, fabrication specialists like Tanaka. Chemists, doctors, network specialists, hackers, science types, farmers, and farm supply. Beans are just as vital as bullets, maybe moreso. A broader skillset gives us more options."

"Dante Neumeier had a sister in Third SpecWar. He was outside Tani at Merrill base, but Lorin should be around. I think she's a reservist now and coaches Olympic biathlon. I'll look for her first and see who else she knows." Ministrelli got up from his table and slipped out the back.

Sixteen sleepless divs later, the UN had a functional, armored base established right on the coast. The headquarters sprung up on a bare patch of coastline adjacent to the East Sea, behind a triple wall of modular cargotainers, dropped tens at a time by massive interface shuttles. The invading UNPF engineers worked in a hurry, moving the modular 'tainers into an armored steel perimeter, while unloading their contents. Each 'tainer's walls opened to expose tents, preloaded bunks, machine tools, comms equipment, fuel bladders, pallets of lethal and non-lethal ammo, and more. Their new facility was a short distance from Jefferson Starport, along Highway One. The ground troops had quick access to the highway, the starport, and more troops, vehicles, and logistical support was ferried in-system by the div.

That meant Donahue's team of partisans had a target. They'd wasted no time, checked their maps, identified choke points, highlighted vulnerabilities, and concluded the Thomas McLaren Memorial Bridge had to go.

"Initiating in five!" Tanaka shouted from a second-story apartment balcony and was rewarded with a series of *whumps* when he hit the ignition. Two hundred meters distant, the grain truck transporting bulk breakfast cereal they'd parked beneath the bridge detonated with a convincing imitation of a fuel-air bomb. The sealed trailer tank made for an excellent pressure vessel, and the first concussive charge served to pulverize and aerosolize the highly flammable contents. The second, *incendiary* charge followed a bare fraction of a second behind; with the grain dust, oxygen, and spark, the trailer exploded, sending flame and thick black smoke out from beneath the bridge. As impressive as the fireball was, that wasn't the important part—the important part was that it was burning and would *continue* to burn for some time. Einarssen and Gatons hit the lights on their borrowed fire-suppressant pumper truck and parked a hundred meters back from the inferno.

A UN patrol headed down the freeway saw the smoke pouring out from beneath the bridge and sensibly halted in place. There was no civilian traffic on the freeway anymore, so after a near seg's deliberation, they reversed their course, returned to the nearest off-ramp, and followed the south Parallel Road to the underside of the overpass, where they found the pumper truck and two crew watching the blaze. The lead ILAWAV pulled to a halt and a field officer with a nametag that read "Gonsalves" disembarked, with two troops as "bodyguards."

"What are you doing?" Gonsalves shouted.

"We got word there'd been . . . an industrial accident," Gatons answered. "So we rolled out to respond, like we always do, but on the drive here it occurred to us you guys are supposed to be the new government or something. We had a contract with the City of Jefferson, but clearly, they aren't in charge anymore, so before we go involving ourselves in someone else's business, we need to be sure we're getting paid. I've heard about how you guys do things on Earth and we don't want to get blamed if UN property gets damaged, you know."

The O-4 Captain just stared at them for a moment, speechless, before he pointed an accusatory finger at them.

"PUT THE FIRE OUT!"

Einarssen, who was wearing the higher-ranking epaulettes, merely crossed his arms. "I'm afraid I'm going to need to see some kind of proof you can pay for our services, before we're going to do that, *sir.*"

One of the bodyguards racked the charging handle on his rifle and raised it to his shoulder.

"Do as the captain orders, now, you capitalist, mercenary scum!"

Einarssen and Gatons raised their hands in response, immediately. Tanaka, watching them through a rifle scope, noticed the guard *hadn't* had his weapon readied, *and* it was still on safe.

"I thought you were supposed to be here as benevolent liberators or something?" the retired Rescue Tech complained. "We'd like to help, but we have bills to pay, pump trucks aren't cheap, and the UNPF doesn't have any kind of account or credit established. Without the proper liability waivers and contracts signed, we could end up being liable for the bridge if we try to help without some kind of documentation. And if you *shoot* me, you ignorant *ape*, you're no closer to getting your problem solved and my dashcomm, which is streaming live to the net right now, will be proof you *executed me* out of hand. Put your gun down, *Private.*"

Behind them, the fire's effects started making themselves known, and a tarry, semi-solid chunk of plascrete the size of a car powerpack fell off the bottom of the bridge, crushing the cab of the truck.

"See? That's a problem." Gatons pointed to the rubble in the street. "Right now, we're just a couple guys with a pump truck at the right place at the right time. Sign the tablet, and we can get to work."

"Fine! Just . . . fine. Hold on." The officer spoke into his radio for a moment, then handed Einarssen the handset.

"Hello? Yes, this is Loki Mizchiffsen, contractor with City Safety's Fire Rescue team. Hello, sir, how are you? Not great, to be honest, this looks pretty ugly but we're going to need liability docs signed and—hold on, sir..." Another chunk of falling plascrete impacted on the roadway beneath the overpass. "Yes, sir, sorry, it's just I can't hear you over the bridge disintegrating. That's right, disint—it's collapsing, sir. Yes, sir, the McLaren Overpass, we're about two segs out from your headquarters. Yes, it's rather urgent, I'd suggest you send someone out to confirm what Captain Gonsalves here is saying, but maybe don't take the freeway, if you get my meaning? Sure, if you don't need to come out here yourself, you can send me a payment code to my comm, here's the number..." After another minute of wrangling with the senior officer on the other end of the radio, Einarssen managed to get three different UN comm codes, a thousand credits down-payment wired to an account, and the names of four senior UN officers, all good intel to pass up the chain. "Yes, sir, that's a good start, I'll call back if there are further issues."

Fenris handed the radio handset back to field officer and whirled a finger in the air to signal the "fire department" to move onto the next phase of their plan. The pair of them mounted up, and they wheeled the truck forward, but halted, and reversed in a hurry.

"What is it *now*?" Gonsalves demanded.

"Hazmat, sir! Look at the placards on the rear of that truck!"

The captain dialled up the magnification on his visor, and visibly recoiled when the *Radioactive* placard came into focus.

"If we roll in there and hose that truck down, we'll either cause an even worse explosion, or the evaporated particulate will get caught on the wind and everyone on your base is going to go down with cancer in another year or two. Your guys should probably get into their radioactive suits, you have those, right? We've probably already been here too long and need to go, like, *now*," Gatons said, looking worried.

"That doesn't make any sense," the UN officer objected. "If it was radioactive, our Geiger counters would be lit up!"

"Unless the fissible material on that truck was getting wholly converted into a less dangerous isotope because of the fire, which would mean slowing the reaction by applying water to it would spike the radiation and cause a runaway chain reaction!" "Loki" smoothly lied. It was entirely bullshit, but they didn't make nuclear physicists captains in the UNPF. "You might need to just let this one"—another chunk fell from the overpass, and daylight was cutting through the hole the fire had melted in the road surface—"burn itself out if your counters aren't registering anything. I'll refund your advance, sir, and call out the hazmat team." He made a show of checking his comm's time and brightened. "They should be able to get here in…a quarter-div or so."

"I don't speak Gray-annc-ian you idiot, how long is that in minutes?"

"Forty? Forty-five?" Einarssen replied. "The backup team is pretty spread out and comms have been spotty."

"Forty-five minutes for a *hazmat team?*" the officer cried. "There won't be a bridge left! Why so long? On Earth they'd be here in ten minutes, maybe less!"

"Well, they're the secondary, civil team, sir. The primary team operated out of Heilbrun base, but, well…"

That stopped the captain cold, his features frozen.

"Fine, call out the backup team," Gonsalves spat.

Fenris called Tanaka, who played the part of the backup team. Fenris did a convincing job of explaining just how serious this was, and then he passed the comm to Gonsalves.

"Thank you for respecting Mister Mizchieffsen's concerns, Captain. The ID numbers on those placards indicate that truck was hauling Lithium-8, a dangerously reactive isotope. As I'm sure you recall from science class in school, Lithium reacts even more violently with water, and attempting to put out the blaze with good old-fashioned dihydrogen monoxide would have only made things worse. Sit tight, my team is on the way, we're only twenty segs out. My colleague there will refund the deposit and we'll arrive with the proper documentation ready to go. Can you and your troops secure the scene until we arrive?"

"Yes, fine, he can go." The officer waved Einarssen away dismissively, and hung up on Tanaka. The fire truck departed without further issue, and the UNPF officer ordered his troops into their BCR suits, to check their Geiger counters, and to guard the underpass where the truck was still choking out thick black smoke.

Ten segs later, Einarssen withdrew the thousand credits in cash, closed the account, pulled the service chip from his comm and tossed the chip in the trash.

Ten segs after *that*, Gonsalves started to wonder where the hazmat team was. Five more segs passed before he tried to call the comm code Einarssen had given him but got an error. He was *still* trying to call "City Safety" back when the overpass completely collapsed.

A div later, Gonsalves's company commander was *not* impressed to learn that their freeway access had been severed by a truck full of cornflakes.

Three more days passed, and the Freeholders' deception, harassment, and delaying operations were in full swing. There had been more losses—Gonsalves recognized Gatons while he was out pulling yet more utility covers, and despite a chase through a suburban neighborhood, the UN team sideswiped his vehicle with an ILAWAV, wrecking it. They took Gatons prisoner, and the young signaller disappeared into the UN's already overburdened holding facility.

Gonsalves left the damaged truck in place, since the UN clearly couldn't trust anyone with a tow rig, and that night Tanaka lead a small team out to recover the stolen covers and retreated back to his shop. It was the first time since they burned the overpass that he'd left his fabrication shop, and it hurt that he was staying put, fighting the delaying action, rather than retreating from the city with Aoife and the kids. They'd fled the city for a friend's ranch a hundred klicks past Delph' and wouldn't return to the city until the UN was gone. A single handwritten note, passed from Aoife to Minstrel, to Donahue, and on to Einarssen finally wound up in his hands.

We're safe. Do what you must, the Freehold needs you. We'll be okay.

All our love,

It hadn't been signed—that way, if somehow the paper was intercepted, it wouldn't provide the UN with any details on who it was from or to whom it was addressed. And worst of all, she was right. As a combat pioneer, he'd been trained as a fabrication specialist, building tools and equipment on the fly for Blazer assault groups. He carved up the dense polymer access covers and broke them down into all manner of things. Imitation mines of a half dozen designs and colorations. Urban assault prybars. Hollow-tipped caltrops and spike belts for heavy-duty vehicle tires. Disposable polymer knives, hatchets, and tomahawks, which would escape notice with rudimentary metal-detection equipment.

He even took some of the access covers, sliced them thin like a butcher would a salami, and had the covers returned, one-eighth as thick as they'd been. The brittle polymer would crumble and shatter as the heavier armored UN vehicles rolled over them, turning into deadfall pit traps. He even had a plan to rig them with explosives once the UN got around to making "checking the covers" an SOP.

As saboteurs trickled into his little fabshop, Senior Sergeant Hamilton issued the equipment, the assignments, and the routes, with sources, feeds, livestreams, and apps sending real-time info to amend plans on the fly. Cecil was flexing his brain, developing more and more devious ways to harass and hurt the people who had invaded his home.

Speaking of flying...

Fenris dropped the last of his most recently stolen utility plates on the stack and came over to see what Tanaka was giggling about. The design itself was simple, the physics were well within structural tolerances, and the results would be devastating. "You're grinning like Loki is whispering in your ear."

"You would know, Lord *Mizchiffsen*," Cecil replied. "Witness, the ultimate clay pigeon thrower."

"What...wait, how big is—"

"Big enough to throw access covers," Tanaka cackled, "which I'm hereby renaming Cecil's Flying Frisbees of Doom. Two passes on the lathe carves the edges into an aerofoil, like a chakram or a discus. The arm spins, and centripetal force slides our ten-kilo pigeons down the length of the arm. Four revolutions later, it lets fly at two hundred meters per second. The whole thing folds down under a cover in the bed of any air truck with landing jacks. You have any idea how many air trucks with landing jacks exist in this city?"

"You mad bastard," Fenris breathed. "It's glorious."

"You damn betcha," Tanaka replied with a half-crazed grin on his face. "I've got one last little upgrade to make to the killer frisbees themselves, and then we need to test them out, somewhere quiet, away from aardvark eyes. I need to tune the aerofoil for maximum lift, minimize wind effects and measure the ballistic arc. A good ways south, along the coast, I think, where I can lob a few out to sea to calibrate the aiming device."

✧   ✧   ✧

Private Darryl Payette was not at all happy with his first week on Grainne. They'd promised him a quiet rotation of mostly guarding the gate to the Jefferson base. It would be straightforward, they'd said. Land with an overwhelming show of force and begin civil-military cooperative ops to restore a proper socially democratic government. One week in, though, he'd already watched a dozen heavy urban patrols roll out, the quick-reaction-force lift off shortly afterwards, and survivors straggle back in. *Most* of the time. Without the freeway intact, they had to divert through the city, where the streets had live and bogus mines scattered, rooftops concealed snipers, and people dropped rocks, big heavy rocks and boulders, from balconies.

He already despaired how he was going to survive another six months of this. No one had attacked the base itself just yet, but duty squads had quickly been escalated to duty platoons nonetheless. It was nearly midnight, Earth Zulu time, and it was time for his platoon to muster in the yard for their assignments. That the local sun, Io, was rising in the east, was an artifact of the planet's twenty-eightish-hour day.

He saw it coming first, in the third rank behind his platoon mates. Movement in the corner of his eye caught his attention, and he looked up. At first, it looked like the nose of one of the fat-bodied lifters, ferrying equipment to and from orbit. But the scale was wrong. Whatever it was, it was arcing in towards them, silently, and getting larger in a hurry.

"INCOMING!" he yelled and broke formation to run for cover behind one of the heavy armored cargotainers. Not everyone reacted quickly enough, and the disc, a meter across, cleared the now-double-stacked cargotainer wall, hit the dirt and *skipped* like a rock on a pond. It took out Sergeant Second Class Northington at the knees; the projectile pulverized his legs, swept them out from under him, and carried on to take out Corporal Higgins next. Higgins went down with a flailed chest, and then it was up on its side and rolling until it hit the 'tainer where Payette had hidden. The troops scattered for cover, and Lieutenant Cho screamed for a gunship to provide overwatch. A second disc crashed through the base, smashed everything in its path and crushed Lieutenant Julie McCoy's hand below the wrist.

When all was calm, a skywatch was up, and there were no more of the *things* flying in, a wounded and angry Lt. McCoy ordered Payette to examine the disc. Payette looked curiously at the top, which read "CITY OF JEFFERSON" around the perimeter. Flipping the disc over, he was puzzled by the shallow, perfectly circular dinner-plate-sized dome centered underneath. He rotated it until the text on the dome was upright.

"FRONT TOWARDS U.N.P.F."

The mine exploded, and Payette's tour of Grainne came to an abrupt end.

Cecil knew he could only get away with such an over-the-top overt attack so many times. His Flying Frisbees of Doom had an effect all out of proportion to their actual deadliness, and the UN hunted the airtruck carrying the launcher with vigor. It was clunky, inefficient, and brutal, so of course it immediately went to the top of the UN's hit list, as though its mere existence somehow threatened their #1 rank in all three categories. Cecil could see their Most-Expendable-Private cringe through the spotting scope, as the kid reached for the "cornered" airtruck's door latch. He was right to be scared. Fenris had abandoned it on a skyscraper's rooftop and when the young Aardvark opened the cab door, the truck detonated and his constituent parts were blown out into open space, twenty stories up.

Cecil, a kilometer away on a different rooftop, tucked away his spotting scope into his briefcase. He might resurrect the FFoD launcher someday, just to give the UNPF troops flashbacks once they'd relaxed a smidge. For now, it was time to get home to his wife and kids. He abseiled down the office skyscraper's unpowered, unused elevator shaft, tucked his harness away, and met Greg Donahue outside in a ground truck. Tanaka slipped into the passenger seat and flashed Donahue a wordless thumbs-up. Donahue threw the truck into drive, and threaded their way through alleys and side streets, avoiding arterial roads and frequently open utility access points.

Donahue asked, "You ready to shift your AO? I promised your lady I'd see you home safe and sound once the initial crush was over. If it's not now, it's never, and I am vastly more frightened of Aoife Tanaka's wrath than I am of the UNPF."

"Fair," Cecil conceded. "Put it that way, *I'm* doing *you* the favor."

"Yes, you are," Donahue said with a wry grin, and pulled

the truck over. "You know how to reach me. Keep those fabber designs flowing and stay safe."

Donahue shifted into park behind an air truck. It bore brackets on the sides to hold branding placards, allowing for quick and easy changes. Cecil admired their graphic designer's work, for a moment. The side plate read "Business Occupational Health Inspection & Compliance Agency"—BOHICA—and the logo was stylized enough to make one wonder if it was intended to be quite that... phallic.

Brad Ministrelli had adopted a form of urban camouflage—a business suit, this time—and leaned against the door, ready to whisk Tanaka away to the anonymous wilds. His face was solemn, emotionless, like a mask. They lifted without a word and were ten minutes out of Jefferson before the handler spoke.

"Serious question—did you actually destroy a freeway overpass with *cornflakes*?"

Tanaka allowed a smirk to cross his face. "It was a team effort, but, yeah."

Health and Safety Enforcement
Jonathon D. Green

Communications Specialist 2nd Class Clara Chabron spoke clearly and calmly into her headset. "Grainne Station Andersen, this is the UNCS *Maria Cutchet* on approach. Please respond. We will be docking to perform HSE inspections and an initial provisional census to better provide for your needs. You are required to comply with this action and any follow-on actions as directed by our inspectors."

Cutchet was a flagged and armed transport of the Bureau of Health and Safety. This was the start of a Health and Safety Enforcement inspection of the Grainne system's primary asteroid track habitats. Anderson Station was a "burrow" or partially hollowed asteroid mine that produced metals for the Grainne Colony's industries. Once the petty junta of the fascist oligarchy was suppressed, the residents of this asteroid would be producing minerals for the colony's expansion under UN direction. Captain Balza was confident that the fighting part of this police action would be over in a matter of days and once the citizens no longer had to fear the moneyed power of the former rulers, reintegration would go swiftly. Clara hoped he was correct, but she was getting worrying reports from some of her Bureau Academy classmates about the planetside resistance and the problems they were encountering. The previous ship on this duty, the UNCS *Enrique Casas*, had been destroyed after it collided with another habitat. Clara wondered how that was even possible, but not being one of the ship handlers, she figured that someone had failed to properly follow docking procedures and catastrophe had resulted. With a Nordic-pale hand, she fussed with one of the soft rubber

29

beads at the end of the cornrows hidden under her hijab, then repeated her call to the asteroid.

"How much of what happed to the *Casas* have you heard?" asked her tablemate, Machinist 3 Geoffe Galloway. He was a large and gregarious man who barely met the HSE physical fitness requirements for shipboard duty. He was looking at her with a strange expression on his darkly tanned face. They were seated at one of the mess deck's conversational tables. The cheerfully bright lights from the overhead glinted off the polished white surfaces. If not for the omnipresent vibration of the ship's engines and the obtrusive labeling of vacuum safety lockers, they could have been at any of the military dining facilities on Earth. The other clue was that there were no chairs, only stools bolted to the decking.

"I heard that they collided with the Connover Habitat and were lost with all hands. And the population of the habitat," said another tablemate, Inspector Ngome Battu. She was a tall and slender Kenyan who worked in the ship's training certification office and was the lead Health and Safety Inspector on the ship.

"Yes, but why did they collide with the habitat?" Geoffe asked. Clara suddenly recognized the expression that was foreign to his face. Worry.

"They probably failed to hold enough distance from the habitat and gravity took over." Battu shrugged. "The pilot probably needed to be recertified and lied about his currency. It's the innocents his failure killed that are the true victims. This is why I keep on you both to keep your records up to date."

"That's not how it works. This wasn't on a planet where there is gravity. How does a modern ship with modern equipment collide with a stationary habitat?" Geoffe shook his head, "I heard from a buddy planetside that it was not a habitat, but a Grainne military base, and they blew themselves up rather than surrender." He looked around nervously. "He also said that there was no record that it was a military facility. Who knows how many more bases like that are out there?"

"Your 'friend' needs to be spending more time on their duties and less on rumormongering," Battu said. "I think that, if that rumor was true, then that is all the more reason for our intervention in this system." She gestured profoundly with her spork, "If there was a secret military facility hanging over the heads of the oppressed peoples of this colony, then that would explain the fanaticism our troops are encountering. They are fighting for their lives, because if they don't their overlords would simply drop a rock on them."

"Then our job of inspecting and certifying these habitats is even more vital." Clara nodded, quoting the recent interview from one of the Civil Affairs pundits. "The more of these locations we make safe, the less threat is hanging over the heads of those we came here to help."

"Exactly." Battu looked sternly at Geoffe when he chuckled.

"I agree," he said, raising a hand in surrender. "I'm just repeating what I heard from a friend. But you're both right that our work here is vital to the effort."

"You should spend less time repeating what you heard, and more time staying current on your qualifications. I noticed that you need to update your SHARP compliance within the week. Shall I schedule you for the afternoon seminar tomorrow?" Battu held his gaze for a long moment.

"I have the duty tomorrow afternoon, can I do it the day after?"

"It is either tomorrow afternoon, or you will be out of compliance because the next scheduled seminar is in two weeks."

"Then I guess I'll get someone to cover my shift tomorrow and be in the seminar." Geoffe grumbled and glared at his tray. Battu was being petty, Clara thought, but she didn't want to get on the wrong side of the person in charge of her personnel records. That could cost her a needed promotion or award at a critical point in her career.

"Since you are watching out for us, is there anything I need to get current on?" she asked.

"Not so long as you keep up with the correspondence course on cultural sensitivity." Battu smiled at Clara. "Now I think that we should all concentrate on our meals and then get back to work."

Clara reviewed the communication logs from her lunch break and several responses back from the habitat. This was confusing as they were on different frequencies and all claimed to be coming from separate groups, all claiming that they were the true leadership of the habitat.

Fuck off, you Aardvarks! We don't want your kind here! a brash young female voice screamed at them, on one channel.

This is the Resplendent People's Commune of Celestial Peace.

Please join us at docking bay B2 for our welcoming ceremony, said an elderly male voice.

Maria Cutchet, this is Baker Space Mining, Pull alongside and dock at Gantry Nine. I'll have one of the kids run you back in a skiff and we can talk about your plans, a woman's voice intoned in a bored manner.

UNS Maria Cutchet, this is Andersen Control, we have you on our screens, and will direct you to use vector Able-Victory-Niner in the appended chart. You should also monitor this channel for periodic course updates, we have several ore containers on ballistic courses that might intersect this plan. Please note that we are not rated for direct docking of a ship of your class, please stand clear One Zero Kilometers from Bay Zero Able and use lighters to transfer between yourself and our station. A bored male voice came from the speaker. *Cutchet, Andersen Control, be advised that there are some personnel on station with private comms who may try to contact you. They are not authorized to give guidance and vectoring. Nor are they affiliated with the Station Advisory Board. Andersen Control, over.*

UN Ship on approach to Habitat GA1-8985564, Stay away! This station has had a biohazard containment vent and you need to note us as such on the charts. Please Gods, stay away, I don't want to see this happen to another human being! This from a tremulous male voice.

This is Major Thomas Kinkade of the Democratic Separatist Revolution! Please be advised that we are the true government of this asteroid, and need your help suppressing a Grainne rebel-sponsored terrorist cell. Send an armed shuttle to Airlock 7 and I'll put your men to use. Another male voice, gravelly and sure of command.

UN Ship, I am Arch Druidess Shenan Kinkade, of the Druidic Space Republic. My husband has attempted a coup and is trying to oust me from power. I do not have ties to the Freehold, other than my residency fees. I beg you do not fall victim to his power grab. He is the one with ties to the Freehold military and he is attempting to ambush you! Dock at Airlock 6 and I'll personally welcome you aboard. Another woman's voice, scared, but full of conviction.

Unidentified object at heading 351-mark-213, cease approach or you will be terminated. This was a mechanical computer-generated voice.

Clara stared at her console in shock. Were any of these responses legitimate? Or was the habitat full of insane people?

"Captain Balza, I have a wide range of responses from the habitat. I'm unsure which is from a legitimate authority." She spoke to her commander.

"Thank you, Ms. Chabron. I'll let Mr. Mallory sort this out. We still have the better part of an hour before we need to dock. Please route the logs to the First Officer." His voice held a note of amusement. As if one of his junior subordinates was unprepared for their job and was actually willing to admit it.

"Aye, sir," she replied and packaged up the logs and transferred them as ordered to the ship's first officer.

"Specialist Chabron." The ship's first officer, Mister Denzel Mallory's voice came across her headset. "Please contact Andersen Control and ask them to clarify what vector we should be on. I think that they are the closest thing to an authority on this habitat."

"Aye, sir, Contacting Anderson Control for clarification of vectors."

"Thank you, Ms. Chabron." His voice held no amusement, only businesslike approval of a subordinate doing their job.

"Andersen Control, UNS *Maria Cutchet*, on approach, please clarify our approach vector."

Maria Cutchet, Andersen Control, Approach vector is Able-Victory-Niner as shown in our transmitted ephemeris, hold fast at one zero kilometers from bay zero able. Contact Andersen FlightOps on channel Point niner-five for lighter operations. Andersen Control, over. The same bored voice, rattling off the requested information with neither urgency or hesitation.

"Mr. Mallory." She contacted the first officer. "They repeated the vector and hold off, and advised with communication channel for local flight operations for the shuttles."

"Excellent. Monitor the habitat for further broadcasts, but only speak to Andersen Control or Andersen Flight Operations. I think they are obviously the representatives of the habitat's leadership."

"Aye, sir."

Over the next three hours of the approach, Clara monitored all the transmissions from the habitat and wasn't sure what she was listening to. The DemSepRev allied with the Church of Resplendents and attempted to enlist the aid of the research station in their fight against the Druidic Space Republic. In retaliation, the DruSpaRep courted the mining company and the automated warning system. The young woman whose original transmission was the first received continued to spew profanities and blamed the UN ship for all manner of atrocities. Andersen Control and Flight Ops were consummate professionals seemingly unaware of the hostilities brewing under the surface of the habitat.

"I don't know how these groups have been able to survive out here so long. If half of the accusations between the various groups are credible, then we may have to request an intervention company to keep the peace once the census is over," she confided in Geoffe.

"How likely is that to happen?" he asked. The original concern she had noticed in his manner earlier was more pronounced.

"I feel confident that we could get troops here relatively quickly. Captain Balza has some pull with General Huff. He thinks that it is unlikely that we will need them though. If we can get in and see what is really going on, we should be in better position to clear this up." She looked at him. "What have you been hearing that has you worried?"

"We keep getting painted with low-level targeting radars. It's intermittent and low strength, but it's almost constant. Why wouldn't that be worrying?" he stated abruptly.

"I told you when you asked me about it, that those aren't real targeting radars. They are surplus radars used by the miners to register claims and function as navigation beacons. Captain Balza had me ask Andersen Control about them when we started picking up the pings." She sighed, shaking her head. "If they were an actual threat, why would they be targeting us and not firing?"

"We might not be in range of their weapons? They might want a better flight profile on us to better target critical systems? I don't know, from what I hear from my buddies groundside, they are vicious fighters and have no respect for the rules of war. They hide troops among the civilians and carry out terrorist attacks against noncombat troops."

"Where are you hearing about terrorist attacks?" Battu asked, walking by the table.

"Nowhere." Geoffe quickly looked down at his tray. Battu chuckled low in her throat and murmured to him.

"Come by my office when you get off duty. I can schedule

a private seminar to make sure you are current." She laughed a bit louder and then sauntered off.

"What is going on between you two?" Maria asked.

Geoffe grimaced and bit into a twist of vat-protein. "She informed me that due to low registration numbers, tomorrow's SHARP seminar has been canceled and I'm automatically registered for next month's."

"Doesn't that mean you will lose certification for a few weeks?"

"Yes," he snarled. "But she told me that I would need this seminar to get myself up to date before this deployment. I laughed and said that there was always a SHARP seminar on the calendar. Once we were deployed and she didn't have to abide by the base calendar, she canceled all the seminars so I would lose that certification." He sighed, poking at the food on his tray. "I thought it was simple power games, and that at worst, I'd owe her a few maintenance favors for her to schedule an emergency seminar."

"Was that what she meant by coming by her office after you are off duty? That almost sounds like she's trying to ..."

"Yes, she is going to use this to put me in a compromising situation, and then threaten me with a SHARP violation if I don't come across."

"She canceled training seminars to get you to sleep with her?" Clara was shocked.

"Yes."

"You need to report this!" Clara hissed at him.

"There are two problems with that," he said, raising a finger on his right hand. "One, *she* is the SHARP Compliance Officer. All the complaints and problems end up on her workstation.

"Two," he raised another finger, "I'm not the most handsome man on the ship by a fair number. She's female and attractive, so they'll assume I'm the aggressor."

"But you could use me as a supporting statement." Clara gestured to herself. "I could say I heard her threaten you."

He shook his head and sighed. "No, because then you would be on her shit list, and you don't want that. And remember from your SHARP training, all the advances come from men. Women are not the aggressors. There is no way to write a SHARP complaint that has a female aggressor." Geoffe gestured with his utensils.

"Why would she even do this?" Clara asked, dejectedly.

"Because Ngome Battu is addicted to power. I flouted her

power by not taking the course on her schedule. Now, I pay the price of this *'Oppression.'*" Geoffe pushed the food on his tray around a little more, then sighed.

"You need to be careful of her, Clara. Learn from my errors, before you make your own."

Clara found it unsettling, especially since Battu had casually mentioned to her that it wouldn't look good for the ship if the communications specialist wasn't current on her cultural sensitivity training.

"I think I need to get some rest before we close with the habitat," she said, hastily clearing her half-eaten tray from the table.

The next morning brought new and interesting conversations from the habitat. Apparently, overnight, as the *Maria Cutchet* slid closer to the habitat, it had experienced significant changes.

"UN Ship, this is General Shenan Kinkade of the Dominius Spiritual Reserve. Do not continue your approach. You are suspected of being in collusion with the heretical forces of the Democratic Separatist Revolution. We will not tolerate outside interference in our internal issues."

"*Maria Cutchet*, this is Sifu Kinkade, of the Reformed Scientific Directorate. Despite my wife's claims, we are a peaceful commune seeking only unity with the great void. Please join us in bringing this truth to the habitat."

"Incoming ore hauler *M. Cut*, welcome to Benzel Foundry. Please send a manifest and we can get you a good slot in the foundry queue."

The tide of change progressing through the situation on the habitat began to crash together more often as the UN ship moved closer. First it was the struggle between the Kinkades, which grew to encompass other factions, then there was some base ideology shift and it became less about politics and more about some strange religious schism. Then it became some bizarre conflict between contentious academic communities over how a common word was defined in a scholarly paper. It was a whipsaw of alliances and escalations and shifts in ideologies. Clara could barely keep up with who was espousing what position at any given moment.

Even more frustrating was that when these changes stared impacting the normally bucolic communications of the Traffic Controllers. At first the changes only caused slight variations in the approach, traverse around this orbiting beacon on a portside track, as opposed to a starboard track from a previous communication. Over rather than under, all small and trivial differences. As they got closer, the conflicts caused more significant changes. Divert to a different track for several markers then come back to the original flight plan, to avoid an incoming ore hauler. Change to a different track completely, and approach from a different angle. Divert almost completely away from the habitat, circle around at a massive distance and reapproach from an almost opposite direction. Sometimes the ship's sensors could detect another ship in the vicinity to explain the diversion, sometimes they could not.

As she relayed these directives to the captain or the first officer, she saw that their frustration with the situation grew. She had to relay a request from them back to the traffic controller for expedited approach to the habitat so that they could help sort out the situation. Each time the request was denied, with either no reason given, or some seemingly reasonable situation that required the course change. When the decision was made to disregard one of the diversion commands, they were quickly contacted by Andersen Control with warnings that they were entering an area of space filled with navigational hazards. The captain immediately corrected onto the new course, and the dance began again. Another meaningless diversion, and the decision was made to ignore the directions. Again, there was a navigational hazard indicated. This time, the captain studied the charts and decided that there was no real hazard on the track. Ignoring the calls from Andersen Control, the ship was directed on a supposedly clear track to close rapidly with the habitat.

Fifteen minutes later, the close approach radar lit up with multiple small objects directly in their path, all of which were moving fast enough that they posed a real threat to the ship. Some of them would be deflected by the particle shielding, some destroyed by defensive weapons, but not all of them. A significant fraction of the objects were on a vector to intersect with the *Maria Cutchet* and were sure to cause significant damage.

"Damn and blast!" the captain swore, his calm reserve frayed by the preceding day's worth of seemingly random course changes and directions from the habitat. "Denzel, where did those come from?"

"I don't know, sir," Malloy said. "Ms. Chabron, please contact traffic control and ask where those rocks came from."

"Aye, sir!" Maria responded.

"*Cutchet* to Anderson Control, Where did those hazards come from? They were not logged in your advisory."

A completely new voice spoke in response. "*Cutchet*? Who are you? And this isn't the channel for Anderson control. This channel is most often used by the local miners to run roleplaying games or community theater."

"Excuse me? What?" Her voice was incredulous. "I've spent the better part of two days following directions on this channel from someone claiming to be Andersen control." The first officer and captain were now looking at her, only hearing half of the conversation. "We have been getting detailed approach vectoring from them." She didn't mention the newly discovered fictional schismatic struggles on the habitat.

"*Cutchet*, someone has been pulling your leg. Phase shift the channel by four points and refresh your encryption keys. That should put you in contact with the actual controllers." The barely contained laughter was bubbling in the voice. "I have to say that I wasn't sure who the new player on the channel was, but you precipitated a massive new storyline. Thanks for the inspiration and the laughs. Lorekeeper clear."

"Ms. Chabron," the captain ground out. "What is going on?"

"Ah, Captain, it seems that we were given the wrong communication protocols for this habitat. We have apparently been interacting with a community theater troupe during an improv event. I have the new protocol and will be contacting the habitat momentarily." Sweat dripped down her spine as she rapidly changed her com settings to match the new information.

"Grainne Asteroid Habitat Andersen Station, this is the UNCS *Maria Cutchet* on approach. Please respond."

"Maria Cutchet, Anderson Station, glad to finally have you on comms. Would you kindly explain your approach vectors, and the transponder squawk. I'm sending a plot of them from our position and would greatly like to hear your reasoning for this approach. Also, perhaps why you decided to fly through the edge of a marked VDAM field?" a vacuum-cold voice responded immediately.

"What do they mean by explain our vectors? And what marked VDAM field?" Mr. Mallory murmured.

Clara glanced at the vector plot the station sent and froze

at the image on her screen. She heard faint murmurs from the astrogation section, then a sharp intake of breath.

"Ms. Chabron?" the captain asked.

"Sir, it appears that the vectoring that we were given was an extension of the theater. And that certain parts of the local charts that we were sent were redacted."

"And what makes you say that?"

"Sir, we apparently drew an object with our flight path, and were intended to fly into a Volume Denial Dispersed Mass Weapon effect," came a response from the astrogator.

"Son of a . . ." the first officer choked out from his own station. He could see her screen and the image of crudely drawn phallus on the screen. Tagging the flight path was a transponder note "Kess Ommak."

"I think apologies are in order." The captain spoke. Clara was unsure who was going to be apologizing, but she was sure that there would be a lot of them. "I think I will speak with the station directly."

"Yes, sir."

The captain had a long and fruitful discussion with the actual Station Control and the ship was vectored to the station soon afterward.

"UNS *Maria Cutchet*, Anderson Control, please be advised that any and all personnel who wish to enter sovereign Freehold of Grainne space will need to submit to basic entry exams or at least provide records from Ceileidh Station that you have gone through entry scans. Anderson Control, over," the new controller advised once they were at approximately twenty kilometers from the station.

"Anderson Station, *Cutchet*. The so-called Freehold of Grainne was a rogue state and the UN is reasserting civilized control over this system," the captain responded. "You are required by UN Charter to submit to our inspection and census so that your needs can be provided for."

The signal was silent for several minutes.

"*Cutchet*, Anderson. Fine. If you want access to our hab, you get a screening. We are a healthy and clean station, and I'd like to keep us this way. Anderson, over."

"Anderson, *Cutchet*. You do not get to dictate terms to duly authorized representatives of the UN. We are the ones in charge.

You will direct our shuttle to a docking point and cooperate fully with the census team. Do you understand?"

More silence for several moments then, "*Cutchet*, Anderson. *Murum Aries Attigit*. Received. Vector your shuttle to Docking bay Alpha 02."

"And that, Mister Mallory, is how the UN deals with uppity civilians." The captain swiped the com screen closed with a flourish. "Send in Inspector Battu and her team. I dislike the games that were played upon us and will have them understand that my authority will be respected."

"Aye, sir," Malloy responded with a tight grin.

Maria knew that the civilians on the habitat were going to pay dearly for the antics of those few who had pranked this ship. She just hoped that this satisfied Battu's sense of power so that she could clear her own certifications before she was noticed again.

Inspector Ngome Battu waited impatiently for the bay to repressurize, so she could proceed with her crusade to show the barbarians that the UN way was the only way to do things. She had stared down the technician who attempted to tell her that she needed to wear the helmet for her environmental suit. "The docking bay is obviously designed to be a shirtsleeves area. Therefore, we have no need to wear those." She looked around the shuttle's cabin. "I don't want anyone to be in a helmet when we don't need to be in one. Those are for emergencies and this is obviously not one." Turning back to the technician in her way. "Kindly open the door as soon as the bay is repressurized. We have a lot of work ahead of us if we are going to bring this habitat into UN compliance."

"Inspector Battu, I'm getting some strange readings from the external chem sensors. I'm not sure if the air in the bay is safe to breathe. I really think that we should use the environment suits, or at minimum breather gear. Or perhaps having the helmets on hand for an emergency?" Piloting Technician Charles Lee stated his case one last time.

"Did I fucking stutter?" Battu raged. "I said we wouldn't need them, and if it was dangerous, why aren't the toxicity sensors going off? If the air out there was hazardous, the sensor would have alarmed, not given some vague, uncertain response. Now open the door."

"Aye, Inspector," Lee responded stiffly. He had said his piece and pushing further with this particular person would do nothing but wreck his career. He carefully stowed the helmet he had been offering to Battu and tucked a rebreather mask into his cargo pocket.

"And you can stow that rebreather also, or I can write you up for theft, insubordination, and failure to obey lawful orders," came over his shoulder. He sighed and replaced the rebreather in its rack and moved to the door controls.

As the door hissed open, a blast of oddly scented air forced its way into the shuttle, causing Lee to sneeze violently. There was a cloying sweetness mixed with a sharp, almost peppery smell to the air. There was obviously a leak of some kind that was interfering with the circulation system. Battu seemed to not notice as she strode purposefully toward the lock across the small bay. The two supporting clerks followed behind her reluctantly. The three security troops who had wanted to be the first out had to rush to reach the airlock before Battu did. Her insistence on being the first one out of the shuttle had superseded standard practice for them to secure the area first. Lee shrugged at the circus leaving his shuttle and turned back to his copilot Piloting Technician Sandra Chester.

"We should probably turn this thing around so we can leave as soon as they get back," she told him.

"At least as soon as most of them get back. That bitch needs to spend time sucking vacuum. There is no reason I need to qualify as an administrative assistant, but she thinks that if I don't I'm somehow shirking my 'civic duty.' That is why I pay my taxes, so someone else does the paperwork. I'm not paying someone for the privilege of doing my own taxes," he replied.

"You need to keep shit like that inside your head, Lee. She will make your life hell if you don't let her have her way. And if you don't care about your life, she will make mine hell for having such a disrespectful superior." She shrugged. "And anyway, the course is easy, and once you certify you get to send all those TPS Forms back with a 'denied' on them. You just need to make the system work with you."

"You can play games like that." He snorted. "I don't have the patience for it. I just want to drive my bus and go home at a reasonable time." He sighed heavily. "My grandfather had the right idea. He immigrated to Grainne years ago. Took part of the family to live here. I once thought I should have joined him."

"Once?"

He waived a hand at the bay, indicating the whole system. "Not looking like a great retirement location at the moment."

"Which is why we need to make sure we top up our air and water here, that way you won't have to fill out requisition forms to fill up when we get back to the *Cutchet*."

"Amen to that."

At the airlock, Battu hammered her fist onto the access button beside the door. She was feeling particularly irritated by these shirkers and the stupid games they were playing with people's lives. Allowing people to pretend to be legitimate government personnel over open channels is unacceptable. To have someone pretend to be airspace control on an open channel was a safety violation of the highest order. Yes, the controller did guide them on a path safely through a dense asteroid field. And the controller did issue proper safety holds to keep the ship from harm. The one that the captain had ignored was to allow some debris that the ship itself had perturbed to clear their path. The controller used proper procedure and standards but had perverted them to write an offensive message. This was the more insulting part of the incident.

"Open this door in the name of the United Nations Health and Safety Directorate!" She yelled at the door. The strange smell in the air was becoming irritating. It smelled like the traditional foods her grandmother made for the family on holidays. None of her family had the spine to tell the old woman that no one wanted to eat ashy ostrich egg and charred vat-grown warthog intestines. "You are in violation of UN Regulations regarding air quality. I need to inspect your air-handling systems immediately, for your own safety."

One of the clerks coughed behind her, and she turned to glare at the woman. Motes of contaminant were visible in the bays' harsh light. Turning back, she leaned into the intercom button. "Open this door immediately. This census and safety survey begins now and you are not going to enjoy it."

A scratchy voice replied, "Keep your pants on, lady. There is only me and Stabby at the bays. Everyone else is either out working or trying to put their shit in order for your stupid inspection." There was a high-pitched electronic shriek that followed his words. "And Stabby is not too fond of your tone. Give me a seg to clear the lock and you and he can discuss your entry visa." The intercom cut off abruptly, and no amount of shouting, threats or pounding on the controls brought it back.

Almost two minutes later, the door snapped open, driven by incredibly powerful mechanisms designed to work against massive pressure differentials. Inside the lock stood a contraption that looked like the inside of an AutoMed Box, dressed in a lab coat with a stethoscope hung from the sensor node. A pair of angry looking eyes were drawn on the sensor node and one of the operating arms held a tablet that displayed text: I AM DOCTOR STABBY. I WILL PERFORM THE ENTRY SCAN. PLEASE REMOVE ALL CLOTHING AND ENTER THE LOCK.

One of the security troops snickered, drawing a glare from Battu. She slapped the intercom again. "There is no way we are stripping and submitting to your scan. We are the ones in control here."

Stabby's sign flickered and new directions appeared: HOW ABOUT JUST A BLOOD DRAW? WE DON'T WANT ANY FOREIGN PATHOGENS ON THE STATION. IT MIGHT DAMAGE OUR HYDROPONICS BALANCE.

"No," Battu stated.

Again, the sign flickered: THEN YOU DON'T GET ENTRY. BLOOD DRAW AND SCREENING IS IN THE HAB CHARTER AND WE AREN'T VIOLATING THAT FOR YOU.

"No," Battu said again, and turned to the head of the security troops. "Can you move that thing?"

The electronic shriek echoed in the lock. Stabby raised his other arms and several cutting tools were evident and began to move in a weaving pattern that covered most of the area in the lock. The sign blinked again. PLEASE DON'T MAKE ME HOSE THE LOCK OUT. WE DON'T HAVE THAT MUCH WATER. A SIMPLE BLOOD DRAW AND YOU GET IN. The smells of sweet and spicy intensified.

"Ma'am I think we might want to take a step back. That looks like inside of a surplus MD-08 Emergency Trauma box. Those are designed to remove damaged armor from around wounds. I don't have the correct tools to neutralize it," the security specialist said.

As he said it, the lights in the lock began to flicker. The scratchy voice spoke again, "You can force the issue with Stabby, let him run the tests, or fuck off back to your ship." The lights in the bay began to flicker, out of sequence with the lock.

"Fine, back to the shuttle to get some tools to wreck that menace and then we will get this habitat into compliance," Battu growled. The lights were beginning to give her a headache, such that she was starting to see halos around objects in the bay, and there was a little streaking to the dust motes in the air.

Something was wrong. The lights were starting to change color, and everything was beginning to blur together. She stumbled as she stepped towards the shuttle. One of the security troops retched suddenly. One of the clerks tripped and fell down. This wasn't supposed to happen.

"Not feeling too good, are you? Maybe you should let Doc Stabby take a look at you." The scratchy voice spoke again. But there was a echoey quality to the statement. "I'm sure that a blood test and a round of Sober-Up will make you feel right as rain."

"Everyone back to the shuttle. There is an emergency kit aboard." Battu didn't think that this was her voice, but it was an order, so it had to be her. It couldn't be anyone else. She tried to follow her own order, but the deck tilted suddenly, and she was falling.

"Seriously, guys," the scratchy, echoey voice spoke again, "if you signal a willingness to submit to the scan, we can clear this up really quickly. All you have to do is let us do a quick blood test to make sure you are healthy and free of pathogens, and we can get you cleaned up and feeling better."

She watched as the security troops tried to run back to the shuttle. The security lead almost made it before he tripped and hit the decking. Battu thought she could smell the sound of his vomiting. It smelled like candy apples. Another of the security troops was walking in a circle, trying desperately to angle towards the shuttle. The clerks were lying down. Battu wasn't sure if they had fallen or just sat down and collapsed. The older woman was laughing and waving her hands in front of her face. The younger man was crying and begging for the spinning to stop. The last security trooper was standing unmoving in a puddle of his own making. The last thing Battu thought was that these people were insane because of something in the air.

✧   ✧   ✧

Blazer Robert Harley McCombs watched the video feed of the shuttle bay, as the UN Troops succumbed to the gases that had flooded into the bay and popped a throat lozenge into his mouth.

"What the fuck did you put into the air, Skippy?" he rasped.

"My own concoction of Twitch, Sparkle, Retch, Satan Pepper OC and Nitrous Oxide with a glycol transmission booster," came the cheerful reply from his niece, Janine "Skippy" Billisdotter, already suited up in two layers of environmental gear. She was apparently not fooling about how insidious the chemicals were.

"Is it safe to go in there?" He gestured vaguely to the video monitor.

"I've got a temp lock on this side of the airlock. If you carefully break it down like they showed us in hazmat school and dispose of it, nothing is getting back into the hab. Once I shove the garbage into the shuttle and load the demo charge, I'll open the bay and lock to vacuum. That should vent all the nasty stuff. Then I set the autopilot on the shuttle to RTB expeditiously. Once that shitbird is out, I come back to the lock, skin out of Jensen's oversized E-Suit, hand it over to Doc Stabby for decon, and lock back in through the new temp lock you will put in place." She ticked the steps off on her gauntleted fingers. "Easy peasy." She waddled to the polymer bag that was partially secured to the inside of the airlock in question.

"What about anyone who wants to go through the screening?" he asked quietly.

"It is too late for that. They needed to step up before they started soiling themselves. I'm sorry, but this is war and those aardvarks are invaders. Even without a formal declaration of war, they are nothing more than pirates attempting to board a nonmilitary habitat against our civil-safety procedures. The law is on our side." There was a cold metal in her voice that brooked no argument.

"Why in Goddess's name did you happen to have this mix of nightmare fuel on hand?" Robert asked, changing the subject.

"Remember the open bid the FMF posted for next-generation slow-acting, pervasive incapacitance agent? I was going to submit. It seemed like a fun problem." The doubly suited figure shrugged. "Extra cash isn't a bad thing, and I was wondering what to do with the stuff we got from the cousins in the islands. I like the occasional sparkle trip, but that shit is *potent*. I don't feel like I should have to schedule a long weekend to have a hit of it. The rest I cooked up in the empty biolab."

"Why are you here on the family mining concern and not teaching somewhere?" he asked.

She pointed to the rainbow painted ripper skull mounted on the wall. "Because this is home and I hate teaching." She hissed a sigh. "And because Earth couldn't let go of the idea that they are the big dick, this is the only home I have." She turned to face away, shaking her head. "Susan was in Jefferson when they started. She was supposed to be getting things ready for the annual camping trip. She got a reserve recall to report to Heilbrun when they bricked it." She reached a gauntleted fist out towards him. "Go, Team Death Skull."

He bumped the stump of his wrist against her fist and raised it over his head to point behind him, mirroring the motions of his niece. "Rainbow," they said together.

He snorted a hollow laugh and nodded at the lock. "Fuck 'em up, kiddo. We had a lot of family at Heilbrun."

"Aye Aye." And then she was sealing herself into the lock and on her way to turning the waiting shuttle into a fireship. They might not be able to protect the Freehold, but they were by Goddess going to avenge her dead.

UNS *Maria Cutchet* was lost with all hands after a reactor breach in the Grainne asteroid belt. Investigation showed that their flight plan prior to the incident was erratic and in violation of accepted practice and standards. Due to the death of the command crew, no further actions were taken.

Trouble in Paradise

Kevin J. Anderson and Kevin Ikenberry

New Sapporo Spaceport
Meiji

Ellwood clung to the night shadows between a triple-stack of shipping containers. The usual clutter he expected from a United Nations customs-and-clearance zone was absent, which made it hard to stay hidden behind the concertina wire-topped fence.

It wasn't just the New Sapporo spaceport—the whole planet of Meiji was obsessively clean and neat. Between his failed, rushed attempts to secure passage on any outbound freighter, Ellwood had tried to stay hidden in back alleys and fringe zones. But even those places were as clean as the meticulously maintained thoroughfares of the main city. Now, with time running out, he'd given up going to ground. Instead, he stuck close to the spaceport, hoping for a chance to make his move.

He had to get off this planet.

Three weeks of repeated unsuccessful bids to catch an outbound ship soured his mood. If not for his Blazer training and experience, he would either have been discovered by the UN patrols or would have died from starvation or exposure. Time was running out. He needed to go home.

He drew a long breath and held the chilly, damp air in his lungs. Meiji's perpetual clouds covered the night sky with a blanket of amber-tinted gray. The cold temperature and annoying mist tried to penetrate Ellwood's confidence. He *would* find a ship, and he *would* make it home to Grainne. And he swore he wouldn't be too late.

All things are a matter of heart and time.

Ellwood exhaled and closed his eyes for a second. His father's words rang through his mind like a bell carillon. The last news he'd had from Grainne was of his father's illness growing worse, the family gathering at the old man's bedside. Ellwood pictured their somber faces over the sallow, living cadaver which was all that remained of the vibrant farmer after years of cancer. He simply couldn't believe the old man would go out like that. No, his father was supposed to remain strong and resilient until his last breath.

Ellwood had promised him that he would return from the war. The old man wanted nothing more than that, and Ellwood would cling to that promise with fierce determination.

If you want something enough, you will do anything for it. Anything.

The cold breeze shook him from memories as another late-season storm approached. The locals refused to call them typhoons because they rarely brought a storm surge or funnel clouds, yet the powerful winds and rains could suspend ships landing from orbit, with commensurate effects on interstellar shipping. The wind brought a repugnant stench from the nearby lichen farm outside the spaceport's fenced restricted area. Oddly, though, the smell of the lichens—one of Meiji's primary export crops—only made him recall childhood memories. As a young man traveling to Earth with his father, Ellwood was familiar with the stink of processing mills...

Hang on, old man. I'm coming. As soon as I can get out of here.

To do so, though, he'd have to brave more than the odor of a lichen farm. The only shuttles still on the tarmac occupied berths along the outer border, but an impatient glance at his chronometer gave him a measure of hope. For seven days now he'd observed the UN soldiers patrolling the spaceport, and he knew their rigorous patrol schedule. They did not deviate.

A personnel carrier rolled past at the prescribed time. As the security personnel ended their shifts, a four-minute window would open. Ellwood prepared for the four-hundred-meter move from the terminal fencing to the outer berths.

Eyes closed, he visualized his path through the maze of container stacks. He slowed his breathing and sank down into his Blazer training. Physical exertion meant little. He could easily complete the run in the time allotted but avoiding the security cameras as they swept the area would be the greater problem. He relished the challenge, glad to maintain his carefully honed edge after months away from duty.

Ellwood inched closer to the end of the rusted and dented transport container, where he could peer at the first unmanned security tower. The three closed-circuit television cameras panned from left to right in an orderly, laconic fashion. He'd timed the delay precisely. Each sprint between concealed positions would take him no more than three to five seconds.

That brought a rueful smile. *Never forget your training.* As a basic infantry soldier, before his time with the Blazers, he'd learned the simple three-to-five second rush. The sergeants had taught him to remain in a covered, prone position and identify a new objective a short distance away, one he could reach in less than five seconds, then return fire before moving again. Repeating the process, one brief dash at a time, would theoretically allow a soldier to move forward under fire.

As a Blazer, though, he'd learned that technique was bullshit. The best option to move forward under fire meant keeping the enemy cowering in their positions with direct fire.

Yet, like everything in his short career, there was a time and a place for each skill he'd learned. The run to the outer berths would be no different. He would make it, one way or another.

Five.

Four.

Three.

He pushed his shoulders off the container, turned to the open tarmac, and drew a long, deep breath.

Go!

Ellwood reached full speed in five steps and got to the first container stack in another twelve. In the clean shadows, he hustled to the opposite end of the container and glanced at the cameras before timing his departure and arrival at the next container. He repeated the simple task without glancing at anything other than his watch. After a minute and a half, hopscotching from place to place, he'd covered half the ground. The extra time gave him a long look at the containers near the remaining ships on the tarmac. Slim pickings. Instead of the forward stack close to the loaders for the ships, he saw the containers were back against the fence line and set for departure. Not what he expected.

He spat a silent curse into the wind and ran for the next container group. The only explanation was that there had been a change in the departure schedule. If containers were too close to a freighter's powered lift engines, that would cause mass destruction on the tarmac, and the UN would never allow that.

Change of plans, but he could deal with it. A minute later, after adjusting course for the relocated containers, he skidded to a stop in the shadows. A uniformed crew member carrying a slate computer appeared at the opposite end.

Morton.

"Where have you been?" the man hissed. "The *Dahlonega* is warming to boost now. I can't get you aboard the *Willis* either! You're too late."

"The hell I am," Ellwood grunted between breaths. "I'm earlier than you told me to be."

"Departure time changed two days ago. You didn't get my message?"

Ellwood swore and shook his head. "Ain't got a slate, asshole. Been stuck here. How am I supposed to know?"

A curl of breeze carried cigarette smoke to his nostrils. He recognized the scented tobacco; a brand popular in the exchanges of the UN soldiers' compounds. No sooner had Ellwood recognized the scent, then Morton turned toward the open space and marched toward the ships, leaving him behind. He called over his shoulder. "You better get your ass moving. You know what to do. Could be your last chance."

Ellwood didn't argue. He sprinted in the opposite direction, curling around the containers to hug the fence line. Above him, three strands of concertina wire wrapped over the crumbled stone wall. The lower section of discarded antiquated steel containers had seen better times. Rust-rimmed holes dotted several of them. Other voids seemed cut by laser torches. Undoubtedly emptied of their goods and no longer viable for hard vacuum, the decommissioned containers had been used to brace others against the vectored thrust of the transports.

Through a fist-sized hole in the stone wall, Ellwood could see a row of barred concrete cells on the other side of the barrier. The structures were open to the sky above. In the darkness, there seemed to be movement, but he couldn't discern who, or what, it might be.

Hyper-alert, Ellwood crept deeper into shadow and reached for the pistol tucked inside its makeshift holster. A flitter of movement at a rusted container five meters away made him freeze. A small human head poked out and glanced in both directions. A child.

The little one turned back to him. Ellwood tried to smile, tried to ease the wide-eyed kid's flash of panic. "Hey! It's okay. I'm not going to hurt you," he whispered. The boy did not seem to understand, and Ellwood mentally slapped himself. The child looked Japanese, and Ellwood switched effortlessly. *"Konnichiwa?"*

With surprising speed, the boy slithered out of the container and sprinted thirty meters away before sliding on one leg and ducking under the stone wall. Before Ellwood could even move forward, the child disappeared into the stockade on the other side of the barrier.

His brow furrowed. *Why would a kid be in there?*

From the tarmac, the unmistakable whine of lift engines spooling up propelled him forward. The *Dahlonega* pulsed her lift thrusters to idle, and the gentle breeze around him became a hurricane. Ellwood dropped to the ground, pressing his face into the alkaline-smelling soil, and crawled forward. As Ellwood peered inside the stockade, he thought the ragged breach in the barrier seemed too small for even the child to have gone through.

UN soldiers with their rifles at the low-ready patrolled around rows and rows of open cells wrapped in heavy bars. As the *Dahlonega* fired her lift engines behind them and the winds tore sheets of dust and trash into the maelstrom, many of the guards covered their faces and turned away from the blast. Blue-tinted light illuminated the far, dark corners of the interior space, and Ellwood could see that the cells on the other side of the wall teemed with children! Some even younger than the boy he'd seen, the oldest maybe eleven or twelve years. Girls and boys sat together in squalid conditions, in utter contrast to the usual cleanliness of New Sapporo. Some sobbed in muted voices with blue-lit tears streaming down their faces. Others, the older ones, sat glaring at the armed guards around them.

As he realized what he was seeing, Ellwood fought a rising wave of rage at the depravity of the UN. Beautiful, clean, perfect Meiji, like so many things, was too good to be true. A child screamed inside the compound, but no one moved or responded. The familiar actions and reactions of both guards and captives indicated long-term incarceration, as if they'd gotten used to the situation. What the prisoners had done did not matter to Ellwood. They were only children and had no caring adult in sight.

Though he'd been trying to get out of here for weeks, to get home in time to say goodbye to his father, Ellwood forgot his desperate plan to run to the *Dahlonega*. A prison compound full of kids, right here on the edge of the New Sapporo spaceport—in plain sight, but not on any public records.

Ellwood wasn't going anywhere until he understood what was happening here—and did something about it. There would be other ships. There had to be. He needed to go home, needed to escape and get to his father's side.

But he also needed to be here. Now. How could he just leave these children?

Another little boy cried inside the stockade, and the guards barked commands. Chaperones, civilians by their dress, flinched and scurried toward the unseen child. From his hiding place, Ellwood stared at the back of a nearby guard's head and wished he had a bayonet to fling. Instead, he lowered his face to the crook of his right elbow, covering his eyes from the flying dust. As much as he tried to tell himself it wasn't his fight, Ellwood knew better.

His father would have insisted he stay.

Tyrants were owed their due. Ellwood closed his eyes and let the last vestiges of hope turn to the simmering fuel of anger. He muttered, expressing the anger that came from several different directions. He was going to miss his last chance to get out of here. "Oh, you fucking bastards."

UN Forces Cantonment Area
New Sapporo

Sora Hasegawa waited.

Only a few years before, Hermann would have been at her side to place the ancestral string of pearls around her neck. The final moment of careful preparation, long practiced and disciplined by her family's custom, should have been an intimate moment of trust and love between husband and wife. For every state dinner and official reception they'd attended in their eight years of marriage, he'd known and understood the simple ritual.

But during the last two years, especially following his promotion to command colonel at only forty-three, his fixation on rank and duty had wedged itself between them. Sora had demurred to his needs, since her family's interests in the United Nations centered on profit from interstellar shipping. Like Hermann, her family's interest in her was dwindling. Sora knew her role, yet dissatisfaction grew in her heart. More than once, she'd stared in the mirror and watched the gentle acceleration of age while wondering if there was anything more to her life.

She wanted something more.

Hasegawa Interstellar would belong to her when her parents died, but that time did not seem at all imminent, since both were in their seventies, rigorously healthy and vibrant. While Hermann's rapid acceleration up the chain of command undoubtedly meant they would be recalled to Earth in two years, Sora no longer knew if she wanted to go. Hermann's first star appeared likely, given the UN political climate. Only results mattered. He'd married the heiress of Hasegawa Interstellar, after all. She had thought their bond was more of love and respect than profit and gain, but that was proven wrong by Hermann's greed.

While she finished dressing, by herself, Hermann talked loudly into his comm in the bedroom. He'd been staring out the windows toward the spaceport. The approaching storm outside would not likely delay the landing of the *Chitose*, a shuttle from the *Hokkaido*, the flagship of Hasegawa Interstellar, but it could complicate the arrival of the Undersecretary for Colonial Expansion. It might cause difficulties for him to arrive for the dinner in his honor.

Difficulties would be too good for them.

Catching herself at the surprising mental remark, Sora drew a sharp breath, but did not rebuke herself for it. Hermann had his own plans. He wanted her to impress upon the undersecretary how much they needed continued commercial and strategic support for UN operations on Meiji. The Hasegawa shipbuilders on Earth were angry and tense because of the continued incarceration of immigrants from Earth and, worse, the separation of minor children from their parents. Hermann, though, justified the action to ensure proper bureaucratic order. Workers were a necessity on Meiji, workers the UN could trust—meaning those without ties or ideations of the Resistance against Earth. No matter where they came from.

Yet, she could not trust the United Nations. On the advice of the general secretary, Hermann and his advisors drafted a temporary policy to secure the loyalty of the immigrant workforce building the Meiji fleet. The UN could hold minor children for six months, with a fee of five thousand marks each. If a family wanted their children, it was not enough for them to pass multiple security investigations and submit to routine searches and continuous observation. The fiscal aspect, Hermann argued, would keep them in line. Living on Meiji was not inexpensive. But Hermann wasn't satisfied with simple extortion. Should the working parents fail to attend the required wages, they faced deportation themselves. Any children would remain wards of the state until the age of seventeen when they would be conscripted into the Meiji Defense Force, a subordinate command under Hermann's control as command colonel.

She'd argued that he was perpetuating war, and Hermann had laughed and told her the answer was not so simple. War provided opportunities, and those opportunities would benefit Hasegawa Interstellar and themselves, personally. He'd kept his own role in the war at arm's length and prided himself in the docile Meiji environment, but he didn't realize his errors. The first gentle flames of the resistance burned in the quiet alleys and the establishments near the docks . . . and Hermann didn't see it. Heartsick workers, wanting family more than money, would not be ignored much longer. While her husband and his advisors plotted a way to line their pockets in relative peace, the war slow-marched toward them. Her summoning of the *Hokkaido* would speed events up considerably.

With a sigh, Sora grasped the ends of the necklace, raised it to her neck, and clasped it with practiced ease. Each time she wore it, and Hermann wasn't there to fasten it for her, she imagined her mother fainting dead away. The thought made her smile as she straightened the necklace along her skin.

From the bedroom, Hermann ended his comm and called, "Are you ready, Sora?"

"*Hai*," she replied, before switching to English as Hermann preferred. "Just putting on my necklace."

Her words had the desired effect, and she was pleased he caught the small, barbed reminder. Hermann sighed heavily in the bedroom and appeared at the vanity door a moment later, stepping behind her. His white uniform contrasted against her simple, elegant black dress. His longish blond hair rakishly swept back and coiffed perfectly, also in striking contrast to her long, straight hair, pulled back in a matching pearl clasp behind her neck.

His lips draw tight and blue eyes turned serious. He met her gaze. "I forgot again."

She nodded but did not reply.

"You're upset with me." He tried to smile. "I neglected my duty, Sora. I am sorry."

"Thank you." She nodded again and did not take her eyes from his. "I will be downstairs in a moment. Please ask Mako to come in? I will need her help to finish my preparations."

Hermann smiled. "Of course, love." He turned to go but paused in the doorway and spun around with parade-ground precision. Business again, not loving partner. "You are prepared to ensure that Hasegawa takes sole possession of the shipping routes from Meiji to Caledonia? And take responsibility for subcontractors and partners along the other major routes?"

Her voice became formal, too. "I cannot speak for subcontractors, Hermann. Their policies, and those of any partners, are governed by the board of directors. Neither I nor my family have any impact on such agreements."

"Those shipments must be guaranteed, Sora. The UN will pay handsomely to guarantee that these agreements remain in place."

She smiled softly, not trusting herself to speak.

He took that as an answer. "How much longer will you be?"

"Five minutes. It will be faster if Mako comes in."

Hermann flushed and left, and a surge of emotions threatened to bring tears to her eyes, but she held them off, as usual. With fists curled at her sides, Sora stared at her reflection again. *Is this how you're going to live your life? Or are you going to do something about it?*

Mako promptly entered the outer suite dressed in a black jacket and pants, the diplomatic uniform. The younger woman's face showed concern, but she said nothing.

Sora asked, "Do we have communications with the *Hokkaido*?"

"Yes, Miss. The shuttle *Chitose* will deorbit in an hour and thirteen minutes. Landing in just under two hours."

It would have to be enough time. "And Yuichi?"

Her aide's face clouded. "Yes. He reports the children are healthy and ready. They know he's coming for them."

Her pulse began to beat faster. "The storm will provide cover. Have him readied and alert the others." Sora could count her trusted confidantes on one hand. Roles needed to be played. Sora lowered her voice to a whisper. "Tonight is the night."

"Oh," Mako said, then she finally smiled.

New Sapporo Spaceport
Meiji

As the ominous storm coalesced over the spaceport, Ellwood realized he could follow the boy or get back into a hiding space he'd located in a nearby container. He glanced at the hole in the fence the boy had crawled through, back toward the stockade. He couldn't follow the boy. At least, not yet. With the cold rain soaking his borrowed coveralls, Ellwood crawled instead for the container and studied the hole. He could make it. Barely.

Flat on his stomach, Ellwood wormed his way into the dark hole leading into the hiding place. His shoulders caught the raw edges, and just when he thought he was stuck, a twist of his upper body sent him the rest of the way through. He crawled upright in the pitch-black night and froze. Someone else was inside. Smelling acrid tobacco smoke, he turned and saw the glowing end of a lit cigarette. Ellwood made out the barest image of a man's face.

"You in the wrong place, *gaijin*."

Ellwood made no move. "What place am I in?"

A rifle bolt slammed into firing position, likely chambering a round as well. "You not UN."

He clamped his tongue between his teeth. "What makes you say that?"

"A feeling." The cigarette pulsed again, and now he saw the man smile. "If not UN, you Resistance?"

"What does that matter?"

The man laughed. It was a harsh, short burst, but quiet enough not to carry. Rain pounded against the sides of the container. A cascade of thunder rumbled like a full battery artillery barrage outside. "You from Grainne, then?"

Like I'm going to tell you, dogfucker.

Ellwood brought his hands up slowly with his palms toward

the man. "I don't want any trouble. I'm trying to get a ride off this planet. To get home. My father is sick."

"But you a soldier, yes?"

His hands free and open, Ellwood watched the cigarette glow to confirm the man was three meters away at worst. In the darkness, and unless the man snapped some kind of torch to life and blinded him, he could cross the distance and disarm the man before he could fire a shot, much less aim.

"Are you with the Resistance?" Ellwood asked, risking a half step in the man's direction. The man made no move other than another long draw on his cigarette.

"From Caledonia. Gave up trying to get back. Thought the war couldn't find us here on Meiji."

"You're here because of the children across that wall?" Ellwood asked. He brought his trailing foot along under him, inching closer to the man.

"Punky. We give them food and water. The little ones can crawl in and out. UN guards no pay attention to them." The man sighed. "Families broken so the UN make credits from them. War would be too good for the fucking UN."

Ellwood blinked and sucked on one cheek. "They're holding the children for ransom?"

"Extorting the parents. Same thing. We trying to help them."

"Who is 'we'?" Ellwood asked.

"Can't say. You wanna help? I get you a seat off Meiji."

Ellwood chuckled and shook his head. "You expect me to believe that? A man hiding in a dark container? You could be a plant or an informant just as easy."

"If I was, I'd have shot you or called for help. Especially with you creeping forward like a Blazer." The man smiled again around the cigarette. "Oh, yeah, I can see it, *gaijin*. Plain as the shock on your face."

Ellwood couldn't hold back a smile. He laughed and nodded, stepping forward a little more intending to knock the man's rifle away. Another rifle cocked from behind him in the gaping darkness. He mentally cursed himself for losing situational awareness. Someone else was there. Someone fantastically good.

"Not another step, *gaijin*." The voice was deeper and gruff. "Blazer or not, we kill you here and now unless you help us."

"Help you do what?" Ellwood turned toward the voice. A

match crackled and spat to life, ignited a candle, and a soft yellow glow filled the space. A large Japanese man in gray-and-black striped fatigues—the Meiji Defense Force uniform from two decades before—approached from behind. The man with the cigarette was a young boy, no more than twenty.

The candlelight revealed rations and water cans. There were crates of weapons, too.

"You thought Meiji was a paradise, right?" The second man frowned. "The war is here, too, but it's a different war. One for profit. We will end that tonight."

"By freeing the kids? Returning them to their families?"

"That's part of it." The man smiled at him. "My name is Yuichi. This punk is my son, Keiko. There are others who will help us free them."

Ellwood squinted. "I saw at least ten guards inside the holding area. Those aren't great odds."

"As I said," Yuichi replied, "there are others. We have friends inside. Some of the locals aren't too trustworthy so we not tell them everything. But they take good care of the kids, so we get them out, too. They know we're coming soon. And we have firepower arriving shortly."

Ellwood nodded, realizing that the storm would provide excellent concealment. The children already had a known way in and out of the stockade. All they would have to do was widen the hole, but once free, they would be on the wide-open tarmac of the spaceport, and easy targets. Unless...

He smiled. "Your firepower is approaching from orbit, then?"

Yuichi grinned. "Smart man. The UN perimeter towers would cut us down otherwise. We bring the children and caretakers through the hole, and the shuttle deorbits and provides cover as we move them to Hangar One. From there, the others will take them and get them to their families. Once to safety, we get them underground. Hidden. The UN chases the empty shuttle. Maybe they blow it up. But here? Here we get the rest of Meiji to stand against the UN. Show our people we can win. We do not need the UN here for the protection they promise. The UN only wants our lichens and our money. You understand this, yes?"

"The UN is now willing to take the children to profit from those resources, too." Ellwood shook his head. For a moment, he thought of his father in his hospital bed. The old man would expect him to do his duty, just like a Blazer would. He couldn't turn his back, now that he knew the situation. "There are certain things I can walk away from, Yuichi...but not if it's harming kids and especially not for money."

Keiko opened a crate to brand new Meiji-made XA-4 4mm rifles with 15mm grenade launchers still in their shipping configuration. Next to them were magazines and boxes of ammunition. "Even seen those? How fast can a Blazer prepare and load an XA-4?"

Ellwood picked up the rifle he'd handled only in training. He turned it in his hands and worked a finger under the wrappings with a grin. "You're about to find out. While I do, tell me that your extraction plan is more than the two of you blowing a hole in that wall and running like hell. I got the rest of it—getting the kids underground and all. But you gotta get them outta the stockade first."

Yuichi grinned and pointed to several scraps of paper on the wall. He squinted and made them out as maps of the neighboring compound. "We show you."

UN State Dinner
Headquarters Palace
New Sapporo

Diplomatic functions. Hermann had discussed them when they were first married, but Sora hadn't really understood "mandatory fun" until she had suffered through glacial speeches and watched the seconds tick on her watch. As Hermann ascended in rank, she had to endure more and more such events. Her practiced facade, smiling and bowing to all manner of dignitaries (whether or not she liked or admired them) had grown tired. Her fatigue, she recognized, came both from so many events per month and from her own discomfort with the situation on Meiji.

Now, away from the receiving line and watching the torrential rainfall through the windows of the main hall, Sora cradled a glass of wine and waited. Big band music wafted through the party, but not loud enough to interfere with normal conversation. Pretending to sip her wine, she closed her eyes, remembering fondly her first dance with Hermann at his family's traditional wedding ceremony. For the music, she'd chosen "String of Pearls" by Glenn Miller, much to the satisfaction of the elder Hasegawas.

They'd marveled over her exquisite taste and keen ear. As much as she loved the music of that era, her choice didn't come from her own tastes, but she played her role. Even as a young woman, Sora had put her own feelings and emotions aside for the wants of her family. Her marriage was their desire, and while Hermann had once been charming as he pursued her instead of his career, over time her unease had been replaced with discomfort and now abject dissatisfaction.

In her blurry reflection, she saw Mako approaching, and her throat went dry. The time had come. Her assistant's instructions had been to observe Hermann closely. When he noticed that she was not at his side and came looking, then Mako would appear to intercept him.

"Miss?" Mako asked. "A Hasegawa Interstellar vessel is approaching, but it is not on the arrival manifest. They have requested your presence."

Sora consulted the offered slate and studied the message carefully. She felt rather than saw Hermann approach from behind. "Is everything all right, darling?" His warm was warm, but she could hear the annoyance.

She shook her head and forced a tremble into her voice. "The *Chitose,* a shuttle from the *Hokkaido,* is arriving within the hour. The board of directors have sent me a sealed message."

Hermann's brow furrowed. "Why would they not just send you an encrypted message when they reach orbit?"

Sora willed tears to her eyes and did not respond. Mako filled the void with the answer Sora wanted him to hear. "Command Colonel, private and personal messages are sealed by the board and are traditionally delivered by hand. There are formal reasons they do so. The last time such a message came, it was the death of the Honored Grandmother."

Hermann's impatience washed away in an instant. He placed a hand on her shoulder, and Sora flinched. "You should leave before any loss of decorum, love."

She let a tear slide down her left cheek. "Yes. I am terrified the news is . . . my father."

When he nodded, she noted a flicker of light in his eyes. In that instant, her hatred for the man came full circle. Hermann believed her father would leave a portion of the company to him as well, despite her position as the sole heiress. His only care for her was that she would not ruin his diplomatic party or his reputation with a sudden burst of emotion.

"Go. Take my car to the spaceport and then go home, where you can have all the privacy you need. Send it back for me, and I will join you as soon as the dinner is complete." Hermann forced another smile and when he saw another tear race down her cheek, he added, "I'm sure it's nothing."

A million retorts swirled in her brain. "I will have to return to Earth."

"Do what you must if you have more pressing matters. I will be fine here without you, Sora."

She reached up and kissed his cheek. "I know, Hermann."

Of course, you will.

She walked directly to the front staircase and down into the foyer. Several sets of eyes followed her. As she reached the first landing, she turned to Mako, who was ever-present at her left shoulder, and nodded once. The signal was simple and clear: *Don't speak.*

Outside, under the covered entranceway, the sound and smell of the pouring rain surrounded them. The noise blotted out everything as they ducked into Hermann's dedicated car, with the flags bearing his command colonel's rank mounted on each front fender.

"Spaceport—all possible speed, on Command Colonel Sturm's orders," Mako snapped to the driver.

Trying to control her pounding heart, Sora sat back in the seat and looked out the window as the car sped through the rain. Fifteen minutes later, as they reached the spaceport, Sora peered around the driver's head through the front windshield to see the military checkpoint. She stole a quick glance at Mako, who nodded.

They had hoped the driver would follow established standard operating procedures. With her husband's car and insignia present in the floodlights, the checkpoint guards collected themselves and formed up to salute the vehicle. A sergeant stepped forward and spoke to the driver. Sora saw the young man's shoulders sag, but she couldn't tell if it was relief or annoyance.

No soldier ever wants to stand in the cold rain any longer than they have to.

Hermann's sayings over the years had all played into her plan.

It took only the right weather and the right men and women willing to put their lives on the line for these children. Hermann wouldn't hear complaints from the workers. Without a voice, the strained families of the imprisoned children had no choice but attempt rescue even at great cost. Sora hoped they would be successful without loss of life, but things seldom happened flawlessly. But she could hope even if her husband always told her it wasn't a method. It was all she had left.

Through the vehicle window, Mako pointed at a descending ship's amber thrusters firing gently above and approaching the spaceport through the storm. "There's the *Chitose*." With a quick glance, Sora confirmed it to be on approach to the far end of the field, near the UN compound. While not as fast as other shuttles, the *Chitose* had wide, capable bays.

It would work perfectly for their purposes.

The sergeant stepped back into his shelter from the rain and gestured. The diplomatic car rolled through the checkpoint and sped across the military portion of the tarmac. As it approached the far checkpoint, another group of soldiers made the same frenzied run into the rain. The customs and courtesies of the service were predictable to a fault. Now it all worked on Sora's behalf.

The detonation of an explosive device on the wall of the stockade near the lichen farm caught all of them by surprise. Torn between their duty to defend their position and also to respectfully receive the command colonel's wife, they froze.

As shockwaves and fire expanded from the explosion, Sora shouted to the driver, "Go!" Without questioning, he stomped the accelerator pedal to the floor and rocketed through the gates as the checkpoint guards dove out of the way. "Get to the *Chitose*! It's the safest place on the field!"

New Sapporo Spaceport
Meiji

Sudden torrential rain muted the dust and smoke from the explosion as the platter charge brought down a section of the stockade wall. Ellwood watched Yuichi and Keiko dart into the breach, firing at the known guard positions. No hesitation. They meant business. They'd practiced their attack, marking the position of the predictable UN guards and set their timing accordingly. For resistance fighters, their discipline was commendable. While it wasn't quite the method he'd learned as a Blazer, their initial attack appeared successful. Less than fifteen seconds after they'd charged into the stockade, the first children scrambled through the hole blasted in the wall.

Ellwood called out to them in Japanese. "Here! Follow me!"

The first boy ran toward him, closing the distance quickly, with more children at his heels, panicked, desperate, but filled with hope. A few adults came through with the next wave looking addled and shocked, urging the children ahead of them. The kids understood the plan and dashed to salvation, quickly lining up behind the container. Ellwood heard the methodical firing of the two rifles, creating chaos among the unsuspecting guards in the stockade, and he knew Yuichi and Keiko were having the effect they'd wanted . . . but he also knew it couldn't last. They didn't have much time. Through the rain, he saw the approaching ship bearing the familiar paint scheme of Hasegawa Interstellar. The markings indicated the ship was the *Chitose*.

As the massive shuttle flared on its final approach, landing engines blasted the surrounding tarmac with hurricane-force winds. The rain swirled into a blinding mist, obscuring everything around them. Ellwood grinned. The shuttle was much more than a diversion.

As he did his best to round up the fleeing children, Ellwood watched the *Chitose* pivot on its maneuvering thrusters, which eased the wind along the planned escape route. Leading the kids, he ran for the next container stack with the children right behind him. In the distance, he saw a group of ramp hands waving their lighted cones—the signal. The children sped around him in silence as the roaring rainstorm covered even the slap of their footfalls through the puddles. Ellwood turned and counted them going past.

More than fifty! Damn, all those children held hostage!

"Go!" he cried, and the steady stream of children continued out of the mist and past him. The amber-tinged light of the *Chitose*'s engines shone down on small, strained faces. Yet they kept coming. Another fifty.

The rattling gunfire increased from the stockade—the stunned UN soldiers finally returning fire, still not knowing how many rebels were attacking the facility. The children raced past him, following their leaders to the safety of the hangars where others would speed them to their waiting families while the *Chitose* and the raiding party, himself and the others, helped them escape. Ellwood hoped they could divert the attention of the UN soldiers a few more minutes.

The line of children grew more ragged, groups of two and three interspersed by longer distances. Two young teens limped past him, and Ellwood saw blood running down one's torn pant leg. Spurred to action, he turned and ran back for the entrance, passing a few last children. An aircraft's turbine engine roared to life as he passed the end of the container, and a blur of movement caught his eye in the same instant he collided with a silhouetted figured. He sprawled across the wet tarmac, rolled, and came up with his rifle pointed at the figure on the ground. She pushed herself up to lean on her arms.

A woman? She seemed utterly incongruous here, wearing a soaked black evening gown. Her long, dark hair was plastered across her face. She wore high heels, one of which had fallen loose as she tumbled.

"Who are you?" he demanded. "What are you doing here?"

Her face turned to his, and he felt a shiver of recognition run down his spine. A string of elegant pearls encircled her neck, and Ellwood wondered if her husband, the command colonel of the New Sapporo garrison, had purchased them for her. The photos of the two of them adorned propaganda posters all over the Meiji terminal areas with bold slogans of "Together We Thrive." Sora Hasegawa, shipping heiress, wore a traditional neo-*kimono* and Command Colonel Sturm stood in his impeccable dress whites.

Now she was at the spaceport, in the middle of a raid. Unarmed. He pressed forward with the rifle's barrel pointed at her chest.

The flagship's shuttle, which belonged to her family, pivoted as it landed. Sora Hasegawa stared up at it. Ellwood gasped in realization. He spoke in broken Japanese. "You're here for the children."

She climbed to her feet as if trying to regain her dignity and replied in fluent, unaccented English. "To get them home."

Ellwood jerked his chin toward the landing *Chitose*. "You brought them here as a distraction? Just for this raid? Big risk."

"If all the children get out it's worth it." Her eyes flickered past him, alarmed.

The young rebel Keiko staggered out of the dust and waved a bloody hand. "Blazer!" The boy had taken at least three bullets in his legs and one arm but was still on his feet.

Desperate to rescue him, Ellwood ran and yelled over his shoulder to Sora. He had to trust that she was an ally. Right now, he had no other choice. "I'll get Keiko! You get the children to safety!"

He ran for Keiko. The boy limped toward him, his rifle threatening to slip out of his grasp. He stumbled and fell forward, but Ellwood caught him with one arm. Forcing the words out, Keiko said, "My father . . . still inside."

Ellwood hefted the boy, draping a thin arm over his shoulder, but the young man's legs wobbled. "Get up, Keiko. You gotta get up!"

"I'll make it." The boy tried to smile, but there was no way he would walk—

"I have him," Sora barked in Ellwood's ear. "You seal off the stockade wall."

Before he could respond, she raised Keiko's arm and pivoted under it, taking his weight on her shoulders. The shipping heiress, despite her fancy gown and pearl necklace, was remarkably strong and determined. The dichotomy of her elegant garb walking a soaking, camouflaged soldier to safety disoriented him. Ellwood stepped back as Sora and the boy limped over to the hangars where the ramp hands moved toward them.

A firefight raged inside the stockade. Without his son's rifle, Yuichi was vastly outnumbered. Ellwood hesitated, torn. The urge to simply follow the plan overwhelmed him. He had to whisk the children into hiding so the *Chitose* could boost away. The UN would assume the Hasegawa spacecraft had taken their charges. Ellwood couldn't turn his back on them.

If this isn't my fight, I don't know what is.

Dammit.

Ellwood ran. A few straggler children passed him, and he yelled at them to move, pointing through the rain as the squall intensified. The *Chitose*'s timing had been perfect.

Reaching the barricade of containers, Ellwood flinched as flashbangs detonated along the wall. Even muted by the wall, the light still made him flinch, but he could see a shadow bounding out of the glare and mist—Yuichi carrying the body of a small girl. Wounds dotted her chest and legs, and Ellwood could see that the other man bore similar injuries. He staggered forward, then collapsed to his knees in the rain.

Ellwood was there in an instant, reaching for him. "Come on, Yuichi. Get up."

"I can't, Blazer." His head turned too slowly to face Ellwood. His dark eyes danced back and forth and struggled to focus. "Take her." He had barely kept himself alive, forced himself to keep going, to carry the child.

Ellwood saw that the girl was dead, her face a porcelain mask of peace despite the horrible pain she must have felt.

Yuichi didn't know. He struggled to stay upright. "Take her! I will keep them back."

"No, Yuichi. You're in no shape to do anything but get to safety. You need the medics. You just have to get up. I'll take her, Yuichi. Get to the hangars!"

Yuichi reached up, and Ellwood gingerly removed the little girl from his arms. He checked for a pulse and found none. As he did, the older man scrambled to his feet and lurched toward the hangars in the swirling cascades of rain. Two workers appeared in their dark, soaked clothes. One took Yuichi's arm and assisted him. The other bit her lip and took the little girl from Ellwood's arms.

"*Arigato*, Blazer," the older woman said. His identity was out, for better or worse. If the UN started asking questions, it was only a matter of time before they came for him.

Not without a fight, they won't.

Ellwood spotted movement, and his rifle came up without thought and swung toward the figures emerging from the hole blasted in the stockade wall. As soon as he identified their UN uniforms, he squeezed the trigger in short bursts, knocking them down. Now it was time to defend what Yuichi and Keiko had done.

He strode toward the hole as more UN soldiers pushed through. Again, Ellwood fired. His face twisted in sudden anger at the United Nations, the war, and how it had kept him from his ailing father. Years of frustration surfaced, coming to a head, and he used that to his advantage. Relentless, Ellwood took cover at the corner of the containers, working his way toward the damaged wall. He had to keep the enemy at bay.

"Come on, you bastards!" Ellwood yelled over the thundering

rain. Several rounds struck the container wall near his head, and
he ducked out of the way, letting them fire wildly in his direction. To his left, in the wide-open space of the outer bertho, Sora
Hasegawa walked toward the *Chitose* with her arms above her
head, waving. Somehow, even drenched and bedraggled, in the
middle of a firefight, she managed to look elegant.

What is she doing?

She turned toward Ellwood. Deep in shadows, he couldn't
be sure she was looking at him, but at the same time he felt
her eyes on his with a deep intensity. Her left hand, still raised
over her head, made a circling motion. Her right arm pointed
at the stockade wall.

Ellwood slipped around the corner and fired six quick shots,
hitting at least one soldier in the tight, smoke-obscured space
between the container and the stockade wall. The enemy would
keep coming. More rounds slammed into the container wall next
to him. Too close. They knew where he was. It was a matter of
time until—

WHUMP! WHUMP! WHUMP!
WHUMP! WHUMP!

He turned back to see that the woman had disappeared as the
familiar chorus of the Mark-32 20mm grenade launcher lobbed
round after round into the UN stockade. He saw the launcher
mounted and manned inside one of the *Chitose*'s open cargo
bay doors. Now that all the children were gone, the shuttle's
crew kept the UN attention on them by fire. The diversion was
almost complete, the rescue successful, but he needed to give
the ramp hands more time. The last few children and the last
of the workers crept toward the hangars as rebels ran to collect
them and get them away. They just needed a few more seconds.
He wouldn't need to delay the UN soldiers long.

With covering fire from the *Chitose*, Ellwood reloaded his
weapon before bursting forward and charging up the narrow
chute between the containers and the stockade wall, intent on
killing anything in his path.

Five steps into the confined space, Ellwood reeled as another
barrage from the *Chitose* detonated along the top of the wall. The
blast scattered hot debris across his face and arms. He retreated
to the corner of the container in time to see the wall give way

and collapse outward. An odd, sudden silence created a calm eddy in the storm.

In the distance, Ellwood heard a cacophony of Meiji's famous wind chimes tolling in their random symphony. He'd not been into the city to see the iconic structures. His sole mission had been to get home.

Focus, Blazer.

Muzzle pointed into the swirling dust and rain, Ellwood waited for a target to materialize. Seconds passed. His eyes swept across the collapsed wall again and again, but there was nothing. A burst of gunfire from behind snapped his attention around. The UN forces had given up on the stockade and now they were attacking the *Chitose* itself!

The shuttle's shielding took the brunt of the UN small-arms fire with indifference. From the open bay, the grenade launcher continued to fire. A few of the crew lay prone on the lowered ramp and fired various small arms, whatever they had, into the UN forces charging their direction.

Ellwood raced to the nearer line of containers, the same place he'd tried to meet Morton so he could arrange a ride home. In the shadow, the command colonel's wife huddled in the rain. Seeing her fearful expression, he understood what had happened. The *Chitose* hadn't had time to fully descend and scoop her up, to snatch her away from here. Sora Hasegawa had chosen for them to be safe enough to boost, to maintain the illusion, while she waited for her husband's forces to collect and arrest her.

Ellwood approached her cautiously, expecting her to be despondent. Her head snapped up, and she glared at him with fierce, dark eyes. "What are you still doing here?"

"Getting you out of here," he blurted. It seemed the proper thing to say, realizing she was a woman who had betrayed everything she'd known.

"You are a Blazer." It wasn't an accusation, merely a statement of fact. "Keiko told me."

"I was." Ellwood knelt beside her, taking cover. "I'm not sure what I am right now, except trying to get home."

"To Earth?" Rain ran down her face. The urge to wipe it away nearly overwhelmed Ellwood.

He shook his head. "Grainne. My father is dying."

A pained look crossed her face. "My father will die of shame when he learns of my betrayal. I have given up everything."

Ellwood nodded. There was no other response that came immediately to mind. Then he said, "You saved the children. We'll get them back to their families."

"For now." She sighed. "There is no guarantee that Hermann and his zealous assistants won't continue their abysmal policies."

"No, there isn't," Ellwood agreed. "But, the Resistance has come to Meiji. The rescue of the children will only embolden others to join and keep up the fight. I thought your family had a contract with the UN. Why did the *Chitose* fire upon them?"

"A contract is merely a document." She sighed. "Like my family, Meiji wanted nothing of this war. They tried to remain unaffiliated. I've learned that between good and evil there is nothing neutral. So, I made a choice. I pray it was the right one."

Pressed against the damaged shipping containers, some bearing her family's name, the heiress looked impossibly...human. Her gown soaked through, Sora pulled her knees to her chest and wrapped her shivering arms around them.

Before he could say anything, she looked up at him. Her brow furrowed with a question and then a soft smile formed on her lips. He watched her tilt her chin down to her chest. She brought her hands to her neck and unclasped the string of pearls. As she placed them into one palm, her expression was serene and troubled at the same time. Her eyes came up as she held out her hand. "Get on board the next ship you can. These will pay for you to get home, Blazer. Tell everyone what happened here."

"My name is Ellwood." He stared at the pearls before reaching out and taking them gently. He strung them between his hands, knowing they would more than finance his way, letting him acquire a second set of identification and commercial fast transport in the general direction of Grainne. "And you're Sora Hasegawa, shipping heiress."

She bowed, as if it were a formal introduction back at the diplomatic reception.

Ellwood leaned forward. "If we're going to get out of this, we must move fast. There's another way. Something more important."

Sora brought her chin up. Still close together, he felt her breath on his face as her beauty almost stunned him silent. "We?"

He thought for an instant about his father and imagined the

old man in his hospital bed, smiling and laughing. Ellwood hadn't fallen all that far from the tree. His father would understand, and if he died before Ellwood could make it home, the old man would agree it was for a noble cause, the greater good.

Opportunities are like lightning, son. They rarely strike the same place twice. When you see a good one, for yourself or to stick it to anyone who stands in your way, do it.

Do it.

He extended the pearls, reached for her neck. Uncertain, Sora swept her hair out of the way and he secured the strand back in place and put his hands on her shoulders. "The rest of the galaxy will know about what happened here, Sora. We'll make sure of it."

When she smiled at him, the crusty deployment-caused layers around his heart crumbled. There would be no going home. At least, not yet. Here, as unlikely as it was, might be something worth fighting for, after all. His father would understand.

Ellwood stood up as the gunfire reached a crescendo behind them. He pulled her along with him. At the touch of her hand, the ripple of electricity down his spine was unmistakable, and when she didn't immediately let go, his heart jumped in anticipation.

Sora kicked off her expensive shoes, and he chastised himself for underestimating her. "Let's go."

They started for the hangars and the rescued children as the maelstrom of rain and wind whipped around them. Bright light suddenly bathed the tarmac, extending their shadows ahead of them as they ran. He smiled at her as the *Chitose*'s ascent engines fired and the shuttle rose into the sky. By the sounds, carnage rolled behind them in the blast, but he didn't risk glancing away from the beautiful woman.

"Welcome to the Resistance, Sora."

The Humans Call It Duty

Michael Z. Williamson

Cap slipped through the undergrowth. He was stealthy, for there were things that would kill him if they found him, men and animals both. He surprised rabbits and bouncers and other prey as he appeared like a ghost through the leaves, and they scattered before him, but he was not hunting now.

The sound of Guns had alerted him from his patrol. They came from somewhere near his friend, and he hurried to investigate. Guns were an indication of hunting, and David was alone, with many enemies in the dark woods. He increased his pace, mouth wide to reduce the rasp of his breath, and squeezed between two boles, then under the dead, rotten log he'd passed on the way out. His patrol had only been half done, and he hoped David would understand.

He drew up short. The scents in his nose sorted themselves. That one was Gun smell, and not from David or another friend. That was smell from David's Gun. That was the smell of David, and the smell of blood. Cap dropped flat on the forest floor and eased his way under a brushbush. He gazed deeply into the dappled murk and widened his ears and nose. The Enemy was not nearby.

He moved quickly, striding forward, dreading what he would find. There was a dip in the ground, leaves hastily tossed to cover it. A few scrapes revealed a hand, then an arm. The sweet-sour smell told him already, but he kept digging until he saw the face, then more. It was David, dead. Cold flowed through him as he stared at the body, ragged holes blown through it by Guns. All David's harness and gear were missing. The thing he called a

71

Comm was gone, and Cap knew that was bad. If an enemy had the Comm, he had to get it back or destroy it. He didn't know why, but that had been one of the things drilled into him from an early age. A Duty, it was called.

He whimpered in pain, for David had been his friend his entire life. Somehow, he had to do what must be done, and return to the fenced Home where David and he lived. He wasn't sure what happened after that, but he knew what he'd been taught, and knew he had to do it. First, he reburied David's body, sad and wishing other humans were here. They knew what to say for the dead, and Cap couldn't say it for them.

Standing and peering around, he spotted the route taken by the Enemy. He would come to that soon enough, but first, he had to do what David called a Datadump. That tree there should work, and he trotted toward it. He scrambled aloft until the branches would barely take his weight, swaying in the late evening breeze. He pressed the broad pad on the shoulder of his harness and sat patiently. It was a human thing, and he didn't know what it was exactly, only that he was to climb a tall tree and press the pad every day at sunset. That too was a Duty. It beeped when it had done what it was supposed to, and he eased back down the limbs and trunk, flowing to the ground like oil.

Now to the hunt.

The path the Enemy left marked them as amateurs. David and his friends left much less sign of their passing, although he could still follow them easily enough. There were some friends, those who David called Black Ops, who were almost as adept as he, and could kill silently and quickly. He wished for their company now. They were hunters as he, even if human, and would understand his feelings. But those fellow hunters were not here, and he must tread carefully. It was his Duty to his friend to continue doing what he was trained to, and to recover the Comm. After that, it would be a pleasure to kill those who had killed David. That was his Duty to himself.

There they were. He dropped into the weeds and became invisible, watching them patiently. There was no hurry, for they could not get away from his keen hunter's skill. He sat and listened, grasping what few words he could, and waiting for the right moment.

"—odd to find one rebel out like this, along our patrol route," said one.

"They're all weird, if you ask me. They don't want law, don't want schools, and don't want support. Why anyone these days would be afraid of the government is beyond me," said another. He felt like a leader, and Cap guessed him to be the Sergeant. There were eight of them, so this was what David called a Squad, and Sergeant was the Squad Leader. They were enemies. He was sure, because the clothing was wrong, they smelled wrong, and David's people had Squads of twenty.

"It is their planet. Was," said another. He carried a large Gun, the kind for support fire. He was another primary target. "I guess they were happy, but a strange bunch of characters," he agreed.

"Well, we've got a prize, and a confirmed kill, so that should make Huff happy." He was turning the Comm around in his hands. He made a gesture and handed it to another, who stuffed it into his harness. Cap made note of that one's look and smell as Sergeant continued, "He wanted to prove that initiating lethal force was a good idea, and this should help. We'll sweep another few klicks tonight, then pick up again tomorrow. Jansen, take point," Sergeant said.

"Sure thing, Phil," said the first one.

The Squad rose to their feet and trudged away. They might imagine they were stealthy, compared to city people, but Cap easily heard them move out, three person-lengths apart, Jansen first, then Gunner, then Sergeant, then the rest. Cap appeared out of hiding, and followed them, ten person-lengths back. He stayed to the side, under the growth, and avoided the direct path they were taking. The Squad had Guns, and he did not, but he had all the weapons he needed, if he could get close enough.

It was only a short time until one said, "I'll catch up. Pee break."

"Shoulda gone before we left, geek," Sergeant said.

"Sorry. I'll only be a few seconds."

Cap watched as the Enemy stood to the side and relieved himself. He jogged sideways along their path, hidden by leafy undergrowth, and waited until the last man passed by his chosen target. He crouched, braced, and as the man fumbled with his pants, threw himself forward. His victim heard him, and his head snapped up in terror. He was wearing the Goggles people wore to let them see in the dark, but it was too late. Cap swept over him before he could scream, unsheathed, cut, and landed rolling. The body gurgled, dropped, twitched and was still.

One.

Cap slipped quickly away, through more brushbushes, and carefully climbed a tree. He wanted to be high enough to see, but low enough to use the limbs to escape if he had to. He peered through the woods, eyes seeing by the moonlight, and waited for the Enemy to respond.

They weren't a very good enemy, he thought. They hadn't noticed yet. That was good, he supposed, although a part of him was insulted at the poor competition. He dropped lightly back to the ground and returned to the kill. Sniffing and listening carefully, he made sure no one was nearby, then hoisted the body up and dragged it carefully off. He buried it under a deadfall, where the ants and flies would take care of it and erased any sign of his passing. There was no time to rest, but he'd taken a few bites before burying the body. He could go on.

The Enemy had finally figured out that one of theirs was missing. In pairs, they stumbled noisily through the brush, whispering his name, "Misha!" They weren't talking into their magic Comms yet, that could reach people through the air. They might soon call for others, however, and that made Cap consider things more urgently. From his perch high in a graybark tree, he kept watch over the Enemy's movements. That pair was closer and separated from the others by a slight ridge. He eased back down and concealed himself under a tangler, where he was unlikely to be seen. They could see heat, but they would not see him. Even faced with Goggles he could be invisible.

They were heading off to the east. Cap followed along behind at a safe distance. Could he take two? Perhaps he should wait. But there was little time, and the Comm had to be found. It had to. He edged closer.

One paused, pulled off his...no, her, he smelled...Helmet, and drank from a Bottle, leaning against a tree. There was risk from the other, not far away, but Cap took the chance and jumped.

A bite, twist and roll, and her neck was broken. That injury not even people could often fix, and not out here. He heard a yell and the cough of a Gun firing, and heaved himself up and away, bounding into the heavy darkness, the growth a whisper alongside him as he slipped his feet surely into gaps. No noise from the hunter. That was the way.

"Phil! Guys!" the other yelled. "It's an animal! It got Lisa!"

Two.

Cap shot away under the weeds, found a tree and raced aloft. He could barely see through the tangle of leaves and was worried about their Goggles. He was hot now, and they had seen him. Did they know what he was?

They were distressed. He knew it from the increasing loudness, the shaking in the voices, the reek of fear from them and their indecision. He would win this yet. He didn't know all of what he heard, but he knew the harness was recording it, and he caught some words he did know.

"—call for evac!" said one.

"We can't!" said Sergeant. "The rebels know we are out here, that's why we walked all this way. We are supposed to find those roving missile teams."

"I know why we're here, goddammit! But that thing killed Lisa and Misha!" one argued.

Sergeant replied, "You're going to call in and abort because of an animal? Any idea how that will sound? And evac is for the wounded."

"It's still out there!"

"So now we know. We shoot it when it comes back, add it to the count," Sergeant said.

"I don't think—"

"I don't care what you think!" Sergeant interrupted. "We'll bivouac here, take a look in daylight if we can, and continue from there. Shoot anything that isn't human. Var, you and Jaime take first watch."

"S-sure, Phil," "Uh-huh," the two replied, not sounding happy. In a short while, the other four tucked cloaks around themselves and leaned against trees. Var and Jaime walked around the clearing, eyeing each other and the blackness. Cap dropped to the ground and crouched. He meant to kill Jaime if he could, then drag him off.

Jaime had the Comm.

It was halfway until dawn before the chance came. Cap didn't sleep, simply watched and waited, though the day had been draining and disturbing. Patience was a tool of the hunter. The Enemies tossed restlessly before slipping into disturbed slumber. At the darkest, coolest time of night, Var muttered something to Jaime, then sat against a tree, took off his Goggles and rubbed his eyes. That made him almost blind. Cap moved without hesitation.

He leaped over a log, dropped into a slight dip, and exploded out of it. Here is where it was dangerous, if Var was looking. He wasn't.

Jaime was just turning, not from suspicion, but from fear of the woods. Cap caught him on the back of the neck and bit hard. A swiping pawful of claws tore his throat out and quieted him to a wet, breathy sound, and he dragged the body up the slope and into the dip.

A shout, a cough of a Gun, and a Bullet cracked past his ear, like a rotten bluemaple branch snapping. Cap knew what Bullets were and flinched. He ran as fast as he could, hampered by the limp weight of his kill, and felt a sting in his tail. There were other shouts and shots, but none came close, and he ran until his legs and lungs were on fire. He crawled under a featherfern and pulled the corpse in with him, then opened his mouth wide to quiet his heaving breaths and listened for pursuit.

Three.

The Enemy was shouting now, scared. They hadn't followed him because they were consumed with their own fear, their fear of him. Cap knew what pleasure was, and that was pleasure. He took a look at his tail and found some short length had been shot away by the stray Bullet. It stung and throbbed badly. He would accept it. He had the Comm and had done what his friends wanted.

"*Jaime has the rebel comm!*" one Enemy shouted.

"You make it sound like it chose him on purpose. We'll find it during the day. We have a sensorpack," Sergeant replied.

"I tell you that cat thing is hunting us and knows exactly what it's doing!" was the response.

"And I tell you it's a dumb animal. It's been hit, look. Here's a blood trail. Grab your gear and we'll follow it."

"*Are you insane?*"

The voices became confused. Cap didn't understand the words, but the fear was clear. They would look for him, but not yet. Not until it was light. Very well. He could hunt in light, too. Rising, he dragged the body further away. They might follow this trail, and he had to confuse it.

The creek was refreshing and cool, and he followed it upstream for some distance, splashing softly in the rippling pebbled shallows. He dragged his burden up a rocky shelf, back into the woods, and found a good spot, near some firethorns. No one went near firethorns. They would spring and sting their prey with a painful bite. He checked again to make sure the Comm was still in Jaime's harness. It was. The fabric was too tough for him to tear, but he yanked at the straps with his fangs until he was able to wiggle it out. He paused, turned to the body and ate noisily and quickly, until he knew to stop. If he filled up, he would be unable to hunt. He tore out a final warm, quivering mouthful of flesh, shredded it with his teeth and tongue, and swallowed. Salty and rich, and he savored it. The taste of his Enemy's death. The rest of the body went into the firethorn bed, where it could fertilize them, and the Comm went several hundred paces away with him. He bit hard, until the case and a tooth cracked, then bashed it against a rock until it was open. It had to be destroyed, and he wasn't sure how good the enemy's tools were at finding it. He urinated in the open case and buried it as deep as he could in a damp depression that was overgrown with weeds.

He was done. The Comm was safe, and he could rest, then transmit his last Datadump and work his weary way back to Home. Hunger and fatigue gnawed at him to do that very thing, but another part was still awake. That part was sad, angry, and mean. It meant to avenge David's death, and it did not want to be ignored.

And there were only five of them left. Rest could wait. The Datadump could wait if need be. Some Duties were more pressing than others.

Dawn was breaking, and Cap was near the Enemy again. They looked ragged, drained, and fearful. He would help them feel that even more. They'd found no sign either of him or the Comm with their tools, and that meant Cap had done well. He felt pleasure, and a hint of satisfaction. They had killed David and taken the Comm, but he had killed three of them already and destroyed it. But it would not bring David back. He whimpered in loneliness.

They were trudging back the way they'd come, and he followed them behind and above, slinking from limb to limb on the overhead path they had yet to suspect. He detoured where the trees thinned but kept the Enemy always in sight. It was an old game that he knew from instinct and training. When Leopards had been taken from their Old Home to this New Home, they brought their skills with them. The Ripper of the forest might be stronger and faster, but Leopards were better trackers. And Cap, or Capstick, as David had called him since he was paired, was one of the best Leopards in the Military.

Below, Sergeant said, "Look, it's daylight, we should be fine. We'll set mines there," he pointed, "and there. You watch, Cynd, and wake us in two hours. We'll move again, then rest again, okay?"

"I think so," the female Cynd said. Cap watched as the Squad shuffled about the area. They were placing the small boxes he recognized as explosives. He'd seen those in training. They were smaller and different shaped than his people's, but he knew what they were. He paid rapt attention to the placement.

Then the Squad lay down to sleep again, leaving her to stand watch. But she did stand, not sit, and he wasn't sure of his chances.

He watched as she moved around, alert and careful. There was a smell of not quite fear. Eagerness. Worry, that was it. Cap knew how to do this. First, he must move away and out of sight.

Slipping through the growth, padding slowly and cautiously so as not to rustle, he edged around their clearing. There was one box, at the base of a tree, standing on its legs. It took only a moment to bite it gingerly between fangs and turn it the other way. And it was so thoughtful of them to paint the back side yellow.

Another patient turn brought him to two more. The last of the three was stuck in a tree on a spike. It took some figuring on what to do, as it was wedged in tightly. But it shifted a little when he gripped it, and he was able to rotate it around its mount.

After that, it was no trick to get back in the trees, on the high branches. They would take his weight and afforded him a path to the edge of the clearing. Lower he slipped, quickly and quietly, until he was following a long run over a graybark limb that overhung the area. He crouched on the perch and waited. Whenever she faced away, he slipped a few steps closer. Cynd was walking back and forth, and sooner or later would pass under him. The others snored, alertness dulled by fatigue. He would have a few seconds. That would be enough.

Cynd was walking toward him. She would pass underneath...
now. Reaching down like a stretching spring, Cap got as low as
he could. His paws were bare meters above her Helmet visor,
unseen in her restricted vision. He let go with his rear claws
and dropped, feeling weight pull him down.

She wore Armor and her Helmet, but her face was exposed,
and her legs. He knocked her flat under his weight, felt the breath
whuff out of her, and locked his jaws over her face. She gasped
for air, and he knew she was trying to scream inside his mouth,
as a yearling would. Her hands scrabbled for a weapon, but he
pinned her arms down with his paws, letting the claws sink into
the flesh and holding them tightly. As her gyrations increased,
he unsheathed his rear claws and gouged deeply into her thighs.
Hot wetness splashed, and the body underneath thrashed and
thumped. He was intent on the kill, but his awareness was still
with him, and he heard another voiceless scream of distress and
the sound of gear.

With no hesitation, he rolled off Cynd, and charged away,
legs pumping and lungs heaving as he drove around the trees in
long bounds. Bullets came after him, and he dodged back and
forth, stumbling over a rotten stick, rolling through a patch of
ground ivy, and away.

Shouts were followed by loud *BANGs* as someone detonated
the mines. The explosions tugged at him, wind snapping at the
leaves. But if they were bad for him...

His ears were ringing slightly, but he could hear shrieks
and shouts, swearing and confusion. The heavy growth would
have stopped most of the metal stings from the mines, but they
had to have been disorienting. And frightening. That was what
he wanted. He wanted them afraid, wanted them to know, to
understand and regret.

This was not their home. This was his. And he would protect it.

There was the sound of pursuit. He listened, head turning,
to localize the noise. There was one, that way. He stretched out
his hearing again.

Only one, shooting blindly and crying gibberish under his
breath. Taken by panic, Cap thought, and the smell agreed. He was
coming this way, but only from luck, and there were no others.

He could handle one.

As the Enemy came over the hummock, Cap sprang out of

the leaf bed, his deathsnarl tearing the air and terrifying the animals. The Enemy stopped, wide-eyed and color draining from his face. Smell told Cap that Enemy had voided himself, and as he tried to swing his Gun around, Cap took him.

First, he crushed the wrist that held the Gun with his jaws, while scratching for the face to distract him. Bones splintered, the Gun fell, Enemy screamed, and Capstick turned his attention elsewhere. The other hand was bringing up a Knife, and Cap rolled off, pivoted, and leapt back. The blade tore his lip as he hit, but he shattered that arm, also. The Enemy was sheathed in Armor and a Helmet and Boots, but the thighs and the groin were exposed, and Cap sunk his fangs deep into soft, warm flesh. Enemy howled in agony and thrashed, cried and shook, whimpered and twitched, and was still. Cap ate a few more bites to keep his strength up, and trotted off in a circle around the area, ears alert for voices.

Four.

"She has to have a trauma team! Phil! *Abort the goddamn mission!*" Gunner screamed.

"Yes!" Sergeant agreed. "Hold on, okay?" A moment later he continued, "White Mountain, this is Silver Three. Abort! Abort! Abort! Require immediate extraction and medevac." There was another pause, and Cap knew the message was being turned into a squeal before the Comm sent it, so no one would know they were sending it. The magic squeals only other Comms could hear. If he'd only been able to find friends, all these would be dead. Now they would get away. That saddened him. But he might get another yet.

Sergeant spoke again. "Understood, White Mountain. We can make exfil point in thirty minutes." Click. "Okay, let's destroy the excess gear and weapons and bury them... Guys, where's Jansen?"

They worked themselves into another panic, and Cap again knew pleasure.

People had good ways to deal with wounds, and Cynd was strapped to a Litter they built. She moaned, and was still alive, but Cap knew he could fix that in a moment's time. All that were left now were Gunner and Sergeant and one called Wes. Wes and Sergeant carried Cynd, and Gunner led the way. They were heading north again, and Cap used the arboreal highway to follow them. Sometimes he led them. He knew where they would go, for a Vertol could best reach them on the Bald Hill.

The three Enemy were jogging quickly through the forest. Cap slipped into the lower branches, flowing along them like an elemental force, silent and determined. They were sweating and gasping for breath and had taken off their Helmets to get better vision and cooling. That was good. He could see Gunner curve to the right up ahead, and eyes wary, he tensed for action . . . now!

A leap, a tuck, and Wes's head was in his teeth. He somersaulted over, the world twisting, gripping as tight as he could, and felt the neck snap. Sergeant screamed, and Gunner tried to fire, but Sergeant was in the way. He moved to the side, and Cap dodged the other way as Sergeant dropped his end of the litter and tugged at his Gun. Cap tasted brains and sprang away, rolling off the path and into the soft, leafy fronds of a downweed patch, which hid him as he slid down the hill and over the edge of the ravine, roots and tendrils snagging him. Guns sounded again, and he winced at pain in his side. He had been hit, but it wasn't bad. Nor would it matter if it had been bad. He was hunting. He had an Enemy to bring down.

Five.

He circled again, listening.

"—can't leave her here!" Sergeant said.

"Do you want to try getting to a weapon before that *thing* rips your throat out? Mother of God, have they bioengineered those things?"

"I'll carry the back, weapon slung, you do the same up front. Drop her if we have to. At least she'll have a chance!" Sergeant said.

"You didn't hear me, Phil, *I'm not carrying anything!* I'm making that rendezvous, and they are never sending me back without a full platoon. You file any paperwork you want. I'd rather spend the war in jail than have that thing rip me to death. I liked Cynd, but she's not going to make it."

There was the click of a Gun being readied. Sergeant spoke, "Sergeant Second Class Willen Rogers, pick up that litter or I'll shoot you right here!"

"You really are insane, you know that?" Silence. "Alright. Sorry. Nerves. Let's get the hell out of here." The sound of their feet indicated they were carrying the Litter, and Cap felt pleasure again. He would finish this, despite the wound. He might die as he killed them, but David would be avenged.

They were still heading north, and Cap kept back a bit. Sergeant was watching the trees. He was the tricky one, and Cap would save him for last. He wouldn't die quickly, and Gunner might shoot him while he fought with Sergeant.

Ahead was the upper branch of the creek. They would have to cross there, and that's where he'd kill them.

His side hurt severely, and he licked at it, tongue rasping through the fur. It tasted of blood, and the bitter tang of other damage. But he wasn't dead yet, and there were still things that must be done.

He rose and moved. He motion was tight and slower than before, but he ignored the pain and glided along the boughs.

Bald Hill, as the humans called it, was not the highest point around. It wasn't really a hill, just a jutting end of a smooth ridge. The creek flowed past it from the highlands, and Cap would have to be ready, as once they crossed the water they'd be where they could be found and would have clear space to protect them. He urged himself forward, breath gurgling slightly. The wound in his side had hurt his ribs. No matter. He sprang nimbly from tree to tree, skirting the two Enemy and their burden.

This was good, he thought. They must cross here, with the Litter, as the ground sloped instead of dropping off. He would wait . . . there.

The Enemy was close now. He could hear them muttering to reassure each other along with their tortured breaths. They would have few more of those. He waited under the cut bank of the creek, just upstream from the crossing. Their voices resolved through the chuckling sound of the creek.

"—get across and we can rest," Sergeant said.

"Thank God," Gunner heaved out between strangled gasps. His voice was unclear yet. "We'll need . . . ready . . . for when evac arrives. How do we . . . what happened?"

"We tell them exactly what happened," Sergeant said. "There's enough evidence in the monitors."

They stopped at the beach and prepared to cross, and Cap took the moment to swim closer. A projection covered him, and he waited for them to splash into the chill water, the same water that tore painfully at the wound in his side.

Now. Their Guns were slung, they were knee-deep in water, and they couldn't move as quickly as he did. He clambered up the bank, unheard over the water, and sprang, muscles releasing like a tensed spring.

He was on Gunner and clawed his throat out. Six! Sergeant dropped his end of the Litter, and Cynd tumbled into the water to drown, next to the worms of red leaking up from Gunner's wounds. Seven! Cap turned, and saw Sergeant raising his Gun. He ducked and leapt, using Gunner as a base and felt the burn of a Bullet through his shoulder. It spoiled his attack, but he clawed Sergeant savagely with his right paw, tearing his arm and chest. He tried to force him under water, and Sergeant fired again with his other hand. He missed.

Cap sprang lightly back to his feet in the rocky shallows, sending agony through his side and shoulder. Sergeant was scrabbling for purchase and wasn't looking as he pounced again. He shoved the man's head under water in the deeper pool and leaned on it to hold it there. Gurgling sounds came, and he knew death would follow soon. He ignored the pain in his ribs, and the new pains as his Enemy cut him with a Knife. He shrieked, but pressed lower, closing with the blade until it could cut no more.

He fed on the pain and pressed the attack. He could feel his foe weakening and knew it would not be long now. Exhaustion was taking a toll, though, and he lacked the strength to attack again. Blood loss was making him weak, and spots before his eyes told him he was fading. But his Enemy was faring no better. He slipped under the water again, and emerged coughing, before falling back once more. Cap crept closer, begging strength from his tortured body.

They clashed again, Cap desperate to finish this, his Enemy desperate to survive. As they wrestled, he felt death hovering nearby. Or was that the sound of a Vertol?

It was a Vertol. Cap snarled in outraged frustration. The Gunners aboard wouldn't shoot yet, but he had to leave or die. He drew back, dragging the limp, almost dead Enemy with him, keeping the man between him and potential Bullets. He slipped under water and headed for a moss-spattered rock, needing to get behind cover. Bullets like a deadly hail stirred the water, and he sank as he'd been taught. There was the cut in the bank, and there was the rocky shelf he'd taken on his way in.

Another burst shredded the growth as he fled, while burning with rage at not killing Sergeant. He could not dwell on that now. He had to escape to make his Datadump, survive to fight again. Let the Enemy keep Sergeant and Cynd alive. They could tell them how the fight would go. Not only the soldiers, but the human settlers and their dogs and even the Leopards would fight.

Cap waited under a featherfern, eyes narrowed to cold slits, and held motionless as the Vertol passed over, then again, then a third time. They knew he was there but couldn't see him. Cap had played this game before, even though it wasn't a game now. Despite their tools, people couldn't find Leopards. Not one time in a hundred.

The Vertol flew over again, even lower, then the sound of it echoed away across the hills. In moments, the normal sounds of the northern forest returned, and Cap raised himself, all cuts and aches and bruises, to end his mission. It was nearly sunset, and he still had to hurry.

High in a tree, Capstick spent some time recovering from the exertion, feeling his heart thump, sensing his blood boil, hearing his thoughts roar. His injured shoulder was an agony that he would have to accept for now. At Home, it would need Surgery. His ribs might, also, and the wounds to his skin and tail. Then there was the pain within. He was weak, ill, and hot, but he would rest to recoup his strength and press on. The human doctors could heal him, as they had before. People were good at such things. His thoughts were interrupted as his harness clicked and began its Datadump, and he heaved a deep sigh. He knew better than to roar in anger, pain, frustration.

David was dead. He knew other people, but David had been his friend his entire life. He could not yet think of existence without him. Loss...emptiness...he had no symbols to describe it properly.

Cap still had a purpose, however, and that would give him strength. But fatigue and exertion and his wounds called to him to rest. He would do that now. Tomorrow he would travel gingerly and painfully back to Home. There, he would be paired with a new friend, and he and that friend would hunt the invaders remorselessly. Perhaps the manhunters from Black Ops would join them. If not, he would teach his new friend what loyalty meant, and they would hunt as a pair.

The humans called it duty. To him it was simply the way things were.

Solitude

Jessica Schlenker

"Well, Brandon, be a dear and introduce us!" chirped an unfamiliar woman wearing a blue hat, from just behind Payload Master Brandon Davidson of the *Sri Lanka*. Davidson, who had just opened his mouth to say something presumably not an introduction, closed it with an audible click.

Reginald Baxter loathed her perky, falsely cheerful falsetto already. He steadfastly stared at Davidson, not acknowledging the woman. Davidson visibly suppressed a wince. "Baxter, this is Maria Sanchez, of the United Nations' Office of Health and Safety. Ms. Sanchez, this is Grainne Asteroid Mining Complex One's hydroponics specialist Reginald Baxter."

"It's *Maria*, and I'm so pleased to meet you, Reggie," she chirped, extending her hand. Reginald noticed the carefully manicured nails, which rivaled those of any high-end courtier and bespoke of her complete lack of familiarity with hands-on work. He did not extend his hand in return, instead clenching the order tablet.

"Ms. Sanchez." he acknowledged as he kept his focus on Davidson. "I have the supplies you ordered, Payload Master." He offered the tablet to Davidson, who took it and led the few meters to the pallets.

"I was surprised to discover you lived on this station alone. That's quite a safety violation," Sanchez continued, speaking over the conversation regarding supplies. "I'm afraid that can't be continued now that we're in charge of the system."

That finally forced Reginald to respond. "Mr. Hayes constructed this facility based on UN requirements to facilitate trade with

UN parties, and there are provisions for a single individual with my *documented—*"

"*Disability,*" Davidson interjected. "As Mr. Hayes informed you, Ms. Sanchez, Mr. Baxter has a documented *disability* which makes it difficult and even painful to interact with other humans beyond the most minimal of requirements. We have all been briefed by Medic Phillips on how to interact and assess his situation to minimize concerns. He is monitored remotely as unobtrusively as possible. Please desist. You've seen for yourself that Mr. Baxter is healthy and hale, and you've reviewed his *medical* records and orders. Now, please, return to the *Sri* so that we do not unduly distress Mr. Baxter further."

The woman huffed but finally left. Reginald felt himself relax slightly. "Disability?" he asked quietly.

Davidson shrugged. "We all like some peace and quiet on occasion."

Reginald snorted. "And why the hell is she here? Leons didn't mention a trade delegation inspection, and *that* mentioned as being in charge. Hayes wouldn't sell out."

Davidson paused. "I suppose it makes sense you haven't heard. The UN invaded Grainne. Rumor is the spaceport is half obliterated. Most of the military installations got kinetic strikes, and trackable military ships were disabled or destroyed. I've seen handheld video of the Jefferson base. It's nothing but rubble."

"What the hell?"

"Hayes might have more information, but the UN has control of communications right now."

So Reginald couldn't even ask. Lovely.

They completed the checklist and mutually signed off, releasing payment. Davidson paused at the hatchway. "Let me know if you get overcrowded?"

Reginald scowled. He lived alone in Mining Complex Delta, or MicDees, for damned good reason.

Two days later, it became apparent that Davidson's suspicion held true. The computer alerted him to an unannounced, unscheduled docking. Video showed several people wearing blue hats.

He hailed Mining Complex Command. "MMC, I have unscheduled visitors. Please advise."

Sally Leons answered, her expression blank. "Ms. Sanchez

has 'offered' the use of 'unused' space in the crew quarters of MicDees to certain UN-affiliated groups. They are expected to interact with you regularly for your own good."

Reginald drummed his fingers on the desk. "Do they have *any* notion how bad of an idea that is?"

Sanchez peered over Leons's shoulder, which explained the carefully neutral expression Leons wore. "You just need acclimation and socialization, Reggie, and I'm sure you'll adjust. Humans are social beings, after all."

He would rather flay his own hands and shove them into buckets of salt. But Leons must have realized the gist of his response, because she was shaking her head ever so slightly. He bit back his response.

Sanchez smiled, an oozy, smarmy expression which further aggravated Reginald. "I knew you would listen to reason if you weren't given a way to escape it. The crew assigned to the station should introduce themselves shortly."

Leons's expression made it clear what *she* thought of the situation. "Please inform myself or Mr. Hayes if your *disability* becomes unmanageable. Preferably before you take steps to mitigate it yourself."

Before he increased their insurance costs, he assumed, if the insurance was even functioning still. "Understood. Baxter out." He didn't wait for acknowledgement; he never did.

The UN "affiliates" were still milling around the docking area when he approached. It was better to initiate contact on his terms. "Who is in charge of this group?"

The others cleared out from in front of an older woman. "I am. Civil Manager Heidi Brichenstock. Are you our ... host?"

"I am Hydroponics Specialist Baxter. I believe you have been led to believe there are spare ... *accommodations* on MicDees. That is not precisely accurate."

"I'm sure we'll make do," Brichenstock assured him. "I've been provided the official plans for the facility."

"They are more than ten years out of date."

She looked unsurprised, not even resigned. "It wouldn't be the first time. I do work for a bureaucracy, after all."

He almost liked her. He shrugged. "You have been warned. This station also does not have sufficient crew-support quarters or supplies."

"I did notice that." She hesitated. "I also was informed you have a disability, the nature of which I was not given details. Is there anything I should know?"

"As I recall, the official diagnosis was 'anti-social.'"

She blinked, then nodded. "I will ensure that my people understand to limit their enthusiasm for following Ms. Sanchez's instructions regarding *socializing* with you, then."

"I am sure my boss's insurance would appreciate that."

She looked confused but did not question why insurance would be involved.

MicDees's first life as the initial administration office for Hayes's endeavor included sufficient support, including bathroom facilities and cooking capabilities, for a respectable crew. The complex had been replaced by the MMC and retrofitted to be primarily hydroponics. The remaining crew quarters, designated for emergency use only, were skeletonized, and most of the facilities were converted into hydroponic support and the necessary attendant activities.

Reginald rediscovered how much he *loathed* sharing a bathroom with anyone, let alone some of these utterly piggish UN office workers. He griped to Leons about the complete inability to maintain the most minimal of hygienic standards. After the third time that Sanchez peered over her shoulder to chirpily inform him that "didn't sound too bad," and that he'd "adjust in due time," Leons found a UN regulation that enabled private communications, completely encrypted, to Medic Phillips.

Phillips took over the task of keeping Reginald from losing his frail hold on his temper. Before two weeks was out, this required nearly two hours a day of Phillips listening to Reginald rant and rave while making notes.

But, despite the UN's much vaunted love of processes, procedures, and proper protocols, the combined forces of Hayes, Leons, and Phillips could not convince Sanchez to remove her administrators. Brichenstock's complaints about the insufficient facilities also prompted no movement or mitigation response.

Reginald wondered if Sanchez was a sadist, getting off on inflicting unnecessary discomforts on, well, everyone. Did she hate Brichenstock? Reginald himself? Or was it some perverse kink?

Not that it mattered. *If that damned video next door didn't shut off...*

He yanked himself back under control. He'd promised Phillips and Leons. He owed them a lot. He could keep trying, he told himself, grinding his teeth as the barely audible fake laugh track came from the break room next to his administrative office. He heard Brichenstock chastise her people for the volume, and it went down. *She* seemed to feel sympathy for him and was at least trying. He still almost liked her, an odd feeling for him.

A snippet of conversation made it through the door. "I know the guy keeps the areas he uses *spotless*, but the place could really use some *color*," a female voice said.

"Oh, definitely. Maybe even a mural in the rec?" replied a second female voice. "Ocean views would work."

The first laughed. "You and your oceans."

Reginald had a superior idea, one which suited him better than ocean scenes. They could get the hell off his station.

His hydroponic checks weren't completed for the day, but he retreated to his quarters anyway. Every time a door or hatch moved, every barely heard conversation as UN personnel went past, every single sound that wasn't either the slight mechanicals of the station proper or caused by himself, he twitched. He dug out the long-unused sound suppression headset, from back before he fled groundside. It cut down on the persistent slight echo, whether real or just in Reginald's ears, that resulted from the movement of other people in his domain.

The headphones worked for about a day. The pressure of the headset on his ears finally pushed him to pull it off for just a moment. The very first thing he heard was that insufficiently bedamned laugh track on whatever insipid video was being played in the breakroom.

He fled to the hydroponics chambers, which Brichenstock had declared off limits to her crew, despite Sanchez's smarmy encouragement that they "get the freshest air possible." Plants fared better under at least slight gravity, so the hydroponics chambers existed on the outermost side of the station, under the gentle spin. Having a "down" sometimes helped, but today, nothing soothed his nerves. Even the softly humid air, redolent with the scent of growing plants, failed to bring him the normal serenity.

Here, though, he could at least *pace*. And pace he did, for hours, while he manually tended his charges. After every last task was completed, he stayed in the chamber. He was too wound up for the most calming of his music choices. Hunger and exhaustion finally pushed him to return to his quarters.

He found a carefully situated packet at the entrance hatch to the hydroponics chamber, with a note taped to it. Paper was even scarcer on the station than elsewhere, and this looked to be torn from someone's diary or journal.

> *My apologies.*
>
> *Phillips contacted me to check on you without actually checking on you, and when I reported that you appeared to be pacing in Hydroponics, he directed me to acquire the items here.*
>
> *I explicitly did not enter your quarters, so these may not be up to your usual standards.*
>
> *Phillips explained how long you've been isolated, and a little more clarification. If I'm about to toss one of these idiots out an airlock, I can only imagine how hard this is on you.*
>
> *I'm attempting to get this group relocated . . . anywhere. I'm in contact with my upper management about the situation with Ms. Sanchez, as well. She is unaware of this, which is one reason for this being handwritten.*
>
> *Phillips requests that you communicate with him via your standard method.*
>
> > *Heidi*

The packet contained a set of the emergency crew supplies, including a handful of the choicer meals. The meals he didn't recognize had UN markings, and he assumed she'd raided her own crew's backup supplies. He did not dare contact Phillips today.

Two "nights" in the hydroponics section left him calm enough to contact Phillips.

"Are you still in hydroponics?" was Phillips's first question.

Reginald panned the camera, so Phillips could see for himself.

"Right. Brichenstock has made progress cutting around Sanchez, but until there's an incident, that's as far as she can go."

"What does that mean?"

Phillips shrugged. "It means you can't, how was it Brichenstock put it, 'shove anyone out an airlock or anything else quite that drastic.' She's sympathetic. Seems she's quite the introvert herself."

"'Introvert'?" Reginald snorted. He knew damn well he made the average introvert look like a social butterfly.

Phillips grinned at him. "Just be your normal, charming self then, I guess. Hayes requests that no important equipment be damaged, however. We have limited capability for resupplying under the circumstances. Scuttle we're getting from groundside is that the resistance is using up all the electronics they can get their fingernails into."

Reginald nodded, then blinked. "Wait. What? How are you getting rumors with Sanchez breathing down your neck?"

Phillips smirked. "Seems that you aren't the only one with 'mental health discretion' requirements out here in the boonies. Handy little loophole, that." The pious expression Phillips wore for a moment nearly made Reginald laugh. "After all, it is my sacred duty to 'do no harm,' and to ensure that everyone remains healthy. These are 'trying times,' and everyone has to 'do their part'!"

Phillips mimicked Sanchez's voice so well, Reginald actually flinched. "I see. And my part is to get these idiots off my hydroponics station?"

"We need you to keep feeding people. From your perspective, nothing really has to change. Except, of course, removing your ... irritations."

"Got it. Baxter out."

Reginald cautiously returned to his quarters. He encountered no one directly, but certainly heard traffic. When he arrived in his office, he found Brichenstock waiting for him.

"I do apologize for intruding," she started.

He waved her off. "I'm okay for now. Thank you for the supplies."

She relaxed a little. "You're welcome. I wish I could do more."

"And I'll try to not kill anyone."

She winced. "That's why I'm here. Phillips told me about what happened back groundside."

"Does it worry you?"

She stared at one of the displays and didn't answer immediately. "They're basically kids," she sighed. "I mean, I'm not *that* much older than they are, maybe ten years older than the oldest of them, but they're basically kids. Decent-meaning ones, at that. Puppies who like numbers."

"But there has to be an incident, doesn't there?"

"And I'm asking that there be no lasting damage to whichever puppy needs its nose smacked with a shoe."

"I will do my best to not actually hurt anyone. That . . . incident . . . was . . . a very long time coming, and I've gotten better control since then, too." He actually meant it.

"Thanks. I know you can't *promise* anything. I know how it is."

He must have shown his doubt, because she half-smiled. She pushed up a sleeve and traced a faded scar along her forearm. "I know how it is," she repeated. "And I will protect the puppies." She left.

Reginald had not considered that her support was rooted in more than a sympathetic disposition. He, for one of the very few times in his life, actually wanted to talk to someone to find out about *them*. It was an odd feeling, but he didn't suppose it would last long.

Over the next several days, Brichenstock continued to intrigue him. He knew, and she knew, that until his tolerance was breached irrevocably, the situation would continue. Knowing that there were *plans* and an *endgame* for his torture to be ended . . . brought him a curious level of peace, and his temper rose more slowly than it had previously. *Her* temper, however, seemed to have made up the balance. She snapped more frequently at her "puppies" and rode on them hard for previously innocuous situations. He heard a couple complain about it while they walked past his office, or he wouldn't have suspected.

It was his turn to check on *her*. It felt . . . odd. Very, very odd. It had been a long time since he felt compelled to reach out to someone for any reason, rather than having it forced on him by external dictates.

He checked with the computer for her whereabouts and discovered she was pacing in a quiet-even-for-MicDees wing. He'd paced that passageway a few times himself and went to stand in the most conspicuous but least intrusive spot to wait for her. She glanced at him when he leaned against the bulkhead but kept pacing for several more minutes.

She eventually slowed and sighed. She leaned against the opposite bulkhead. "I know. You're supposed to have an incident, not me." He tilted his head at her and waited. She shrugged. "You haven't stayed on top of what's going on down on Grainne, or even in the system, have you?"

He shook his head.

"When I took this position, we were told ... I guess it doesn't really matter what we were told. What we *thought* was going to happen, or anything. The ... expectation was the regular person on the street, or ship, or whatever, was going to open their arms and happily accept the UN's oversight."

He snorted, and she half-smiled. "Right. I believed them. Why shouldn't I? I didn't know better." She paused. "Jump Point One is destroyed. Your Resistance took a Skywheel down."

"Wait, what?"

She nodded. "And you're out here, just feeding spacers and trying to be left alone, with a sadistic bitch from theoretically my side trying to force you to socialize with us, and if that's not a microcosm of this whole fiasco, I don't know what is."

She paused. He recognized the expression, or at least thought he did, of assumed dispassionate distance. "I never really explained what we're doing—what my team does. OpSec and all that. We basically just run payroll. There's been a flaw in the program for, I don't know, longer than I've worked on the team. Occasionally one user would get someone else's info, things like that." He blinked, and it was her turn to snort. "Has never been fixed. So, against policy, I've always kept an offline backup, personally. I didn't trust the online backups."

"And?"

"I caught someone using an account that should have been expired out years ago, making edits two days ago. Major edits."

He raised an eyebrow, and she looked at the ceiling. "I overwrote my copy with the new 'master' version in the system."

"You ..."

"And then I deleted my copy. Shouldn't have it anyway, after all. 'Policy should guide us in every step,'" she singsonged with obvious sarcasm.

"Sanchez?" he asked.

"The very same. Coincidentally, also the individual who appears to be utterly incapable of following policy in any other matter." Brichenstock shrugged. "Honestly, given everything else, I expect to throw that problem on her, too. Upper levels are ignoring everything else so far." She tilted her head at him. "You've lasted a bit longer than I expected."

"There's a plan."

She nodded. "That was a risk of letting you know about it, I guess."

"What about you?"

She shrugged. "I'm technically just a contractor. If they get too mad at me, they'll ship me home. I might forfeit the short-term bonus pay, but there's jobs enough I can do back on Earth."

The answer felt off, somehow, but Reginald couldn't place what made him think that. She shrugged. "Thank you for listening to me. I should go back before someone wonders where I am."

Reginald assumed Brichenstock had shared the bit about the database knowing he might share it with Phillips. For her sake, he only did so a couple of days after the conversation, once he was reasonably confident that she had settled down a bit.

Phillips gave him a long look after he relayed the information. It was unnerving.

"What?"

Phillips shook his head. "Nothing, Baxter." But even Reginald could tell it wasn't nothing. "How's your temper been?"

Reginald shrugged. "They're really starting to get on my nerves again."

Phillips nodded. "Just remembers Hayes's request."

"Will do. Baxter out."

Of course, it wasn't necessarily the people alone getting on his nerves. That *damned* laugh track might get someone killed directly. Every time he heard it, the red would start seeping into his vision, and he'd start seeing heads smashed in, almost hallucinations of slamming people into walls to kill them. He hadn't experienced *those* in a long time, and he was more than a tad concerned. The effort involved in not wrecking things increased every time, and he knew it was just a matter of time before the necessary "incident" occurred.

Reginald's nerves were already humming with frustration and anger when the computer announced an incoming message from Phillips. "Baxter here."

"Sanchez is on her way over," Phillips started, "and she's pissed at Brichenstock."

"The database?"

"She thinks Brichenstock corrupted it to make her look bad,

or some nonsense. She's caught some heat from letting them out of her direct supervision."

Reginald felt almost joyful for a brief second. "She's coming to take them off ship?"

Phillips shook his head. "That certainly didn't seem to be in her plans. I'm not completely certain."

"...she isn't intending to stay here herself, is she?"

"Just let Brichenstock know. You have a couple of hours; Davidson is her ride again, and he's feigning 'difficulties' to buy you some time."

"Understood. Baxter out."

He checked with the computer to locate Brichenstock. She was in private quarters, so he sent a comm query.

"Brichenstock here." She looked disheveled and a bit disoriented, as if he'd woken her up.

"Sanchez is en route, and apparently pretty angry at you."

Brichenstock shook her head and looked more alert. "About damn time there was some kind of response from her."

"She might be coming to stay on MicDees for 'direct supervision,'" Reginald replied. He felt this was the worst possible outcome of "response."

Brichenstock smiled, not a particularly nice smile, and shrugged. "Let me handle it, although I'd recommend you be there as well."

"Might not be a puppy needing its nose whacked?"

"Sometimes you have to discipline adult bitches, too," Brichenstock agreed.

Brichenstock met Reginald at the primary airlock after Davidson alerted MicDees of the ship's approach. "Allow me to handle her as much as possible," she told him.

"And let you have all the fun?" he replied.

She snorted. "For the purposes of the UN, a 'peaceful' resolution, where I run roughshod over her, is best." She not-smiled again. "Although I highly doubt it will happen, I must make the attempt."

Sanchez only waited for the airlock to pressurize because she did not have access to overrides. Her typically smarmy smile and coifed appearance were missing, and she looked more like the snake that Reginald treated her as. "Brichenstock, how *dare* you report problems without consulting me first." Reginald noted the lack of first name usage.

Brichenstock shrugged. "You were provided reports and status updates. Your inability to read is not my concern."

Sanchez hissed. "I will have your career."

"For proving you don't know how to do your job? Hardly. You won't be the first I've gotten removed from that role. Ah, Payload Master, greetings."

Davidson's appearance distracted Sanchez from her diatribe, and Brichenstock prompted, "I believe, Ms. Sanchez, that you were about to request an *in-person* tour of the facilities which I have *repeatedly* filed complaints as being inadequate *per contract* for my personnel."

"I—" Sanchez started.

"—want to keep getting promotions?" Brichenstock interjected. "We all do, hence my suggestion. In fact, Mr. Baxter, would you do me the kindest favor, and show Ms. Sanchez around?" Reginald gave her a look, and she not-smiled. "Perhaps start with the corridor near the chemical storage?"

Reginald gamely agreed. He felt impressed with Brichenstock's sudden control over the situation and wondered why she hadn't exerted it before. Sanchez looked confused and flummoxed as she found herself being herded off and out of the bay. Reginald faintly heard Brichenstock speaking to Davidson and hoped the conversation would result in the UN crew's removal.

Sanchez was mercifully quiet at first and appeared to be looking around the station. Near the transition between crew and working decks, she asked, "Why is it so barren?"

Reginald didn't consider his home to be barren and replied as much.

"It's bland, with no color. UN specifications do require sensory enhancement for long-duration space life," she answered.

"I like it this way." He shrugged and opened the hatch into the working decks.

Despite being the primary individual concerned, Reginald scrupulously ensured that all the hazmat and warning signs decorated the appropriate areas. The chemical storage section was carefully maintained. "Why do you have so many liquid chemicals?" Sanchez asked, picking up an MSDS binder.

"Water is the restricting resource on a station, and each type of plant requires different supplements. Some plants require different mixes depending on their lifecycle to ensure the most productivity. I find it easiest to mix the solutions in volume, and Hayes has some of the bare chemicals brought in from the reduction plants. Recycling or using the chemicals here is essential for cost efficiencies."

Sanchez stared at him for a moment. "That was a long speech for you."

He started ushering her in the direction of the hydroponics entrance. "I like plants."

"But not people."

"Correct."

"You have to get used to people at some point," she replied. "This team must stay on the station. It's safe—"

"They can't stay," he stated bluntly.

"Well, Brichenstock will obviously be removed from her role, but the rest of the team will remain here."

Reginald ground his teeth and glanced in the direction of the chemical loading bay airlock, at the end of the corridor. She looked in the same direction. "What's that?"

"Nothing important," he said as dismissively as he could.

Sanchez glowered. "I'll determine that for myself."

Reginald shrugged with all the nonchalance he could muster and gestured in that direction. She engaged the inner airlock door, and Reginald stayed outside the marked swing radius. Several meters deep, the airlock could handle large pallet loads, a holdover from the days when MicDees was the only part of the mining facility. Sanchez moved to the far door, frowning at the outer airlock's control panel.

The outer airlock's indicators correctly showed the other side was depressurized. "What is in there?" Sanchez demanded as she punched buttons, randomly for all Reginald could tell from here. The video feed from the bay had failed years ago, and repair was deemed noncritical.

"A loading bay, generally unused," he answered her question curtly.

She frowned in irritation. "I want to inspect it."

"That will have to wait," he replied coolly.

"I want to inspect it immediately," she demanded, raising her voice. She turned back to the panel.

"I suggest waiting," Reginald replied. He did not permit his tone to vary and based on the way her lip curled when she glared over her shoulder, it was aggravating her to no end. He took satisfaction in needling her as much as she had harassed him these last weeks. He noticed error messages showing up on the corridor's interface, and assumed she'd hit something she shouldn't have.

"Now," she hissed.

"I wouldn't if I were you." *Do it, bitch.*

"Now," she snapped as she keyed the airlock to cycle. He caught a brief glance of Sanchez's expression as the hatch swung shut. She didn't even have the sense to be afraid, just puzzled. He watched as the pressure readout dropped to zero.

Reginald gave it about ten minutes before keying comms to MMC. The emergency gear inside the airlock should have been sufficient, had she paid attention.

"MicDees to MMC, Baxter here."

"Leons speaking."

"Ms. Sanchez appears to have attempted to inspect the chemicals loading bay without protective gear. The airlock emergency gear has not triggered."

"Well, hell."

Brichenstock was summoned to the passage, as was *Sri Lanka*'s captain. They had been working on loading her team onto *Sri Lanka*.

"I didn't mean for you to *actually* throw her out of an airlock." Brichenstock sighed.

"Her lack of reading comprehension is also not my fault," Reginald replied. "I hope the paperwork is not too onerous."

Province of Man

Jaime DiNote

Because your own strength is unequal to the task,
do not assume that it is beyond the powers of man;
but if anything is within the powers and province of
man, believe that it is within your own compass also.
—Marcus Aurelius

1.

Bullets whizzed through the thick, yellowing underbrush, striking the trees with loud cracks. United Nations Peacekeeping Forces Lieutenant Sam Overstreet bounded between the ancient wooden pillars, making his way to a wounded comrade. While traversing the sparsely populated Saorsa Valley was slow under the best of circumstances, the bulky and bloodied first aid bag strapped to his chest made movement especially treacherous. Sam made the final sprint to his objective, taking advantage of a short lull while the rebels reloaded. He threw the aid bag to Captain Talia Jackson as he shouldered his rifle to return fire, panting from exertion and heat, "Who the fuck thought blue helmets were a good idea out here?"

Sam fought to control his breathing through the adrenaline and exertion of the sprint, the extra gravity taxing him more than it should have. He took aim and shot into the last area he'd noted as a firing position. He quipped to the injured company executive officer between bursts, "You know, this could be such a beautiful planet."

Captain Jackson winced as she slapped a clotting agent on

her wound and wrapped a tight bandage around her upper arm. "There's something wrong with you, man. Keep shooting!" she ordered.

"What?" Sam pressed, firing another volley toward the enemy. "Just look at that sunset! Magical."

Having staunched the blood flow, Jackson pushed herself up to retake her firing position, the rifle's low recoil and the discarded autoinjector lying next to her allowing her to stay in the fight. With a pained grunt she barked, "Shut the fuck up, Street!"

Some people just don't appreciate nature, Sam wisely took the cue that discretion was the better part of valor and toned it down.

Within minutes, the exchange tapered off and Sam hollered, "Cease fire!" The command echoed throughout the unit, and an uneasy silence followed.

Each platoon immediately dispersed to fulfill post-engagement duties. First platoon established and secured the perimeter, tended to the wounded, and documented the dead. Second platoon moved into the brush to collect intelligence and take any wounded combatants into custody.

The NCOs consolidated the remaining ammunition, redistributing it as needed. While lethal force was strictly prohibited, even the UN admitted that their Peacekeepers would need to defend themselves in such an openly hostile environment. Thus, in its infinite wisdom, the UNPF had deployed them to the field with a basic rifle and minimum combat load, one fifty-round magazine per soldier, along with a full complement of nonlethal munitions.

Sam stood next to Captain Jackson as First Sergeant Rachel Goodwin handed her a reloaded magazine and reported the casualties. "Ma'am, five wounded this time, four are ambulatory. Two dead."

"Who?" asked Jackson, inserting the magazine into her rifle.

"Nuwayver and Hughes."

"Shit," Jackson swore. "No wonder Street had the aid bag. Hughes was a good medic, too. How many did we get?"

"Third squad's checking that now, ma'am," 1st Sgt Goodwin replied.

Jackson checked the counter on her rifle. "Whoa, First Sergeant, there's only eight rounds in here."

"What did you expect? We haven't been resupplied in a month," Goodwin reminded her. "That nonlethal shit is useless and it's not like we were swimming in ammo when we got here. How long did you think one full mag apiece was going to last?"

Jackson threw up a hand to the First Sergeant, indicating her point was made. She was right—they had tried the nonlethal approach, per UN law and regulation. When the webs snared more trees than rebels, and the stunners accomplished nothing more than pissing off a nest of feral cats, the commander gave the order to abandon nonlethal altogether.

The three walked to the casualty collection point. Jackson spoke to the acting squad leader, Sergeant Second Class Palacio, gathering information for her report and checking in with her men. Sam took the opportunity to help to keep their spirits up through the pain.

"Halt!" They heard the security team shout at an approaching person. "Who is it?"

"Lieutenant Ansbach and second platoon," came the reply.

"Blackbeard!" the soldier shouted, issuing the challenge.

"Pirate!" Lieutenant Second Class Jennifer Ansbach responded with the password, annoyed.

"Approach slowly and be identified."

"Fuck you, it's me!" She flipped off the smirking Peacekeeper pulling security as she passed him.

Once Lt. Ansbach was through the perimeter, she took off at a sprint toward the XO. "Captain Jackson! You need to come with me."

"What is it, LT?"

"Prisoners, ma'am."

"Street," Jackson called, "let's go."

They followed Lt. Ansbach to their prisoner collection point inside the company perimeter as she quickly briefed them on the most promising intelligence prospect they had found yet.

"Two males, one approximately mid-forties, the other about twenty. One female, looks maybe fifteen. We found them making their way back to their base, probably going for reinforcements. All wounded to some degree, we're offering what medical aid we can, but it doesn't look good for the elder male. Figured you'd want to question him while you can."

"Good work, Jen."

As they approached the casualty collection point, they saw the older man lying on the ground, blood turning his light blue shirt a deep crimson. The young girl held his hand, allowing the ground forces to render aid under her suspicious watch, her blond hair held back by the long braid running down her back. The younger man sat a few meters from them, receiving a splint on a broken tibia and a bandage on the bullet wound that caused it, trading insults with the Peacekeeper working on him. He was a handsome man, obviously strong, with short, dark hair and the kind of build that one develops after years of hard physical labor. If he'd been smaller or weaker, he might have lost the leg.

"I got this. Street, you go talk to the young guy."

"Yes, ma'am." Sam veered off toward the young man, instinctively putting on his kindest, most disarming smile.

The young man was still arguing with the acting medic.

Oh, an ornery colonial. Who could have seen that coming? Sam thought sarcastically. He could see the Peacekeeper guarding the young man tighten his grip on his rifle, and Sam took this as his cue to intervene.

He placed a calm hand on the Peacekeeper's shoulder and said, "Stand down, Sergeant Price. I think I'd be pretty riled up too in his place, wouldn't you?"

"Yes, sir," the sergeant snarled, never breaking eye contact with the young colonial. He reluctantly removed his finger from the trigger guard and placed it alongside the receiver.

Sam slapped the sergeant on the back, "There we go!" He turned to the injured colonial, "Now that we're all calm, tell me, what's your name?"

The young man spat at him, "Eat shit, aardvark!"

Sam repeated the phrase aloud slowly, thoughtfully, "'Eatshit Aardvark.' I've never heard that name before. What is that? Lithuanian?"

The young man stared at him like he'd grown a second head. "What do you people want from us?"

Sam stepped toward him and squatted down to look him in the eye, still flashing his friendliest smile. "Well, Eatshit, I'm Lieutenant Sam Overstreet from the United Nations 429th Peacekeeping Civil Affairs Regiment. I'm sorry we had to meet under these circumstances. Our mission here is to meet with local civic leaders to discuss exactly how our people can help your people. We're here to have a dialogue; try to get us all on the same page so we can work together for a better Grainne."

"We don't need your help. We don't want your help. We were doing just fine until you assholes stormed our farm!"

"Everyone needs a little help now and then, Eatshit. We have reports of Colonial Ground Forces hiding out in this area and we'd hate for you to get caught up in all that."

The young man gritted his teeth and inhaled deeply, "Name's Jeremiah and we are obviously not FMF! The only people on my property were my parents and siblings; just the seven of us." His eyes shimmered with tears as he forced words through a tightened throat. "And now, thanks to you, my mother, two brothers, and my baby sister are all dead."

"I'm sorry—" Sam started, having lost his friendly smile. Now all he could feel was shame and pain for this young man.

"Don't!" Jeremiah shouted at him. "Don't even try it. Since when is an unarmed six-year-old girl an enemy soldier? You slaughtered my family! I hope the resistance sends you all home in bags. Now get the hell away from me so I can say goodbye to my father."

Sam said nothing, simply nodded to the others to give Jeremiah some room. He offered the young colonial help to stand, knowing he'd refuse it. Instead, Jeremiah chose to crawl the few meters to his only surviving family. He held his father's hand, saying a tearful goodbye, and then cried with his remaining sister once the man's final, ragged breath left him.

Jackson approached Sam, "You get anything?"

He paused, still reeling from the sight of the decimated civilian family in front of him, then shook his head, "No, ma'am. He says they're just farmers."

Jackson's voice dripped with skepticism, "They're all 'just farmers.'"

"Maybe that's because this is a *farming community*? When was the last time we encountered an actual Colonial soldier?"

"Even if they are civilians, that doesn't mean they don't funnel information and supplies to the resistance. Come on, we're losing daylight. We'll question them back at base. Wildlife will be out soon."

"Ma'am, I don't think they're inclined to answer many questions." Sam knew he was being borderline insubordinate, but he silently implored her to show this family some compassion.

Jackson looked him dead in the eye, "They never are."

She turned away and made a wide swooping motion above her head like a vertol's main rotors, giver her soldiers a focal point as she called to them, "Bring it in!"

Sam continued watching the family while Jackson gave the company their marching orders. The girl, whose name he still didn't know, was trying to help her hefty brother to his feet as the POW escort team pulled her away to restrain her hands.

"For your safety, ma'am," they said without a shred of emotion or patience, pushing her roughly toward the formation.

Jeremiah lost his balance on the uneven terrain and fell bodily on his injured leg, screaming out at the sudden sharp pain.

Sam moved forward to secure his bloody, loosened bandage. Jeremiah gritted his teeth through obvious pain as Sam tried to keep him calm. "It's alright, Jeremiah. You're going to be fine. We'll get you back to our base and fix you up. Let me see if I can find you some pain meds, okay? I'll be right back."

No sooner had he stood up to find the aid bag than he saw Sergeant Second Class Jeffrey Price level his rifle at Jeremiah. Without a word or hesitation, Sergeant Price fired a single round through Jeremiah's forehead.

Sam stood in shock, unable to breathe. His vision narrowed at the sight of unmitigated gore splayed on the ground before him. He barely registered the distant sound of the young woman screaming for her brother before his world widened once again.

"What the fuck was that?!" he screamed and lunged for Sergeant Price.

Jackson was by his side in an instant, holding him back. Price spoke calmly, emotionlessly, as though he'd just squashed a spider. "He moved to attack you, sir. You're welcome."

"That's bullshit and you know it!"

"Stand down, Overstreet!" Captain Jackson ordered him. "Look, there's nothing we could do for him anyway. It's getting dark and we still have to climb a fucking mountain. Pretty tough to navigate these woods after nightfall and we still have *our* wounded to carry. We got to move, and we don't need another casualty slowing us down even more. We'll deal with Price back at base."

She let go of him and motioned for the specialists to search the body for intel before moving him next to his father.

"Stick a few grenades under the bodies," 1st Sgt Goodwin called to her troops. Sam tried to protest, but she continued with a smirk that never reached her dead, gray eyes, "For the wildlife, of course."

Sam still stared at the body, sick to his stomach at the carnage he'd witnessed. He tried weakly to speak, "Ma'am..."

Jackson shouldered her rifle and surveyed her company, looking once more at him before walking away, "Shit ain't so fucking funny now, is it, Lieutenant?"

2

Sam spent the next day alone in his quarters, the recycled air blasting him with the smell of sixty other inadequately washed asses. At least it was cool. Well, cooler than the sweltering outside. He stared out his small window. The usually breathtaking mountainside view seemed dusty and dingy through the emotional tempest raging in his mind.

The ersatz outpost was securely nestled into a rocky plateau in the upper foothills above the Saorsa Valley. It was small and sturdy enough for brief exercises, but was never intended for long-term missions. After some field expedient modifications, the unit managed to turn the Standard Pop-Up Rigid Shelter System, or "SPURSS," into a one-hundred-meter compound, complete with housing, office space, supply room, infirmary, and detention cells.

Sam's mind raced, reviewing and processing the previous day's events. He'd seen death, even killing, but never had he so closely witnessed cold, calculated murder, and he admitted to himself that he was ill-equipped to handle it. *What the hell am I doing here? I'm not supposed to be patrolling villages. I'm a legal assistant, for God's sake!*

Confused and angry, he let his thoughts wander back over the month they'd been stranded on an inhospitable mountainside and how far his once respectable unit had fallen in that time.

This was not at all what he'd imagined when he volunteered for this deployment. His job was simply to shadow his law school mentor and fellow reservist, Lieutenant Major Darin Cantrell, in keeping the unit's legal paperwork in order and the commander out of trouble. Sam was good at his job, but he knew there was more to being a good soldier than simple administrative busy-work. During Sam's previous two years at Vanderbilt Law, he'd taken every possible class Darin offered and came to regard the prior enlisted special operator-turned-JAG as both a warrior and a scholar. Sam desperately wanted to follow in his footsteps.

Sam thought he'd hit the deployment jackpot when Darin told him about the commander. Major Beau Lemaire was one of Darin's oldest friends and a direct disciple of General Huff, often lauded as one of his "High-potential Officers." This made him practically a shoo-in for stars someday, and Lemaire got there by being among the most "by-the-book" officers in the UNPF.

Sam learned quickly, however, that the greatest lessons are often borne of adversity.

He thought back to his first command meeting on the ground.

Four Weeks Earlier

The senior leaders and legal team gathered in Maj. Lemaire's office. It was a small room with too few chairs and far too much dust. Normally a stickler for uniform dress and appearance, Lemaire looked rumpled and dirty, with worry lines creasing his forehead. The uncertainty was palpable as the commander cleared his throat to speak.

"Ladies and gentlemen, as you know, an electrical storm hit our outpost three days ago, destroying our primary powercell and damaging the backup in the process. The strike caused a power surge and fire in the equipment room which fried, literally, our communications equipment, and killed Privates Yates and Dixon. As such, we currently have no way to contact MOB Unity, the TOC, or anyone else."

Lemaire looked to Lt. Maj. Cantrell and took a breath before continuing. "What you may not know is that early this morning, fire watch sentries reported distant, high altitude flashes in the general direction of MOB Unity," he paused to read from his notes, "accompanied by a reentry streak and a large, rope-like object falling to the surface."

"Skywheel?" Capt. Jackson ventured a guess.

"That's what it sounds like, Captain."

Lt. Ansbach spoke up, "What does this mean, sir?"

"It means that Unity is probably going to have their hands full cleaning up wherever that filament landed, and it may be a while before they can get to us. Once they realize we haven't checked in, they should send a crew to check our last known position. Might take a week or so. In the meantime, we're on our own. We can repair our backup powercell, we have supplies. We're going to be fine. We are going to continue working to reestablish contact, but we also have a job to do. We can't get home, so let's do what we came here to do and meet with these locals. Understood?"

The tiny room resonated with a strong "Yes, sir!"

"Captain Jackson, get your team together. You move out in two days. Lt. Maj. Cantrell, you're going with her."

"The JAG?" Jackson asked, confused. "Why?"

"You're an excellent soldier, Captain, but Lt. Maj. Cantrell is an expert at interpersonal relations and diplomacy, and quite frankly, you're not. Learn from him. Dismissed."

That first patrol set the tone for their time in the Saorsa Valley. Like most encounters, it started out tense and cold, with the locals giving just enough lip service to get the UN to move on. No one knew who fired the first round, but that rarely matters when bullets are flying. One Peacekeeper fell almost immediately, and Lt. Maj. Cantrell insisted they break contact. It was over in less than a minute as both sides retreated to safety.

The first combat loss was a sucker punch to the entire company. Everyone knew it would happen eventually but seeing it on the first patrol was hard for them all. The most devastating blow came later that night.

Lt. Maj. Cantrell's injuries, like everyone else who made it out, were minor, mostly cuts and scrapes. He never even mentioned them. However, without the ability to monitor him properly, they were unable to detect the impending heart attack brought on by the stress of battle. His peaceful death in his cot that same evening truly brought home the reality of their predicament.

They were alone.

As the weeks came and went without contact beyond the valley, isolation affected everyone differently. Captain Jackson focused on physical fitness. Several of the enlisted relieved their stress in an unauthorized bare-knuckle fight club, courtesy of 1st Sgt. Goodwin, who ensured the chain of command tacitly ignored its existence. Others turned to sex for human contact. For his part, Sam simply socialized with the troops; "smokin' and jokin'" as the old saying went.

It seemed to affect Maj. Lemaire the most, though. After Cantrell's death, Lemaire's staunch adherence to regulations started to fray. He let go of little things at first; grooming standards and fraternization rules grew laxer. His normally meticulous attention to detail when documenting personnel actions slipped. He even participated in some interrogations personally. It was unlike the commander, but this was uncharted territory for everyone, so Sam and the other officers shrugged it off; some behavioral changes were bound to happen.

The Peacekeepers avoided killing whenever possible, but they detained as many as they could for questioning. Maj. Lemaire was convinced the next interrogation would reveal the hidden insurgent assets. The interrogators were simply being too soft in their methods. He therefore pushed them to get answers by any means necessary.

Sam even got in on the action sometimes, as he was present at every interrogation to ensure they followed procedure. The first time he smacked a POW upside the head for some particularly vulgar threats toward a female specialist, he was surprised at his actions and horrified at his enjoyment.

Another prisoner received a closed fist punch to the gut after a tense exchange. Emboldened by the lack of discipline and a growing storehouse of anger at the death of his friends, Sam waterboarded a POW.

Once.

Sam was scowling, mid-pour, when the gravity of his actions finally struck him. He dropped the bucket to the ground, snatched the filthy, piss-soaked rag off the man's face, and marched straight to Maj. Lemaire's office to surrender himself for disciplinary action.

Maj. Lemaire's words echoed in Sam's head, "He give you anything?"

Sam was astounded at his reaction. He barely stuttered out, "N-No, sir."

Lemaire looked back at the pad on his desk. "Damn. Well, keep trying."

"Sir, we've questioned every man, woman, and child we've come across. No one has known anything about Colonial military units or resistance cells. I think it's time to reconsider our approach out here."

"Don't be ridiculous, Overstreet," Lemaire said dismissively. "They're out there, and we're going to find them. Now get back to work."

That was the breaking point for Sam. He returned to his bunk angry and disappointed. He'd committed a war crime; he'd tortured a POW. He sat at his desk with a stack of legal pads and wrote down every detail he could about every interaction the unit had with the locals. *No more*, he thought. *I can't stop it, but I can document it.*

3

The day after the encounter at the farm, Sam forced himself, yet again, to press pen to paper and record the actions that he and his unit had taken within the cloisters of that unassuming valley. The combat deaths, while tragic and painful, didn't bother him nearly as much as seeing a civilian executed in cold blood. He'd had enough. Price deserved a bullet, but a cell would suffice, and Sam was determined to see Lemaire put him in one.

Sam was reading back through all his notes when he heard a sharp knock on his door, breaking his concentration.

"Street!" Captain Jackson's voice boomed from outside the thin door.

He flung the door open, angry at the interruption.

"Boss wants to see you." Jackson stared at his flushed face and bloodshot eyes but didn't acknowledge them. "Now."

"Yes, ma'am," he answered. He took a deep breath, grabbed his notebook and weapon, and set off for the commander's office. It was late, but Lemaire's work hours had become as erratic as his behavior.

Sam was mentally rehearsing what he planned to say to the commander when he rounded a corner in the POW holding area. He approached the detention cells and saw Sergeant Price exit a room, adjusting his belt.

Immediately suspicious, Sam listened closely, and heard faint crying from within the cell. It was the colonial girl that they'd taken into custody the previous day. He stopped Price, and already knowing the answer, asked, "What the hell is going on here? You know no one is to be alone with a detainee. What were you doing in there?"

Price said nothing but flashed a self-satisfied smirk, drew a blood-streaked finger under his nose, and pointed at Sam, winking.

Sam saw red. Without thinking, he grabbed his rifle and smashed the butt of it into Price's smiling face. Price's nose gushed blood and he staggered back. Sam attacked again, swinging his rifle like a club into Price's stomach. Price lurched over, spitting blood on the dirty floor. Sam grabbed his collar and threw him headfirst into the wall. Price fell to the ground, dazed, and Sam landed a couple of solid kicks to Price's torso.

He lifted Price's head by his uniform collar and snarled in his ear, "Get up, shitbag."

Price unsteadily got to his knees and Sam pulled him to his feet, keeping a hand on Price's collar and the muzzle of his rifle in his back. He half dragged the disoriented NCO the last twenty meters to Maj. Lemaire's door, fighting the temptation to pull the trigger the entire way.

Ignoring all customs and courtesies, Sam opened the door and dropped Price at the incredulous commander's feet. Without waiting for permission, he spoke simply and harshly, "Sir, this man goes into a cell. Now. And he does *not* come out."

Lemaire, for his part, didn't seem the least bit surprised or shocked. He slowly rose to his feet and crossed his arms. "What's his crime, Lieutenant?"

"Murder, torture, and sexual battery of a minor." Sam let himself get a good top-to-bottom look at the major. Lemaire hadn't shaved in at least a week, and a splotchy, salt-and-pepper beard hid his lips. Once pressed and sharp as an arrowhead, Lemaire's camo jacket looked like he'd just picked it up off the floor, like a drunk college kid who had finally run out of clean clothes.

Lemaire stared at Price for a moment, without a hint of warmth in his eyes. "Those are very serious charges, Lieutenant. Wait outside for a minute, please."

Sam stepped into the hallway. Mere moments after shutting the door, he heard muffled voices, rising in volume and cheap furniture smashing against other solid objects. He couldn't understand the words being spoken, but "wall-to-wall counseling" is a pretty universal language.

It lasted several minutes. When the two men emerged from the office, Price sported a few new injuries and was missing a tooth he'd definitely had before going into that room. Lemaire's rumpled uniform was smeared with blood where he'd wiped his knuckles on a pant leg. The commander was panting when he called after the junior NCO, "And you're on latrine duty the rest of the week. Clean yourself up, I don't want any more blood on my floors." He cleared his throat and addressed Sam. "LT, come on in."

Sam watched Price limp down the hallway, flabbergasted that he was walking free. "Sir, where is he going?"

"The med tent for a bandage and then to his bunk. He's got a long, early day tomorrow." At Sam's incredulity, he continued, waving a dismissive hand, "Don't worry, we'll have a guard at his door."

"Wait a minute. That piece of shit murdered a man in cold blood—"

"He protected an officer from an enemy combatant," Lemaire corrected.

"He's permanently injured detainees with unauthorized, unwarranted use of force—"

"He used enhanced interrogation techniques," Lemaire excused.

"And he just now *raped* an underage civilian in our detention cell!"

"That's why he's on extra duty for the foreseeable future. Look, he's a sick fuck, but the reality is we don't have the manpower to cover down if I lock him up. It hurts us more than it hurts him. It's hard enough to keep an effective force in the field when we lose someone in combat. I simply cannot justify locking someone up when I could just work him like a dog." Lemaire straightened some folders on his desk and threw out, almost as an afterthought, "I'll have First Sgt. Goodwin keep him away from the prisoner areas. There, feel better?"

Sam tried to respond. He tried to scream that this was nowhere near sufficient. No words would escape his lips. *Goodwin?* Sam laughed internally. *That psychopath?*

"That's not why I wanted to see you anyway," Lemaire continued. He sat heavily in his chair and took a long swig of something in his coffee cup, wincing as he set it clumsily on the desk. "Do you know why we're out here, LT?"

"Yes, sir," Sam started, hesitating in order to collect his thoughts after the sudden subject change. "We're here to bridge the civil-military divide. Win hearts and minds, provide humanitarian assistance—"

"Yeah, if possible," Lemaire interrupted. He sipped from his cup again. "You've read about Operation Midnight Kestrel. The larger UN mission is to pacify this planet. If we can get these colonials on our side, great, but one way or another they're going to fall in line. To do that, we need information about these people; information they've been reluctant to provide."

"There are ways to go about that without violating LOAC."

"How? You've made direct contact with the locals, spoken to them. How much do you think we're going to get by asking nicely and offering bandages?"

Sam stared at his commander, concerned where he was going with this.

"You know that we're completely cut off out here. The commo section thinks they're close to creating a beacon, but we've got nothing so far. MOB Unity still hasn't attempted to find us. There hasn't even been a fly-by. Not one air recon sortie. Do you understand what I'm saying, Sam?"

He remained silent, afraid to speak.

"I'm saying no one is coming for us. Regimental HQ was on Base Unity, and it's probably gone. Wiped out, I bet. There is no backup. If we show an ounce of weakness, these rebels will roll up here and slaughter every one of us. If we want to make it out alive, we must depend on each other. It's important we're all on the same page."

"I agree with that, but a lot of the actions and behaviors here ever since we lost Lt. Maj. Cantrell have been wholly unacceptable even by the most lenient of standards."

"You're still relatively new here, and I know you'll be graduating from law school soon. Darin, Lt. Maj. Cantrell, always spoke highly of you. Said you were a good kid, real smart." His voice came out tight, just above a whisper. "Said you were a lot like him."

"I miss him too, sir. He was a good man."

They shared a moment of mournful silence while Lemaire poured Sam a mug of whiskey from a bottle Sam was positive he'd seen confiscated from an elderly man two weeks ago.

"Do you know how I met Darin?" Lemaire asked before Sam could refuse the offer or ask where he'd got it. Sam shook his head.

"We were on M'tali together, back with the 83rd Special Observation Group. I was a cherry lieutenant, just like you; didn't know my ass from a crater, not that I understood that. Before he went to law school, he was my platoon sergeant. One day, out on patrol, he got a bad feeling. He told me to hang back. I didn't listen. I stepped around a corner right as the bomb went off. He must have heard something because before I felt the heat from the blast, he'd already yanked me back and covered me up. Took a bunch of shrapnel in the process. Later on, after the medics released him, I asked him why he did it. You know what he said? He said, 'You're a thick-headed son of a bitch, sir, but being a hard learner shouldn't *have* to be a death sentence. Stick with me, kid, I'll never steer you wrong.' And he never did. Not once."

"That sounds like him." Sam laughed and toasted his friend's memory.

"I understand that you may find some of our investigative techniques distasteful."

"Not distasteful. Illegal. We have to get information where we can, I get that, but—"

"Do you think they wouldn't do the same to you? Because I assure you, these rebels are sadistic monsters who will not hesitate to slice you open and jump rope with your entrails while you watch."

Sam deadpanned, "That's awfully specific, sir."

"Well, let me show you why." Lemaire pulled out a hard copy file and handed it to Sam.

Confused, he took the folder and perused the contents, feeling more nauseated with every page.

"Long story short, what you're looking at is what's left of my cousin's legs." He let that sink in for a moment. "Right before we left, I got a message from him. He's pretty well squirreled away in Emotional Health, but he managed to get this to me. I made a hard copy before the UN could intercept and delete it. Take a good, long look, LT. You're looking at what happens when hammer meets bone, from toe to knee."

Sam's eyes widened. He hadn't planned on drinking the whiskey, but that was an image he'd drink away under the best of circumstances.

"That's just one example of what these people are capable of. Make no mistake, we are at war. We may not have vertols and artillery, we don't even have crew-served weapons, but we are in the shit. And this," he shook the folder, "is what we're fighting against."

"I understand, sir, but there are still limits. You keep saying we have a job to do. Well, so do I, whether you think I'm qualified for it or not, and that job is to keep you out of prison. The Geneva Convention, Mars Accords, law of armed conflict clearly state—"

"I know the laws!" Lemaire shouted. Mugs rattled and pens fell as his large fist hammered the desk like a gavel. "Here's what *you* need to understand: those laws don't apply right now! We don't have the luxury of locking ourselves in that tiny box of approved rules of engagement. Out here, we follow the law of Four Point Three Millimeter. We engage, detain, and question these rebels under the law of Four Point Three. And, if necessary, we shoot them under it!"

As he shouted each numeral, Lemaire drove a finger into the wood of his desk, harder with each repetition. After a brief silence, Lemaire ran a frazzled hand through his growing hair, trying to regain his composure. "I'm not unreasonable and I'm not a monster, Sam. I'm not asking you to kill anyone, I won't even ask you to question anyone. I understand not everyone has the stomach for this line of work, and that's okay. You never have to set foot in an interrogation room again. I need to know you're a member of our team, though, so I have one simple assignment for you."

Knowing he wouldn't like it, Sam asked anyway, "What is it?"

"That farm your team raided yesterday is now, supposedly, empty. The rebels have probably been using the buildings to stash weapons, medical supplies, food, equipment; all things we need here. You will go with Captain Jackson's team and recover everything you possibly can. If they have a vehicle, use that to transport it all back, and then burn those buildings."

"Sir, that property belongs to the girl in our detention cell. Where is she supposed to go when she's released?"

"That's not your problem. Our supplies are all but gone and no more are coming. I doubt we have a spare cryo pack for Price's face right now. That house is our only shot."

"I understand we need supplies, but there has to be another way. Some of the junior enlisted have already managed to barter a deck of cards for some vegetables. We could do the same."

"I'm not begging for a goddamn thing."

Sam took a deep breath. "Sir, as your legal advisor, I can

defend gathering supplies. It's still looting, but there are mitigating factors in play. However, destroying her home is completely indefensible. Why not just occupy it until we get out of here? The UN has been doing that since we arrived."

"I considered it. However, we can't leave this place unsecured and we don't have the people to guard two locations. A full third of our people wouldn't survive the movement over there. No, we can't occupy it, and we can't leave it available to the insurgents to turn into a stronghold."

Sam hesitated before speaking, "I can't go along with that. You know as well as I do, there is no enemy military operating in this area. Our post hasn't been attacked once and we haven't encountered anyone in a uniform of any kind. We haven't had an intel update in over a month and everything we've learned on the ground here contradicts our pre-deployment briefings. Have you considered that the intel we have is just wrong?"

"Do you really think a bunch of damn farmers could take out this many of us? We're the goddamn UN! No, if they're not insurgents, they're linked to them, and we're going to find out how. You're either going to help us do that, or you're a liability."

Sam didn't like that word. "What do you mean 'liability'?"

"All we have is us, and we *cannot* afford to have anyone on our team that we can't trust when shit hits the fan. Rumor even has it that you've got some of the junior enlisted questioning orders and second-guessing our intelligence. I can't have an incipient mutiny, Sam."

"What are you getting at?"

It suddenly got very quiet. Lemaire stared stone-faced at the young lieutenant and slid a handwritten note across his cheap field desk. "Go ahead, read it. Aloud."

Sam took the paper warily and read his commander's words:

Dear Mr. and Mrs. Overstreet,

It is with profound sadness that I must inform you of Sam's passing. His platoon was ambushed during a routine patrol. Several men were critically wounded and Sam, without regard to his own safety, bravely reentered the fight to pull as many as he could to safety. Regrettably, he succumbed to his injuries before the medics could reach him.

Sir, ma'am, Sam sacrificed himself to save nearly a dozen of his men. His loss is a terrible one, but his heroism will live on. I only hope you feel the same pride in his memory that I do.

I am so very sorry for your loss.

Respectfully,

Maj. Beau Lemaire

Company C/429th Peacekeeping

Civil Affairs Regiment, Commander

A chill came over Sam as he stared at the handwritten letter. He looked at his commander, his eyes betraying his terror and indignation. "What the hell is this?"

"Loyalty, Sam. The most important quality in a tactical unit is trust, and right now, you don't have that. These soldiers need to know that you have their back, that you'll support them when we do get home. I can't have anyone here that won't. So, you've got two choices: you can fall in line, however distasteful you may find that, or," he tapped the paper, "you can go home a hero. Dismissed."

Sam stood, staring at his commander through narrowed eyes. "You know Darin would never have stood for this."

"Darin's not here anymore, son. I'll give you a few days to think about it."

"Thanks for the drink." Sam downed the last of his whiskey, unceremoniously dropped the mug on the desk, and walked straight back to his bunk.

4

As his head hit the black duffle bag he used as a pillow, Sam's predicament fully sank in. Sam was grateful for the drink he'd received, but he could use three or four more to help process the decision in front of him. He'd figured out pretty quickly that he wouldn't survive this deployment unscathed. If the unit had the resources handy, Sam would have already made an appointment with Mental Health. Now, however, the odds of him surviving this deployment at all were shrinking by the hour.

Truthfully, he had no love for the Grainneans. Sure, waterboarding was technically torture, but he'd just seen with his own eyes the unspeakable things they did to their prisoners. Rebel depravity was legendary. All Lemaire wanted him to do was torch a few buildings. He could easily do exactly that, with zero repercussions. It wasn't as if Sam was innocent anyway. If he reported the violations going on at the OP, he'd have to report himself too, and his career would be over before it even began. His commander was offering him protection. It was a conspiracy, but protection nonetheless, if he could bring himself to go along with it.

A gentle knock broke Sam from his reverie. He opened the door to see Captain Jackson. "Ma'am?"

She was still in uniform, but with an unbuttoned blouse, barely concealing an object between it and her black t-shirt. Her battle-worn expression never changed as she pulled the unlabeled bottle from inside her blouse just enough to show him. "Let's talk."

He stepped aside to allow her in. "Ma'am, what's—?"

"First off, cut that 'ma'am' shit out. We're off the record. For this conversation only, it's 'Talia.' Second, I talked to Lemaire. I know what you got in front of you. I thought you could use a friend to help you figure it out."

"Friend?" Sam said, surprised.

"Yeah, a friend. You know, someone who's not *actively* trying to kill you. Ever heard of one?" she shot back handing him the bottle.

He looked at the clear liquid a moment before pouring two small glasses, "So, *friend,* where'd you get this?"

"Tactical acquisition."

"You stole it from the property room."

She took her glass from him, "You gonna report me?"

"Seeing as how I'm soon to be a war criminal or a dead man, I think I can let this one slide. Cheers." He took a large sip, coughed, and nearly spat it across the room. Sucking air only made it burn worse as he choked out, "Holy shit! Is this fucking paint thinner? How do you drink this stuff?"

"Grainnean moonshine. Seems they do everything a bit bigger here, like the fucked-up wildlife." She actually let a smile show as she took a long swallow, "You want me to find you some juice to cut it with, junior?"

"Could you?" he said, still coughing. "Shit."

They laughed a moment, letting their nerves calm.

"You know what your problem is?" Talia said, her arm draping over the pile of body armor next to her on his cot.

"A shitty career counselor?" Sam joked, wondering if the moonshine would eat through his glass before he could drink it.

"Shut the fuck up, Street." She shook her head at him and continued, "There's no gray in your life. You live in world of black and white, absolute good or absolute evil. Life doesn't work like that."

"You're saying some of this stuff going on here is excusable?"

"I'm saying you need more information before you can decide to excuse it or not. You know why I joined the UN?"

Sam shook his head and steeled himself before taking another small sip.

"I grew up, what you might call, 'hood-rat adjacent.' There are still some rough neighborhoods in the greater Philadelphia-Baltimore megaplex, and I had friends, even family, get sucked into the life. Drugs, guns, running from man to man, just trying to get by. Some did, a whole lot of them didn't. I spent too much time visiting jails and cemeteries, and all for dumb shit. Hundreds of years of this shit. I was not going out like that."

Talia took another swig. "My best friend growing up, Sheena, got into the party scene pretty deep and never left. Last time I saw her was about ten years ago, right before I left for the academy. We were at this bullshit party and they were passing something around, I don't even know what it was. A pipe came out and I left the room."

She stared into her glass, swirling the noxious liquid within it, "Next thing I know, cops bust in, half the people are restrained. A couple guys were on the ground twitching from the tasers. Sheena and me hid in a back room, waiting for the adrenaline to die down. When they searched the house, this older fat-fuck cop found us. We were just waiting for them, on our knees, facing the door, hands up. I was clean, but just getting arrested would have cost me my slot. I was freaking out, but Sheena had been around enough to know all the dirtbags. She ended up negotiating an exchange with him: if he let us go, no record of us being there, she'd make sure he went home a happy man."

Talia shrugged her shoulders and made a sound that wasn't quite a laugh, but not quite a "humph" either. "Long story short, he came out about five minutes later, panting like a dog, bright red, wiping sweat off his neck. He ushered us outside, gave us some fakeass directions as a cover, and sent us on our way. Said two nice girls like us should be more careful, it's easy to get lost around there."

"So, let me get this straight, your friend traded sexual favors to get out of jail, and that inspired you to join the UN?" Sam said, confused.

"No, man, pay attention! She didn't give a shit about jail! That girl could do a month in lockup standing on her head. She did that for me, because she knew I actually had a ticket out. You understand what I'm telling you?"

"That Bos-Philly-Balmo continues its ancient tradition of dirty cops?"

"Motherf—!" She threw a kneepad at his head, exasperated. "Such a damn smartass. I told you this because sometimes, a situation requires you to make sacrifices you normally wouldn't, including your dignity on occasion. Sheena made some bad choices, a lot of bad choices, that don't make her a bad person."

She let him think about that for a minute while she sipped her drink.

"There are a lot of good people in this unit. We're all just trying to make it to the next day."

"Good people like 1st Sgt. Goodwin who boobytrapped a civilian casualty? Like Price who murdered a man and then raped his sister?"

"I'm not arguing about them. Price is a piece of shit; always has been. I tried getting him kicked off the mission, but Goodwin wasn't having that." Talia paused, "To be honest with you, Goodwin scares the hell out of me. She's also the reason these soldiers are ready and able to do this job. She's been in this unit longer than anyone and trained almost everyone here, me included. She's smart and resourceful, and these people will follow her straight into hell."

"So, they should get a pass on things the goddamn *system* commander has specifically forbidden? I should ignore things that have been illegal for centuries?"

"I'm saying you can't report one person without reporting everyone. You'll never make it stick. No one is going to say a goddamn word and there are no recordings to prove anything. I'm not proud of everything I've done here, I know you're not either, but we can't deal with that right now."

Talia paused, and Sam instinctively knew that whatever she said next would be the complete and honest truth. Her voice grew low. "I don't know about you, but I want to go the fuck home, and I promise you I *am* going home. I'll do whatever I have to. I like you. I think you're a good kid with a bright future. I want to see you make it too. You got to pull your head out of your ass first. Pick your battles. No matter how much you hate it, you can't win this one."

Sam contemplated her words for a moment as she stood to button her uniform blouse. "Do you think he'll do it? Would he really send me home in a box?"

She sat back down on his rickety field chair. "If you asked me that question two months ago, I'd have said 'Hell no, you're crazy for even thinking it.' There used to be a lot of complaints about that coldhearted bitch Goodwin. She was rough—borderline abusive—but effective enough and no one was willing to take the political risk of firing a lesbian. That's why Lemaire got this assignment in the first place; to balance her out and keep her in check. He was good at it, too! Something with them just clicked as a team and it was great. He hasn't been right since Cantrell died, though. I don't know if it was that or the isolation or something else, but he's different now. I've been with him for a couple of years and I never would have thought this part of him existed. I don't know the Lemaire we got now, but I'd say he's capable of damn near anything."

She stood again and walked to his door.

He spoke as she reached for the knob. "Thanks, Talia. I guess I have some thinking to do."

"Don't take too long. He won't wait forever." She left him to consider his very few options.

5

Sleep didn't come to Sam that night. He paced around his room, even flipped a coin to decide his fate. Logically, he knew there wasn't much to decide. He was a brand-new officer, barely out of training, not even a licensed attorney yet. He was a nobody, and he'd be taking on one of the most well-respected officers in the UNPF without a shred of evidence beyond his own notebook. He knew Talia was right, all he had to do was convince his conscience.

Sam lay down in his bunk, exhausted, wired, and still working off a buzz from the moonshine. He doubted that stuff wasn't pure rocket fuel, but he was grateful nonetheless.

He heard something fall to the ground next to his bed and reached down blindly to retrieve it. Sam knew the moment he touched the leather binding that it was Darin's journal. Sam had collected it and some other personal effects from his mentor's room after his death, intending to keep them safe until he could return them to Darin's wife.

He flipped the book open, skimming the pages, hoping for some kernel of wisdom from beyond the grave. The journal was mostly personal stories about Cantrell's family, but he included information about several clients as well.

Darin Cantrell had been a highly sought-after defense attorney, enormously successful, and as such had many clients at any given time. Darin did, however, document the ones who served to teach a greater lesson than their simple case file might suggest. One example involved an extraordinarily wealthy local businessman-turned-politician, a long-time client, accused of taking indecent liberties with his children's underage babysitter.

Sam remembered the case vividly, as it was one of the first to cross his desk during his internship at Darin's law firm. It was a slam-dunk case; the evidence was mostly circumstantial, and anything incriminating via forensics had been so thoroughly botched that Darin could have easily challenged it. The legal fees alone would have let Darin retire. There was no reason why he shouldn't have taken the case, but something just didn't feel right.

Darin refused to take it.

At great professional risk to himself, he not only "fired" the man and threw him loudly from the office, but also publicly disavowed his client, sending a message to other attorneys that they should avoid the case as well. The average private attorney's nature being what it always has been, Darin mainly succeeded in chumming the waters. The man quickly found himself a less scrupulous attorney and beat the charges.

Sam remembered sitting in Darin's office after the acquittal, his curiosity eating at him.

"I have to ask," Sam started, unable to contain himself another minute, "Why? He beat the charges, he's still in office. The only thing firing him accomplished was getting someone else paid. What gives?"

"You completely missed the point. This outcome was a foregone conclusion from the beginning. Never any chance of it going another way," Darin explained.

"Then why not just take the case?"

"Just because it was inevitable doesn't make it right. I represented that guy for years. I considered him a friend. He was always a little slimy; you don't get where he is without bending some ethical rules, but he'd never done anything so blatantly criminal before. I really wanted this to be another false accusation, Sam. I was hoping that her parents were just trying to shake him down for money, like the others, but you saw the case file. You saw the photos and read the medical reports. Did any of that look consensual to you?"

"I don't know, I've known some pretty freaky chicks," Sam offered.

"Were any of them fourteen years old? Because last I checked, a *child* can't consent to being 'freaky.' As soon as he tried that tired 'she seduced me' bullshit, I was done with him. I'll burn this place to the ground before I go to court for someone who fucks kids, consensual or not, and I'm *damn* sure not going to further traumatize a child for a fucking payday. There's plenty of scumbag lawyers in this town, they can have him. I may not be able to retire right now, but at least I can sleep just fine."

"But she was traumatized anyway."

"Can't be helped. Just because I can't make it right, doesn't mean I have to be a part of it."

Sam silently absorbed his words.

"Remember, kid, it's easy to do the right thing when you benefit from it. It's when doing the right thing costs you that you learn what kind of person you are."

Sam closed the book and lay back down, staring at the blackness outside his window. *So, what kind of man am I?*

He thought about his parents, his girlfriend, and his dog back on Earth. He wanted to see them again. He wanted to settle down, get married, and have a bunch of smartass, brown-haired kids just like him. In order to do that, he had to live, and he'd have to look himself in the mirror every day, knowing what horror he had allowed to continue.

Sam spent the next few hours finishing his documentation of the goings on in the Saorsa Valley and writing letters to his family. Knowing they'd likely never read them, he begged for their forgiveness anyway.

When he was finally spent, he watched the first rays of sun break the horizon. He dragged himself, too stiff and sore for his twenty-six years, out of his chair and back to Lemaire's office, the light and humor drained from his eyes, replaced with resignation.

He banged his fist on Lemaire's locked office door. He pounded the door hard enough he thought he might break through it. Sam didn't care what was going on in there. He had to do this before he could talk himself out of it.

He raised his hand to pound again when he heard shuffling from inside.

"Yeah, I'm coming," Lemaire's voice came weakly.

When the door cracked open, he noticed Lemaire's bloodshot eyes and the smell of stale whiskey wafting from his dirty clothes. Sam fought a sneer as the last vestiges of the respect he once held for this broken man faded away.

Officially dispensing with all formalities, Sam rolled his eyes and clenched his jaw, "I'm in."

Lemaire's expression never changed. "Glad to hear it. Report to Captain Jackson. She'll get you spun up."

Without a word of acknowledgement, Sam spun on his heels and walked away.

The next three days were some of the most intense Sam had ever experienced. Commissioning into the Judge Advocate General corps, he intellectually understood that his combat training was inadequate, but training for an actual mission with Captain Jackson and her team showed him just how badly the UN prepared support personnel like himself.

As a last minute "tag along" on the mission to Jeremiah's farm, he simply fell back on his basic training skills. Sam had some natural athletic ability and could hold his own with a rifle. Jackson and Goodwin taught him to clear a room and not flag his teammates with the muzzle of his weapon. His skills improved dramatically, but it was perfectly clear to everyone that Sam would never be first in the stack.

The morning of the mission, Sam felt completely nauseated from nerves. He hadn't crossed the line yet, but in a few hours, he'd

be face-to-face with his point of no return. He packed his necessary gear and stashed anything sensitive or private into a hidden
compartment in his footlocker, including the journal. Gripping the
small book one last time, he willed the worn leather to give him
some of Darin's courage and strength of conviction. With one last
steadying breath, he hid the book and replaced the false panel.

Time to go, he thought. He grabbed his pack and rifle, then
set off to form up at the gate.

As usual, the trek down the steep mountain slope was treacherous and slow, the loose rocks threatening to give way at the
slightest misstep. The wet, fallen foliage made the journey even
more dangerous.

On one particularly bad step in the high gravity, Sgt. Palacio
slipped on a large, dewy boulder and tumbled several meters down
the slope, grunting as he bounced and rolled. He only stopped
upon colliding with a well-placed tree.

"I'm good!" Palacio called up to the squad, giving a wobbly
thumbs up.

"Just sit, Palacio," Jackson yelled back. "We'll make our way
down to you."

"Papa was a rolling stone," sang Sam, invoking his ancient
Temptations collection. "Wherever he laid his hat was his home."

"Shut the fuck up, Street!" Jackson chastised.

After regaining Palacio, they proceeded down the mountain
unobstructed by man or nature, though the heat, god, it never
ceased. The squad was mostly silent, save for a few comments
here and there as the soldiers egged each other on. Sam tried to
crack more jokes; it was the only way he could calm his rapidly
fraying nerves. Jackson, however, quickly quashed unnecessary
conversation, making it clear to all of them that she was in no
mood for frivolity.

Sam swallowed hard as they approached the outer perimeter
of the farmland. Even here in the mountains, the hot air did
nothing to cool the nervous sweat on his neck. While much
had happened since then, the sight of young Jeremiah's murder
remained fresh in Sam's memory. He tried to push it down and
instead took in every detail around him. He searched for any
indication of insurgent involvement, hoping to find something.

The teams dispersed around the property. Some gathered food
from the fields, others ransacked the main house for weapons

and medical supplies. A third team searched the barn and other outer buildings for vehicles and other useful items.

Sam supervised the team inside the house. He tested wall panels, floorboards, and checked under beds for rebel caches, praying something would turn up to justify their mission.

All he found were keepsakes and gut-wrenching family pictures. He saw bright, happy blue eyes and smiling faces. He saw two loving parents playing with their children and cooing over babies. Grainne was a harsh, unforgiving planet, and this family had found their little slice of heaven.

Sam ran outside and retched into a flower bed. He heaved until Captain Jackson came to check on him.

"Street, what's up?" she asked, sounding genuinely concerned.

Sam wouldn't make eye contact, tears welling in his eyes. "Ma'am, I can't do this. Everything we were told about this farm is wrong. These people were never a threat. There is no military presence here."

"They killed two of our people. We have every reason to believe they're hiding military resources out here," Jackson responded, her head on a constant swivel. Even through Sam's emotional distress, he noticed that she seemed more interested in making sure the troops heard her than watching for an enemy.

"And we gunned down a child in her mother's arms!"

"Every war has casualties."

"Face it, *ma'am,* Lemaire lied to us!" Sam finally fixed her with his gaze. "There's absolutely zero evidence that anyone from the colonial military or any rebel resistance cell has ever been in this house, much less staged anything here. There's nothing of military value anywhere, no hidden compartments, no cache of munitions or supplies. This was just a family."

She sounded impatient as she said, "All we can do is press on with our mission. They're already dead. We can't help them."

Sam turned and placed his hands on the smooth wooden railing surrounding the porch on which they stood. He imagined Jeremiah and his father sanding the wood by hand while the younger children played. His chest ached in sorrow and he squeezed the fine wood with all his might. "Fine, take the food, take whatever supplies you can find. But I'm not torching every single tangible memory an innocent girl has of her family. I won't destroy her home. I won't be a part of this."

Jackson threw her hands up, exasperated. "Why do you care so much? What's so damn special about this girl?"

Sam's voice was calm and peaceful, "It's not about her. Sometimes the line between right and wrong can blur, but this isn't blurry. This is definitely wrong. I've decided what kind of man I am, and I will not go along with this."

Jackson noticed 2LT Ansbach and two of her troops standing to the side, waiting to update the captain on their progress in the barn.

Jackson's voice dropped to barely above a whisper as she moved in close to Sam. Her eyes boring into his. "You know you can't win this."

Sam nodded, "I know."

Jackson sighed and dropped her gaze. "I understand."

Jackson signaled Lt. Ansbach to approach. She'd be available in just a minute. Turning back to Overstreet, she gestured behind him, "Go on and help the guys inside load up supplies. We're about done here."

Sam met her eyes one last time, "Thank you, ma'am."

Jackson didn't respond, just nodded in the direction he should go.

He placed a hand on the door handle and Jackson pulled her sidearm. She pointed it directly at the back of Sam's head. Her hand shook as she took a deep breath and squeezed the trigger.

The report was deafening, and she watched through blurred eyes as Sam slumped to the ground.

She bit her lip to fight down her emotions as she turned to face her troops. She looked Lt. Ansbach in the eye, almost daring her to say something. Wiping the tears from her eyes, she forced her voice to project a confidence and disinterest she did not feel.

"Let's get to work."

The Strongest Link

Jamie Ibson

May 210
Jefferson, Capital Region District (Occupied)

Brad Ministrelli parked the airtruck on the north side of Liberty Park and nodded to two ten-year-olds he knew lived in the area. They drifted apart as he unloaded crates of produce. The older of the two returned and gave him another curt nod. Rifles went into foam cases, and he popped the false floor off the gun compartment to withdraw a squat, rectangular cooler. Several of the apartments next to the park sat quietly, tragically empty. Brad's colleagues had lived here, but they were gone now, killed by the opening salvo: weapons of mass destruction, fired from orbit, without warning, without mercy.

His absent friends still had contributions they could make, though, and in the days and weeks following the occupation, Brad and others went quietly about securing the homes and apartments. Now, the vacancies were caches, comms points, sniper hides, and safehouses. This building manager in particular was a veteran, and he had quietly agreed to keep the units "occupied" despite the loss of income.

There were tiny villages, towns, and farmsteads all over the Capital District, and one by one, as the network came online and surviving FMF troops, reservists, and veterans checked in, they made their needs known. At first, he simply introduced himself with his team callsign, and delivered food, weapons, and ammo. Sometimes, someone needed moving, and he moved them. Anyone with a particular skill, ability, training or access to specific resources was noted by higher authority and tapped for whatever they could provide as the opportunity came.

Earlier that morning, he'd received direct word from an old friend who supplied and maintained farm equipment. Through a source "believed to be reliable," David McClellan of McClellan & Son Farm Supply supplied Minstrel with The Cooler. David's words echoed in Ministrelli's ears.

"*. . . the aardvarks are going to start using nanoviruses. This box has a sample of one, supposed to be a symbol of good faith.*"

Once upstairs, he removed the rear casing from his comm and fitted an in-line encryption token into the exposed guts. He jacked the modified comm into what had been Jésus Salvatore's entertainment system and waited as it accessed the secondary datastream, the one piggybacking behind the vid feed.

:: Minstrel; Authenticate 3SWCLC, Winters, Betty, :: he typed. Encryption let him send and receive signals, but the computer engineers who were organizing the resistance were profession-ally paranoid, and they regularly checked and rechecked ID for anyone using the backdoor network. Establishing his identity and trustworthiness had been a delicate dance. Now that they had a working relationship, providing his callsign, last posting, his CO, and his previous partner's name were enough.

His comm sat blank for thirty seconds before a line of text appeared.

Beth :: Authenticate Donor Kebab, Brutus, Blue ::

He checked his notebook. Beth had given him a list of iden-tification passwords and phrases, as well. In this case, she cited her favorite food, dog's name, and favorite color. Satisfied with her response, his fingers hovered over the keyboard as he tried to summarize his situation.

:: I have precious cargo that might do well at the Roberts Institute, :: he wrote. :: It is live and perishable. ::

Having to be indirect was awkward, but there were key phrases to avoid in the name of paranoia. The Roberts Institute was one of the cutting-edge schools of medical technology at the Jefferson University. It specialized in all things nanite: muscle builders, implants, nanoviruses, and counters.

There was a lengthy pause off air. He assumed a human in the loop was consulting elsewhere before replying.

:: How large is the cargo? ::

Brad cracked the lid on the hard-sided cooler and regarded the interior.

:: I have twelve one-by-five cent vials. ::

Another long pause, then:

:: Standby, liaising with other resources ::

He waited again, comfortable that he'd been correct.

:: Secure eleven vials and advise where they've been cached. Get one vial to Dr. Sykora for analysis. Dr. Sykora belonged to the Freehold Science Alliance; the asset who destroyed JP1 also belonged to the FSA as well. We believe the FSA is friendly, and members can provide SME support ::

:: That's pretty vague, any further details? ::

:: Negative. Updates as they happen. /Beth ::

Brad "Minstrel" Ministrelli was nonplussed. "Updates as they happen" euphemistically meant, "If we do hear something, we'll get back to you, but don't count on it."

Minstrel spent the rest of the evening securing vials in various safe houses. Each one was a stark reminder of everyone who'd died in the strike on 3rd Army's primary base. Once he'd sent their locations to "Beth" he found a café that offered public net access.

Finding entries on a "Doctor Sykora" was easy but did little to identify him. There had evidently been several Doctors Sykora over the last hundred plus years, dating all the way back to the first few decades of colonization. One Dr. E. Sykora had premiered using Orbital Defense systems to cut roads back when Grainne was a young, barely colonized ball of wilderness. Her texts were required reading in many disciplines, including the FMF's "Applied Kinetics" training school, where combat engineers, blazers, and operatives learned to blow shit up on the fly. Other Sykoras had been involved in weapons design, industrial fabrication, medicinal applications of nanites, and virtual intelligence over the last hundred fifty g-years. Minstrel refined his search, sorting the research papers by date, concluded that Dr. Dominik Sykora was who he was looking for. The medical nanite research was dated June 42nd, 208 and Dr. Sykora did indeed work out of the Roberts Institute.

He hadn't spent much time on campus, aside from attending the occasional lecture on the latest in animal behavior studies, and that was a completely different facility than the Roberts Institute.

Once he'd located the primary building, he followed the directory directions down a maze of corridors until he came to the Nano-medicine Research Laboratory. Most of the door was frosted privacy glass, but a head-height porthole let him see a woman working at a desk on the far side. She looked up, and he opened the door and took a step in. There were a handful of workstations, with multiple screens each; the woman was the only person present, however.

"Excuse me, lady, I'm looking for Doctor Sykora," Minstrel began. "Doctor Dominik Sykora, the author of the paper on nanites as a means to deal with implant rejection?"

The lady narrowed her eyes. "Who are you?" she demanded. She was slender, had fair skin, Slavic cheekbones, and her blonde hair was tightly tied into a bun. Blondes were rare on Grainne, and her exotic looks would have been more at home on Novaja Rossia or in Eastern Europe on Earth. The lady reminded him of one of the militia leaders he'd met in the Darkwood Hills, the one with the North American accent.

"I'm...a friend," he said. He cursed himself inwardly; having no formal *spy* training, he supposed someone who knew what they were doing would have had some witty line to disarm the lady's suspicions.

"I'm not sure I believe you, *friend*," she said. Sarcasm dripped from the last word. "If you were a friend of Doctor Sykora's, you would have known Dominik died last week in a firefight with the UN. *'Collateral damage,'* they called it," she spat bitterly.

"I beg your pardon, lady," Brad apologized. "I have...well, I had need of the doctor's expertise. The UN is going to hurt a lot of people, and I want to stop them," he said. "The physicist who destroyed JP1 signed his final transmission as from the Freehold Science Alliance. Public nets suggest Doctor Sykora belonged to the same group. I had hoped that meant he was an ally."

"Lock the door," she said, and he did. "I was Doctor Sykora's assistant. You have thirty seconds to convince me to help you."

"What would you say if I told you the UN isn't satisfied with orbital strikes, and their next major attack will be a bioweapon?"

"I would say, you're too late," she said harshly. "There's already a pneumonic infection making the rounds, first signs began exhibiting a few weeks ago. It's awful."

"Is this it?" Minstrel asked and placed the 5cm vial of viscous coffee-colored liquid in its protective polymer sleeve on her desk.

"Are you *INSANE*?" the woman near-shouted, jumping to her feet. "What is *WRONG* with you?"

"It's doubly-sealed, and I'm desperate," Minstrel replied defensively, backing away. "I had hoped, with a pure sample, Dr. Sykora could analyze it to formulate a counter." The woman seemed somewhat mollified but remained suspicious. Brad continued. "I'm sure one is possible. They aren't going start spreading around a disease they can't immunize against."

The lady gingerly picked up the vial, peered through it, and weighed it in her hand as though weighing the risk.

"How can I trust you? I only met you two segs ago. You could be a UN spook."

"There are some things you just have to take on faith, lady. It seems I have to put my faith in you, though, so let me volunteer this: I was assigned to the Jungle at Heilbrun Base. One of my teammates studied advanced veterinarian techniques here at the Roberts Institute. Before the invasion, he came here regularly for training updates and to refine the boosters...for our partners."

"Okay, stranger, would this teammate of yours be from Logan?"

Brad searched his memory. "Honest answer, I don't recall where he's from, we joined almost eight years ago, and he doesn't talk about his folks. And please, call me Minstrel."

"Not good enough to convince me you're one of the good guys. What's your friend's cat's name, Minstrel?" the lady pressed.

"A panther named Shadow. He had a too-aggressive leopard named Wraith as well, but Wraith didn't make the cut."

"And your cat's name?"

"I...don't have one, anymore." Brad swallowed hard but met her gaze evenly. "Their names were Elvis and Betty, but they died in the strike on Heilbrun. Now I'm just making it up as I go along."

The woman seemed satisfied with that and nodded.

"Call me Nicki. Come with me."

Nicki guided Minstrel through the front office to a changing area with shower cubicles.

"Clean up and get out of those...street clothes," she said, with a moue of distaste for Minstrel's rough work clothes. She pointed to a pile of sterile scrubs. "It's a sterile lab, and you need to scrub up. *Thoroughly*. When you're done, there might be something that fits you there."

She disappeared around a corner, and Minstrel heard her turn on a shower of her own. He stripped, stepped into the shower, and took a moment to glory in the near-scalding hot water. A dispenser mounted in the stall had several strong soaps and shampoo, so he washed his hair, beard, and body from head to toe. When he exited the stall, he found scrubs that fit and dressed. Nicki was already changed and waiting for him by a sliding door.

The door activated, and he followed her into a sterilization hall that bathed them both in UV light. They reached the exit and Nicki paused, looking at a screen.

"You have implants," she said. It wasn't a question. Minstrel saw a display highlighting the implants he'd received upon graduating from cat school.

"Yes," he replied. "Handlers get nasal and cochlear implants to improve our sensitivity to scent and sound. Helps us understand our cats better. Not as good as cats, but much better than a normal human." She was nodding along as he explained. "But you knew that."

"I did, but I'm still testing you. You passed."

Once into the lab proper, he sat where directed, and watched as the woman slipped the vial into a receptacle. Through a viewport, he watched as the vial was taken inside the machine, and a syringe withdrew a tiny sample of the dark brown liquid. The arms moved about inside the large, boxy device, and a few segs later, Nicki scanned some preliminary results on her screen.

"Those...*monsters*" she cursed under her breath. Minstrel sat quietly, with an attentive, questioning look on his face. She turned to face him. "This isn't the pneumonic bioweapon." Brad was crestfallen and opened his mouth to speak when she continued. "It's something new. Your sample contains spores that irritate the hell out of the body's mucous membranes and skin, like poison ivy, but worse. Much, much worse. But there's something else going on here too that is causing an error in the diagnostic. I'm going to need the rest of the evening and all day tomorrow to conduct a proper analysis. Come back tomorrow, around...seven divs," she said, turning her back on Minstrel and attending to her diagnostic.

Her brusque manner was off-putting, but Minstrel wasn't happy just walking back out the door so soon after arriving.

"Can I get you dinner? Bring it back here for you? I realize this is one helluvan imposition that I just dropped in your lap, and there isn't much I can do to make it up to you."

With an exasperated sigh, she pushed back from the controls.

"Fine. Combo number thirty-two at Darmawan's. Chorizo enchiladas, four-cheese Satan pepper blend. Beans, rice, guac, pico de gallo, and their house beer. Make sure they know it's for Nicki and not to wuss out on the heat."

"Can do."

There was little foot traffic on the streets. Three months in, Jefferson had been fully occupied with UN "Peacekeepers" patrolling the streets. Even in the few short blocks to Nicki's suggested cantina, he saw three foot patrols of occupying UN troops and two airborne drones, quietly humming along fifty feet up.

Natalena Darmawan proved to be a master chef of traditional Indonesian/Mexican fusion, once they got over a...miscommunication. Minstrel got some heavily spiced peanut chicken satay skewers and brought back dinner. One patrol stopped him, demanding to know his business. He called himself a "research assistant" and showed them the contents of the bag. With nothing more dangerous than some Satan pepper sauce, he was "allowed" to proceed after an admonishment to get himself some "proper" ID.

The skewers were excellent, the jasmine rice fragrant, and pepper sauce tangy. Nicki, on the other hand, let her enchiladas get cold. Eventually she emerged from the sterile laboratory environment and showered again. Minstrel found a kitchenette a few doors down from her laboratory/office, and when she appeared again, dressed, she accepted her reheated plate without comment. Minstrel sipped a beer of his own as she chewed.

"So the Darmawans pass along their compliments," he said. "They said you don't come around as often as you used to, and the next time you did, it'd be on the house."

Nicki froze, mid-bite. "Mm-hmm?" she answered with her mouth full.

"Yep. Food was excellent, made me wish I'd eaten there before. I suppose Jefferson, being as large as it is, I can't have dined everywhere." Nicki took another bite. "I'm sure you can just imagine their surprise when they asked what brought me by, and I explained how I only just learned of Doctor Sykora's unfortunate demise."

"Oh?"

"Indeed. You can imagine *my* surprise then when Natalena put a scattergun in my face and asked if ordering *combo thirty-two with chorizo for 'Nicki' was some kind of a sick joke.* Now, I've had a gun in my face a couple of times, but this was the first time a forty kilo Indonesian lady had me dead to rights for ordering *dinner.*"

"I'm sorry, I—"

"It seemed to me we were perhaps having a *failure to communicate*, and I explained that I had met his lovely assistant Nicki, and she had given me the order. Natalena explained that Doctor Domini*ka* Sykora was a slender blonde, a hundred seventy cee-em tall, and a brilliant researcher down at the Uni just like her father. You must think me an *idiot.*"

"Of course not, I . . . well . . . I had to be careful," she finished lamely.

"Do you actually know Mike Pieters?" he demanded. "Or were you just fishing for intel?"

"No, I do, he and I did pre-med together. We were flatmates," she protested. When Minstrel cocked an eyebrow, she looked away. "And, yes, we dated. For a long time. I was shocked when he went into the FMF instead of private practice. He could have written his own ticket. I guess it was never about the money, for him."

"No, it wasn't. For Mike, it's about taking his gift and doing something amazing with it. Our cats are smarter, faster, stronger, and tougher than they've ever been. The implants he designed help them heal from injuries that would otherwise kill them. Their median reaction times are up to three percent faster since he got to work, and there are even a few that are beginning to show signs of genuine sapience. What have you done for the resistance lately?"

Nicki shook her head and appeared to choose her next words carefully.

"I am a patriot, Brad, and I'm sorry I deceived you. I do have friends and colleagues who have been disappeared by the UN. I'd call it paranoia, but it isn't paranoia when they're really after you. I will do everything I can to help."

"Not unreasonable," Minstrel acknowledged. "Thank you."

"From my preliminary workup tonight, the UN has something very new, very different, and very crafty. I'll think about it tonight, and I'll get back at it in the morning. I assume you have somewhere to sleep?"

"I'll figure something out. Seems ridiculous to fly a hundred and fifty klicks home but my truck bed is comfortable. I'll meet you here at . . . three divs?"

"See you then."

It was oh-dark-thirty when gloved hands dragged Minstrel, still in his sleeping bag, from the tent he'd erected in the bed of the airtruck. Bleary from sleep, his hands instinctively clutched for the sidearm that no longer rode his hip until his shoulders and head cleared the edge of the truck, and his torso fell to the ground. Air whooshed from his lungs on impact, and he gasped for breath.

He clawed his head out of the sleeping bag and was blinded by a pair of flashlights aiming down at him. The quiet hum of stunners cooled his initial, violent impulses.

"Who are you?" a gruff voice with an aardvark accent demanded. "Why are you out past curfew?"

Minstrel tried to sit up, but an electric jab from one of the stun batons laid him out flat. He collected his thoughts and coughed out an answer.

"Bradley Sukarno. Visiting from out of town," he wheezed. "I didn't know about any curfew."

"Who are you visiting?" the same voice demanded. "They should have told you about the curfew."

"I arrived late," he lied. "After Iodown, didn't want to disturb anyone. Can I please get up?"

"No," the second voice said. This one was higher pitched but still stern. Probably female. "We're taking you to lockup for the night, you vagrants and transients are more than likely terrorists. Roll onto your front and stick your arms out like a T. Do it now."

Shit.

Still inside the sleeping bag, he feigned having more difficulty rolling onto his front than was necessary until he kicked himself free of the bag completely. Shutting his eyes against the lights, he focused on what he could hear instead. There were only two of them, he was sure of that, and they were both to his right.

Amateurs.

He heard the low hum of a security personnel car nearby,

but otherwise, the park he'd stopped at was quiet. How bad had things gotten that the UN had security personnel assuming policing duties and rousting "vagrants" from *public* parks?

Spreading his arms out to his sides as ordered, he waited for the instant the first binder clicked on, before jerking his arm in to his side, pulling the UN troop down and close. Minstrel heard the hollow *thunk* as the UN trooper's head collided with the rear bumper of the air truck, and then the second UN troop reflexively triggered her stunner. The actinic lightning struck her ally, crackling as the stunner blast lit the air. He jerked rigid and Minstrel surged to his feet, shoving the disoriented one towards the second with the binder still latched to his wrist. The two UN troops fell in a heap, and Minstrel was on them in a second.

The UN still liked to believe it was a "liberating" force, and as such, did its utmost to limit the equipment their troops carried. "Non" lethal and "less" lethal were standard issue, but only if applied *properly*. He dug a telescoping baton free from the stunned man's belt and flicked it to extend it before whipping it around to crash into the back of his exposed neck below his helmet. The *crunch* was muted, and the male officer collapsed on top of his partner, pinning her in place. Snapping the baton around in a figure eight, he brought it down backhanded across the windpipe of the female. Her arm was trapped, extended, and Minstrel dropped a knee over her upper arm, preventing her from reaching the parrot mic that sat on her shoulder. Not that she would be able to speak with a crushed trachea, but getting any kind of a signal out with the comm would be enough to summon backup.

"This isn't your world," he hissed and watched the light fade from her eyes. He rolled her partner over and confirmed he was out too. He stripped their vests and belts of valuable gear and removed the one binder with the dead woman's key. Minstrel dragged the bodies back to their patrol car. Lifting the overweight dead guy was a pain, but Minstrel got him into the driver's seat and then heaved his partner into position next to him. He cast about hurriedly in the rear of the vehicle, spying a large foil evidence bag, useful for isolating electronics from any outside signal, and slammed the trunk shut. With the bodies in place, he popped the pole for his tent and threw his sleeping bag into the front seat. He'd need to be gone soon; if they'd followed procedure, they would have called in their location and what they were checking before rousting him. He scanned his truck—no identifying marks, no vehicle ID or number plate, just a plain silver airtruck with an open bed. He rummaged in the civilian rucksack, where he kept his field kit, and pulled out a firestarter.

Dead simple to make, the paper muffin-cup firestarter held a fifty-fifty mix of sawdust and candle wax. He lit the paper and carefully placed it low in the cab of the patrol car. Greasy polymer smoke was drifting from the windows as he pulled the air truck away. He listened to the UN comm as someone tried to check on the two troops. There was dead air for a few seconds, and they checked again. After the *third* status check failed, they sent a drone to check on them. A seg later, panicked voices came over the comm as the drone showed the car, fully engulfed. Brad checked his map and confirmed he was already six klicks from the scene. He pulled the battery from the enemy comm, sealed the device away inside the foil evidence bag, and tossed it on the seat next to him. With any luck, it would be some time before they realized the dead officers' gear was missing, and the foil would spoof any passive transponders or external instructions. Their encryption protocols would be beneficial to the resistance, so he retrieved his own comm and coded an old friend who lived in the south end of town.

"Hey, handsome," she greeted him at the door. "Anasazi" was a statuesque amazon of a woman with a thick mane of raven hair that hung to her hourglass waist. Even at 1.5 divs, she looked like she'd stepped out of a beautician's, and Minstrel leaned in to peck her on the cheek. "You're gonna tickle me with that beard," she complained, but the smile didn't leave her face. "I've missed you!"

"I hate it," he admitted. "But it does help with their facial recognition systems."

"You look...rugged," she enthused. "*Very* manly, I approve. How goes? Have you been in town long? Can I pour you a drink?"

"It goes, no, and yes," he said. "*Very* yes." She brought him inside. Seconds later, she presented him with a frosty beer bulb, and he sprawled on the couch.

"I'm sorry to crash your place this late," he began, but she shushed him.

"The UN doesn't sleep, so neither do we. This doesn't sound like a social call."

With a sigh, he brought her up to speed on everything he'd been doing since they last saw each other. Anasazi, real name Siobhan Ceallaigh, had been an FMF Rec Spec. After Anasazi's four-year hitch was over, she turned professional escort and quadrupled her pay. The sex industry crashed to a halt under the UN occupation, but it seemed she knew everyone who was anyone, and very quickly found herself a full-time spy. She choked on her drink when Minstrel related his misadventure identifying Nicki.

"Dammit Brad, you should have called me. I could have arranged a proper intro and saved everyone the trouble. A lady doesn't kiss and tell, but for you, I make an exception. Nicki was a client of mine, a while back," she admitted. "It's been a while, but I know her well."

"She seems intense."

"She's brilliant, and sometimes that comes with a social cost. For a while, it seemed I was her only social contact. She's dedicated to her research. She managed to blend work with play when her man, Doctor Endah Taliin, came along, that's about when we stopped seeing each other. But Endah *was* killed by the UN a week ago, and she's retreated into her shell again. I'm not surprised she came across as cold. She's a brilliant researcher but wanted nothing to do with the resistance and seemed to think the UN would just leave her alone. It's awful that that's what it took to get her to notice what was going on everywhere else, but at this point, it's easier to find people who've lost someone than someone who hasn't."

After continuing his story and telling her about his rude awakening, he turned over the equipment he'd looted.

"You continue to impress, Bradley Ministrelli. What are your plans for the rest of the night?"

"If you don't mind, I'm going to put my tent back up in the truck out front, roll out my bag, and rack out."

Siobhan looked hurt. "I certainly *do* mind. Why on earth would you sleep in your *truck* when there's a perfectly warm bed *here*?"

"I didn't—I wasn't—I didn't want to presume," he stammered.

"You are a bundle of nerves and have been flying solo for months, mister. You need a shower, a massage, and you need to get spread. For that matter, so do I. *Strip*."

❖   ❖   ❖

Brad woke in the morning to Iolight streaming through the windows. The heavenly scent of bacon sizzling on a griddle wafted through the air, and he blearily made his way out of Siobhan's bedroom and down to her kitchen. She was dressed, made-up, and looked like she'd just stepped out of the spa.

"Half a div of scorching sex, bacon for breakfast, being served up by the smartest, savviest, sexiest superspy I've ever met. Marry me," he proposed, with a mischievous grin on his face.

Siobhan smiled and pecked him on the cheek. "Ask me again when the war's over, handsome. Plates are there." She indicated as she lifted the bacon off the grill.

"Where did this come from? Last I heard the UN was clamping down on proper meat, they want everything converted over to vat-grown abominations instead."

"I've been saving it for a special occasion. We'll head out as soon as we're fed."

"We?"

"Of course. It's been ages since I saw Nicki in person, and with a *proper* introduction, her fears should be allayed somewhat."

"Good morning, Doctor Sykora," Siobhan greeted her as she strode into the lab office. The doctor seemed a bundle of nerves and jumped when she heard her name.

"Good...morning?" she asked, more than said, as she turned to see the speaker. "Siobhan!" she cried and hugged the taller woman fiercely. "How *are* you?"

"Very well, thanks! May I introduce my dear friend Bradley?" she said with a grin on her face. Puzzled, Nicki turned as Brad entered with a sheepish grin on his face.

"Your dear...friend..." Nicki repeated, looking back and forth between the two of them. "You two...?"

"Yes." Anasazi nodded. "I've already given him shit for not coming to me first. Let's catch up inside, shall we?"

The morning passed slowly for Minstrel. Nicki continued her examination of the sample he'd supplied and ran a variety of tests he didn't understand. He lacked sufficient expertise to be of any value in the lab and was relegated to running errands, picking up equipment and supplies from elsewhere in the lab facility, and keeping Nicki and Siobhan fed. Anywhere he went off campus, uniformed UN troops occupied street corners, guarded checkpoints, and harassed Freeholders. Larger armed drones and light gunbird vertols buzzed overhead. The hostility on the street was palpable, and Brad actually ducked into a cocoa shop when someone skeeted a hexrotor out of the air with a shotgun. He sheltered there for half a div more while the UN overreacted outside and emerged to find most of the checkpoints had added troops in power armor on-site to intimidate the civilians into sullen compliance.

Feminine laughter greeted him from around the corner as he returned with hot jambalaya for three.

"So then he says, all serious-like, '*I'm looking for Doctor Sykora from the Freehold Science Alliance.*' And he has no idea that the FSA was a *varsity social group* for all us freaks and geeks." Minstrel felt his cheeks flush, but he rounded the corner anyways. Tears of laughter were streaming down Siobhan's face, and when she saw Brad, Nicki tried to stifle her own laughter. Brad smiled, and she let out another chuckle. "But I suppose you know now."

"This has been . . . a learning experience, and a rude awakening," Brad allowed. "I am not trained for this, but I *am* learning quickly. How did the rest of this morning go?" The lighthearted atmosphere suddenly chilled, and Nicki looked downcast.

"Frustrating. Frightening."

"How so?" Brad asked.

"It violates every moral code of the field." She scowled, jaw tight. "I've got a full workup on what it is and what it does. The superficial irritation isn't a virus, it's an allergen—urushiol. It causes contact dermatitis like some earth plants. It might itself be lethal for sensitive individuals. That's just barely the beginning," Nicki said. Her skin had gone pale, and there was a sheen on her forehead, as though it stressed her just to speak her findings aloud.

"The bad part is, they've embedded a virus within it. The irritant will last six, maybe eight weeks once a person contracts the condition. It's been designed to be more robust than the natural stuff and can be deployed via crop duster, in a spray, or for that matter, they could airburst it from artillery shells.

"The virus, however, is hidden within the allergen like a nightmarish matryoshka doll and will take effect as the spores' effects wear off. The immune response attacks the RNA shells and releases the virions. That's a hemorrhagic plague that will disintegrate the infected person's blood vessels from inside out. A week or two later, organs begin to fail, massive subdermal hematomas, and you die. Maybe your lung's alveoli and capillaries go first, and you drown. Maybe your eyes rupture, and they can't stop bleeding. Maybe your aorta blows. Doesn't matter; the point is that it's fucking monstrous. Ebola was stamped out on Earth centuries ago, but this looks like a highly weaponized version of it. None of our standard counters will touch it."

Brad considered the problem and concluded it was time to lay his cards on the table.

"There is a group of hackers, electronics intel specialists, geeks and/or Black Ops troops running a secondary net behind the scenes. I don't know who they are, but I trust the FMF troop who put me in contact with them. I report in, receive instructions or requests for materiel, transmit and receive data. Each time I do, I run the risk that the UN figures out how we're getting the messages around. They're clearly... fallible, since they *didn't* know the significance of the FSA, they just knew that Dr. Meacham was a friendly who'd made the ultimate sacrifice. They hoped that because you and he both belonged to the same... social group," Minstrel grimaced, while Nicki smiled, "that meant you were a friendly too. When they gave me *your* name, I didn't get so much as a first initial. So there are gaps in their intel, but they *are* connected to friendlies of all sorts, all over Grainne. Hell, maybe the halo too, I don't know. Maybe we give them a copy of the data, see what they can shake loose?"

Siobhan was nodding, and eventually, Nicki did too.

"I don't like admitting defeat," she said. "But you may be right."

Siobhan had a safehouse not too far from campus, and the trio left the lab together. She activated a map overlay on her civilianized comm and showed it to Minstrel.

"You're not the only one with geek friends. There's... fifty thousand? Nope, sixty thousand now, of us residents tracking UN checkpoints. When they establish a temporary control point, a user pins it on the map. If you live anywhere within a half-kay radius of the CP, you get a notification on the coordinates. When they tear the CP down, users can mark it clear. Once multiple sources confirm it's gone, we remove it from the overlay. But the overlay naturally interfaces with the navigation side and plots a route around them."

Brad shook his head. He could have used an overlay like that a long time ago. Evidently Siobhan and he moved in different intel circles, because he'd never heard of the overlay. They'd have to start sharing best practices, starting with this link. He could think of a bunch of other active partisans who would appreciate something like that as well.

They arrived safely, and Minstrel logged in with the entertainment vid again. After exchanging bona fides with Beth, Minstrel summarized their problem and asked for help.

Beth took her time replying, but eventually, the reply came:

Send the analysis for distribution. Reports from CRD indicate the allergen, local nickname "the runnies," has gone live. Secondary tasking, use all available assets to produce standard multi-use medical nanos in bulk and prep to distribute to known militia groups.

The clock was ticking.

Beth's report took the matter from "urgent" to "critical," and the trio concluded "all available assets" included begging help from mutual friend Sergeant Michael "Specter" Pieters, who was out near Delph'...somewhere. He was a fully qualified veterinarian and nano expert who could fabricate and program them in bulk. If worst came to worst, some models in Nicki's simulator suggested a course of medical nanos could delay but not stop the virus, potentially buying them time. Minstrel was pleased to learn Anasazi was already tied into the rest of the Jefferson handler team through Amber Riggs. The veterans and volunteers who supplied the missile teams connected with the leopard handlers, the handlers provided much-needed pathfinding and wilderness survival expertise in the Dragontooth Mountains and hunted vertols from the safety of the wilds.

Minstrel's comm's range was limited when not connected to the standard network, so they followed the hills and slopes of the range up to the peaks, flying barely above the treetops until the ocean disappeared over the horizon to the east. From here, they'd get the best possible coverage and the broadest possible broadcast. "Specter, this is Minstrel, over," Brad sent for the fourth time.

"Minstrel, this is Frosty," a familiar voice replied, and Brad

sighed in relief. Rick Winters was the team's senior sergeant who ran with two leopard brothers, Ronny and Buck. After exchanging *another* authentication, "Frosty" sent him the handler team's most up-to-date encryption key so his comm would communicate with Pieters and directed them to his AO. Thirty kilometers on, Brad broadcast again.

"Minstrel? This is Specter. Is that you buzzing around overhead?" Pieters asked. *"I'm with Fritz and Riggs. Magnus is hurt, and we're trying to extract on foot. Your timing couldn't be better. Stand by."*

"Blow an LZ, and we'll pick you up," Brad replied. Pieters replied in the affirmative, and Brad circled until he heard detonations and saw trees topple. He swiftly dropped the air truck below the massive treetops and came to a gentle rest, perched precariously across a pair of parallel pillar trunks. Three handlers emerged from the treeline carrying a stricken leopard on a rough nuggetwood stretcher. They already had IVs running and the shirts that made up the stretcher fabric were darkly stained.

Pieters hopped into the bed of the airtruck with his patient, and Amber Riggs and her cat Sheerah joined them. A liquid black shadow flowed out of the trees behind him, and Shadow jumped over the tailgate to join his partner just before Pieters dropped the truck's rear door. Two handlers and three cats made for a crowded interior, but it made sense—Amber wouldn't leave either of her two cats behind, while Mike was the best veterinarian they had. With the interior sealed away from the outside wind, Minstrel popped the rear window, and Riggs leaned in. Her face was taut and dirty from weeks of rough living, with leaves and twigs in decorating her mud-caked mane of dirty blonde hair. Both handlers had lost a lot of weight.

"Where are we going?" she shouted over the turbines.

"I know a place!" Nicki shouted back. "Sit tight!"

Minstrel's airtruck touched down on the outskirts of Fall Creek, and Dr. Sykora led the way into a large log cabin. She brushed cobwebs out of her face, a good sign that indicated the cabin hadn't been disturbed. Minstrel, Riggs, and Pieters carried their stricken patient inside the cabin, and downstairs. Pieters did a double-take when he realized his old ladyfriend had held the front door, and introductions were rapidly made as Pieters hung IV bags from the basement's rafters. The cabin had a stainless-steel game table in the basement, some surgically sharp game-dressing tools, a well-stocked medical kit, and plenty of disinfectant. Surgery was a long, tense affair, but handlers spent a good deal of time in cat school learning to be the veterinarian version of a blazer combat medic. With Mike operating, Brad and Amber assisting, and Nicki programming nanos on the fly, they stabilized the wounded leopard and left him to rest.

"What happened?" Brad asked when they'd cleaned up. "And whose place is this?"

"It's . . . mine, I guess?" Nicki answered. "It was Endah's. He loved to come out here and get away from the city life, he found it peaceful. Sometimes he hunted, and the fishing here was excellent. We obviously haven't been out here since the invasion. Now he's gone, I suppose it's mine, more or less. I'm the closest thing to next-of-kin he had even though we never made it official."

"Well we appreciate you letting us crash," Mike replied. "It's good to see you again."

"Likewise, but I wish it wasn't under these circumstances," Nicki replied. "What happened to your cat?"

"There's some kind of off-planet smuggling op," Amber replied. "We haven't had a single resupply since February that didn't come by way of airdrop. Ammunition, consumables, field rats, shoulder-launched anti-air missiles, the works."

"Only this time, we got sloppy," Pieters spat in disgust. "We had a rule—one missile per launch site, to do otherwise exposes us. Well, this time we had more than we could carry away and launched three from the drop site in a hurry. We downed two, but the third swept around, pinpointed us, and we had to leg it. The next wave was an Avatar incendiary strike and a sweep by a Special Unit in that fucking clamshell armor."

Riggs stroked the wounded leopard's fur and looked sadly at her cat's wounds. He was dopey, conscious but sedated. "Magnus didn't understand you can't fight powered armor with teeth and claws. The UN was . . . a tad miffed. We got one of the suits, but it was a close thing, and then we ran. Another mistake like that will cost."

Pieters shook himself out of a reverie. He was running on a mixture of adrenaline and stress, but Brad could read the puzzlement on his face as he took in Brad, Siobhan, and Nicki in this cabin basement. "Now, what in the Goddess's name is so important you had to pluck me and mine out of the field?"

Beth: Assets have cracked your earlier conundrum RE precious cargo counter. We are distributing this widely, and full details have been published on the nets, in the Halo, and word will reach other systems in fifteen days. Make best use of it you can; getting results was... costly.

The message was etched into his retinas. Beth was, as usual, being understated. He worried what "costly" meant, but he assumed it meant casualties. The infodump itself meant nothing to him, so he handed it over to the doctors immediately.

"Goddess..." Pieters cursed quietly.

"You see it too?" Nicki asked soberly.

"What am I missing?" he asked, clearly out of his depth.

"The good news is, we can fab a cure now," Mike said. "Whoever your source is, they were thorough. Anyone who's been given this nano can have blood drawn to start a culture within thirty divs for anyone with the right blood type."

"What's the bad news?"

"It's going to be a slow process. The first reports of the runnies came out three weeks ago, meaning we've got four or five left before the blood plague does its thing and starts killing us in job lots," Nicki continued with a grimace. "We should stick ourselves with the first set of counters, so we can draw blood and get secondary cultures going at the same time. Let's get to work."

In addition to being experts on the subject, Doctors Pieters and Sykora were decent instructors and had spent a morning teaching Minstrel and Anasazi the finer points of processing basic medical nanos. Riggs had elected to remain at the cabin, caring for Magnus and the other leopards, and besides, they wouldn't have hidden on campus very well. That then freed both the experts up to make the vastly more complex counter to the runnies. For seven and a half divs a day, they sourced supplies and cranked out nanos that had been, until the UN's occupation, produced on an industrial scale and distributed as widely as possible. They had to avoid being conspicuous at all costs.

It was Yewday, and Mike had agreed to remain with Nicki in

the lab as Ministrelli and Siobhan got out, stretched their legs, and grabbed lunch for all five. When they returned to campus, Minstrel spotted a large cargo hauler emblazoned with a logo.

McClellan & Son Farm Supply

"That isn't right," he whispered. "Hold on."

When they neared the truck, Minstrel greeted the man, extending his hand.

"You John's new help? How's he doing these days?"

"Oh, ye know," the man replied, giving him a quick limp-wristed handshake. His Scottish brogue was so thick it was nearly impenetrable. "Doin' his best tae keep on keepin' on, what with the UN and all."

"No doubt. Give him my regards, would you? Tell him Brad Steele says hi?"

"Aye, will do, have a good 'un."

When they had some distance, Ceallaigh lowered her voice.

"What was that all about?"

"John McClellan died three and a half years ago, on Mtali," Brad replied. "His *brother* sourced the original sample of the allergen. If they rumbled David somehow, they might know we have the sample. If they know we have the sample, they might be looking at labs that could analyze it. Did you see how he shook hands? No way he's Freehold."

"Dammit."

"Keep your head on a swivel. Methinks shit just got real."

Brad and Siobhan kept their eyes wide as they strode purposefully onto the university grounds. Parked cars and trucks, ordinarily innocuous, now seemed suspicious. There were more drones overhead, and groups of students now looked more like undercover UN troops. Brad looked up as a wing of Sentinels flew by, high overhead, then realized he was exposing his face to any drones looking down at him and tucked his chin again. He couldn't tell where his survival instinct ended and paranoia began; blood hammered in his ears, and he recognized his body was getting ready to fight whether he wanted it to or not.

The airtruck he'd arrived in was parked on the far side of campus, and a detour would delay them, unacceptably so. They passed another nondescript aircar where a pale Caucasian man sat with another with darkly tanned skin and wavy black hair.

The former stood out, especially, as any long-term exposure to Iolight would have imbued him with a permanent tan.

Once is an accident, twice is a coincidence, third time will be too late.

Siobhan saw them too and pulled out her comm. "I'm calling them," she said.

Mike Pieters fumbled his phone as it buzzed.

"Yes?"

"Get out." Ceallaigh's voice on the comm was harsh but urgent.

"What?" Pieters asked.

"Get out. Get everything we have, and get out, now. They're coming."

"We can't just..." Mike argued, but Nicki grabbed the comm from his ear.

"If we leave now, we lose a third of our counter-nanos."

"You don't leave now, we lose it all. We've got spooks and surveillance teams all over campus. Take the north exit, then west, we're coming to you."

The UV sterilization chamber slowed their exit from the lab, and the pair emerged already peeling their scrubs off and tossing them into the recycler. Nicki poked her head out the door and quickly ducked back in.

"Shit. Director Kaur is coming this way with four more. No uniforms."

Nicki considered her options for just a moment and grabbed Mike's comm again.

:: Too late, incoming, :: she typed. She glanced around the lab for something she could use as a weapon.

The comm beeped in reply.

:: Stall them ::

Nicki took a deep breath and guided Mike towards the showers. "I recall, once upon a time, you had a thing for getting hot and wet and soapy. They're coming, but we have to buy them time."

Mike resisted at first, unsure whether she meant what she'd said, but as the words registered, he followed his former ladyfriend into the showers, where they got the water running.

The door opened. "Doctor Sykora?" a feminine voice called out. Nicki looked at her old boyfriend, who just nodded in understanding.

"Doctor Sykora?" the voice called again, but they didn't acknowledge.

"Check the shower," a male voice ordered. Nicki mouthed the words "Trust me" and Mike nodded. She pressed herself up against Pieters under the stream of water and gave him a deep kiss as she wrapped her arms around him. She was warm, and slippery, and her lips were soft; Mike regretted that their careers had taken them different directions. It had been a long time since he'd held her like this, and he suddenly found himself missing her a great deal. All too quickly, they were interrupted.

"Oh!" the female voice started, and Nicki jumped back, "surprised" by the woman. "Oh, dear, I'm sorry to, well, to interrupt," she apologized, and Nicki did her best to feign indignation.

"Can I help you, Director?" she enunciated, hands on her bare hips.

"I beg your pardon, and yours," Director Kaur apologized to both. "But there are some men here from the UN, and they need a word. They're quite insistent."

"Let us rinse off the soap and dry, and we'll be out in a moment," Nicki said, and Kaur nodded and turned away. Pieters delayed another thirty seconds before shutting the water off, and the two emerged while toweling off. Nicki took her time drying off, giving the UN aardvarks an eyeful, knowing how repressed they were when it came to nudity and sex. As anticipated, the shock value caused a few wide eyes, appreciative stares, and then one soldier cuffed another other upside the back of his head.

"Eyes front, you. You know what the cultural brief said."

"But, Sarge," the younger man complained, and received a poke to his chest.

"And no rank!"

Pieters filed all that intel away for later and dressed quickly. He knew how twitchy her nudity was making the men, and every second that passed meant the other three were closer. They paid him almost no mind, but the aardvarks from Earth couldn't take their eyes off Dominika.

"Now then," Nicki said as she pulled on her top. "What do you want?"

One of the men stepped forward and flashed a badge. "I am Captain Nicholas Devers of the 12th Military Police Company.

You two are under arrest, the charge is conspiracy to commit terrorism. Place your hands behind your back."

"Excuse me?" Director Kaur protested. "You said nothing about arresting—"

"I don't have to explain myself to you," the MP snapped. "Now, get out of the way or be arrested for obstruction."

Kaur backed away as two of the men with Devers reached under their jackets to remove binders.

"You ready?" Minstrel asked as they turned the hallway corner, and Dr. Sykora's office/lab door came into sight.

"Just fuck 'em up, I can handle it," Anasazi declared. Minstrel reached into the bag from Darmawan's, withdrew a bulb, and popped off the cap.

"Honey! We brought lunch!" he called as he backed through the doorway. The first UN goon he saw opened his mouth to object, but Minstrel already had the bulb held out extended, and he squeezed, spraying Satan pepper sauce into the closest target's eyes and mouth. A second thug's eyes widened as the attack registered, then he too was coated in sticky, red, fiery salsa.

Minstrel dropped the bulb and leaped at the third, the one who seemed to be in charge, as Pieters went low, slamming into a fourth from behind in a low rugby tackle. They crashed to the floor, and Pieters grabbed a stickyweb gun on the MP's belt and fired three times at near-contact range, pinning the UN troop's head to the floor.

Minstrel and the captain went down in a heap, but the UN officer was overweight and outmassed Brad by forty kilos. From beneath his bulk, Brad grabbed the captain's too-long hair with his left hand, cranked his head back, and slammed the heel of his right through the captain's jaw, breaking his neck and ending the fight. He leveraged the body off himself and rolled to his feet.

Siobhan webbed one of the goons suffering from pepper spray, and Nicki decked him with a vicious elbow to the base of his neck. Minstrel dodged aside as the last hostile finally cleared his own less-lethal sidearm and lifted it to fire, but Siobhan took three steps forward and kicked upwards between his legs like she was punting a football. The sudden, unexpected impact crumpled him to the ground where he keened in agony. Pieters webbed him in the face, muffling his screams and ensuring he would suffocate, then did the same for the other UN troops as well. Stickywebs were only "less" lethal, after all.

"We need to leave. Now," Minstrel panted.

Nicki shook her head in the negative. "We'll lose a third of the counter if we go." If the dead and dying UN troops leaking and thrashing on her office floor bothered her, she made no show of it. Director Kaur, on the other hand, stood in the corner with tears streaming from her eyes.

"What have you done?" she stammered. The foursome all looked at her, forgotten in the melee, then Pieters pointed the webgun at her.

"Turn around," he ordered, "and put your hands on the wall." Kaur complied, and Mike shot her in both hands, pinning them in place with the last of the stickyweb. "This way, they don't blame you," he said by way of apology. "Maybe. There will be more coming."

Siobhan's checkpoint app proved a lifesaver. She watched in real time as the plainclothes spooks' uniformed backup raced to the scene, but they reached the airtruck and slipped away before the UN could close the net. This part of the city was too hot for Siobhan or Nicki to remain. DNA sniffers would go over the lab and then any random checkpoint became a lethal liability.

After reclaiming their gear and their stash of counter-nano, Siobhan posted Nicki's analysis of the runnies, and the cure, to every anonymous forum she knew. The UN would try to deny their use of bioweapons, of course, but the information wasn't for their benefit. They fled west and outside Fall Creek, Pieters reunited with his anxious panther. They disappeared back into the forest with Riggs, to go back to the hunt. It hurt, to let his colleagues go back to their hunt while he was errand boy, messenger, and general go-between, but intellectually he knew he was now a force-multiplier, not a trigger-puller. Through his work, everyone else became that much more effective, and there was some satisfaction to be found in that.

"Where will you go?" Brad asked. "You can't stay here anymore, not after that."

"I have family in Taniville," Siobhan answered. "Barring a flight to Caledonia, it's the safest place for us to disappear." It was also at the far end of the continent, a ten-thousand-kilometer trip, and Brad winced.

"You could stay with me, stay on the move. Goddess knows you're better at this spy shit than I am."

"You know I'd love to," she replied. "But the last I heard, Tani hasn't been able to organize itself in the slightest. I'll look up some old friends from First Army and keep doing what I'm doing. I'll be careful, you just promise to do the same, you understand? And when this is all over, you can propose to me again. It'll give you something to look forward to."

Brad smiled sheepishly, kissed her deeply, and shook hands with Nicki before the women departed. He took a deep breath and got back in the battered air truck to start making his rounds.

His first stop was at the farm in Darkwood Hills, with the blonde woman who'd resembled Nicki—except, she didn't resemble Nicki anymore. Her skin was patchy and raw, scabs wept pus, and she moved as if every joint was inflamed. So did everyone else, for that matter.

"I've got something you want," he said and handed over the first case. "Twelve doses of counter-nano to the runnies."

One of the men objected. "Only twelve? There's forty people around here."

"All I can spare, friend," Brad apologized. He hurt for them—they were obviously suffering. There had been a handful of children running around the last time he'd been here, but they were conspicuous in their absence. "I have other people to supply. But if you draw blood in three days, anyone compatible can use it as a starter culture. These doses will take effect immediately, symptoms will heal naturally in a week, overnight with a reconstructor nano, and I have *eighty* doses of that you can have. The cultured version takes about two days to work fully, then another week for natural healing."

The man who had objected, a woman Minstrel took to be his wife, and another couple began unloading. Minstrel caught a moment to ask the blonde woman about the children, and she teared up.

"This isn't our first go with their bioweapons," she spat. Her North American accent had been obvious the first day he'd met her, and he wondered how she'd come to be hiding out here, of all places. "The last one gave everyone pneumonia, and Riga choked to death in her sleep. That's her father, Dak."

Minstrel nodded. "Just make sure *everyone* gets the counter, lady. *Everyone*. It's lethal if untreated." He spared her the horrific details, so long as she was clear on the consequences.

"Thank you," the blonde woman said quietly. "I don't know how you came up with this, but you've already proven yourself the strongest link in *our* chain of command, I don't know what we'd do without you."

Minstrel went to the bereaved father and embraced the man, briefly.

"Dak, I'm sorry about Riga. If I could have done anything about it, believe me..."

The haunted farmer stepped back and looked upon him with reddened, gummy eyes and weeping sores. Minstrel had seen that look before. It was a simmering cauldron of rage and hate, and he'd seen it staring back at him in every mirror after they'd bombed Heilbrun. He'd raised his kittens from birth to be his sidekicks, battle partners, and his kids. The day they'd died, he would have killed every man, woman and child on Earth, if he'd been offered the chance. Dak, apparently, was a stronger man than he, because the man's features softened after a moment, nodded, and he turned away.

"If any of you need relief, to come off the line for a while and get your hearts and heads sorted out, even for a day or three, say the word," Brad told the blonde woman. "I'm tied in to a lot of people, people with safehouses and resources and help. I can make that happen. Better to trade distance for time than flame out and lose everything. Every*one*."

"That's the last thing Dak would want." She stared at her host's retreating form as he disappeared back into the farmhouse. "He'd see it as defeat."

"Understood," Minstrel replied, "but the offer stands. Some wounds, a nano can't heal."

The blonde thought about that for a moment. "I think we're a bit—" The blonde abruptly hacked and coughed, spitting out a wad of bloody phlegm, "past that point."

"You may be right. The others look to you. Veteran?"

"Active, Third Mob logistics. I was on one of the last flights out before they hit the base." She extended her arm, and Minstrel shook it Freehold style. "I'm Kendra, but my old recruit instructor called me Icebitch."

"Who was that, if I may ask?"

"Senior Sergeant Joe Carpender," she answered, and Minstrel gave her an incredulous look.

"Very pleased to meet you then, Kendra. Joe was my section commander before he lateraled to Mirror Lake; I know what he was like, so if he was your RI, you have my respect. My friends call me Brad, and I'm sorry I couldn't get the nanos here any sooner."

"Thank you, Brad. I know we look like hell right now but give us a week's relief from these fucking spores and we'll be back in the fight." Kendra looked to the farmhouse where Dak's remaining family waited inside. "They ain't seen nothin', yet. We're just getting started."

Bidding War

Michael Z. Williamson

Jeremy Bravo sat in his office, sipping cocoa, wondering how to get money. His office was in a fenced compound north of Jefferson, not far from what had been Freehold Forces Heilbrun Base. It was readily reachable by transport, but remote enough to avoid random gawkers and idiots wanting a "tour" of Ripple Creek Security Operations. It housed their offices, standard training facilities, lodging for times of duress, such as now—their families were recently moved into the adequate housing, which could double as additional training facilities if necessary, equipment and maintenance, and their armory, still intact as an authorized UN contractor, at present.

It was understandable that retailers, factories and even banks had trouble during an occupation, especially with UN bureaucrats trying to create government regulations where few had existed. For a military contractor to struggle during a war, though, was... frustrating.

Ripple Creek should have their choice of contracts, and if the war was anywhere else, they would. Even here, they should be able to pick up all kinds of protection gigs.

While there was a goldmine of executive protection to be done, the contracts were not viable.

He absolutely would not accept UN contract work in this system. This was Ripple Creek's base of operations, and goodwill with the locals was essential. Besides, quite a few of their employees were Freeholders, too. Getting between warring factions of your primary employer and your neighbors was not a wise option.

He had plenty of notes out for outsystem security. As far

as that went, the company worked for a number of multinats, bureaus and private individuals. Those contracts were in effect and supporting themselves. That didn't cover the margin for the rest sitting idle, though.

The UN's primary concern was here. Every bureaucrat in the system was terrified of being captured and/or killed in brutally bizarre and creative ways. The Assassins Guild—technically the Professional Duelists' Association but call a spade a spade—were taking a slow, methodical toll on a number of BuState, BuMil, and others, even BuEdu and BuTreas managers. Every insurgent group had tags for the lower administrators and would happily take the bigger ones if they found them. So, most of the high-value targets were hiding here in Jefferson, in their offices, terri-fied to set foot in the street, but required to do so periodically.

If they sent flunkies, the flunkies died, too. So the flunkies pleaded ignorance of the finer points of the mission until the ranking admin wankers had to respond.

Every one of them wanted a personal security detail. The UN wasn't willing to pay top rates for those high-level but noncritical personnel. He didn't want to be in the middle of that goatfuck. Nor should he accept the second-string rates being offered for first-line PSD work. He also didn't want to get on the UN's bad side by refusing. He was running out of excuses, and the last two feelers had wound up at MilBu intelligence, forwarded to theater leadership, gleefully insisting they could *absolutely* employ his personal security details if they were available. At about fifteen percent of their usual rates.

Choices were disappearing fast. Things were getting critical.

Then there was the new power bill from the UN Interim Civil Electrical Cooperative, which was about twice the usual bill from the former Capital Power Systems. The UN added all kinds of environmental, service, monitoring and other fees that didn't do a damned thing for him, just drove the cost up. He also had communications about wanting licenses and certs on the company weapons, their professional standards—of which they had plenty, but not under the UN bureaucracy except when contracted to them, etc.

Lasman Khaima came through the open door for a morning conference. He was bigger, broader and darker than Bravo, and looked more like what people expected of a hired goon.

"What do you think, boss?" he asked as he dropped into a deeply arched chair that whuffed as it compressed.

Grimacing, Jeremy replied, "I think everyone needs to polish up a résumé for store security or a nonfield job. We're running out of options."

Khaima replied, "The problem is if we keep sitting on a fence, we're going to get a stick up our ass." He flicked out a pocket-knife and started cleaning his nails.

Jeremy took a sip of his drink and nodded. "Absolutely. But there's no good outcome if we get between the hostiles trying to stop bullets. We'd lose people for too little money."

Khaima said, "Did you see the local reward for Scott Loughery went up again?"

Jeremy hadn't. "To what now?"

"One fifty K, preferably alive."

He exhaled, almost a whistle. "Damn. That's a good fee." Loughery was Chief, Grainne Interim Governmental Infrastructure Development Function. Joseph Mattias, billionaire and braggart, had openly put prices on the heads of several bureaucrats he felt were interfering with his prosperity and glamorous life-style. The Duelists' Assn. had gotten three so far. A private sharpshooter got one. Two others had encountered significant IEDs. In response, Mattias had a price on his head, but enough money and contacts to evade, avoid, and pay off any attempt on him so far.

Khaima nodded and said, "Yeah. How would you feel about protecting him?"

"If they'd pay that per week, I'll actually consider it." That would be twice base rate for someone in that status.

"Can we haggle? What are they offering?"

"Fifteen K."

Khaima spluttered. "Per *week*? I knew they were offering crap, but that won't even get you a good entry control team from Fortis."

Jeremy nodded. "Right. And we'd still be defending a scumbag from our neighbors who have reasons to want him dead. Bad juju." On the other hand...

"Nothing outsystem?"

"Travel costs are killing every deal. We have to get out of here via UN-controlled routes, which are slow and expensive. You add a half mil in travel expenses and we stop being competitive.

Everyone calling needs either sooner or can find good enough for cheaper. All the action is right here."

"Which we can't take."

Jeremy scowled and chugged the rest of his chocolate. "Right again. We have the permanent contract with Prescot, the standing consult with the Caledonian royals. The ten or so others you know about. Every new offer is right here, not enough, and especially given the PR nightmare."

"The only thing I'd jokingly suggest is we take out Loughery discreetly. That money will feed us for the month at least."

"That's where we're going."

Khaima was wide-eyed. "Boss, I was joking."

"I'm not. A buck's a buck and if our primary employer isn't paying, they stop being an employer. They might hinder contracts or file criminal charges. If we take their coin our friends have to try to kill us, and damn, will they be personally pissed. We're boned either way, so we may as well make sure we have a safe place to live for now. If we don't have principals to protect, we have to create some. There's also the possibility that if we're discreet enough, they start hiring us to protect them from what we'll do if they don't hire us."

That got a grin from Khaima. "Protection money. We really don't have a choice. We need money, the Unos aren't paying. So who do we send to do this?"

"We do it personally. You, me, Truitt, Grey, Tombala, Mahmoud. Find out where this value-added screen monkey is, and we'll go get him."

Finding Loughery was easy. He was conveniently in Jefferson, along with most of the bureaurats trying to create a new nation, just like all the other nations.

Getting him wouldn't be easy. He had a security detail of mixed bureau security and MPs. They were not as effective as Ripple Creek, but they were good enough to stop bullets. That meant murder charges from the UN, because there was no feasible way to separate him from them. Then, RC would have to unass the area with him, and even if he was compliant that would be a noticeable act.

Jeremy personally did the first recon. It was convenient that Mattias owned a building in the area. On the other hand, he owned a lot of buildings. Atop one of the railed rooflines, Jeremy carried a box of tools and monitors, and pretended to slowly and methodically monitor and adjust climate-conditioning equipment. It was even the right time of year to tweak it, after it came online, before it hit full capacity. While doing so, he placed microcameras. Those fed into delicate, spider-silk thin transmission lines, reinforced with monofilament, that dropped down a ventilation shaft where a company tech would wire it into a shielded line they could check with the right code.

Mattias also had his HUMINT element, which was a combination of every private comm camera he could get access to via several dark network hackers. That was made easier by the number of people voluntarily taking as many images and video as they could to help keep a live update on UN operations.

Loughery had a regular schedule from his apartment inside the Gray Zone to his office at the edge, where he was forced to deal with mere humans, and worse, humans not subserviently minded to him.

Once before, though, he took an armored limo and security team to a coffee shop rather far out of downtown, almost in the Delta district on the river.

And apparently again this week.

They went over the findings back in their compound, in a room with no windows and with everything swept and scrambled. It wasn't as secure as some military sites, but no one should be suspect and nearby, and the perimeter was kept secure.

The meeting was composed of Bravo, Khaima, explosive technician Oren Truitt, intel specialist Derek Tombala, pilot/driver/operator Sarina Mahmoud, and Jack Grey, the senior shooter and protection expert on hand.

Jeremy confirmed. "So he goes there every Berday?"

Tombala said, "Twice at least. He's meeting an intel source." He had a file open with notes.

Grey asked before Bravo could, "Do we know whose intel source?"

"Mattias says it's someone the Freehold insurgency trusts to furnish intelligence useful to us."

Khaima noted, "But not whether they're an honest double or just being fed?"

Tombala shook his head. "No. That doesn't really matter to

us though, does it? Apparently, it's military intelligence, so not even Loughery's job. He's trying to horn in on their operation for the glory."

"So pretty much no one is going to miss this asshole. Right. So make sure the source isn't hit in the crossfire. But also make sure he doesn't identify us. Slug him? Her?"

"Him. Pudgy little nerd. Easy enough to gap Loughery while that kid's whimpering on the floor."

"It would be, but Mattias is paying for him alive."

Tombala got very serious. "Boss...I mean, there's a difference between security and abduction, but they're sort of two sides of the same chip. Murder's a much bigger difference, but it's easy. Anyone who's got a kill on file should be able to put a round through his brain without much hesitation. Then we just disperse. Dragging him with us..."

Bravo explained, "Yes, it's going to be exciting, and we hate excitement. But, we love money, we need money, and that's what we're being paid for."

Shrugging, Khaima said, "Okay, then, let's work on E and E."

"First, obviously, no discussion with anyone, even family. We don't have a contract so there's no reason for anyone to even think anything is going on. That's what we want."

Grey commented, "We better plan an exercise, though, if we and others are moving around."

"Right. So, the rough plan is ingress the location, eliminate the security detail, egress with the target. Second egress is outside of what will be an increasingly broad but more dispersed perimeter. Then we have to arrange a delivery point."

Three days later they were on location at the coffee shop frequented by Loughery and his source. Bravo was in line for a cocoa, dressed like any other businessperson hoping to get by, though his clothing fabric was a bit tougher than those around him and had a certain amount of padding built in. He and Sarina Mahmoud were carrying doccases, standing just behind Loughery and his goons.

In his earbud he heard, "Visual front confirmed."

He let his peripheral vision take in the scene. Grey was at the rear, with a clear field of fire at the goons. Tombala had the two at the front through the door, and there were few bystanders.

Truitt was ready to shoot or obscure as needed, or take out the wall for a Plan C.

He smiled at Sarina, as if they were involved. He even ran a hand up her shoulder. Loughery suspected nothing, and his goons limited their action to returning cold stares against the glares aimed their way.

It was as perfectly set as it could be. Showtime.

There was the waitress. Now, then.

He glanced at the wall, then said, "Damn, I'm going to be late."

Everything exploded in noise, flash and smoke.

One second Scott Loughery was watching his coffee arrive. Business was about to start, and it was going to work in everyone's favor—the locals', the UN's, his. This source had been reliable twice. If this data was good, Loughery's office would set him up with just enough funds to keep him hungry and digging. Loughery would look good and BuMil would owe him a favor, such as more security.

The air cracked. There was a flurry of chattering BANGs and explosions whuffing pressure and dust and he startled and flailed. His entire security contingent was on the floor, all bleeding, most dead, some twitching as nerves accepted the inevitable. He'd seen it in combat video. He never expected to see it live. He heard screams and shouts and watched the locals all dive to the floor.

They all just died. What the fu—

A big man punched Leon Amit, his source, hard. Amit squealed, mumbled and collapsed. The man turned and grabbed Loughery's bag and comm.

A robbery? In daylight? But why hit my—

Rough hands seized him and something dark poked him under the right nostril.

A disturbingly cheerful voice asked, "Does this gun smell like ball sweat to you?"

Adrenaline rippled through him. It was a pistol. The muzzle did smell faintly of sweat.

I could die at any moment, he thought. Cold chills and nausea coursed through him.

"What do you want from me?" he asked, trying to hold exceedingly still and sound completely submissive, because he was.

"Let's go for a ride."

His abductor turned, and Loughery turned with him completely compliantly, hoping the backup force wasn't far away. Of course, they had dozens of personnel to support, but maybe they were near.

There was the door. It would be perfect if they arrived right now. He could dive out the door and hit the ground. It opened and a rush of hot, dry air blasted in.

A hand slapped him in the balls. Not hard, just enough to sting and make him gasp. As he did, a puff of vapor engulfed his face. He could smell it, rubbery and musty, and feel it burning. He felt a sneeze coming, and saw *his* car pull up, the trunk opening. The sneeze and his eyes both shut down in a swirl of color and twanging waveforms.

Bravo and Khaima lifted Loughery and dropped his head into the trunk, then rolled the rest of him in on a preplaced sheet. Grey bent over with a pair of sharp forceps and extracted the tracking chip from Loughery's right hand. He flicked it into the gutter. Eyes ahead, they walked briskly around the car and Khaima let his boss into the back then took passenger front. Grey and Truitt, slightly older and dapper, got in passenger middle and rear carrying classy luggage, and Sarina Mahmoud strode around the front and into the driver's seat. In moments, everyone had rifles laid out, and Truitt had a rocket projector.

The limo didn't look out of place here, the number of people was roughly correct, and they'd done their best to not act suspiciously. It was probable that no one had seen anything untoward, and unlikely that any locals would tell the UN if they did. Even acknowledging trouble could lead to being flagged and interrogated. The usual local reticence was reinforced by the intruding Earth culture.

Sarina rolled off.

"I had to adjust the seat," she commented. "Driver was the tall one."

"Noted."

Getting into the Gray Zone could be difficult. It required ID, a documented tasking, searches, and protocols of equipment. Getting out, though, was far less complicated most of the time.

That was about to change, since the moment Loughery was noticed missing, things would lock down. However, that would happen in stages, starting with a search for this limo.

From the back, Bravo ordered, "Drive it like we stole it, which we did."

Sarina replied, "Understood. Within all legal limits so as not to attract attention."

"Exactly."

Driving like a criminal was easy and obvious. Refraining from doing so even under duress took courage and training. That was their stock in trade. If nothing else, this was a nice exercise to keep their edge honed, and they would get paid.

At any time, a number of UN officials were in armored limos, others in staff cars, and a handful in air-capable vehicles. No one had twigged yet, but as soon as someone did, they'd try to disable or override the vehicle, or barricade with whatever force they had. The faster RC relocated and changed vehicles, the better.

Sarina took a right at the corner, past a small shop that was closed and gone, an economic victim of the invasion. She took a left, two rights, another left and had relocated them from the art district to a business zone. Very quickly, she pulled into a parking block, then punched the motor and skidded all the way to the third level. Above that level the block used motorized sorting. Here and down were parking for odd-sized vehicles.

On the third floor, a company-hired driver backed out of a space and gave Mahmoud room to park. At once, the doors popped open, the team climbed out into hot, dank air, popped the trunk, rolled Loughery into the sheet, loaded the wrapped bundle into the hatch of an adjoining Bufori sedan, got in, and backed down to the landing. There Sarina spun a turn, and they departed the block.

At the perimeter of the Gray Zone, traffic was slowed, but moving steadily. The Freehold had no provision for government override of vehicle controls, and this was one more thing that vexed the UN greatly.

Mahmoud reported, "Crap, they're starting to check vehicles."

From the back, now changed into a different suit, Bravo asked, "What are they using for barrier?"

"Two armed goons."

"Do you think you can ram if necessary?"

She replied at once, "Yes, how hardened is this thing?"

"Small arms shouldn't hurt it."

She nodded. "Okay. Do we have a backup outside?"

He thought through the list. "I can have Rosten do it. He's

already out of the zone." Rosten also had no idea what was going on. He'd been told to go to a location, wait for instructions. This happened all the time, exercise and real world. The man had no reason to expect real world, as there was no contract. He and the other staged personnel were useful backup who couldn't betray anything.

Sarina said, "Okay, here we go."

One of the UN perimeter patrol waved them closer, looking slightly intimidated by the expensive, chauffeur-driven vehicle. Mahmoud dropped her window. City dust and heat flowed in.

The guard was Eastern European, but his English was respectable if accented. Through the window he said, "Good afternoon, respected people. I am sorry to delay you. We have a security issue and need to check the vehicle."

From the passenger seat, Khaima raised his eyebrows and sounded incredulous as he asked, "You do realize who this is, right?"

The guard replied, "Sir, I do not."

Khaima pointed into the back with his thumb. "This is Rajer Pierson-Alton."

"Sir . . . I apologize, but I don't recognize that name."

The big man carried on through. "CFO and Vice-President of Lola Aerospace? The company that builds half of your landing craft and handled the upgrade contract on the Guardians?"

Bravo took the cue and called from the back, "What do they want, Sherise?"

Sarina replied, "Sir, they want to inspect the vehicle for something."

"Do they have a valid warrant?"

Khaima said loudly, "Not that I can tell."

The young guard stammered, obviously overawed by the claimed status, and leery of creating a scene. Traffic was piling up behind.

Jeremy could almost see the wheels turning in the boy's head. His senior sergeant came over. The MP gestured and talked while the supervisor wrinkled his brow and looked at the car.

There were frowns and hesitations, and Jeremy was trying to decide if he should signal Mahmoud to floor it, when the soldier turned and said, "Sorry to have delayed you, sir. Please relay our apologies and have a good day."

He pointed and the two gunners raised muzzles and half-saluted.

Khaima nodded and replied, "Thanks for keeping us safe, soldier."

Mahmoud eased forward and through the checkpoint.

As soon as the window was up, Tombala pulled a scanner.

"They didn't drop any bugs that I can tell."

Grey was looking behind as he added, "But they did figure out their error. There's screaming on the net about stopping us."

Bravo said, "Then let's make that next vehicle swap."

Sarina nodded. "Yeah, where are we going?"

"Remember the shop/warehouse we rented about a decade ago, for cash, to run a scenario?"

"Yes. On it." She changed lanes, got onto the freeway, and yes, this section did not have the destroyed bridge. She exited at the next loop, then resumed multiple turns, heading generally in the direction of the site.

Tombala announced, "There's a vertol overhead with parasite UAVs, trying to find us."

Bravo and Mahmoud both said, "Understood" simultaneously, and she took another turn, slowed as if looking for parking, then eased back into traffic.

Tombala updated with, "The drones are dropping lower. Also, our own net sent me a snapshot of vehicle pursuit. One Eel, two armored DT5s, and an AMG truck that is probably UN."

While turning yet again, she asked, "Who are we meeting?"

"I've directed Rosten to be ready. Once there, we have three ways out."

Mahmoud nodded. "Right. I'll program this to continue. We'll need to bail fast."

Khaima said, "Don't forget our payroll."

"I won't."

Accelerating now, Mahmoud said, "Here we go." She turned into the industrial park, and there was the garage.

Tombo asked, "Can you do anything about that drone astern?"

Oren Truitt said, "Yes, but I want to wait until we're close."

Bravo said, "We're close now."

"As you say, boss."

Oren leaned his grey head out the window, pointed his launcher, and it thumped.

A moment later there was a sharp BANG. Sarina took a sharp yank of the wheel, off the road, and the car rolled into the open bay doors.

Truitt confirmed the drone dead. "It's down."

Bravo shouted, "And stop. All out!"

The Bohemian Fire Drill took six seconds. Doors flew open, operators leapt out, the deck lid was still rising as Khaima grabbed Loughery's body like a sack of meat, thumped it into the cargo compartment of a five-year-old TesGen crew truck that rolled up alongside, and they all piled in as Sarina slammed the driver's door and the Bufori rolled off on auto. She hopped into the crew truck driver seat.

A few seconds later, Rosten punched the button on a kitted-out Dinocorp Lightning, sending it back into the city. He closed bay doors and grabbed a cycle, exiting through a personnel door.

It wasn't going badly so far, but Jeremy had hoped to be here before the first swap was identified. If they had a drone gap of even a few moments, the chase should be focused on the Bufori, and possibly the Lightning. The longer that pursuit chased those, the better the odds in the current transport, worn enough to be unremarkable.

"Okay, get us into commercial traffic. Do we need a fake?"

Tombo said, "We seem to be good for the present." A moment later he added, "No, here come drones."

Jeremy had eyes on a feed, Tombala watched two others and listened.

"They got the Bufori," Tombala announced. "It did take them awhile. They had to make sure it was empty and not boobytrapped."

"Good. What are they doing now?"

"They're reviewing, and I think they're going to pick up the Lightning. Yes, that's what they're tracking. And now us."

"Continue to drive normally. As soon as you think we're clear, Oren, blow the Lightning."

Tombala said, "Roger. They're piling on it now. We seem to be tertiary."

"Perfect."

Truitt asked, "Blow it now?"

"Yes."

The man grinned and keyed a code.

The car didn't just blow. It discharged several fragmentation warheads that shredded two of the drones and caused pursuit to slam to a halt. Then it incinerated hot. That was going to require an emergency response. The UN had learned not to trust local responders, so it was going to take time.

Bravo shrugged. "Of course, they now know we're the probable."

Oren said, "Meantime they have a fireball to deal with."

"Yeah, splitting resources is good, they're limited, but they're also determined. Ready with countermeasures?"

From the middle, Tombala replied, "Ready." Truitt was the supporting fire, Tombo was the spotter. They were in good practice and showed it now.

Almost at once, the tech noted, "I'm tracking a drone. As soon as you can deploy a net, do so."

"Firing."

CHUNK.

Tombo nodded. "Got one, there's another steering around."

Bravo said, "Fire at will."

A louder bang came from an AA launcher, then twice more.

Truitt sounded satisfied. "Got it."

Tombo had more news. "There's a cop following, and two armored patrol cars. The bastards are using our vehicles, of course."

This was not going well, and Bravo exclaimed, "Oh, fuck it. How many missiles do we have?"

Oren held up two fingers. "Two. Our only two at present."

"How did they track us so fast?"

Tombo said, "I assume he's got a secondary transponder."

"Well, we need to fix that."

"Do you think he'll talk?"

"Without hesitation."

"Get us into some steel. The plaza under the Freibank building?"

Sarina said, "That could work. There's a parking stack."

"Keep us on ground level," he nearly shouted in warning.

"Of course."

"Okay, move, move!"

They bailed out again and popped the hatch on the cargo box.

Loughery was awake. He was obviously terrified. He panted and gasped and was flushed.

"Are you going to kill me?" he asked, sounding panicky.

"Nah, we were just paid to deliver you. Or will be. It works on the honors system. You probably don't know what that is."

Carefully, the man replied, "Sir, I am a very senior official. I am very valuable as a hostage."

Bravo grinned. "Oh, we know who you are. It took us most of a day to unass the area and remain unseen. We'll meet our client soon."

Khaima was the biggest. He leaned over and brusquely asked, "Loughery, where's your second transponder?"

"Eh? I only have one." He rubbed his hand where the wound was. "You removed it."

Tombo shrugged. "Well, if you don't know, the easiest thing is just to amputate both hands. You won't need them where we're going."

Loughery started blubbering. "I really don't know!"

Bravo muttered. "I believe him. Well, shit. We just need to find the code to burp it. Can we get that?"

Tombo fumbled with a transpinger. "I suspect we can. I don't know how fast."

Bravo was getting antsy. "Make it fast or take the hands to make sure." They weren't going to lop off his hands but keeping up the fear factor couldn't hurt.

The man blubbered and twitched.

"Okay, I think I have a pingback. And it's in his ass, of course."

"Cheek, or actually in his ass?"

"Cheek. Left."

"Oh, good."

Bravo took delight in grimacing at Loughery. "Bend over. This is gonna hurt you a lot more than it hurts me."

"Wha, uah..."

He wrestled the man over his knee, presented the left ass cheek, and Grey sliced the pants open with a scalpel. He probed for a spot, nodded, and jammed the blade in. He was only a battlefield medic, so it wasn't a very neat job.

"OWWWwwww!"

"Shut up, pussy," Grey ordered, as he reached in with forceps and pulled.

Khaima struggled to hold the man still as he whined and cried and squealed.

Grey squirted clotter into the small wound, and said, "Done."

"Okay, get back in the box, Payroll."

The man, if he could be called that, whimpered and cried.

Mahmoud nailed it and they departed the underground, back into traffic.

Tombo said, "We have to assume they'll orbit search to find us."

Bravo acknowledged, "Yeah. Also, if we do this again, we toss them into a Faraday bag first."

"With DNA diffuser."

Shortly the man added, "There's pursuit all over the area."

Jeremy had an idea. "Can you get that transponder into a stream from here?"

"Maybe."

"Wrap it in this." He handed over a glove to add some mass.

Sarina said, "We're about to cross the Industrial Stream. It flows past the air and spaceport from here."

"Perfect."

Window down, Tombo heaved, and the package sailed over the bridge and dropped out of sight.

A few moments later he added, "Drones are following that."

Grey commented, "Good. They might find us afterward."

Bravo said, "Yeah, we're not going back to the office."

"Was this worth the money?"

He reconsidered, but yes. "Money for now, proves which side we're on, sows chaos amongst our new enemy, and proves our capabilities. Long term, it was our best bet."

The young man shrugged. "Reasonable. Well, not, but neither are the circumstances."

"Right."

Sarina asked, "Do we steal another car?"

"No, we're swapping again. All these are borrowed, by the way. For the cause."

Truitt asked, "Will people still be willing when their cars get seized?"

"I'm told the nerds scrambled the records, and we're borrowing a lot that are contracted to the UN anyway."

"Borrowing?"

"They can have them back when we're done. Like this one."

Tombo noted, "They've backed off. Interesting."

"Yes, they don't know what happened yet. They'll need a human in the loop for that decision. Get ready to drag his ass."

"Roger."

An utterly nondescript cargo van waited under the sunshade

in front of another empty warehouse. Too many of those since the UN came along. Bravo felt anger over that.

The change was anticlimactic. Their hire, who knew only that he was driving a vehicle for cash, climbed into the contact truck cab and took off. The team stuffed Loughery into a metal tool chest in the van's cargo bay, climbed into the van with only Bravo and Mahmoud up front, and cruised away.

It was half a div driving slowly and normally before they reached the edge of the agricultural flats. There were numerous gravel and dirt drives and access roads to houses, shops, and fields. Eventually, Bravo saw a ping and said, "Turn there."

Sarina took them down the gravel. It was well-graded and relatively recent and crunched under the wheels.

"That's our meeting." He pointed to two men sitting under a sunshade sipping cocktails. On the far side of the clearing were a work truck, air-capable, and an upscale but not opulent Skoda sedan with stretch seating.

She said, "So that's Joseph Mattias."

Bravo remembered she'd never been on one of Mattias's details.

"Yup. We've contracted to him before, but always on the other side—protection."

They slowed, stopped, and climbed out into the faint haze and bright Iolight. Khaima and Grey dragged the toolbox.

Without preamble, Jeremy asked, "Got the cash?"

Mattias handed over a small case. He said, "I do. And given your reputation, you can even count it with hands on."

Jeremy took it and glanced inside. There were bundles of UN Marks and several prepaid cash cards.

Mixed funds. Excellent. He replied, "That's not necessary, sir. Your reputation is sound."

Mattias barely smiled and gave a fractional nod. "Thank you."

"Which doesn't mean this is a date."

Mattias laughed cheerfully, turned to the other party present and asked, "Mr. Bandara, are you ready?"

"I am." The scarred man looked over at Jeremy. "He's in the crate?"

"Yes. You wanted him alive."

Sarina tapped a key on the lock, which popped open, then grabbed the corner of the side and flicked it. It fell open to reveal Loughery, squinting at the Iolight and whimpering. The whimpers got more urgent.

Bandara smiled very thinly. "Very good. You gonna stay for the show?"

Mattias replied, "You know how much I love watching you work, but I've got events to plan, people to have killed, and the UN to blame for it. I'm swamped."

The lanky, scarred man nodded. "Make sure you get some rest in there."

"I will. You'll deliver him back to the UN?"

The duelist—well, assassin—replied, "Eventually."

"Excellent. Have a good day."

Mattias turned to the Ripple Creek element.

He said, "I have a bottle of imported Caledonian whisky in the car. Will you join me?"

Bravo replied, "We accept, thank you, sir."

Mattias walked with them. Apparently, he wasn't sociopathic enough to enjoy watching even that kind of asshole die. He was willing to pay for it, however.

Behind them, Loughery's voice turned panicky and incoherent. When Bandara asked, "Which knife do you want?" Loughery began an inarticulate, blubbering scream.

It became staccato with shouts, then gurgled to nothing.

No one looked back.

Into the awkward silence, Jeremy turned to Mattias and asked, "We'll need something else for next month, and we do have more personnel available. Do you have a list?"

Mattias replied, "I do. None of them will be missed."

The Bugismen

William McCaskey

June 210
Duterte City, Nusantara

"Can't beat a posting like this," a UNPF lieutenant crowed to his compatriots as he leaned back in his chair and patted his stomach. The noise from the street below was muffled through the restaurant's second floor windows, but the din from the kitchen would rise and fall with the swinging of the serving door carrying with it the spiced aroma of cooking belecan.

"It's a wonder you can pass tape, James," another retorted.

"James may be a fatass, Schriner, but he at least finds us good places to eat. You spend so many marks on cards and hookers it's a wonder you aren't on emergency funding," a third said, laughing.

"Give him a break, Arturo. At least he paid us back on that last loan," James cut in.

"About that," Schriner began.

"Are you fucking kidding me?" Arturo interrupted. He slammed a fist on the table causing the passing waitress to jump and eye the three warily. "You ask for another fucking loan and I'll skull drag your ass back to the barracks and slam your dick in a door."

"Why would you even lead with that? I was going to ask you to spot me for lunch, I need to make a draw from finance after I spent what I had on hand last night." Schriner eyed Arturo. "You need to get laid."

"Man's got a point, you're wound a little tight," James agreed with Schriner.

173

"Luckily, we're right next door to where the Grainne military trained their whores." Schriner grinned as if he had solved all the world's problems.

"Expensive and reserved for flag ranks and VIPs." Arturo ticked off his fingers.

"All off the books and against policy. General Order One," James interjected.

"Only the fully qualified 'specialists' are reserved," Schriner explained. "The trainees are open for business; get it set with the right clerk and you can even have the fee autodrafted from your pay. Streamlines the entire process. Don't let the MPs see you walk in or out and don't bring them into the barracks."

"Trainee whores doesn't make much sense," James snarked, reaching for another pineapple tart from the plate at the center of the table.

"They call 'em 'Recreation Specialists' but classify them under 'Emotional Health.' This girl from the mainland, or did you get a local?" Arturo added.

"Whore's a whore regardless of what they call it," Schriner scoffed. "Local, not a raghead though. It's a wonder people can even stand living near those types. She had some interesting stories to tell, though. Threatened me with something, sounded like the bogeyman."

"Did you get clarification?" James asked.

"Why? I wasn't paying to hear her talk. Tell you what, you cover dinner and spot me a bit for the game tonight and I'll make sure you both get your ashes hauled with some local strange."

"Shut it, Arturo." James cut the third lieutenant off before he could antagonize their compatriot any further. Looking at Schriner, he finally answered, "Deal."

September 15, 210
Tjibeo Village

"What do they dance for?" the UN major asked the woman standing beside him, as his soldiers broke into teams of two and spread through the crowd.

The woman's gaze never left the dancers, a young man and woman moving within the melody of the flute while the surrounding dancers' bodies followed the quicker beat of the drums. Finally, she answered, "The dance is for their Mahaguru, a recognition of his life and the lessons he taught. They recognize his ties to the Islamic community while still honoring his faith as a Christian."

"And why do you not dance for your father-in law?" the officer asked blandly, his eyes sweeping over the crowd. "Yes, I know who you are, Analyn Richards, and your relation to the deceased," the officer continued without waiting for the woman to answer.

The woman ignored the obvious trap and simply nodded to the two central dancers, "They requested the placement. What business could the UN have at a memorial? You've caused enough damage already."

"The only reason you and your children have not been arrested yet is because your father-in-law's name still carries some weight amongst the upper ranks of the UNPF. However, that weight will quickly diminish once it is known he died causing the death of four Peacekeepers."

"Peacekeepers who were raping a child. What would you arrest us for? You've burnt half my crops and seized production of the other half," Analyn answered, coldly. The tempo of the music shifted and now the central dancers moved quicker while the outer ring slowed their movements to highlight the precision of the dance, the young man in the middle had drawn a still-sheathed sword from the sash around his waist.

The officer waved away the accusation, "Stones, Mrs. Richards. You are the ones that live in the shadow of a training school for whores. As for charges? Production and trafficking of an illegal substance, causing a degradation in UN food production, and incitement of a riot."

"Sparkle is legal in the Freehold, Novaja Rossia, and Caledonia, to name a few of our markets. We don't sell in Earth space. You illegally seize crops and land then offer a tenth of what they made before your arrival, for those who had stakes in the land, the land to work it. Your difficulty in finding farmhands is your issue, not mine. Perhaps you should return to your filthy cities on earth. You are delusional. Despite your provocations, there have been no riots"

The officer seized her arm and squeezed, "Grainne is UN space now, you mouthy cunt. Food production will be used for the supply of UN forces occupying this miserable mudball your father-in-law dragged you to. Food supplies your influence hampers, and this is a riot if I declare it as one. We have questions for you."

The woman looked down at the officer's hand as if an offending odor had assaulted her nose, "Remove your hand, Major. It is an insult to touch a woman not your wife or family here."

The major spat, "I served on Mtali. You aren't one of them and I don't give a damn for raghead customs. Your farms will increase production." He paused and then leered at Analyn, "And perhaps if you are a bit more respectful, your life will become easier under our occupation."

The music shifted again, the tempo increasing for each of the dancers, firelight glinting off the now bared keris in the young man's hand, and the eyes of Analyn.

"And that is why you will never conquer us."

The major coughed, trying to catch his breath. Releasing Analyn's arm, he raised his hands to his throat to test the wetness pooling there and his hands came away bloody. Stumbling back on legs that no longer wanted to support his weight, a strangled gurgle escaped his lips as he tried to call out. Analyn stepped forward and slid around to the major's back, bracing him against her body and supporting him with a false tenderness.

The music stopped suddenly, and the keris-wielding young man stepped between the outer ring of the dancers and took the head from the nearest UN soldier with an easy swing of his blade. Daggers appeared in the hands of the dancers, within moments and a flurry of flashing steel every UN soldier that had accompanied the major was dead or dying.

The major could only stare on in horror, unable to move, as his men died before his eyes. Analyn leaned in to murmur in his ear, "The paralysis you are feeling is quick acting, and in most cases, brief. The handle of the kapak kecil is carved from a hardwood native to our islands and sharpened for precisely this." She paused and pressed the sharpened point of the weapon's haft into the opposite side of his neck, slowly piercing his skin again, leaving the handle of the small weapon within the major's body. "The pain is excruciating, and overexposure can lead to cardiac arrest. You have time enough left for me to share a story."

Analyn caressed his hair with a false tenderness. "Once upon a time, there was an empire that tried to eat the world. Vain enough to boast that the sun would never set upon their borders. They thought they knew how to inspire fear, to maintain control. They came to an island nation, a birthplace of kings and empires. They raped the women and pillaged the land. They stole great treasures and spat upon centuries old customs. But it was on this island that they learned what it was to be truly afraid. Pirates wielding black magic, the kind that could steal a man's soul, called the island nation home. One by one, the empire's soldiers were slain, with silent blades, or disappeared in the dark of the jungle, never seen again. Slowly, news of these horrors crept back to the seat of the empire's power. Whispers, 'Beware the Bugismen.' The empire fell, only to be replaced by others. Time passed and the world grew smaller but the children of the Bugis never forgot their history, or their treatment at the hand of would-be conquerors. When the time came, they left their island and sailed a darker sea for a new home." Reflecting light drew the major's eyes to the blade of the small hand-axe in Analyn's hand, the sharpened point of the wooden handle wet with his blood. "We remember, and we do not suffer threats from would-be conquerors." She pressed the tip of the blade against the right side of the Major's throat, "Beware the Bugismen." Analyn drove the point of the blade under the skin and tore forward, slicing through the carotid artery before dropping the major to the ground, like so much trash.

Around her the crowd was bundling the bodies of the UN soldiers, uniforms and weapons were left with their former owners to be laid with them when they were left to be found. "They died without lifting a finger." The young man's voice drew her attention away from the dead, his keris sheathed and returned to his hip.

"They underestimated us. This was only going to work once; you and your sister played your parts perfectly. Well done."

Jacob smiled at the praise from his mother, "We'll need to disappear. The main plantation won't be safe for us anymore."

"Agreed, leaving the bodies near the city will draw some attention away from the village but not enough. Someone will need to get into Duterte to establish contact with the mainland. Let them know we're still here," the young woman who had danced opposite Jacob added as she joined them, cleaning blood from her kerambit with a scrap of cloth.

"I'll go," Jacob volunteered.

The woman shook her head in a manner that reminded Analyn of the twins' father, "Makes more sense for me, I can blend in with the trainees at the Academy. Plus, you were the last to recon for our friends from the mainland. You know where the caches are stashed."

"Tanya, I don't like you going in Duterte alone, the city already took Lolo," Jacob argued.

"Aww, you do care," she teased her twin. "It took nine Aardvarks to kill grandfather, and he killed four of them. We don't know how many he injured but I'm willing to bet none of them walked away unscathed. I'll do what I can to find the video, someone has to have it."

"Fine," he agreed, reluctantly. "If you can, see if you can get your hands on his shillelagh. He didn't come home with it." Turning to their mother, "Will you come into the jungle?"

"I'll go south to Kedah; they need to know the UN is getting bolder and intends on destroying all of Grainne's cultures. On Mtali the Aardvarks tried to use the tribal rivalries to their advantage, worked in some cases. They won't find the same situation here, but they are slow to learn new tricks, and this is a threat to all of us. If the Sultan is expecting them, then he'll have a reception planned for them," Analyn answered, before resting her hand on her son's, stopping him from drawing the keris. "It is yours, Pendekar. Use it to take back our home."

Jacob nodded before hugging his mother tightly. Turning to his twin sister he grinned, "Never unarmed, yes?"

Tanya deftly rolled her chocolate brown hair into a tight bun and fluffed it before slipping her now sheathed kerambit beneath the mass of curls, hiding it perfectly, "A lady never gives away her secrets."

"No, but we know the truth of a Srikandi," Jacob teased.

Analyn smiled at her children's jibes, "With the reserve crops and the contacts in Duterte we can assist our former guests with funding. Perhaps they in turn can bring materials from the mainland for us." The two children nodded as Analyn laid her hands on her children's shoulders. "Come, we've much to do and not nearly enough time to do it in." The three turned from the square, the memorial to their family member complete. The patrol would be found not stripped of weapons. It was a message of utter contempt.

I

October 3, 210

Jacob checked his timepiece as he set his pack against the base of a gum tree and turned to check the path behind them. Half a div till sunrise, they were right on time. Isko and Mamat had slipped away to their own hide while he waited for the call from their contact. Lowering himself down to a knee, the fingertips of his left hand traced across the cassette of his shotgun to reassure himself that he had a jungle load prepped as he let his gaze sweep the undergrowth, paying attention to his peripheral for movement. The air was rich with the taste of salt from the nearby cove, while the waves played a steady rhythm against the beach.

Just ahead of Jacob, Tuah had shed his pack and was performing his own scan. The dim light of dawn filtering through the thinning canopy highlighted the movement of his head as he looked up to search the branches above him. The earpiece of his radio coming to life pulled Jacob's attention.

"Alamo. MacArthur," a familiar voice sounded in Jacob's ear.

"MacArthur. Alamo. Suwanda," Jacob replied as he tapped Tuah's shoulder before slipping past the other guerilla to watch the water. The rest of his team would know their contact was approaching from monitoring the radio, but this was a sight that never grew old for Jacob.

The only indication was the brief change in the rhythm of the waves before the vessel broke the surface and made its way towards the beach. Jacob smiled, as he always did when seeing the tiny sub. The UN deluded themselves into believing they controlled the skies and space but had forgotten the oceans.

In the three segs it took for the sub to beach itself and the four-man crew to disembark, Jacob and his three accomplices had reconvened and were waiting, the heavy packs stacked next to them in the soft sand. Mamat, Isko, and Tuah scanned the jungle and the beach as Jacob stepped forward to meet their contact, "Robbie, good to see you still mostly in one piece."

Blazer Robert McCombs grinned and held out the prosthetic of his right hand, "I'm surprised a leopard hasn't drug you up a tree, yet, kid."

Jacob grinned and gripped the prosthetic lightly, not willing to risk damaging the Blazer's replacement limb, "Shotgun is usually a good deterrent to that happening."

"That it is, and you work that beast almost as fast as you do a knife," McCombs commented.

"Mamat's a better shot and Isko's faster with the blade." Jacob shrugged.

"And Tuah?" McCombs smiled, knowing what was coming.

"I'm the smart one," Tuah deadpanned, cutting Jacob off before he could respond and turning to look at the blazer.

Robert laughed as he focused his attention on Tuah and offered his prosthetic again, "As-salaam aliakum, my friend."

Tuah let his shotgun hang from its sling across his chest and took the offered prosthetic in his right hand, "Wa alaikum salaam, Robert."

"Let's get business handled and off this beach," Robert declared turning back to Jacob. "How are the crops holding up?"

Jacob nudged the packs still sitting in the sand with his right foot. "Three hundred pounds of unrefined sparkle and a hundred pounds of coffee. First thing the Aardvarks did was torch the sparkle labs, but I figure you mainlanders can handle that piece."

Robert nodded, "We'll clean it up, and get it offworld." Left unsaid was the understanding that the black-market sparkle trade would go a long way to funding the Freehold resistance, "They left the coffee alone?"

"Their preference for it will make it worthwhile on the mainland," Jacob answered as the rest of Robert's crew hefted the packs to their shoulders and carried them towards the sub. "Is this your final stop?"

The Blazer nodded, "This will top us up, smart move separating out the pickup points. No indications that the Aardvarks picked up on the movement; and we dropped a shipment of materials for delivery to JOMAS."

"Much appreciated. From what my mother has passed on the next batch off the line will be going to Kedah for the tribes in that region. They want to be ready if the UN decides to island hop."

"Sound plan, I wouldn't mind getting my hands on one of those shotguns they put out. Figure fifteen millimeter will work just as well in tight quarters as it does punching through jungle growth," McCombs commented.

Jacob chuckled, "You get your bosses to put in an order and I'll hand you one, no charge."

"Deal. Shouldn't be that hard, considering the numbers your family has trained, don't be surprised if it picks up after we kick the 'Varks off Grainne. Got anything else we need to know about?" the operative asked.

"All the primary fields for anything other than coffee, rice, and bananas have been torched to be converted over to 'approved' crops." The distaste in the young man's voice easily discerned. "Any families that refused to collaborate had their homes ransacked and destroyed. We didn't lose much since we left after my grandfather was murdered, but there are more than most that have few options."

"Your grandfather would be proud of you and your sister. Your dad would be too," McCombs interrupted.

Jacob paused, his eyes tracking out towards the ocean before returning to the blazer, "Where?"

"Mtali. Couple of us recognized the style of blades they were carrying from your grandfather's training course, that's when we asked for your dad to consult. He's the reason it was my hand and not my life, and how we were able to work so well with the natives."

"No one has ever confirmed it, but my gut tells me he didn't come home because of the UN. God knows where I'd be if Lolo hadn't put his foot down to leave earth."

"Your grandfather definitely made a statement. Four dead, nine critical just to kill one old man with a stick and knife. He definitely got the assholes' attention. There's been talk from higher of recognizing his and your dad's contribution to SPECWAR; after the war most likely and long overdue."

"Thank you, Robert. Once these assholes are gone, we'll get the training program restarted." Jacob caught the wave from Tuah and Mamat. "You're loaded, ready to go, and about to start burning daylight."

"True enough. Oh! This may interest you; intercept puts an ADVON party in this region. We think it's to establish a FOB in the area to put down any potential insurgency that attempts to disappear into the jungles."

"And since everything has been focused around Duterte and the surrounding villages, any push into the jungle may not be expecting trouble just yet," Jacob finished.

"Got it in one," the Blazer grinned.

"We're going hunting," Jacob stated as Mamat and Isko each nodded to McCombs and made their way off the beach.

"Godspeed," Robert called over his shoulder as he climbed aboard the sub.

"Inshallah!" Tuah responded as the sub dragged itself from the beach and disappeared below the waves.

Jacob turned his back on the beach, Tuah mirroring his lead, and the two followed their companions inland.

II

October 6, 210

"You baliw, budak," Tuah muttered, tapping the side of his head, as he squatted next to Jacob with Mamat and Isko huddled around the palm-sized speaker set between them.

"Baliw, like monyet. Kid was running so scared he never thought to check his gear for bugs," Isko added as the four leant in to hear the conversation over the rain drumming on the shelter roof.

"Take a breath, Private. You're safe now." A man's voice attempted a soothing tone, though a hint of insincerity could be heard.

A cough echoed from another, this voice trembling, *"Safe, sir?"*

The sound of liquid pouring into a cup was faint beneath the downpour outside, before a third man spoke, *"Drink, it'll calm your nerves."*

"Do as Sergeant Tulley says, kid. Then tell us what had you barreling into camp like the devil himself was on your heels," the first voice instructed.

Moments pass before the once shaky voice speaks up, his nerves apparently settled by whatever had been in the offered cup, *"Two days ago, Sergeant Mikaleson woke us up after he realized the watch was gone. Corporals Shannon and Briggs, no trace of them, like they vanished."* Another pause, and the sound of the cup refilling. *"Sergeant says no one gets left behind, so we start searching for them, spent the entire day but there was no trace of them. Night falls so we bed down, watch is set, and then the sergeant goes down, this cat-looking thing on his back. It's all teeth and claws tearing at him, disappears into the jungle before we can get a shot off and Sergeant Mikaleson is just laying there, torn to shreds. Between myself, Davies, and Sammy we were too scared to sleep. I think I dozed off cause at some point I woke up to Davies screaming as another cat was dragging him up a tree. Sammy managed to hit Davies and put him out of his misery."*

"You're condoning the murder of a fellow soldier. Am I hearing you right, Private?" the first voice demanded, the disgust in his voice apparent.

"No, Sir! *There was no way we could have gotten him, and Sammy may have been aiming at the cat. Sammy was the one pulled the trigger, not that it matters much now. Sammy died crossing the river to get back to camp, gator or some shit dragged him under."*

"The jaguar was lured in, but the caiman was coincidence. Wasn't it?" Tuah interrupted looking from Mamat to Jacob. The Grainne crushjaw wasn't exactly a caiman, but it was analogous though much faster.

Mamat, the oldest of the four, simply gave a yellow-toothed smile and pointed to Jacob's wrist.

Jacob waved for silence and tapped the leather cuff holding the agimat against his left wrist. A small smile crossed his face as he acknowledged that he might be crazy, but he had help, before motioning back to the speaker.

"*Three dead, two missing presumed dead,*" Sergeant Tulley mused.

"*Think it was the Boogeymen,*" the private started before the rolling of thunder drowned out the radio.

"*Those ghost stories that Lieutenant Schriner was telling in the barracks. The ones his girl tells him,*" the private explained.

The lieutenant scoffs, "*Ghost stories. Go get some rest, Holmes. You'll feel better after some decent rack time.*"

"*Yes, sir,*" Private Holmes acquiesced, silence falling between the lieutenant and platoon sergeant.

"*Kid's got a point, LT,*" Tulley finally offered, breaking the silence.

"*About Schriner's stories? Agreed, they're damaging to morale, but we've seen no signs of inhabitants in this sector. We'll break camp tomorrow and RTB to Duterte. Some R and R will do the men good, get their minds off the last couple days.*"

"Leaving the CHUs for the follow-on?"

"Sure as Hell not carting them out, ourselves. Leave 'em for whichever company gets stationed out here. It'll save a few Guardian flights, at least until a path gets cut for the Eels."

"Roger that, sir. Chow's on you tonight, by the way," Tulley needled his platoon leader.

"Thank God, 'cause you can't cook," the lieutenant responded goodnaturedly.

Jacob palmed the speaker and shut it down before slipping it into a pouch attached to the cross strap of his bandolier. "This camp disappears tonight."

"Do we go to war?" Mamat interjected.

"Grainne is as much our home as it is the mainlanders. The UN has already shown they will ignore our way of life and see our families starve. We're already at war, and if we get their attention then forces sent here won't be able to harass the villages," Jacob responded.

"Pendekar," the title and the namaste salute, traditional between Silat warriors, was Mamat's acknowledgement.

Jacob turned to the rest of his team, "We're two divs out from their sentries. Twenty-five left in the camp, two rows of three CHUs. Only the back three should be full, and the front far right has their lieutenant and sergeant. Worst case they are all awake and alert, best case every one of the lazy bastards is asleep. We ghost the sentries and work into the middle. The sensor net's about a meter off the ground, pretty sure they got tired of the alarms going off every time a screamer-monkey troop came through the trees; so we stay low we can work right under it. Blades and silent for as long as possible, make sure the cassettes are set for buckshot. Questions?"

"Prisoners?" Isko offered up.

"Not from here, Hakim gets that chore," Jacob answered. With no more questions coming, Jacob looked each of the other three men in the eyes. "Sundown then."

As Jacob shifted to his side of the hooch and dropped the partition to give the three men privacy, Mamat, Tuah, and Isko were unrolling and laying out their prayer mats on the unsteady surface of the shelter's fiberglass floor. Suspending their tents high in the jungle canopy had started as a means of avoiding predators at ground level, but it was proving incredibly effective at avoiding UN patrols as well. Braving the downpour, Jacob monkey-crawled to each of the three corners of the established web to check the spinnerets. The young man still marveled at the devices—when partnered, the system would spin out high-tensile strands that connected and wove to form a web nearly twenty-eight square meters, strong enough to easily support his team. Each of them had carried in pieces of the flooring. The entire structure could be left and returned to months later with the same stability and strength as the day it was constructed.

Satisfied that their current home was stable, Jacob worked his way back to the communal tent. Stopping just inside, he could hear the prayers of his brothers. Peeling off and replacing his soaked cotton shirt and trousers with a dry set, the young man settled himself in the center of his space. Jacob pulled the thong necklace from under his shirt and traced his thumb over the silver coin and the raised engraving of St. Michael, murmuring his own prayer, "The Lord is my Rock. He trains my hands for war, my fingers for battle. My stronghold, deliverer, and shield in whom I take refuge. Saint Michael the Archangel defend us in battle. Be our protection against the malice and snares of the Devil. Amen."

III

Night had well and truly fallen before the four men descended from their elevated campsite carrying only their shotguns, pistols, and blades. Jacob dragged on the ropes, the attached pulleys assisting, to raise the ladders up into the canopy. They would be lowered in the same manner when the team returned, before securing and hiding the cables against the base of the nearest tree. Mamat and Tuah led the way, born and raised in this region, they knew the quietest route to the UN encampment. Isko brought up the rear while Jacob let his gaze sweep upwards using his peripheral vision to watch for movement with his shotgun slung across his body at the low ready; the Aardvarks were the least of their worries in the jungle, day or night. Harimau resembled earth's tigers in general shape, but Jacob was pretty sure a harimau would drag a ripper and the ripper's meal up a tree for his own enjoyment.

The fireteam's travels were muffled by the continued deluge typical of the monsoon season, and the appearance of a dull white glow where there should only be pitch blackness gave away the location of the UN camp. All four guerillas had scouted the camp. The UN believed themselves alone in the region and acted it. The pirates of the southern atolls would have put up a stronger defense. Jacob let his shotgun hang from its two-point sling and tightened it against his chest so it wouldn't shift. Tapping first Isko, then Mamat, and finally Tuah to get their attention, he unwound the running ends of his cord bracelet from around his right wrist. The other three men nodded their understanding and repeated his actions with their own bracelets. The sentries would be the first and quietest.

Jacob stretched out with his hearing as he belly-crawled at a snail's pace towards the sentry he had designated as his target and thanked God for stupid enemies. They hadn't cut back the grass of the clearing. Only where they had their camp had the grass been cut, giving Jacob and his brothers a method of approach familiar to all of them. The rain-soaked ground drenched the cotton of his shirt and trousers, causing a slight shiver through his body. Jacob tightened the bracelet before wrapping the cord around his hands to form a garrote. The design had been created by his father for combat use similar to a sarong when battlefield conditions made wearing one impractical. Using his elbows and bare toes to propel himself forward, Jacob finally heard the shuffling footsteps and grumbling complaints of his assigned target over the falling rain. Through the grass, Jacob could make out the figure of the UN soldier, his back toward him, and Jacob steadied his breathing. Quietly, he rose and looped the cord over the soldier's head and around his neck, pulling back quickly as the loop crossed his enemy's throat. A cross kick from Jacob drove the sentry to the ground. His right fist snapped back as his left punched down tightening the cord sharply and Jacob felt it when the man's hyoid bone finally snapped.

Jacob maintained the tension on the makeshift garrote until the struggles ceased, satisfied only after he checked and found no pulse. Lowering the body the rest of the way to the dirt, Jacob unwound his weapon from the soldier's neck and deftly rewrapped it on his wrist. Moving forward, he fought to steady his breathing and the rush of adrenaline that threatened to overwhelm him, loosening his shotgun's sling helped as he neared the jungle side of the CHU shared by the lieutenant and platoon sergeant.

Drawing his belati from its thigh sheath while listening for any movement inside the structure, Jacob wondered how his brothers fared in their own initial hunts, knowing there was nothing he could do for them now. Peering around the corner of the row of pre-fabbed hooches, he caught sight of Isko. Jacob flashed his blade in the light and grinned when Isko returned the signal. Seeing no other signs of activity, and hearing no movement inside the CHU, Jacob slipped up to the door and tested the handle with his left hand. The door swung outward on silent hinges and he shook his head at the audacity of UNPF leadership. The space was designed to easily accommodate five soldiers, but it had been converted into a combination of barracks and office with the two men sleeping on either side of the entrance. The man on the left began to stir, and Jacob darted forward, his belati twisting in and out, punching into the hollow of the platoon sergeant's throat and then repeating the strike again, slightly higher and this time leaving the blade buried deep. His forward momentum slammed his elbow into the platoon sergeant's nose, knocking the man back onto his cot. Jacob tore his blade free, leaving the dying sergeant grasping for his throat in a futile attempt to stem the blood flow. The officer was still sleeping soundly when Jacob reached down and grabbed the lieutenant's hair with his left hand, forcing the man's body to roll towards the opposite wall. Startled awake, but too slow to react, the tip of Jacob's belati slid smoothly behind the trachea; with a sharp twist and a forward punch, Jacob severed Lieutenant Arturo's throat.

Jacob wiped his blade clean on the man's bedsheets as panicked wheezes followed Jacob out the door. Isko was nearing the door to the middle CHU, when he caught sight of Jacob he pointed over his shoulder and held up two fingers. Jacob answered with two of his own then waved him towards the door as he turned to pass between the CHU he had just left and the one Isko was about to enter.

Gunshots ripped through the silence that had lain over the camp, and shouts of alarm echoed from the one of the rear CHUs. Tuah's shout cut above the rising cacophony, "Allahu Akbar!"

"Shit," Jacob swore as he resheathed his belati. Hands moving to his shotgun, a quick pull had the harness releasing its tension, allowing him to raise the weapon into his shoulder's pocket, while pressing the selector slide from safe to fire. The door to the center CHU swung open and before the UN soldier had completely emerged Jacob lashed out with his foot aimed at the middle of the swinging hatch and kicked it shut, a thud and grunted curse telling him the object had made an impact. Jacob rounded the shuddering door, two shots shredding the chest of the lead Aardvark, sending him reeling back into the shocked arms of his comrades. Shoving his weapon around the dead man's body Jacob fired three more shots into the tight quarters of the CHU's interior. Rounds designed for use against jungle predators proved incredibly effective against unprotected flesh, if the rising screams told him anything. Stepping further into the room Jacob counted the bodies, some still, some moving. Five. The first lay in the doorway where his companions had dropped him and the other four were clustered nearby. One was struggling to extricate himself from the pile, his arm stretching as his fingers grasped for a nearby rifle. Jacob stepped on the hand, ignoring the pained scream ripped from the soldier's throat as he let his shotgun hang from its sling and drew his Merrill. The pistol bucked twice in his hand and two rounds punched through the back of the Aardvark's head.

The sounds of further combat from outside drew his attention, holstering his pistol and dropping the half-spent cassette from his shotgun Jacob slapped a full one into the port and stepped through the door. Mamat and Isko were finishing off two UN troopers, but a third was raising a rifle to shoulder while the Freeholders' backs were turned.

Rushing forward, shotgun forgotten on its sling, Jacob led with a kick to the back of the soldier's right knee, and she screamed. His left hand snapped over her head, fingers plunging into her eyes and peeled her head back, holding her in place. His right fist cracked her jaw while the following elbow dislocated it completely. Dropping his elbow back down to crush her nose, the following hammer fist demolished the cartilage, leaving the woman's face a bloody mess as she whimpered from the brutal onslaught. Her rifle slipped from her fingers as they spasmed.

Jacob's rage drove him further. Aardvarks had taken his grandfather and threatened his family. Lightning had no mercy when it struck, and neither would he. His right hand, wet with the soldier's blood, chopped down on her throat, silencing her whimpers as the momentum carried his arm away from her body. Jacob released her head and eyes as his forearm reversed and swung back to clothesline the UN soldier across the throat, driving her roughly to the ground. Jacob pivoted on the ball of his left foot, his right rising, the drive of his arm turning his body, and as her head struck the ground his foot fell and crushed her throat. The entire attack had taken less than three seconds, and when it was over Jacob saw that the last of the UN forces had been dealt with.

"Where's Tuah?" Jacob asked as he, Mamat and Isko approached, Mamat favoring his left leg.

"Meng amuk?" Isko offered, though the shrug in his shoulders showed his own questions.

"Last CHU then, that's where I heard him shout from," Jacob directed as he turned to stride towards the source of the initial gunshots.

Rounding the open door, Jacob stopped short marveling at the carnage his fellow guerrillas had wreaked.

Mamat slid past and stepped completely into the bloodbath. Pointing to the body of a decapitated UN soldier, a rifle still clutched in dead hands, "Appears one slept with his rifle nearby, he probably died first. Tuah went amuk. They tried to dogpile him, look at how the bodies fell and the cuts. Even dying, Tuah was a master with the keris." Mamat stopped and knelt down next to Tuah's body, wiping the blood from the younger man's eyes and closing them. "Insha'Allah," the older guerilla spoke softly.

"Insha'Allah," Isko repeated.

"He comes home with us," Jacob stated as he leaned down, picking up Tuah's keris he slid the sword into his sheath and offered it to Mamat, who took it.

"The camp?" Isko asked.

"Let their dead lie where they fell. The UN will come investigate and find nothing to help them. Meanwhile, we'll continue to strike and bleed them," Jacob replied as he rolled Tuah's body up onto his shoulders. They'd trade carrying him back to the campsite and call for a boat to meet them near the coast to transport them back to the Beo region.

They Also Serve...

Michael Z. Williamson

Reconnaissance is a critical, if nonglamorous aspect of military operations. The better the information available for intel, the better the battle planning. Jacob Drafts knew this and took the task seriously. He'd served years ago, before any of the recent fighting, but remembered his training.

None of which made it fun to lie in the cold and damp after an early fall rainstorm, watching a UN convoy at a rest halt.

The UN element was well protected, with gun trucks front, rear, and middle, drone escort, drivers to take over in case of system error—which had happened to several, thanks to Freehold hackers—and sophisticated layers of sensors, including audio, visual and IR, weaponfire sensors, the works. Most of the troops wore body armor. They'd learned that quickly.

There were dismounted security elements posted, while the unit set up a privacy screen for a latrine area.

Frank Tait, his neighbor, muttered, "Are they seriously putting up a screen to take a leak? Just whip it or squat and go." Frank wasn't a vet but was a very capable hunter. He could hide anywhere. He was very good for a man of twenty G-years.

Jacob said, "Yeah, a lot of Earth cultures are very, very repressed on nudity, even in the field or for medical exams."

"How can a doc examine you if... never mind." Their voices were low enough they shouldn't be detected, but less talk was better, even a kilometer out.

Getting back to the task, Drafts took a survey of the troops through his glasses.

"I count twenty-three vehicles, sixty-five individuals. Sixty are regular UNPF. One is Space Force, probably an Intel attachment. Two are Airspace Force, probably intel or documentation. One is BuJustice, probably to coordinate with intel on captive ID, one is a BuMil contractor, probably regulatory oversight, or possibly environmental management. Fifteen of the regs are Russian, eight South American Combined Force, twelve are Federal Europe, four East Asian Co-Prosperity, the rest are North American."

"You can tell all that from here?" Tait asked while squinting in the direction of the patrol. He'd written it all on a single sheet of notepaper. Nothing went on electronic devices, even if not connectable to a network.

"Yup," he muttered. "Positive ID through their uniforms."

Tait asked, "You can read their insignia at this range?"

"No. They're each wearing their distinctive element camouflage."

"'Distincti...' are you fucking kidding me?" Frank barely kept it at a whisper.

"Each force, branch, and region have their own uniforms."

"For their home environments?"

"For each environment they plan to be in," he explained. "Six of the Russians are in Temperate Woodland Fractal pattern, nine are in Mixed Terrain dot pattern."

"God, Goddess, Goat and dildo. What the fuck were they thinking?"

It was a good question. It was not only a ludicrous OPSEC failure, an INTELSEC failure, and a cohesion failure, it had to be expensive as fuck, and logistically bulky as all hell to have that much support for clothing.

He shrugged very slightly. "No clue. It's retarded, but that's what a bureaucratic government gets you...hold on."

A couple of the loiterers were talking. He carefully swung the sensor mic that way and picked up the convo.

The younger one, European, at left asked, "Why would you want to stay here? It's wilderness." He sounded northern. Danish?

"Yeah, that's part of it," the older one, a North American sergeant, replied.

"What's to like about wilderness? It's creepy. There's not a habitation within sight, probably not within an hour driving time." Drafts noted the man had cut a sapling to use as a hiking staff. He'd gone about three meters into the woods to get it, and no further.

The American said, "The air is clean. The industry is low. Earth is what, ten years from complete climate collapse?"

"Don't they keep pushing that back?"

"Sure, fine tuning, and holding it slightly back with good administration. It's inevitable. Maybe here, too, but it will take longer."

"It's so heavy, though." The Euro leaned on his staff and grabbed some candy from his pocket. He offered one to the American.

"Thanks. Higher gravity. Think of it as a workout."

The Euro said, "Thinner air. Tougher on the lungs."

"I'm from Colorado. This isn't too bad."

"Okay. Are you in supporting Tremena in the election?"

The American nodded. "I am. I like that she's dedicated. She stopped going to school at *nine*, to devote her efforts to effecting change."

"I didn't realize she started that young. I could deal with her as SecGen. I think I prefer Max Find, but it depends on what they say in the next three months."

"Is that when voting starts?"

The Euro nodded, "Yes, we have forty-five days now."

"Huh. If we're still here, I'll vote through the phone verification." He tapped his pocket. "I really don't get the locals. They don't seem to want any government at all. Textbook fascism."

"I don't understand, either. I know there's a doc about their founding in the background brief."

The NCO nodded. "First we've got to get this load forward. There's a major push coming, I can feel it."

"Yeah, we're hauling a lot of stuff."

"Not just stuff. Lots of it is ammo. Lethal ammo."

"Damn, did Huff get clearance?"

The American leaned closer to his counterpart, but Jacob could still pick it up with the gun mic rested on a hump. "I don't know, and we shouldn't really talk about it, but if you look at the cases, they're all hazmat marked for small arms or fireworks, and these aren't fireworks."

The Euro snorted, "They sort of are."

The American snickered back. "Hah. True. It's going to suck back on base, though."

"Why?"

The American grimaced. "Aw, the LT had to mouth off to Ambaatu."

"But he outranks—"

"Yes, and Amb was being a jackass, but when called out did bring up his background. Then the LT told him," the sergeant looked around to make sure they were alone and lowered his voice, "that after seven hundred years it was time he got over slavery."

The younger troop visibly tensed. "Aw, shit. Dumbkump."

"Yeah, he tried to weasel out of it to the captain that his family was repressed by the Soviets. Which may be. But since he brought up the one, he can't then use the other. It was never mentioned."

"Right. So you were witness?"

The American frowned again. "Yes. I really don't want to get involved, but it's probably on the recorder there, and probably on the truck's, too, and they know I was standing right there."

"Fucking paperwork. It's all we seem to do."

Drafts almost sympathized with them.

"Yeah. It's more trouble than the enemy. Okay, looks like we're rolling. Later."

"Yup, kick it."

As the Aardvarks boarded their vehicles, Drafts took it very personally that some of them wanted to stay here.

Over your dead bodies, he thought.

He and Frank stayed slumped under the bush until the last truck was well onto the roadbed. Patience was a virtue for intel. None of this would spoil in a couple of segs.

This was a new road, cut through the hills and stabilized only the year before, to connect the small inland city of Aikainen to Jefferson. Now it was being used to supply a garrison to keep the locals in line. On the one hand, they needed the road, on the other hand, it was angering to have the enemy use it against them.

Once he felt it was very clear, he said, "Okay, let me call this in."

His comm was already set for squirt transmission. In the cities, there were enough signals not to worry about any individual one, as long as the sender avoided key trigger words. Out here, any signal might be noticed and get an investigation, but short duration bursts minimized triangulation, and he'd be away from here shortly.

He tapped a code, waited for the screen prompt, and said, "Beth?"

Shortly, there was a response of, "Receiving."

Beth might be part AI, might be part human. No one knew. You got a code, you called using it. You were given a code for the next time. If you lost the code or it was thought compromised, you had to ping the general line and get reidentified and reauthorized. It was secure for the rebels. He had no idea who was in operation outside his own unit, other than from occasional leaked reports of casualties and damage, and some scores that were too big for the UN to hide. They were hurting the invaders, but it would take time to organize good strikes against a superior-equipped enemy. Hence the recon.

"Hotel One Five Three. Copy."

The processed female voice replied, "Ready." That was probably automated.

He reported his observations using the reliable centuries-old SALUTE method—Size, Activity, Location, Unit, Time, Equipment. Troop estimate, convoy stop, grid, uniforms, insignia, ranks and probable taskings, the time, and the vehicle types and weapons. He attached the images and audio recording. He knew there were analysts compiling all this and building a good TO&E of the UN forces, and comparing casualties against it. They needed to build a database of numbers, movements, equipment, and disrupt what they could. The standing orders were not to pick fights with heavy combat arms units, or major bases. Soft targets like convoys, political missions, and remote sites were top priority. If they could demoralize the support, the contractors, the bureaurats, it would hopefully drive them to stay on their bases, and then... he had no idea, but that was the orders for now.

He got a single blip confirming receipt of his report, and unpowered and decoupled the comm.

"Let's move."

Three convoys stopped there over a week. The next one had light engineer support and dug in a field latrine with pits and mounted a water tank for handwashing. That was a potential sabotage target, but there was also a sensor mount, and almost certainly some high-level drones coasting on solar charging and eyeballing the area. Wasting resources on that would just reveal their presence and do little to harm the UN.

The second one was a bigger convoy and dropped off more

facilities—a prefab overhead and some shelter sections for perimeter protection. This one was over thirty cargo trucks. The FOB a hundred klicks further, near Aikainen, was expanding. A bit more and they'd be able to handle regular air cargo with overwatch and not bother with ground transport. Not that it mattered. He and his small element couldn't raid this one as it was. They could theoretically snipe, and they might inflict a few casualties and then there would be a force come looking. It was five K to their operations site, six more to their village, but enough sensors would follow DNA and broken brush and reveal it all. They had too many kids to want to risk it.

The enemy were moving in and settling down and the Freeholders were powerless to stop it.

After recon, they trod carefully through the brush. "We'll need to change routes," he noted. "Don't want to wear a pattern through the forest."

"We can follow just under the ridgeline of the rill over there."

"Good idea."

They moved in silence, which gave him time to brood.

The late-night knock at the door was expected, but he still checked the camera. Yes, it was a local delivery, and they were in uniform shirts. Even if no one trusted the UN to abide by its own Law of Armed Conflict, the uniforms helped. Anyone suborned by the UN would try to ditch the shirt or mark them to make it apparent. These were legit. He killed the lights inside and out and opened the door.

"Happy Birthday," the one said, as they both laid boxes down. "Got to run."

And they were gone.

He dragged the two packages inside, pulled the lights up thirty percent, and opened them.

Contents: Three more uniform shirts marked CENTRAL INDEPENDENCE GROUP over the left pocket, since he wanted the adult kids and his wife kitted out while doing any kind of support work. If the UN showed up, they'd already know this was a rebel cell, and there wouldn't be any kind of court to argue the point, but being in uniform offered some protection under Geneva primarily, and also Hague and Mars. It also added to collective credibility of their resistance. They were a uniformed fighting force.

Two automatic carbines. An actual military radio with power cell, very useful. A crate of field rations. They could already freeze dry and inert pack here, but this saved labor. There was a brief update on reported and confirmed casualties to the UN, nothing about the rebels. He glanced it over, then tossed it in the fireplace for immediate destruction. There were several reports on UN expansion, far too few inflicted casualties, and he knew the rebels were taking hits hard.

The supplies were not enough to pretend to fight a war, even low intensity. It was about right for a weekend camping trip with the Scouts.

Still. "Lissa, Megan, Anst, you've got uniforms." He handed over the shirts. Looking at the carbines, he said, "I think I'll give one of these to Tait, and we'll keep the other for now."

Anst said, "Heck, Dad, we've got enough guns."

"We do," he agreed. "Well hid. But half of them aren't in military calibers. Three are outdated and should be backup anyway, and I can always loan them out. We're active troops, we'll keep the frontline stuff."

"Makes sense," the young man agreed. His son was just eleven Freehold years, but thoughtful and reliable. He'd helped with some movements and kept his mouth shut.

Lissa pulled the shapeless shirt over her firm, shapely figure. "It'll never catch on in the Garment District." She smiled.

"I like it," he said. He did. Though he liked her in anything. She was fit, curvy, and sexy as hell. Her profession was process automation. There was little of that out here now. They were only farmers because they had a house in the area and wanted to avoid the city.

Megan's shirt was loose and floppy. She still had the graceful slenderness of youth, though she'd probably take after her mother very soon. Anst was a little wiry but building muscle fast.

"We wear these all the time when engaged in anything related to the war," he reminded them. "Even if it's just loading a truck or delivering a message. We're a declared military force, and hopefully we get treated as such."

They all nodded.

"Tomorrow we'll camouflage print them. Though I'd love a spare khaki so we can work outside and any drones not pay much attention."

"Until they figure out what the color means," Megan noted.

"Yes, Meg, but if a hundred noncombatants all wear khaki, and ten of us have unit patches, it means they have to do a lot more digging for target ID."

As long as they don't just blow everyone away, he carefully didn't say.

The next convoy felt safe enough for the troops to take a longer break, an Earth hour, and hack around in the woods cutting hiking staffs, something most of them couldn't do on Earth. Combat ecology regs notwithstanding, they wanted souvenirs.

This convoy was still bigger. The rest point now had a latrine, they had a semi-staged power recharge, and there was a second sensor tower that would be hard for rebels to work around. It was a methodical buildup as firebases grew further out from the capital.

Tait said, "I swear, we've got enough locals to knock over one of these convoys. If only we had the support to get us close... do you agree?"

"Small arms are enough, but we'd have to be right up among them, and their sensors are better than ours." He pointed to the tower. "That will detect movement if we get close enough."

"It's aggravating."

"Also, they'd have a...wait." He was going to mention fire support. But the UN couldn't.

"What?" Tait prompted.

"They could have artillery or an air strike on location in a couple of segs. But they can't do that if their own troops are in the engagement area."

"Okay."

"How big are your balls for this?"

Frank whispered back, "What do you have in mind?"

"How many different uniforms were in that last convoy?"

"Is this a quiz? It was...seventeen."

"So who'd notice number eighteen?"

The man stuttered. "You're kidding."

"I am not. They lollygag in the woods. When they start recall, walk in, brass balls, get among them so they can't shoot, secure as many vehicles as we can, drive balls out."

"They'll see it's the wrong uniform," he said, tugging at his shirt.

"I guarantee they won't. At most it will be, 'That's odd, it almost looks like Oceania Federation camo.' We use similar colors with a bit more blue. They have no reason to expect otherwise. It's a shame there aren't more troops from off-Earth or we'd do even better."

"And sensors for their ID?"

"Yeah, that's an issue, but it doesn't have a way to spotlight us that I know of. Not in daylight. It might be able to project laser dots, but those are hard to see."

"So we just walk in, and either wait for the freakout or start shooting, hijack the trucks and roll?"

"We need to expect some resistance and casualties," he said with a deep, sober breath. "But yes."

"You're serious?"

"Yeah."

Frank shrugged. "Well, shit, my balls are that big. I'll even crack dirty jokes as we meet them."

Kilometers away from either home or the OP, he powered up the encrypted radio. It appeared to be a rough-built copy of the last-generation EC-45/2, which was more advanced than the '43 he'd trained on, but not as sophisticated as modern gear. It should be secure enough for short, coded transmissions.

He spent a lot of time under featherferns, he realized. They gave a pleasant shadow and were always near a damp spot, but he was used to that. The smell was rather sour, but it faded into the background after he got used to it.

He selected the band, punched for connection, and waited.

It was only moments before he received a reply of, "This is Beth."

He said, "Need permission for an active operation."

"Describe."

He summarized as vaguely as possible, as he'd rehearsed, carefully having no written notes. "We believe we can get among the next element and hijack some vehicles. We'd try for the gun trucks and sensor first, then as many cargo carriers as possible."

The voice replied, "Stand by."

The freq went silent for a lengthy time. He knew what was COMSEC. Even encrypted radios could be cracked or tracked.

It was three segs before a reply. "You are authorized this

operation between four and seven days from now, if opportunity exists. It is important to follow through. This has been added to an op plan."

"MR." *Message received.*

He leaned back and sighed.

He muttered to himself and to Tait, "Okay, so now we're committed to bringing in some goods. I gather Intel has some idea what is on those trucks and is hoping to share the wealth."

His combat element was seven men and two women, and his living room was crowded. Two of them had brought food, so it wasn't going to wreck his supplies too badly.

All were veterans except Frank, whom he could vouch for. All were people he knew had reason to hate the UN beyond the fact it had invaded their home. Three had a record of combat against the UN, two others were Mtali vets. The rest, including himself, hadn't seen combat, but there was only one man who had not been engaged in at least recon and sabotage, and his father had died in the attack on Heilbrun base. There was always risk of a leak in an insurgent cell, but this was as tight as they could get.

They'd be outnumbered about 12:1.

They had two versions of rifles. That wasn't a concern. The four men without military rifles couldn't reasonably carry civilian rifles. It would stand out, given that the convoy had a security element, but was otherwise unarmed. So they had five riflemen and four without.

"You guys will have to start with pistols and scavenge," he said. "But I'll make sure I try to find something you can use ASAP."

"Not a problem." Vitori shrugged, though he looked tense. It was his father who had been lost. "I can go straight for a vehicle. The cab offers some cover once it's been cleared."

"Yeah, it does."

His support element was both his kids, and eight others. They were all young adults of the combat element, so probably very reliable, but young adults were prone to be flaky, persuadable, or just scared. They were to remain uphill until vehicles were secured. Best case, seventeen trucks out of convoys that had been forty or more.

Lissa laid out the upgraded uniform shirts.

"So we took the issue khaki," he noted, "and then transfer

printed a variation of our standard camo. We changed the colors and shapes slightly, so it won't jump out as ours, but it's a good pattern for these woods. We've all got unit ID." He pointed to the sewn-on tag that read CENTRAL INDEPENDENCE GROUP. "And our Provisional Forces official notice to all parties and the International Red Emblem states that we can camo the shirts to suit, as long as they're this base style, and/or are tagged with the unit. Not that I expect the Aardvark fucks will give a crap, but we've gone through the motion."

He paused, then said, "More importantly, it's similar to several UN elements that I'm informed are on planet, but none that I've seen so far on these routes. We won't have similar-looking hostiles. That makes IFF easy. Looks like a Freeholder, don't shoot. Looks like anyone else, shoot. The end."

Vitori asked, "The next convoy is in the afternoon?"

"I expect so, based on pattern. They've always been daytime. They have a laager to reach for night. Worst case, if we tie them up, they'll be out after dark, and maybe someone else can fuck with them. Now, here's the patterns of vehicles I've seen so far..."

He switched to drawing charts and schematics of the vehicles and their stops. All by hand, all to be burned once done.

He and Frank waited behind a rock, which had been far enough uphill to be ignored by every UNO so far but was close enough to what they considered as their limit to let him move among them in a handful of seconds. The rest of the element were scattered near trees and in a depression just slightly higher up. They were uniformed, wearing commphone headsets clipped in place, and five of them slung rifles, while four had hidden pistols. Behind them were the additional drivers including Megan and Anst. They were to wait for the attack to resolve before boarding.

He watched discreetly, trying to decide if he should let the Aardvarks see him moving about, or wait for the last moment.

That was a better choice. They would figure out the ruse eventually, and they sucked at woodcraft. They had no idea where each other was and shouted back and forth.

He heard one.

"Ramon?"

Ramon replied, "Yeah, down here by the... sort of ditch. A gully, I think."

The first said, "I see you. Check out this mess of baby trees. These are good stuff."

Ramon was enthusiastic. "Hell yeah! Start chopping. We'll keep the best and trade the rest."

Man, the Aardvarks loved their hiking staffs. Though he had to admit that bluemaple saplings were strong and had nice grain.

It was a pity it wasn't a few weeks later. The Rippers would go into a mating frenzy and eat their share of Unos. Then in spring they'd be scrambling for food for the newborns. He planned to remain inside during those times. It was a beautiful early fall, instead, varying from cool to warm, and pleasant. Io was ahead of the convoy, shining along the roadway.

Over a vehicle loudspeaker, someone announced, "Five minutes until Mount Up. Everyone return to convoy."

He drew a slow, deep breath, checked his rifle, clicked his phone to local broadcast, grabbed his own fresh-cut hiking staff, and rose carefully. He started walking downslope, and the rest of the element followed in staggered formation.

He was nervous about the fact they were in different pants, khaki or brown, or tan under the printed camo overlay. The colors didn't set right. The shirts all had the same pattern, but the printing had been done in sections 40cm square, and the edges of the pattern butted together. They also had different weapons and no helmets, though a lot of the convoy weren't wearing theirs anyway. It wasn't perfect, but it was probably good enough.

It had better be. The key was to act determinedly nonchalant.

Troops milled about, occasionally glancing his way then ignoring him. He led the short Freehold squad onto the cut, then the flat of the improvised rest stop. He saw now how much trash the intruders had tossed onto the ground. UN regs prohibited that, and it was a classless move. That pretty much summed them up.

He made a point of not walking too fast, and of nodding preemptively to anyone they passed. They had plenty of time, and it took only a seg to get everyone near the vehicles, and largely between the trucks and the UN crews. There were occasional glances, but no one showed much interest beyond the fact it was an element in a matching uniform, just like the others.

Sergeant Second Class Xander Blaylock thought it neat to be in actual woods. You could tell these didn't have a regular human presence. Well, a few convoys, but no actual stripping and building. They weren't even recovered woods, like those in Environmental Reconstruction Zones. This was raw wilderness.

Yeah, he needed a hiking staff. He didn't really hike, but one would look good on a day walk on the track, and Gibbs in the structural shop could do a good job of carving them into figures. He wanted one with a root bulb so there was lots of material. That sapling there...

He pulled out the pocket saw he'd bought at the Exchange, trimmed off several branches and the top. It was longer than it would be finished, which was perfect. Then he shoved it back and forth, getting a bit of thrill from disrupting an actual tree. From his spare ammo pouch, because they only had one mag each, he pulled a folding trowel, and dug dirt and weed tendrils away from the roots. He hoped nothing here was a skin toxin.

The roots were only a centimeter or two thick, and he was able to saw, rip, pull, saw, and yank until he had the knotty bulb out. And damn, that looked like a spiked weapon. Morningstar? But it would be better carved into some dragon or something.

His radio announced, "Five minutes! Recall and prepare to board!" Then someone repeated the advisory by voice, for extra safety.

Yeah, he didn't want to run late. Support troops had a rep, and this unit was trying to look professional. He banged the sapling base against a tree to shake more dirt off and headed back downslope.

The woods were full of troops. Hiking staffs were the souvenir of choice, and there was even a way to get them back legally. Pay a local a couple of marks, have them print a receipt claiming they sold it, and it was an Exempted Artifact, not an eco violation. Though a handful of people had just taken some pics in the deep woods. Those wouldn't need any clearance.

The Russians and the far north North Americans seemed pretty casual about deep woods, as did the FennoScand contingent. For everyone else, it was an exotic thrill.

He wondered about that element, who were probably Asian, based on the camo. How did this compare to any rainforest preserves?

They had darker skin, buff, so not Southeast. That camo pattern was unfamiliar, but definitely a wet woodland multilayer. It worked very well here. Who wore something like that?

They redrew fast, he'd give them that. They'd already cordoned the rear and were expanding forward around the convoy. They were supposed to be aligned on the left side. No, some of them were armed, so they were the security detail, and the regular troops were mixed up with them.

Had he seen them at the first stop?

A couple of them spoke in firm tones. What accent was that? "Oh, sh—"

Here goes, Drafts thought. This was war, but he was about to execute enemy soldiers with as little emotion as he'd have butchering a hog.

Less. Hogs are of benefit to us and have thoughts and feelings in common.

He let the staff hang on his arm, casually swung his carbine, continued into a raise to his shoulder, and started shooting.

He was amazed at how easy it was. Headshot, headshot, headshot, and three of them were down like sacks, brains splattered inside their helmets. A fourth turned to run and he aimed carefully, getting her above her body armor, right up under the atlas. She didn't have a helmet and the round erupted out the crown of her skull. The body flopped and didn't twitch.

All around there was shooting, and screaming, and then different shooting, as the armed members of the convoy finally returned fire.

Suddenly it was an ugly scramble, with both groups running for the trucks, some of the Aardvarks running for the woods where the support element could safely get in a few shots, others trying to take cover underneath the vehicles. He watched one guy stand flapping his arms and shrieking, mouth open wide, until one of his people put a bullet through it.

He saw movement and dove for the ground, and a stickynet went right overhead. Some of the goop dripped and stuck to his sleeve in a clingy puddle. He rolled and smashed it into the dirt. If he contaminated it enough, it wouldn't pin his arm to his side or a truck when he brushed past.

Someone right next to the vehicle shot the projector operator, but there was a charge loaded, and it fired as the Uno died. The mass of web slammed the Freeholder down, breath knocked out, a bundle of gluey gunk on his chest, but luckily not on his face. It was Vitori. He couldn't help the man at this second, so he made note and kept moving.

The convoy's rear weapon was a stun cannon, zapping out blasts of voltage in blue ionized channels. One charge barely winged Sandra Twana, a Mtali vet, who yelped, shrieked, growled and swore. She was reduced to a limp with everything below her left hip overloaded and unresponsive. He wondered if it still hurt like hell or was numb. She swore again as she stumbled and shot, so it probably hurt. It took her three more bullets, but she hit something and the zaps stopped.

It started so easily and was pure chaos so rapidly. He remembered he'd been counting on the confusion. The UN had no real idea who was who, shooting at whom. His people knew. But when they all clustered together or ran around mindlessly...

At least twenty Aardvarks were down dead or bleeding out, and a lot more of them screamed. They obviously hadn't encountered armed resistance on planet yet.

However, their security element had switched to rifles, and now rounds snapped past.

Despite his earlier pep talk, he felt awful blowing away the unarmed pogs, but they were uniformed military, and this was war. Killing the drivers was an effective way to pin the convoy in place. He got two more. A lot of them were in the woods or across the road cut now, and not effective. Several had been netted by their own security, and one was on the ground in convulsions from neural lash. That left fewer than eight active Freeholders against a similar number of armed escorts, who had much better gear and position.

It was also necessary to gain control of the vehicles. He sprinted for the front, shot at two more Aardvarks and hit one of them in the shoulder as he passed two vehicles. He leapt for the driver side steps on the lead truck. Frank followed to take charge of the gun mount.

A burst of rifle fire cut him off, he flinched, cringed, tottered backward and got behind a wheel fast. Frank...was alive, and under the cab.

Then he heard the angry buzzing sound of escort drones moving in close. They had limited firepower—about like a rifle—but he was unarmored.

He hunkered behind the dual wheel, hoping the drones would

move past. He'd only seen them patrol in pairs front and rear. There were several more now, sounding like horror-sized hornets.

He heard one of the Unos shouting into his commo, "... multiple rebel combatants with lethal weapons. Request support element ASAP. Enemy appears to be wearing Oceania camouflage, note war crime."

He had a moment to think, *and that's how the fuckers will report it in the media. It's not even actually one of our camos, it's just something we came up with. But they'll make us out to be monsters.*

Yes, they had the convoy pinned, but they didn't have control of the vehicles. They hadn't seized any of the support weapons, so now the Freeholders were hiding under the trucks, too. Though some of his people—it looked like Paris and old man Emmett were dodging around risking fire while dishing it out. Good.

He shimmied around and there was an Uno, who raised a thumb and asked, "Truce?"

Huh? Drafts shot him, careful to avoid damaging the wheel.

Another guy dove behind the wheels across from him.

"Fuck, was that one of them?" he asked. "I figured he w— oooooh, shit!"

The kid was out and running further back. Drafts tried for a shot.

Then the truck hummed and rolled.

Only about a meter, but shit, this was bad.

He figured he was safer just outside the wheels, only exposed on half an arc, and there was growth in the ditch that would help. He rolled over and over, let gravity pull him into the hollow.

Apparently, despite a latrine built on site, a bunch of people had pissed here.

He snagged the radio from his back, almost getting stuck to it with the goop, which he rolled through grass, ripping blue-green blades free but keeping that mess coated. He powered the radio up and plugged it into his headset.

"Beth, Operation Rolling Weasel is pinned down and needs support or will have to abort."

The response was almost instant. *"Keep engaged and wait for support."*

Was that just an automated botponse?

He asked, "Confirmed support?"

"*Yes, confirmed,*" was the reply.

Alright.

He got his legs under him, ready to sprint, shouted into his headset, "*Freeholders, continue the attack,*" and dug in feet and moved before the enemy located him.

There was a flurry of fire, and it looked like one of the Aardvark guards was down. Yes. And Genske had the man's rifle now.

It was Simon Says, redone as Sergeant Says. What the hell, it worked.

But as Genske ran, a drone zigged past and shot. But it missed. Barely, but a miss.

Another one homed in on his movement, and he decided to charge it and dodge as the best option. There was no cover handy.

A round cracked past his ear. Another miss. He didn't think another adrenaline dump was possible, but he felt one. Icy shock through his entire body.

The drones weren't very accurate. Or rather, were perfectly inaccurate. Their fire consistently missed by several centimeters. Almost as if...

...Beth had them hacked just enough to make it look good.

He shouted into his headset, "*Stay engaged! We have support!*" He wasn't sure how much, but their orders were to make this work, and even retired, he was still a gods damned soldier.

Beth's voice spoke urgently, probably a processed human operator.

"*Cover, cover, cover!*"

"*Freehold get down!*" he shouted, and dove for the scraped surface, then scrambled back toward the trucks. It made him a slow, fat, target, but the trucks were their mission here. Besides, neither side was going to blow them up.

He heard cacaphonic booms and felt air disturbance. Massive cannon fire. Shit. What did the UN have? And how could he get everyone out?

No, that fire was targeting the forward gun truck. Armor spalled and projectiles splattered. The enclosed turret took hits, as did its gun. Probably a combat kill, no longer effective.

The next burst targeted the power pack, then swept toward the driver compartment. He'd hoped they'd salvage that, but since it appeared to carry non-lethal weapons only, the cargo was more valuable.

He looked around but couldn't see anything. It probably wasn't an armor unit. The Freehold had little enough to start with. Probably some support trucks. He didn't see anything airborne. He squinted forward and saw movement.

Was that it?

One combat buggy, four guys bristling with gear, strapped to it with snatch cords. They all had carbines, pistols, swords, armor, integrated helmet comms, two swivel-mounted MGs on the roll bars, one mounted abaft the driver. That was an entire case of anti-armor missiles on the rear rack. They had to be doing eighty klicks, off road, on coarse terrain.

The forward gunner was targeting the vehicles. The side mount was hosing the shit out of the dismounted troops on the plain.

The guy in the rear stood bouncing on his knees against the vehicle's jolts, waving the muzzle of a launcher and then there was a *BangThump* of it firing and a cloud of countermass debris out the rear. A few meters out the sustainer engine cut in with a *Hisshhh*.

The rear gun truck exploded.

The shooter dropped the launcher, grabbed the third gun, and started pouring fire at the Freeholders.

Drafts tried to hug the wheel even closer. Fuck. The gunner didn't recognize them as . . . no, wait. He was blasting a cordon between them and the UN, and driving the enemy into the woods, back and away from the vehicles, hosing them clear. The enemy were being driven away and running from their own vehicles.

A relayed message from Beth shouted at him to, *"Get aboard and drive! Fast!"*

He shouted into his mic to the support element. *"Board and drive now! Now! Now!"*

He waved a *come on* and swarmed the second vehicle. As he reached it, he tripped and slammed into the corrugated step, breaking his fall with his hands and his face.

Godsdamn, that hurt.

Frank took the other side. Movement underneath resolved as one of the crew, hiding more than anything, behind the wheels. He shrugged, raised his carbine in burning, throbbing hands, paused, and put a round right up the spine. The kid screamed, flopped, convulsed, and died.

Shit. He probably wasn't actually a threat but fuck it. Enemy uniform, battle, shoot.

He leapt onto the step, into the cab, hoping it wasn't on some sort of biometric control. He saw the control panel and realized it had been, but that entire box was disabled. Likely, the troops had made the smart decision that any driver was better than no driver in an emergency. Except, of course, in a hijacking.

He punched start, swiped the instruments to whatever default they were set for, grabbed the shift and shoved it into Drive. He let it idle, eased into the throttle to gauge the motor, and then gunned it hard. The truck dropped into a depression, banged against the far lip, whipping his neck. It bounced out, bounded over the next one, and he was away, driving past the ruins of the lead gun truck that belched flame and thick, oily smoke with the stink of burning polymer.

Then he took a quick glance at his hands. Several scrapes, some raw flesh, a jagged puncture tear. All superficial, all painful. He gingerly felt his face. Upper lip swollen and dripping blood, and two teeth feeling loose and electric on the nerves. His shirt stank of dirt and urine residue from the ditch.

He'd live. He drove hard, Frank shooting out the window at something. Behind him, other vehicles detoured around the deadlined ones, and formed a new convoy.

"Beth, we have a casualty down with an entire stickyweb on his torso. He'll need to be cut loose and probably evacced from the impact. Location approx vehicle five."

"*Acknowledged.*" A few moments later, the voice added, "*The support element has him.*"

He kept driving. He hoped the support element had managed to assist the additional drivers, especially his kids. Now it was even more dangerous, because the enemy knew the convoy was compromised, and could just have air support blow them into cratered debris. Trucks and supplies were only money to Earth. Enemy combatants were worth it.

They had to make it three kilometers undamaged, then turn off.

Into his ears, Beth relayed, "*You have a hanger on. Stand by for fire.*"

The buggy pulled alongside, one of the troops pointed and shot, and nodded into the side mirror. That was it.

Frank asked, "Where are we turning?"

"About three hundred meters ahead, fast." His voice was muffled by the bruised and bleeding lip. He added, "Can you carefully cut off this sleeve with the prison goo on it and wad it up for later disposal?"

"Yeah, hold on." Frank pulled out his pocket tool, flicked open a blade, leaned halfway across Drafts, not bumping his damaged jaw. Carefully he slit and ringed the sleeve. He folded the clean fabric over the glue and placed the bundle on the dash. Jacob's shirt was still sticky with blood from his jaw.

They were just approaching the turnoff, which was barely visible.

Frank said, "That's a trailer track." At best. It was rutted, narrow, and half overgrown.

"Yes, there."

Nothing to do but drive.

Screaming engines overhead marked a UN combat vertol, but it didn't shoot. Probably, they weren't sure how many survivors there were.

But that meant some sort of response would be along quickly. He wasn't sure what all was planned, though he assumed looting of the trucks.

The track narrowed and he slowed, slipping in and out of ruts, driving through low spots and mud puddles, brush and limbs smacking and scraping the sides. Every bump hurt. It was dark under the thick, subtropical growth. It had a familiar smell of humid rot and decay. Orange molds fought with blue and green leaves.

Ahead, someone in uniform held up a hand and he slowed and stopped.

The bushes started moving, and he flipped out, grabbing for his carbine, before realizing they were all either Freehold Forces or local resistance. Some of the shirts were home dyed. Another militia element.

He heard thumps as the hatches opened, and the truck swayed. Damn, they were looting it like lowenas on a dead bison. He wasn't sure how they were carrying it all, then he saw...

Bicycles. And wheelbarrows. Everything was being lashed or carted, and then walked off into the woods. He saw one bike with two rods tied to the bars—one for steering, one for caliper braking. It had two hundred kilograms of ammo crates in the panniers, and one hundred more in the kid car towed behind it.

In under a seg the truck was stripped even of the pioneer tools, and someone knocked on the door. He opened it.

"Commo," a cheerful grin said. It resolved as a very dark

woman in very dark face paint in a home-brewed gray camo shirt. Her tag read DARKWOOD PROVISIONAL GUARD and had two chevrons on the pocket flap.

"Bringing or taking?"

She held up a wrecking tool. "Taking," she said.

Drafts shifted over, and in seconds the chick leaned over him, broke the dash cover, yanked out the entire commo assembly, chopped the power cable with cutters, and shimmied back out.

"I need a medic when one is free," he said, pointing at his lip.

"I'll relay," she agreed.

As he watched, someone loaded two of the truck's power cells into a cart and rolled them off. Damn, this was going to be a stripped hulk before they were done.

In fact, they were done. The movement receded, and everything was quiet.

The road guard ahead waved and came forward.

"On foot, fast. We'll have transport in a bit." He produced a spray canister and let a cloud fly inside the cab. The smell was strong. Drafts deduced it was a DNA solvent to break down residue and make tracking harder.

They slogged through the woods, alternating between game paths, trickling waterways, and across hard ground.

A woman ran up alongside.

"Medic," she announced. "Yeah, that's a mess. No, keep walking." He'd paused but resumed.

"Okay," she said. "General analgesic, and I've got wound spray. Left hand."

He held it up, she spritzed it, and it burned even more. He winced but didn't say anything.

"Right hand."

He held it over and she sprayed that one.

"Now pause a moment, close eyes, this is going to hurt."

He felt her fingers roll his lip up and almost yelled through the grimace. The spray made him twitch and shake. It stank of disinfectant and then his nose lost sensation and smell, too.

"That's it for now. We'll follow up on the teeth later, or your dentist can."

"Fanks," he acknowledged with a grunt. His lip was already going numb. He resumed walking so he wouldn't fall over from pain and fatigue.

He noticed the muscle-powered transport gradually moved onto powerbikes, a couple of terrain buggies, several four-wheel haulers, and eventually a couple of trucks. He hoped it was fast enough and discreet enough the UN didn't track everyone down.

Eventually someone rolled up on one of the four-wheelers, slapped the rear saddle, and said, "Climb on."

He swung his leg over, snapped the belt, slung his rifle across his chest, and grabbed the edge of the right cargo pannier. The guy took off.

The motor was mostly silent. The wheels made a lot of noise. This could definitely be tracked if the UN wanted to expend the resources, but they were a couple of kilometers from the abandoned convoy, which was several kilometers from the turnoff, which was three kilometers from the ambush. He figured the rebel leadership was assuming that was sufficient radius to be statistically safe. How many investigators would the enemy risk when they'd already lost a convoy? And did any components of those trucks remain?

It was of interest to him, but if he never knew, he couldn't tell.

Besides, the ride hurt his teeth. A lot.

It was dusk, near dark, when he was dropped off a few hundred meters from his house and slogged across two fields to reach it. Everything looked normal. Everything was. The kids were already here, mucky but unharmed.

"I got one, Dad!" Megan grinned. "Got his helmet, too!" She held it up.

Anst said, "I think I had the main ammo truck. It was packed."

He grinned at that. "Well done. We'll go over it later." He was proud of them, and now the element had more experienced combatants.

Anst looked sober as he added, "We lost one. Frank Tait said Mr. Emmett got hit. They brought him home to bury."

"Damn. Well, he was a brave man, and we're better to have known him. I just hope he's not tracked too easily. That could bring attention to the rest of us." He realized they'd have to make excuses for the old man being dead, and hope to avoid any detailed exams.

Lissa had food, skin treatment, and quickly found painkillers and a cold compress. She looked like the traditional farmer's wife the UN hated and some troops envied and appeared harmless except for the uniform shirt. While he ate, she cleaned the weapons, checked the loads, and stowed them back in the concealed box next to the house's power and utility conduit, where they were least likely to trigger a scan. She helped him with dinner, and even helped him shower.

Dr. Wrege didn't ask how his lip and teeth got beaten, didn't even make a comment about drinking and mouthing off. He just noted, "They're mostly sound, but there was some impact trauma to the jaw. I've injected some reconstructor nanos and some polymer reinforcement. You need to keep that splint on the teeth for the next day. Sip liquids. It should be fine after that."

"Thankth, doc. How mush?"

"Eh, this one's free," Wrege said without even looking up from his log screen.

"Thankth."

"Don't mention it."

He most certainly wouldn't.

It was back to farm work, dirty, tiring, and lagging due to the previous activities. Even with coordinate machines to handle the crops, the animals required a certain amount of hands on. He was still learning, still toughening up. But he'd rather deal with animal shit than be in the city, that much closer to the UN bureaucrats and their bullshit.

He was back inside late, showered, and sipping some high-proof vodka with vegetable juice to get some minerals and take the remaining edge off his teeth when there was a knock at the back door. He stiffened.

"No, that's them," Lissa said. She went back, nodded at the screen, and opened the door.

He vaguely recognized his woodland chauffeur from the day before, and one of the other wreckers.

The man said, "We have a crate here for you."

This time the crate contained ten UN rifles with three magazines each. Someone else carried in a package in a waterproof cover, which revealed a squad machine gun. Three light anti-armor missiles. A case of mixed standard batteries and powercells. Four sets of torso armor and helmets.

The first one held up a radio.

"UN commo rehacked, can be found when on with a specific search, receiver only. You can listen in to certain transmissions, and its ID range is short."

"Most trif." He grinned. This was a respectable amount of gear for a squad. If another convoy came through, he'd find a different location to enfilade and stop it, away from support. If not, they'd find one of the small outposts and raid and harass it.

They'd been declared combatants in name only. Now they could really fight.

Replacements
Justin Watson

Firebase Lang, North of Delph'
2nd Platoon, Bravo Company 1-87 Infantry

The grenade hissed softly and released a green smoke cloud. From his position kneeling behind a thick evergreen tree, Sergeant First Class Rhys Harlingen watched dreamily as the celery-colored smoke billowed across the cool, grassy clearing for several seconds. Shaking his head to clear it, Rhys looked around at his people and saw that his were not the only drooping eyelids in the patrol. He reached to the man next to him, Sergeant Quinn, 1st Squad Leader, and shook him. Quinn's head snapped up, his brown eyes wide in surprise under his patrol cap.

Rhys made a forestalling motion with his hand to calm Quinn, then indicated with a wave that he should rouse the rest of the patrol. Quinn nodded, chagrin apparent on his dark brown face.

Five days in the bush will do that to anyone. I don't know if it's worse or better that we made no contact with the enemy.

Rhys turned his eyes back to the sandbagged walls and dug-in concrete fortifications of Firebase Lang, waiting for clearance to come over the radio. If they entered the clearing without clearance, a jumpy sentry just might fire on them.

"Blacksheep Two-Seven, this is Lang Golf." The earpiece in Rhys's helmet crackled to life. "I see green smoke, over."

"Lang Golf, Two-Seven," Rhys said. "Confirm green smoke, over."

"Roger, Two-Seven," the guard on radio watch at Lang answered. "Come on in, and welcome home."

215

"Roger, out," Rhys said. He rose to his feet, knees crackling like pinecones in a vice, and waved for his people to follow him. They left the concealment of the treeline and walked out into the kilometer-wide clearing surrounding Firebase Lang. With a little prodding from Quinn, the soldiers maintained their spacing and vigilance right up to the moment they collapsed into a file at Firebase Lang's entry control point.

Per standard operating procedure, Quinn and Rhys stopped at the gate and counted in their six soldiers as well as inspecting them for any critters that might be clinging to their gear, artificial or natural.

"Get a shower and some chow, Quinn," Rhys said. "And put these guys on twenty-four-hour standdown. Meet me at the command post in an hour to go over the patrol report, then you take a standdown, too."

"Sergeant, I don't need a standdown," Quinn said. "I just need a shower and some sleep."

"Your dedication to duty is noted, Sergeant," Rhys said, his voice devoid of inflection. "Ericsdottir can handle her fire team without you for one more day. Shut up and do what I tell you."

"Yes, Sergeant," Quinn said, turning toward the barracks tents.

Disregarding his own grumbling stomach and the filth coating him, Rhys headed for the Company Command Post, a plywood building reinforced by sandbags near the center of the outpost. Captain Shultz would want a quick word, and while the CO wasn't chickenshit enough to jump one of his platoon sergeants for taking a shower before checking in, Rhys knew he'd appreciate being informed ASAP.

Even though all I can tell him is, "We ain't found shit."

Sure enough, Captain Schultz was in the command post when Rhys pulled open the CP's flimsy plastic door. The tall rangy officer sat at a green folding table, scrolling through reports on a ruggedized gray tablet. He looked up as the door open and stood to greet Rhys with a firm handshake.

"Welcome back, Sergeant," he said. "Take a seat. I take it your patrol was quiet?"

"Yes, sir," Rhys said as he settled into a chair, taking his rifle off its single-point sling so the muzzle wouldn't drag on the extruded plastic floor. "We hit all OP locations and saw nothing out of the ordinary."

Schultz nodded.

"Do you think we've stopped the rebels' logistical traffic through our area of operations, or are we just missing them?" Schultz said.

"I don't know, sir," Rhys said. "Since higher pulled the rest of the brigade back to Delph', we have a fuck-ton of ground to cover. They're too good at spoofing our automated sensors and we just can't put enough mark-one eyeballs out there to cover every logging road, much less all the deer trails and other paths that could fit a bike with a small trailer or a mule cart. I got no proof, but my guess is that we're a moderate inconvenience to them at most."

Schultz stared at the situation map on the table between them for a moment, his brow furrowed. He finally exhaled.

"I think you're right," he said. "I'll talk to the Old Man about trying something different. In somewhat better news, your platoon is a getting a few new sets of mark-one eyeballs. Colonel Antoine brought some replacement personnel with the new Eel."

"Cherries or transfers, sir?" Rhys asked.

"Mostly transfers," Schultz said. "Fortunately, only one of them is an NCO, a Sergeant Cogman. There was no one we could get promoted in time to keep him from taking a team leader spot. The rest I divided up, no more than two per fire team."

Rhys nodded, taking it in stride. Their parent unit, 1st Battalion of the 87th Infantry Regiment, was an aberration among UN forces on Grainne, or indeed, UN forces anywhere. For more than a decade their battalion commander, Lieutenant Colonel Antoine, used his family's political capital to plant himself in 1-87 and avoid relief despite his eccentricities. He also exerted heavy influence on personnel coming into the battalion.

As a rule, 1-87 accepted only enlisted men in the lower three paygrades and brand-new officers. Nearly every NCO, company commander, and staff officer in the battalion at this point had been promoted up through the ranks *in* the battalion *under* Antoine's command, ensuring they were up to Antoine's standards. Accepting an NCO from another unit was a wild card.

Nothing for it, we are short on people. Hope he doesn't suck.

"Oh, and the colonel was kind enough to drop off a platoon leader for you," Schultz said, a mischievous smile curving his lips. "Lieutenant Nguyen. He *is* brand new."

Rhys exhaled and ran a hand over his face. Breaking in new

lieutenants was senior NCO business, and if you did it right the result was decent company commanders, majors, colonels, etc. But it was always a pain in the ass. Even the ones with potential, almost none of them were objectively *good* from day one, and took months to develop into an asset. He'd had Lieutenant Lang right about where she needed to be before the rebels had killed her.

Rhys pushed that thought away.

"Where is he now, sir?"

"In the motor pool," Schultz said, grinning. "He was eager to get started. Go get cleaned up and grab some chow and I'll introduce you."

There just weren't enough construction assets to make every facility on Firebase Lang hardstand, so the maintenance bay was a massive green fabric tent with dull twenty-by-twenty polymer planks laid down for flooring. The tent, fabricated from locally sourced fibers, was big enough to accommodate two Eel assault vehicles out of the company's complement of sixteen at a time.

With space thus limited, Eels only stayed parked in the maintenance tent when they required the use of the heavy crane to pull their power plant, or if the maintenance team had to crack open sensitive electronics or other systems that needed protection from the elements. The tent was almost always filled with the whine of hydraulics and the buzz of power tools.

The mechanics and vehicle operators performed all the other maintenance functions out on the parking line of the motor pool. As Rhys approached second platoon's line with Schultz, he saw a short man in fatigues with buzz-cut black hair standing on a ladder in front of one of the Eels. It looked for all the world as if the guy was trying to fellate the four-foot long barrel of the Eel's twenty-five millimeter auto-cannon; his hands gripping its barrel on either side and his mouth pressed to the muzzle.

"BOOM!" The man shouted into the weapon.

Schultz looked sideways at Rhys and grinned.

"He was captain of the Tactics Club at the Academy, you know," he said, tilting his head toward the man on the ladder. "Co-captain of the Combat Weapons Team, too."

"I'll sleep better knowing that, sir," Rhys said, picking up his pace to reach conversational distance with his new platoon leader before Nguyen "Boom-Tested" the gun again.

"Lieutenant Nguyen," Rhys said.

The diminutive officer looked away from the muzzle of the twenty-five millimeter down at Rhys. Nguyen's dark brown eyes were bright and eager, his posture erect and positively humming with youthful energy. Rhys found himself exhausted just looking at the boy.

"Good Afternoon, Sergeant," Nguyen said, politely, then saw Schultz and started to salute, then checked the motion, apparently remembering that they were in a forward area. The effect looked like an epileptic spasm. "Sir."

"Nguyen," Schultz said. "What are you doing up there?"

Before Nguyen could answer, a young woman with Nordic blonde hair and fair skin appeared out of the commander's hatch on the Eel's turret. Ericsdottir pulled herself to waist-level defilade, her newly sewn-on corporal's chevrons were a slightly brighter shade of gray-green against the lapels of her faded and stained battledress.

"Hey, Ell-Tee," she said. "Could you give us another shout? I don't think the scanner got a good reading on that last..."

Ericsdottir trailed off as she saw her platoon sergeant and company commander.

"Oh, hi, sir. Welcome back, Sergeant," she recovered, her voice bright. "The lieutenant was just giving us a hand. The, uh, emitter on the sonic scanner is out, but the receiver still works, so he was helping us test bore and barrel integrity."

Ericsdottir held up a green device that Rhys recognized as a chemical alarm, not a sonic scanner. Her smile took on a sheepish cast as she waited to see if her superiors would play along.

Schultz just shook his head and turned something that sound suspiciously like a chuckle into a cough.

"Nguyen, this is Sergeant Harlingen, your platoon sergeant," Schultz said. "I leave you in his capable hands."

The captain turned and walked away without waiting for a response, shoulders shaking with barely concealed mirth. Rhys turned back to Nguyen and Ericsdottir.

"Good thinking, Ericsdottir," he said. "But I'm afraid I need Lieutenant Nguyen for a minute. Give the scanner to Metz and do the rest of the boom testing yourself."

Ericsdottir's expression fell.

"Oh, I think we're okay," she said, pretending to examine

the readout on the chemical alarm in her hands. "No cracks or fissures detected."

"No, no," Rhys insisted. "Using a nonstandard input requires a larger sample size, you know that. Take at least twelve more readings, Corporal. Good loud ones. Sound off like you've got a pair."

"Yes, Sergeant," Ericsdottir said, handing the chemical alarm back down inside the turret, her expression resigned.

They walked away to the sound of Ericsdottir's much higher-pitched, "BOOMs!" Nguyen smiled amiably.

"I take it I was the victim of a prank just now?" he asked. His accent was American West Coast, his voice in the middle of the tenor range, young and clear.

"Well-spotted, sir," Rhys said.

"Ah, well, I figured I'd take some crap as a new LT," Nguyen said, he stuck out his hand. "Pleased to meet you, Sergeant. I'm Tom Nguyen, though I guess you call me 'sir.'"

Rhys shook hands, the lieutenant's grip indicated he wasn't physically weak. Nguyen's reaction to the prank could be good, could be bad. If he really was secure enough that a joke didn't bother him, good, but if he was absorbing the prank without comment because he was too timid, or too concerned about his popularity, not-as-good.

"Right," Rhys said. "I won't lie, sir, you're joining us at a rough time. We lost your predecessor and a lot of good people just a couple weeks ago. Currently, the battalion is patrolling an area bigger than Georgia. There are no friendly local forces to speak of and we suspect the rebels are massing logistics for something big, but there's not a whole hell of a lot we can do about it."

"Understood, Sergeant," Nguyen said, and Rhys was relieved to see his expression dim. "What *are* we doing in that case?"

Rhys smiled, but it was tinged with fatigue and pain.

"Our best, Lieutenant. We're doing our best."

Crouched under the front window of a department store, Lieutenant Tom Nguyen, or rather his digital avatar, risked a look over the windowsill. When no hail of virtual small arms fire greeted him, he took a longer look. Fifteen camouflage-clad figures, his third and weapons squads, sprinted across the gravel parking lot and into a gray and brown brick building that he'd designated as their support-by-fire position.

The computer-generated village was lit in a convincing facsimile of Grainne's predawn sunlight and Nguyen's VR rig even supplied the drone of native insects, boots crunching on gravel and the *whh heeeesshhhh* of a soft, consistent breeze. The immersive effect was only partially successful, though, as the insects did not sting, his boots did not slip and slide on the gravel, nor did the breeze cool the sweat off his skin. On a subconscious level, his brain noted the dissonance between the simulation's audio-visual and tactile inputs.

"Blacksheep Two-Six, this is Blacksheep Two-Four." Sergeant O'Donnell, the weapons squad leader checked in on the platoon radio net. "Support by fire set, over."

"Two-Four, Two-Six, Roger, stand by, over," Tom acknowledged, his pulse quickening. Computer simulation or not, this was his first training exercise as an officer.

If I can just not fuck this up in front of the CO, I'll be off to a good start.

Turning around in the simulated storefront, he counted the nine surprisingly lifelike representations of second squad around him. The squad leader Sergeant Harris and his two team leaders, Corporals March and Cohen were represented by avatars like Tom's own. For this exercise, the remaining members of second squad were represented by AI bots. Ironically, the movements and facial expressions of the bots were smoother, more realistic than the avatars of the real soldiers participating in the exercise.

"Blacksheep Two-Seven, this is Two-Six, is your element set?" Tom asked, his commo rig auto-selecting the correct radio frequency based on call-sign.

"Roger, Two-Six," Sergeant Harlingen replied. "Overwatch set."

Alright, here's where the simulated metal meets the notional meat, Tom smiled as he made his way to the front door of the department store.

"All Blacksheep Two elements, this is Two-Six," he said. "Commence assault on Objective Gold."

Letting go of the transmit button, Tom turned to the three men and six digital constructs with him.

"Alright let's—"

Tom's vision went pure, plain black and deathly quiet filled his ears.

The young lieutenant unlatched the fully enveloping VR helmet and ripped it off his head, shooting upright from his simulation chair—too quickly as it turned out; a wave of dizziness put his ass back in the chair as his senses adjusted to reality. He took a deep, shuddering breath and looked around, seeing Harris likewise coming out of his VR rig, shaking his ginger-topped head. He was followed shortly thereafter by Cohen and March. Sergeant Harlingen and the rest of the platoon were still sitting tight, secure in their VR rigs.

Rising more slowly, Tom saw Captain Schultz regarding him with a pitying half-smile from the control terminal of the sim center.

"Was there a technical issue, sir?" Tom asked.

"No, Nguyen," Schultz said. "You were killed by enemy fire. Go ahead and have a seat."

Shitfuckingcuntfullofcockbags.

Tom sat on the plastic bench at the back of the company's simulation room, allowing his head to *thunk* back against the prefabricated polymer wall. Stewing in frustration, Tom relished the brief, sharp pain in his skull.

He didn't have long to wait. The rest of his NCOs began shaking out of their VR rigs in ones and twos. Nguyen was unsurprised that Sergeant Harlingen was nearly the last one out, followed only by the smartass blonde corporal, Ericsdottir.

"Alright, Second Platoon," Captain Schultz said from the controls of the repeater holo-display. "Gather around me for the AAR."

Tom wanted to run and hide, but he fought to keep his expression impassive as he approached the glowing terrain model of the repeater display. Once Sergeant Harlingen and second platoon's four squad leaders and six team leaders were all standing where they could see, Schultz hit a few keys and glowing blue icons representing the platoon began to advance across the holographic terrain model from the LZs toward the objective.

"Your landing went as planned," Schultz narrated. "As did your approach and initial entry into the town. You remained unnoticed to this point—"

Schultz paused the display at the point where third squad and weapons occupied their position across the street from the main objective building. Then he zoomed it in on the buildings north of the objective where 1st Squad had assumed far-side security. In a nearby alleyway, a red icon blinked into existence.

"It was at this point in the exercise," Schultz continued, his voice clinical. "That an enemy security element noticed the movement of your platoon. Because Lieutenant Nguyen thought to request jamming support, the enemy was unable to alert the high value target on the objective of our presence via radio or phone comms."

Nguyen opened his mouth to give Harlingen credit for requesting the jammers, but his platoon sergeant stopped him with a miniscule shake of his head. The red icon on the display began to move further down the alleyway and into a two-story building.

"The enemy lookouts moved into this building," Schultz said. "And occupied the second floor, from this elevated position they observed second squad entering the department store south of the objective and engaged them with a recoilless rifle, killing the platoon leader, second squad leader and most of the assault element.

"The enemy's movement to this building was masked from most of the platoon by various buildings except for," Schultz paused, fiddling with the controls for a few seconds, "Alpha team, first squad. Sergeant Cogman, I believe that is your team."

Cogman was a medium height man with a hatchet of a nose and flat gray eyes under a straw-colored crew-cut. He didn't look embarrassed, more annoyed to be called out.

"Yes, sir," he said.

"In that case, this alley was in your field of view, you should've observed the lookouts' entire movement," Schultz said flatly. "Yet you failed to either engage the enemy or report them. Why?"

"I guess I must have missed them, sir," Cogman said, his tone bored.

Tom felt his face warming and his fists clenched at his sides. He had only known Cogman for a few hours longer than the rest of the unit, but he already felt embarrassed at the replacement NCO's lack of professionalism. Tom's gaze flicked to his platoon sergeant and he saw Harlingen's jaw muscles clench violently, but the company commander was talking so they both remained silent.

"You missed them," Schultz said flatly, his tone making it abundantly clear how stupid that answer was.

"Yes, sir," Cogman said, shifting from one foot to the other under the hostile gaze of not just his commander, but every other NCO in his own platoon. "Look, I'm sorry, sir, but we just never took this video game shit all that seriously in my old platoon."

"Maybe if you had they wouldn't be fucking dead," Ericsdottir snapped, her voice filled with sudden, intense vitriol.

"What did you just say to me?" Cogman said, stepping towards Ericsdottir. Tom started to move to intercept, but Harlingen was already between them.

"At-the-fuck-ease, right goddamn now." Harlingen's normally laconic voice was a growl. "Both of you."

"Sergeant Cogman," Schultz said, his voice still flat. "You will treat every training event as if your life, more importantly, your men's lives, depend upon them, because they do. If this is an issue for you, you will not remain an NCO in my company. Understood?"

"Yes, sir," Cogman said, voice subdued with deference, feigned or genuine, Tom couldn't tell.

Schultz continued breaking down the short-lived mission from there, which was mostly a depressing recitation of his platoon's simulated massacre. Tom allowed his gaze to drift from NCO to NCO in his platoon.

Ericsdottir was still glaring at Cogman. He'd pegged Ericsdottir for an incorrigible smartass from day one, naturally, but she seemed a more or less jovial smartass. The anger and contempt she'd shown Cogman seemed to spring from nowhere, and taking a shot at his dead comrades? No one was happy with Cogman, but that was cold-blooded by anyone's standards.

What the hell *was that all about?*

As soon as the After-Action Review broke up, Harlingen called out both Cogman and Ericsdottir.

"Sergeant Cogman, report to my desk in the CP and wait there," Harlingen said. "It appears you need remedial counseling on your duties as a team leader. Ericsdottir, Quinn, stay here."

Nguyen waited with Harlingen for the rest of the platoon and Captain Schultz to filter out. As soon as they were alone with Ericsdottir and her squad leader, Quinn, Harlingen started questioning her.

"Alright, what the hell was that about?" Harlingen said, echoing Tom's thoughts.

Ericsdottir was absent her normal smirk, instead her features were clouded and furtive.

"Nothing, Sergeant," she said. "I just thought Sergeant Cogman's attitude was all wrong."

"Oh bullshit, Ericsdottir," Quinn chimed in. "Something about Cogman has been eating you up for days. Talk."

Ericsdottir chewed on her lip for a long moment. Tom remained silent, not knowing what he would say in any case, but tried to look stern and serious while he let his NCOs do all the talking.

"Last week Cogman was talking with the other transfer, the Pashtun kid—"

"Private Rashid?" Harlingen asked.

"Yes, Sergeant," she said. "Anyway, they were talking about how much they wanted to get some pussy."

Harlingen raised his eyebrows and cocked his head as if to say, *yes, and?*

"Hensley told him the platoon was off limits and the local girls weren't safe," Ericsdottir continued. "Given that a local bitch would likely fuck you just to infect you with something. Told him to get used to jacking off and be grateful the platoon has a great porn stash—not to be confused with a porn 'stache, of course."

"Ericsdottir," Harlingen said, warning tone audible.

"Right, sorry, Sergeant," she said, and her voice lost the momentary levity. "Anyway, Rashid was like, 'that's why you pick the local girls who aren't expecting it.' When Hensley asked him what he meant by that, Cogman said, 'What? You never held down one of those colonial bitches and gave it to her? We used to grab a different one each week and pass them around the platoon.'"

Tom felt his stomach lurch. He couldn't stop his next words. "What the fuck?"

Ericsdottir nodded. Sergeant Quinn's mouth was slightly open in surprise and Harlingen's own expression settled into something harder and sharper than his pro forma deadpan.

"Right, sir," Ericsdottir said. "When we pushed him, he tried to play it off like he was just joking."

"That's not funny, that's disgusting," Tom said.

"No, It's not funny, sir, and he wasn't joking," Ericsdottir said.

"Are you sure about that?" Harlingen said, his normally laconic voice deadly earnest.

"If you're asking me if I can prove anything, of course not," she said. "But, Sergeant, I *know* he wasn't kidding. That sick fuck is a rapist; I can smell it on him."

"We have to report this," Tom said. "We have to start an investigation."

"Wait just a minute, sir," Harlingen said, then turned to Quinn and Ericsdottir. "You two don't talk about this to anyone—not a single goddamn soul. But in the meantime, make sure none of the females are ever alone with Cogman or Rashid. Try to make it look natural if you can. Get out of here."

Tom waited for the two NCOs to leave.

"Sergeant, we have to get an investigation started," Tom said again. "We can't have a fucking rapist in our platoon."

Sergeant Harlingen seemed to age before his eyes, his shoulders slumped, and his fingers went to the bridge of his nose.

"All we know for sure about Cogman is that he's an asshole. We don't know he's a rapist," Harlingen said. "Corporal Ericsdottir's misgivings aside, it's possible he just has a fucked-up sense of humor, which would hardly make him unique in the force. He and Rashid are the only survivors from his old unit so if they say they were just joking, there's no one else to question."

"So we just let this pass?" Tom said, his voice rising. "That son of a bitch confesses to serial gang-rape and we do nothing."

"Sir, calm down," Harlingen said. "We'll tell Captain Schultz what we know; maybe I'm wrong and he or Colonel Antoine can find some traction from their previous assignment. For now, we watch the sonofabitch like a hawk. I'm going to write him a negative counseling statement for incompetence and insubordination during this exercise. If he doesn't square himself away, all I will need is two more negative counseling statements to establish a pattern of misconduct, then I can relieve him and he'll be someone else's problem."

I don't want him to be someone else's problem, I want him to swing from a gallows.

Tom was not, pro-forma jokes about new lieutenants aside, entirely stupid. Ergo, he took a deep breath and tried to adjust his expectations.

"What about the rape 'joke'?" Tom asked. "Surely that's conduct unbecoming, at least. There's counseling statement number two."

Harlingen shook his head.

"Can't use it," he said. "If he challenges his relief, having that on the record against him puts every single dirty joke we let slide up for examination. This isn't a platoon full of Mormons, sir. I'd have to relieve every NCO we have."

"Sergeant, there's a difference between dirty jokes and bragging about gang rape," Tom insisted.

"Of course, there is," Harlingen said. "But unless the judge advocate advisor he gets is retarded, it's enough for them to muddy the waters at the review board. They can claim we singled him out because he was a transfer we didn't want from another unit. Since Rashid is involved, they're almost certain to bring up charges of institutional racism, too."

"The hell?" Tom said, gesturing at the epicanthic folds over his own eyes. "Racism? I'm Vietnamese! Colonel Antoine is black. I've seen every shade possible. I met two other Muslim soldiers today; we're not oppressing them."

"Islam is a religion, not a race, sir," Harlingen said. "More to the point, you and the battalion commander have obviously internalized white supremacy despite your own ethnic heritages. Very sad. It's so common among Americans with minority heritages who don't suck at life."

"Oh, come on," Tom said. "No review board is going to buy that."

Harlingen took a deep breath and exhaled through his nostrils.

"From our battalion or the 87th Regiment at large? No," he said. "But he won't get a board from our regiment since Cogman and Rashid can claim conflict of interest. A *lot* of other units in the UNPF hate 1-87 with a passion. Some would let him off just to spite us."

Tom stared at his platoon sergeant for several seconds, his lip curled in disgust.

"They'd let a *rapist* off," Tom said. "Just to piss us off?"

Harlingen looked extremely uncomfortable for a long moment.

"What?" Tom said. "They would?"

Harlingen shook his head, not in negation, but in disgust.

"Sir, there are units where raping the locals might as well be in the standard operating procedures," he said finally.

Tom felt the air leave his lungs.

"No."

"Yes, sir," Harlingen said. "We're losing this war, badly. Morale is absolute shit and discipline is worse. The brass can't do anything about it, so they'd rather not *know*."

"You've got to be kidding me," Tom said.

"I'm not," Harlingen said. "Colonel Antoine won't tolerate it and his officers and NCOs are loyal enough to enforce his will. But other units' senior leaders just want to get through this deployment alive and with their careers intact. They're not going to draw attention to war crimes in their ranks, nor risk having their men turn on them for fucking up their fun."

"This is so fucked up," Tom said, leaning against the wall and putting his hand to his face.

"Welcome to the war, sir," Harlingen said. "Where the enemy is only half the problem."

The roar of VTOL engines overhead shook Rhys's gray plastic desk, forcing a typo on the evaluation form he was filling out. He glared up at the dull, gray metal ceiling of the CP before returning his attention to the glowing screen in front of him. Backspacing several spaces he continued typing again—

Sergeant Cogman, aside from the incident recorded in attached counseling, has performed his duties in a satisfactory manner this quarter.

The words pained Rhys as he typed them. It was hardly high praise, and in an organization as prone to bureaucratic inflation of evaluations as the UNPF, it was even a de facto negative report. Still, it wasn't the relief-for-cause evaluation he wanted to write. The hard truth was, even by the broadest possible terms, Rhys had no grounds to relieve or even further discipline Cogman.

Sergeant Cogman and Private Rashid kept their acts meticulously clean in the six weeks following the virtual reality exercise. Neither offered anything remotely resembling disrespect to their chain of command and neither made comment, in jest or not, about misconduct toward the locals. They performed their duties well, if not superbly, and neither bitched about anything. It pained Rhys because, whatever he might have told his new lieutenant, he trusted Ericsdottir's instincts. Rhys believed he had two genuine war criminals on his hands.

War criminals or not, though, the replacements were no fools and after the first time Rhys laid down the law, they'd given their leadership no further case for adverse action.

Adding to Rhys's foul mood was the fact that the VTOL that just interrupted his train of thought was returning from dropping off a long-range patrol made up of *his* soldiers. He'd wanted to go with them, but Captain Schultz had pointed out, correctly, that Rhys has been on patrol twenty-eight of the last thirty days. The CO insisted he let Sergeant Quinn take the mission alone since it was, essentially, a muscled-up fire team, not even a squad.

"Harlingen," Schultz said. "If shit kicks off out there, I want you leading the rest of Second Platoon to the rescue, not sitting with your ass hanging out on the side of a mountain with one-sixth the combat power you're responsible for. Nguyen seems to be doing alright, but I don't want to send him into his first firefight without his platoon sergeant."

The CO had a good point, but Rhys hated being at the firebase while his people were extended way beyond their normal patrol radius; thirty minutes away by air, to be exact. Schultz was right about the platoon leader, too. Nguyen had led several mounted and dismounted patrols and done fine, but still no enemy contact. The lieutenant tried to act mature about it, surrounded as he was by veteran NCOs. Rhys knew the kid was dying on the inside to get into the shit, though.

The door of the CP swung open, drawing Rhys's eyes up again. Sergeant Crabbe, the second platoon artillery forward observer and Sergeant Quinn walked in. Rhys nodded at them both curtly, then turned his attention back to the lukewarm evaluation he was writing for Cogman.

Wait, weren't they supposed to be on the patrol?

"What are you two doing here?" Rhys said, standing up from his folding table as they approached. "Why the hell aren't you out with the patrol?"

Quinn and Crabbe looked at each other, eyes wide in alarm.

"Sergeant, the lieutenant said the CO pulled us at the last minute," Crabbe said.

"Wait, what?" Rhys said. "Where's Lieutenant Nguyen?"

But even as the question escaped Rhys's lips he knew the answer.

"He got on the VTOL, Sergeant," Quinn said, confusion apparent on his face. "He had an updated flight manifest."

Rhys shot an incredulous look at the company clerk, a reedy corporal named Barton sitting at another folding table, who was responsible for typing up the lion's share of the paperwork.

"I'm sorry, Sergeant, I thought you knew," Barton said. "The lieutenant said that Sergeant Crabbe and Sergeant Quinn were both down with fever and he needed to get on the bird since they would be at sick call."

"Oh, Jesus Christ," Rhys said shaking his head in disgust as he walked toward the back of the CP, toward Captain Schultz's office to tell him they had a lieutenant rogue and in the wild.

I swear I'm going to choke the shit out of that little bastard for this.

Forty-eight hours on the side of a mountain cooled, but did not extinguish, Tom's enthusiasm for the mission. They had been rotating, two men on observation, two on security, two asleep since they'd arrived. The time asleep in the cave next to the battery-powered heater staved off hypothermia and frostbite, but also revived cold-deadened nerves so he could feel the pain accumulated on watch more keenly. The long Grainne year meant a long, chilly autumn, and they were told to expect winter at this latitude to be brutal. At the observation post they put down pads and mats under the brush and netting they used for conceal-ment, but there existed no way to make lying prone on freezing rocks getting blasted by icy winds *comfortable*. Their only saving grace was that the snows hadn't started yet, so they stayed dry, if perpetually windchilled.

Tom was just settling into his turn for sleep when Welch, their commo geek, came stumbling back through the cave tunnel.

"Sir," he hissed. "Sir, we got movement on NAI Frank."

NAI Frank was **N**amed **A**rea of **I**nterest Frank; a logging compound that regiment's intel section suspected the insurgency's brass used for meetings.

Aches forgotten, numb flesh forgotten, Tom sat bolt upright instantly. He tied his bootlaces with fumbling fingers, redonned his cold weather gear, grabbed his rifle and helmet and sprinted down the tunnel toward the mouth of the cave, remembering to crouch as he emerged so as not to silhouette himself against the mountainside over the rock ledge on the cliff.

It was the dead of night with a sliver of moon to illuminate the ground, but Tom easily made out six local trucks winding their way north toward NAI Frank with his naked eye. Buckling his helmet's chin strap and flipping his optics down, he started magnifying the green and gray imagery, his HUD displaying range to the trucks in decreasing kilometers. He took a kneeling position next to Rosales on the ledge, who tracked the lead vehicle with his massive 10mm sniper rifle.

"I count six vehicles, approximately twenty-five personnel, sir," Rosales said, his voice flat.

"Confirm," Tom said. "Welch, call it up."

For a few seconds, Tom heard Welch talking into the radio and only static answering. Finally, the commo specialist put down the hand mic and looked at Tom, fear apparent in his eyes.

"Sir, I can't get through," Welch said.

"What?" Tom looked back at the commo geek. "Why not?"

"It's some kind of EMI, sir," Welch said. "Electromagnetic Interference."

"I know what EMI is," Tom said, more harshly than he intended. "Is it natural or jamming?"

"I don't know, sir," Welch said.

"Go get the ears and find out," Ericsdottir snapped.

While his commo specialist went to get the Mobile Operational Utility Sensor-E, Tom continued to observe the vehicles. The convoy split into three sections. Two trucks drove to the northern edge of NAI Frank and stopped, while the trail vehicles stopped on the south side of the road, taking up blocking positions. The two middle trucks parked in front of one of the houses in the settlement. The men who got out of the trucks were all fit, bundled up, and carrying Grainne-made weapons openly.

Fucking jackpot, if we can just get the goddamn radio to work.

"Sir, the source of the EMI is one of the trucks on the southern edge of town," Welch said from under a specialized helmet sporting small, circular sensor dishes on either side of his head.

"That's gotta be a powerful jammer," Ericsdottir said.

"Why do you say that?" Tom asked.

"Well, sir, I'm not awesome at geometry," she said. "But we're more than a six hundred meters away laterally, and another hundred meters vertically. If you do that a-squared, b-squared shit, I imagine that's quite a distance."

"Pythagorean Theorem," Tom said, his tone absent as he pondered the problem. "And you're right, whoever they are, they're important enough to have some decent jamming equipment..."

"Yeah," Ericsdottir said, a note of suspicion in her voice. "Too bad there are twenty-five of them and we can't call up the rest of the company."

"Those are civilian trucks?" Tom said, ignoring Ericsdottir's comment, turning to Rosales.

"Looks like, sir," the sniper said. "Might be up-armored but I can't see any signs of it."

"We'll have to risk it," Tom said, pulling out a rope and webbing-set, he began to secure himself in a rappelling harness just as he'd learned at the Mountain Leader course. They'd already anchored long ropes, just in case they needed to get off the side of the mountain quickly.

"Lieutenant," Ericsdottir's normal sarcasm was replaced by the hesitancy of concern, "what are you doing?"

"Get into harness, Ericsdottir," he said. "I'll go first and belay you once I'm down. Rosales, as soon you see me pop a thermite on their jamming gear, start disabling their vehicles, I don't want them to get away."

"You don't want them to *what* now?" Ericsdottir said.

"Welch, as soon as the jamming is off, call in the cavalry," Tom continued, unabated, ignoring his own hammering heart. "Schindt, Rosales, after the vehicles are disabled, cover us. We'll exfil south and switch on our IR beacons so you know who not to shoot."

Tom took a deep breath, and instead of rocking into classic L shape, secured himself to the rope to rappel down face first. He looked over his shoulder.

"Sir, what the fuck are you *doing*?" Ericsdottir repeated, looking at his position on the ledge.

Tom gave what he hoped was a daring grin.

"Get in your harness and follow me."

And with that, Tom stepped over the side and began to run down the side of the mountain, his break hand providing just enough friction to keep his descent controlled and more or less straight. As gravity pulled him inexorably toward the ground and the icy wind rushed through his hair and needled his skin and lungs, taking his breath away, Tom knew he'd never felt more alive.

Now this *is some soldier shit.*

The sentries patrolling the southern edge of town walked winding paths, eyes scanning the treeline. Their expressions were alert and professional, but not paranoid—they were keeping watch but not expecting contact. Each held a rifle and had night optics strapped to their face. They were backed up by a man with a medium machine gun set up over the roof a truck's passenger compartment.

Easing back around the trunk, he motioned for Ericsdottir to lean in closer.

"Shoot the gunner at the truck," he breathed in her ear. "I'll kill the roving sentries. Give me a ten count, then initiate when you're ready. Once they're down, I'll sprint for the trucks and thermite their jamming gear. You cover me."

Ericsdottir's incredulous expression was visible even through night optics, but she nodded, and settled into a prone firing position, rifle shouldered, cheek to stock. Tom did likewise. Because the enemy had their own optics, he didn't engage his IR targeting beam, instead relying on the optic's passive sensors to create his sight-picture. The HUD projected not only cross-hairs, but the predicted ballistic path of his rounds in glowing red. They were close enough that his targets were still on the ascending branch of his rounds. He aligned the crosshairs just ahead of the man, placed the pad of his finger on the rifle's trigger and waited.

CRACK-thweet. Crack-thweet, Crack-thweet, three shots rang out over the night air.

Before the report of Ericsdottir's second round, Tom fired. The rifle recoiled into his shoulder and through his optics he saw the man jerk as if stung. Tom followed up with two more rounds before the man fell, then tracked over as quickly as possible to the other sentry, who was already moving for cover. Tom fired once, missed and fired three more rounds, sending bark from a tree flying off into the night. Glancing at the truck he saw that the machine gunner was slumped over his weapon. Tom's second target was crouched behind a tree thick enough to stop his bullets.

We're running out of time, if the rest of their people make it down here, we're fucked.

"Ericsdottir, covering fire!" Tom transmitted. "I'm going for the trucks!"

Springing to his feet, Tom sprinted through the woods, pumping as hard as a he could to reach the truck. A prominent root caught his boot, tripping him as a burst of fire chewed into a tree mere feet behind him. Tom fell flat on his face but didn't stop. He crawled forward as he'd been taught during his first cadet summer, to break the enemy's tracking. The rocks and spiky evergreen seeds strewn across the forest floor dug into his knees and elbows as he scrambled forward.

Have to take out the jammer, or else we're not going to make it out...

He was less than ten meters from the truck now, pushing himself back up he bounded forward, trusting in Ericsdottir to keep him alive, ignoring the rounds flying back and forth in the woods behind him. Tom's lungs burned from the icy air he inhaled in ragged gasps and his heart hammered inside his chest.

The driver side door on the truck was unlocked when he got there, keeping his trigger hand on his rifle, he yanked open the door and scanned inside. There were discarded coffee cups, empty plastic bottles, cellophane junk food wrappers and—

There.

He recognized a portable jamming unit in the right-rear passenger seat. Climbing awkwardly into the truck's cab, fumbling with cold and a copious dose of adrenaline that shook his hands, Tom retrieved a cylindrical gray thermite grenade from his web gear and a roll of tape. The tape came off its roll with a *crrrreccch* and Tom secured the grenade to the boxy black jamming unit, flicked off the safety clip and pulled the pin on the grenade. Before it ignited Tom hauled himself out of the truck, turned and ran like hell back for the woodline.

As he ran, Tom could hear the hiss of the thermite slagging the jammer.

"Summit Eight-Niner." Tom tried to reach the sniper on his helmet comms. "This Blacksheep Two-Six, clear to engage tar—"

A jackhammer blow to his lower back sent Tom sprawling to the cold dirt and grass, well short of the woodline. For several terrifying seconds Tom couldn't get a breath and all he saw were gold and silver starbursts. When his vision returned and frostbitten air filled his lungs again, Tom rolled onto his back, reaching for his rifle, every movement agony.

"Don't you fucking do it, cocksucker!" A rough, deep voice warned him.

Focusing with some effort, Tom saw one of the insurgents, a tall, burly man in a knit cap, leveling a Grainne-issue rifle at his face, his expression furious. Behind his assailant, Tom saw other armed men running to catch up. Despite the mortal terror coursing through him, a detached piece of Tom's mind forced a chuckle from his throat.

Well, shit, it was a fun ride, if short...

The insurgent's thoracic cavity exploded without warning, spraying Tom with hot, black and red viscera. A split second later a thunder-crack report echoed off the mountainside and through the trees, then another, and another followed by the higher pitched rattle of machine gun fire from far off. Another of the insurgents fell, a large chunk of his torso turned into pink mist, and the rest went to ground as the machine gun kicked up fountains of dirt all about them.

"Move it, sir." Tom's radio crackled to life with Ericsdottir's voice. "You're covered!"

Wiping the blood, entrails, and bits of black fiber from his face with a gloved hand, Tom grabbed his rifle with the other and ran, once again, for the relative safety of the trees, his men covering his hasty retreat with a hail of fire.

Less than an hour later, Rhys shook his head as he walked the logging camp at NAI Frank; six trucks hulled; one burning, the rest with gaping holes through their motor cores, a couple dozen dead insurgents, five, *thank God*, live soldiers and one bloodied and battered lieutenant. Fists clenched at his sides, Rhys stormed toward the cabin where they'd established the aid station. Ericsdottir intercepted him.

"Sergeant, you know if you kill him, they might just stop giving us officers," she said.

"Don't threaten me with a good time," Rhys said. "Why do you care, anyway?"

Ericsdottir looked abashed.

"Well, I mean," she stumbled over her words, looking around at the logging encampment. "Look around. Yeah, he's maybe batshit crazy, but his plan worked. We just killed twenty-five insurgents and he was the only one who got hurt. The LT's got balls."

Ah, there it is, the time-honored seal of approval of the enlisted for a particular officer, he's got balls.

"I'll keep that in mind, Ericsdottir, now fuck off," Rhys said, continuing his march toward the aid station. When Rhys walked into the small log cabin, the platoon medic was examining an enormous purpling bruise on the LT's lower back.

"Will he live, Doc?" Rhys asked in a voice that indicated he was ambivalent about the answer.

The nineteen-year-old medic, Private First Class Taylor, looked back at Rhys.

"Well, Sergeant," he said. "From what I understand that's up to you and the CO. But if you're asking if the bruise will kill him, probably not. I gave him a local so he won't get fuzzy and he can keep pushing. He should get some bloodwork when we get back, though, make sure it didn't fuck up his kidneys or nothin'. You start pissing blood, you tell me, sir."

Rhys smiled in a decidedly unfriendly manner.

"Thanks, Doc," Rhys said. "Give us the room."

Taylor beat a hasty exit, leaving platoon sergeant and platoon leader alone in the otherwise empty logging cabin.

"Lieutenant," Rhys said. "If you ever pull some stupid shit like that again, officer or not, I will beat the life out of you and impale your corpse on crooked rebar as a warning to all lieutenants not to buck for medals."

Nguyen's eyes went wide, then narrowed. Anger and chagrin warred openly across his features.

"I wasn't bucking for a medal. But understood, Sergeant," Nguyen said, a sullen note in his voice.

"He's going to have to get in line," a corn-belt rasp interrupted from the door. "Rank hath its privileges."

Captain Schultz stood in the doorway, looming large in full armor and kit, regarding Nguyen with a razor-edge glare. Rhys straightened to attention, Nguyen followed suit with a wince.

"Yes, sir," Nguyen said, his defiance slipping away. "I'm sorry, sir, I know I didn't ask your permission, but I felt my place—"

"Shut the fuck up, Lieutenant," Schultz said. "You knew what you were doing, you overzealous little shit, and you're going to get away with it this time because it worked. They had maps labeled with multiple logistics caches."

Nguyen, wisely, chose not to respond or react to the news.

"Have your squad leaders start their precombat checks," Schultz said. "We have three hours to formulate a plan and conduct rehearsals, then we're hitting their largest cache. We expect resistance. You've proven you can pull some adrenaline junky bullshit, Lieutenant. Now let's see if you can actually lead your platoon, which I remind you is your fucking job."

The village, "Redbriar," on the map, was comprised of approximately two dozen buildings. A significant minority of them were on fire now, and damned few were untouched by the fight raging between Blacksheep Company and the rebels defending their supply cache. Night optics were unnecessary now as the gray early light, glow from the fires and occasional explosion of heavy ordnance provided ample light for the combatants, even though smoke threatened to obscure whole sections of the village.

Tom Nguyen sprinted down a side street, cold morning air stinging his nostrils and throat, his boots crunching and tossing gravel hither and thither. Per direct orders from Captain Schultz, he maneuvered just behind his third squad, and a missile team from weapons squad surrounded him. Though not under direct fire, he heard the cacophonous reports of machine-gun bursts and rifle fire filling the air without cease, punctuated by the deeper *thuds* of grenades exploding, and the occasional *whoosh-BRUM* of shoulder-fired rockets.

"Two-Six, Two-Seven," Sergeant Harlingen's voice sounded in Tom's ears. "I've got second squad and the guns with me at Building Red Three. Confirmed the enemy center of mass is Building Red Two. We're taking heavy fire from that position, over."

As Harlingen spoke, the men of third squad stacked up on the back door of a wood frame, one story house. Metgers, the alpha team's grenadier, extracted a ten-round mag marked with red tape from his 20mm grenade launcher and replaced it with a blue-taped mag containing solid slugs.

"Roger, Two-Seven," Tom acknowledged. "We're breaching Building Green-Two now. Can you reduce the target, over?"

"Negative, Two-Six," Harlingen responded, "Basement on Red Two is a reinforced bunker. We've got them under heavy fire but they're not suppressed."

Metgers blasted both hinges of the door and kicked it into the building, then stepped out of the way. Four men from third squad flowed through the door, trying to rapidly clear the fatal funnel. Too rapidly, as it turned out, the third man tripped on the lip of the floor tile inside, sprawling on his face with a crash and a stream of profanity.

"Stay the fuck down," Corporal Luzan, a short swarthy NCO ordered, stepping over the prone rifleman and into the building. "Don't mask fire."

"First room clear," Luzan reported after a moment. "Moving on. Get up, Williams, take number four slot."

Tom entered the cleared room, a utility room occupied primarily by laundry machines and a big utility sink. Gritting his teeth, Tom held fast while Third Squad cleared the rest of the house. A gut-shaking *THROOM* outside interrupted the laconic "room clear" check-ins from third squad. Tom couldn't see what had detonated, but fire slackened on both sides for several seconds after the explosion.

"All Blacksheep-Two Elements, this is Two-Six," Tom said. "SITREP."

"Stand by, Two-Six, explosion near Two-One's position, break," Harlingen answered.

There was a brief pause as Harlingen unkeyed his mic before continuing.

"Two-One, Two-Seven," Harlingen called for Sergeant Quinn. "Status. Say again, what's your status?"

"Two-Seven, this is Two-One-Bravo," Ericsdottir's voice answered, hard-edged and tight. "Two-One Actual is gone, booby trap on Building Blue-Three. I've lost contact with our alpha team, too, don't know where they are."

FUCK. Quinn's dead, and we don't know where Cogman's team is.

"Roger, Two-One-Bravo," Harlingen answered. "Get your team in position and put fire on Building Red-Two."

"Looks like we're alone in here, sir," Luzan said, returning to the back room with Tom. "Family must have bugged out when the shooting started."

"Good," Tom said. "Let's get eyes on Building Red-Two and kill those fuckers."

Tom stayed low as he entered the front room, not particularly wanting to draw fire, treading softly on a thick, fur rug betwixt green leather couches. The view out the living room window was dismal. In contrast to what the map depicted, it wasn't a street but an open field more than fifty meters across that separated building Green-Two from Red-Two. Red-Two was a brown, one-story brick structure about the size of two or three houses put together. It was surrounded by a swing set, monkey bars and soccer goals. As Harlingen had described, narrow windows at ground level twinkled with muzzle flashes.

Really, fuckers? Hiding weapons in a school?

Tom thought furiously. Harlingen had second squad and the machine guns in a building to the east, no closer than Tom's element. First squad was halved, somewhere south of them. His element, third squad, augmented by a missile team, was supposed to be the assault element, but he didn't have enough men to successfully rush across that much open field and take a fortified objective.

To punctuate Tom's tactical problem, a burst of machine-gun fire shattered the living room window, sending glass shards tinkling lethally into the room and ripping great chunks out of the leather furniture. Tom dropped prone, trying to become one with the unidentified animal hide that adorned the floor. Another burst peppered the front room, sounding like an overturned nest of malicious hornets.

Shit, shit, shit.

"What do we do now, sir?" Luzan shouted.

Tom thought furiously, trying not to look indecisive but truly at a loss for what to do... until he saw the man-portable missile launcher on Williams's back.

"Williams," Tom shouted. "Tell me you packed thermobarics today."

Williams's face betrayed confusion.

"Yes, sir," Williams said. "But we can't fire in here, the countermass will choke us—"

"I know, load a thermobaric and hang on a sec," Tom said, then he keyed his helmet mic. "Two-Seven, this is Two-Six. I'm going to try and engage the basement with a thermobaric missile. On my command, mass all fire on the south-facing windows of Red-Two so we can get in position. Acknowledge."

"Roger, Two-Six," Harlingen answered. "Say when."

"Okay, Williams." Tom turned to the young missile operator. "Take your first shot just outside the kitchen door there. Aim carefully, you got to get it *in* the basement, but don't wait to see if it hits. As soon as you fire, sprint for the truck there." Tom nodded out the window to a gray four-by-four parked on a side drive. "Remember to get behind a wheel-base. Got it?"

Williams's eyes were wide, but he nodded firmly.

"Okay, LT," he said. "I'm with you."

Tom stood behind Williams at the kitchen door on the house's east facing. Metgers had his hand on the doorknob, looking to Tom for affirmation. Tom nodded.

"All, Blacksheep Two Elements," Tom said. "POUR IT ON THE FUCKERS."

The rattle, crack and buzz of small arms fire rose to a crescendo that even the hearing protection on Tom's helmet couldn't fully mitigate. Bullets and grenades blew pockmarks into the bricks and concrete of the Red Two's southern face with abandon and the enemy's return fire slackened.

Metgers flung the door open, Tom slapped Williams on his armored shoulder and they flung themselves out the door into the smokey morning air. Williams hit the dirt only a few feet from the house, missile tube already on his shoulder. Tom joined him, snuggling into the dirt as ragged return fire puckered the dirt entirely too close to them. Just as he had been taught in Cadet Basic, Tom looked back and around, then slapped Williams on the helmet.

"Clear," Tom shouted. But a loud *THUMP* cut him off as the captive piston launched the missile. Behind him, shredded polymer countermass created a cloud in the air. A split second later the southern face of Red-Two was consumed in fire.

Yes! Tom grinned at the sight.

The short-lived explosion faded, as did Tom's grin when a small geyser of blood gushed from Williams's arm just above the elbow. Both men stared at the wound in shock for an instant before the ground furrowed all about them with the impact of dozens of rounds.

GOD FUCKING DAMN IT.

"Move, Williams!" Tom shouted, grabbing hold of the shoulder on the man's body armor and half dragging him behind the truck. Despite the prodigious amount of firepower second platoon was placing on the building, the enemy rounds followed Tom and Williams, chewing into the vehicle and creating great puckering holes in its body.

Tom crouched awkwardly over Williams, shoving gauze into the bullet hole in his arm as they both cringed behind the rear wheelbase of the truck.

That could've gone better, Tom shook his head as a near miss creased the very top of his helmet, nearly sending him to the ground. He crouched lower, practically on Williams's lap. *What the hell do I do now?*

The missile launcher was still hanging by its sling on Williams shoulder, a green tube with an optical sight and firing mechanism on the top, smeared with blood. One more missile was on a bandolier across Williams's chest.

"Give me the launcher," Tom said. Taking the tube in his hands, he tried to wipe the sight clean, only to realize his hands were coated in Williams's blood. Chivying a bit of undershirt out from underneath his armor, he wiped the blood off the weapon as best he could, ejected the expended load and rammed home the last missile with a *thunk-snap*.

Tom looked left and then right.

Which way would they expect me to go? Roll back or roll past the front fender. Maybe . . . kinda fucked up . . . whatever, we're both dead if I don't.

"Williams," Tom shouted in his ear. "I need you to run to the front wheelbase to draw their fire. I'm going to take another shot. *Just to the wheelbase*. Don't go into the open."

Williams's expression was twisted with incredulity and hazy with pain, but he nodded once more, propping himself up to a crouch. Tom took a deep breath, then said, "Go!"

Tom dropped to the ground and rolled out a scant centimeter beyond the rear fender of the truck and sighted in on Red Two's window slit. The optical sight was still smeared, but it displayed range and elevation alongside the targeting reticle, indicating it was still working properly. Taking one more deep breath, Tom stabilized himself and depressed the firing mechanism, sending the missile on its way.

The missile rocketed right through the basement window and, reaching the back wall, detonated. The warhead consumed all the oxygen in the basement in a millisecond to fuel an incinerating blast that scorched the ground around Red-Two for thirty meters in every direction, setting the playground equipment ablaze. After the final reverberation of the blast, the village of Redbriar was eerily quiet for several seconds.

Rising unsteadily to his feet, Tom gestured for the men still in the house to get up.

"Two-Seven, lift fires," he said. "Two-Three, follow me."

✧   ✧   ✧

The basement was dim enough that Tom and his men had to use flashlights to see. Cold white shafts of light played across shattered and melted firearms and ammo boxes, radio sets, and of course, charred corpses. The air hung heavy with the stench of burnt meat. Tom's heart thudded in his chest as his own beam played across a trio of very small, blackened corpses huddled together near one of the support beams.

Oh, Jesus. Oh, no-no-no-no-no.

Acidic bile roiled up Tom's throat, he choked back on the urge to vomit, putting up a gloved hand to hide the tears forming in his eyes.

I killed kids. Oh, fuck, I killed kids.

A heavy hand landed on his shoulder, causing him to start.

"Sir." Harlingen's voice betrayed, for once, naked compassion. "Why don't you take a minute? I've got this."

Tom coughed and blinked rapidly several times.

"It's alright, Sergeant," Tom said. "I mean what was I supposed to do? Don't put your kids in your fucking fighting position, right?"

Despite his best efforts, the last word escaped Tom's lips with a cracked, pleading tone.

Where were they supposed *to put them, you fucking murderer?* his conscience raged at him.

"Sir," Harlingen said, staring intently into Tom's eyes. "You did what you had to do. No one knew there were kids down here, but even if we did, we had to take out this position. Without the missile, we could've lost the whole platoon on this one building."

"Right," Tom said, coughing and shaking his head. He forced himself to think of his duty. That's all he was doing—his duty. "Do we know what happened to Cogman's team?"

"We think they might have all been caught in the blast that killed Quinn," Harlingen said. "Ericsdottir and her team were trying to reestablish—"

As if summoned by magic, Ericsdottir voice came over the radio.

"Two-Six, Two-Seven, I need you at Building Blue-Five ASAP." She sounded furious and scared at the same time. "I found Cogman and Rashid."

"Are they wounded?" Harlingen asked. "Status."

"Rashid's dead. Cogman's alive and unwounded, but probably

bring Doc Atwell," she said. "Just come as quick as you can, Sergeant. It's all fucked."

Second Platoon maintained two attached medics, one man and one woman. Doc Atwell was the female. Harlingen and Tom exchanged looks as the same horrible thought occurred to both of them.

Oh, Christ, no one was watching Cogman.

It was a short run to Building Blue-Five, a wood frame residence nestled alongside four or five much like it from outside appearance. Rhys had just enough presence of mind to shout, "Friendlies coming through!" as he, Atwell and Nguyen ran through the front door.

They entered another rustic rural Grainne living room with brown upholstered furniture and magnificent, if unfamiliar, racks of horns and tusks adorning several walls. A thin brunette woman sat on the couch wrapped in a blanket, a blank expression on her face, blood on her hands and pants. Atwell went immediately to her. Ericsdottir stood near, clearly observing the colonial woman but not threatening her. Two bodies covered by tan sheets lay on the black fur living room rug, pools of dark blood spreading from both.

Cogman was on his knees, fingers laced behind his head, pants around his ankles, cock and balls hanging in the breeze. Schindt stood behind Cogman, the muzzle of his light machine gun angled so that he could blow Cogman's head off without hitting anyone else in the room. The rifleman and grenadier in Ericsdottir's fire team pulled security, watching out the windows.

Harlingen knew, but he asked anyway.

"What happened?"

"This cunt's husband shot Rashid," Cogman shouted from the floor before Ericsdottir could speak. "So I shot him, then the crazy bitch came at me with a knife. What was I supposed to do?"

"Then you should've shot her, dumbass, not *raped* her, you useless sack of shit," Ericsdottir screamed.

"You guys are such a bunch of faggots over a little local gash," Cogman said. "I swear to fuck—"

"SHUT YOUR FUCKING MOUTH, COGMAN," Nguyen shouted. "You are going to prison for the rest of your life. And I hope your new friends there bore your ass out like an artillery piece, you worthless fuckstick."

Rhys looked at his lieutenant in surprise. He hadn't known the young officer was capable of such raw, palpable rage. Cogman, hopped up on adrenaline and apparently still thinking with his dick, refused to shut up.

"In your dreams, sir," he said. "There won't be a court martial. UNPF will lose the paperwork to cover it up. I'll *readjust* for six months in the psych ward and then be out. Bet my next unit won't care if I'm getting a little on the side, either. So, go fuck yourself, *sir.*"

The local woman appeared to revive at his words, glaring daggers over Doc Atwell's shoulder at Cogman, her nails leaving divots on her brown couch. Rhys hoped they wouldn't have to restrain her. She'd already been through too much.

Nguyen looked him, and Rhys saw the question in his young officer's eyes.

Is he right?

Rhys looked away, shoulders slumping just slightly. Nguyen turned back toward Cogman.

"Get up and pull your pants up, Cogman," Nguyen said, advancing a few feet toward the belligerent NCO.

"Sure thing," Cogman said, standing up, a sneer on his face as he buttoned his pants back up. "Wanna zip-tie my hands? Am I 'under arrest'?"

Lieutenant Nguyen flipped the selector on his rifle to safe, unclipped it from its single point harness on his armor and tossed it gently to Cogman, who reflexively caught it, bewilderment replacing his sneer.

Nguyen drew his sidearm from its holster on his chest in a motion so quick Rhys barely tracked it. The black polymer 7mm pistol came out in a firm two-handed grip and the report of two shots, so rapid they almost sounded as one, deafened Rhys. Cogman's head snapped back, the back of his skull opened to the world. A spray of bright red, gray, and pink flung itself across the rustic home to splatter against the refrigerator. Cogman's corpse collapsed to the black fur rug like a puppet with its strings cut.

For a moment no one spoke. The Grainne widow said nothing, her face resuming its blank expression. The three younger soldiers regarded their platoon leader with a mixture of awe and terror on their faces. Ericsdottir's face shone with open and fierce admiration. Rhys let out a breath he hadn't realize he'd been holding, exhaling loudly, breaking the spell.

Nguyen looked around, his blank expression a match for the widow's now.

"Co-captain of the combat weapons team," Nguyen said in a strange, strained voice, nodding jerkily at Cogman's dead body. Nguyen looked over at the thin rebel woman on the couch, opened his mouth, closed it, then strode rapidly out of the house.

As the door closed behind him, Rhys looked at Ericsdottir and her team.

"Cogman went for the LT's rifle," Rhys said firmly. "The lieutenant had to shoot him. Everything else happened like it did. Got it?"

"Yes, Sergeant," all four soldiers chorused.

"Okay, good," Rhys said. "Let's get ready to reconsolidate."

As the troops stood and moved toward the door, Rhys addressed the widow directly for the first time.

"Ma'am, I'm very sorry," he said. "But we're consolidating all the civilians at the clinic. If you need to clean up first, these ladies will escort you to your bathroom." Rhys indicated Ericsdottir and Atwell.

The woman nodded slightly, rising to her feet. Flanked by the two female soldiers in full body armor, she looked impossibly fragile, but when she met Rhys's eyes, he saw nothing but resolve in those dark hazel orbs.

"You know we won't stop until you're all dead," she said quietly. "We will never, *ever* stop killing you."

Rhys sighed.

"Yes, ma'am, I know."

And maybe we have it coming.

Epilogue

Colonel Madison Kornberg, auburn-haired and straight-backed, sat rigidly in the leather chair proffered her by General Huff. She did not fidget or sigh as the UN's Supreme Commander on Grainne made a show of reading the tablet copy of the report on his desk. As an inspector general, Madison was unused to being on the wrong end of a power dynamic, even when dealing with a senior officer. Regardless, she was determined to maintain her dignity.

"Seven days of ammunition with light and crew-served weapons for two full battalions, various and sundry explosives and other materials," Huff said, looking up finally. "That's quite a seizure. But this business about an officer executing one of his men, I'm afraid it puts a damper on the victory."

"I beg your pardon, General," Madison said. "If you read the report, it's very clear that Sergeant Cogman, after being caught in the act of raping a noncombatant, assaulted Lieutenant Nguyen with deadly intent. The officer in question was clearly defending himself."

Ach, Wes, why am I still covering your ass?

"And all the troops recording gear was blanked so serendipitously because of an EMP weapon, yes?" Huff said, one eyebrow raised.

"That's correct, sir," Kornberg said.

"And your eagerness to accept 1-87's report without further investigation has *nothing* to do with your previous support of Colonel Antoine?" Huff said. "You wouldn't be eager to avoid taking responsibility for your recommendation to retain him in command despite his unit's numerous eccentricities?"

"Sir, there's nothing in that report that strikes me as unfeasible," Madison said, choosing her words carefully. "And, to echo an earlier point you made, without some firmer evidence, I see no need to further tarnish such a significant victory. I hope it's not presumptuous of me to point out that our forces can use any morale boost imaginable at this point."

Madison stopped, hoping she hadn't gone too far.

Come on, Huff, you bastard. You don't want to cause a stink over one lousy rapist...

Huff leaned back in his chair, steepling his fingers.

"Valid points, Colonel Kornberg," he said. "I'll consider them. Dismissed."

Madison stood, saluted smartly, which Huff returned casually, and turned to leave.

"Oh, Kornberg," Huff added. "Tell Antoine that even a man with his connections runs out of top-cover eventually. I better not get another incident report out of 1-87."

Madison nodded.

"Yes, sir," she said. "I'll deliver the message."

For all the good it will do.

Semper Malevolem

J.F. Holmes and Jason Cordova

Dragontooth Mountains, Grainne
December 4, 210

Ernesto Silang was not a man typically prone to hatred.

When the United Nations invaded his homeland and arrested the Citizens in the name of "freedom and equality," he was more annoyed than anything else. With the ridiculous arms restrictions placed upon all residents of the Freehold by the UN occupiers, attaining enough meat for the coming winter became difficult. Not impossible, since he never reported the impressive Merrill M66 15mm precision shooting rifle he had "forgotten" about in the false panel above his headboard, but difficult nonetheless.

When the UN had scanned him for "pathogens and diseases," he had been mildly perturbed. He valued his privacy as much as the next Freeholder. Ernesto figured they had been searching for anyone who was a veteran. He wasn't surprised to discover that they were not worried about a veteran with more wrinkles on his face than hair on his head. Irritated perhaps, but that was all. Even when they accidentally knocked over his wife's urn and scattered her cremated remains upon the stone mantle of the fireplace, he could not bring himself to hate these men and women. They were simply doing their job, albeit in the worst manner possible.

This was not because he was a calm and genial man. He had not grown out of his dislike for any enemy, no. It was for the simple fact that every single ounce of hate left in his body was reserved for Staff Sergeant David Archuleta, Freehold Military Forces (Ret.).

It had begun decades before, when then-Infantry Trooper Archuleta defeated then-Sniper Specialist Silang at the Interservice Sniper Challenge. It had been by half of a single millimeter that Ernesto lost by, and to say that he had been displeased was a vast understatement. However, Ernesto had been a good sport about it at the time and did not complain too loudly in public. Instead he trained harder for the coming year, where once again he lost to Archuleta, this time by one-tenth of a millimeter. The following year was the same result, as was the four straight years after. Ernesto began to detest the other man with a vengeance.

It only grew worse when Archuleta married Ernesto's younger sister, Claudia. Ernesto had been forced to stand there while David and Claudia exchanged vows before the Goddess. As a devout Catholic, it had galled Ernesto to have the ceremony in such a pagan environment. There had been a second ceremony later, at a small cathedral near Delph', but by then Ernesto's grudge had become full-on hate.

Ernesto would bag a fifty-kilo ripper in the middle of winter, and David would manage to get one that was two kilos heavier. Catch an eight-kilo yellow striped snapper in Mirror Lake? David would inevitably catch a nine-kilo snapper in the same exact spot a few weeks later. It was a game of one-upmanship between the two that everyone else found amusing as the two grew older. Ernesto knew that his hatred was not healthy, but at the primal core of his being he could not allow David to beat him. That even meant not letting his brother-in-law outlive him.

So when Ernesto heard from his sister that David had bagged him an "aardvark" from over two kilometers away, the elderly retired sniper finally had enough. Pulling the hidden panel aside, he grabbed his "hunting" rifle and proceeded to go out into the Dragontooth Mountains to bag him one as well. Just to prove a point, he vowed to do it from further out. However, since his brother-in-law also happened to be his neighbor, David tagged along with Ernesto as he stomped out into the freezing cold and snow.

"You can take the green machine, you know," David muttered, referring to the small six-wheeled vehicle they used primarily around the two farms for hauling chopped wood. Ernesto struggled to move through the deep, thick snow and tried to ignore his in-law. The previous day's storm had ripped through the small valley, leaving massive drifts piled high against the walls of the small homes. The branches of the trees around the massive property bowed under the weight of the wet snow, which also made foot travel nearly impossible.

"The contraption would show up on thermals too easy," Ernesto snapped as he shifted the heavy rifle's sling and rubbed his aching shoulder. His heavy winter wear was warm but weighed him down. His green eyes scanned the path ahead and saw that the snow appeared to grow deeper up ahead. He withheld a miserable sigh.

"Actually, the engine has a dampening system that dissipates the heat," David countered as he began to huff as they continued to struggle through the snow. He was no spring chicken either and David always believed that this sort of physical exertion was best left for much younger individuals. "Heat baffles recycle the energy into the engine, so conserves fuel and battery life. It's small enough signature to make it look like a game animal. Also has a heated compartment in the back for sleeping. Enough food and water can be stored in it for up to a month. Two weeks for two people."

Ernesto finally stopped and bent over at the waist. The walk was already kicking his ass and they had not even made it halfway down the rugged driveway yet. He shot a sideways look at David, who appeared to be doing about as well in the wet, heavy snow.

"Get the damn thing," Ernesto told him through wheezing breaths. "I'm not about to haul your wrinkled ass across these mountains."

"Wrinkled ass that was on your sister last night," David retorted as he came to a halt. His hot breath left puffs of steam in the frigid air. "All. Night."

"I hope you die of a pulmonary."

"Almost did, last night. Goddess, my knees ache."

"Screw you. Go get the green machine before we both freeze to death out here."

Eight divs later Ernesto found himself in a comfortable position near a cluster of brush palms. A small boulder lay half-buried in the snow to his left, which gave him something to lean on. The rifle was supported by a small tripod gifted to him by his sister years ago. His mottled white hunting gear rendered him near-invisible to the naked eye while the brush palms obscured his heat signature, thanks to their own excess warmth which was dumped into the leaves. Many Grainne animals found refuge under brush palms during the harshest winter storms.

Iota Persei was beginning to set behind them, the jagged tips of the Dragontooth Mountains casting long shadows down upon the sloping plains below. The region had been hit particularly hard by the previous day's storm, much like their own valley. Many animals had decided to hunker down and wait it out, but the two retired snipers were hunting a far more dangerous prey.

David lay next to him, rangefinder in hand. His brother-in-law had graciously offered to be his spotter for this hunt. Ernesto did not necessarily trust him to give the proper distance, but then again, they were out in the cold together, so any retribution from the UN Peacekeeping Forces was bound to affect them both. If David was going to screw him over, he'd at least offer a little lube first.

Probably.

"Range?" Ernesto asked in a calm manner as he steadied his breathing. His heartrate slowed as he peered through the scope. Far off in the distance was a UN FOB, complete with towers and artillery placements for counterbattery. All-terrain armored personnel carriers were neatly parked in rows near the motor pool, and he could faintly make out individuals standing around in what appeared to be a formation, though it wasn't anywhere close to the exacting standards he dealt with while serving in the FMF. He could even see the shape of a few Guardians in the all-weather shelters. Things were still business as usual for the UN, however. The snowplows were out in force, clearing off the runways and piling the snow up along the outer fenceline in heaps. A predatory smile slowly spread on his face as he found a few tempting targets.

"Two-zero-one-six meters," David replied. He paused before continuing. "That's three meters shy of where I got mine."

Ernesto shifted the barrel slightly and found a new target which was just a little further away. He could faintly make out something shiny on the target's collar. "Is that guy doing all the gesturing with his hands an officer or one of their fancy privates? Nice headgear, nonmilitary issue. Ear flaps pinned up, some sort of religious or political icon in the center. I can't tell."

"Not sure," David admitted after a moment. "Oh, hey. It's a she. Sure looks excited, though. Real excited."

"Range?"

"Two-zero-two-zero," David replied. He paused and gave his brother-in-law a look. "Really? You're going to be that petty?"

"Perfect target."

"Don't miss."

"I won't," Ernesto declared. "I never miss."

"Then why do I always win?"

Taking a deep breath, Ernesto focused on the target. He felt his heart rate slow even further and focused on it. Lub-*dub*. Lub-*dub*. He exhaled carefully through his nose and stopped midway. Lub-

He gently stroked the trigger of the M66. The muzzle brake redirected much of the recoil but not all, which was part of the reason he had set up beneath the brush palms. Their natural heat helped to mask the expended energy from the shot. With a muzzle velocity at just over nine hundred meters per second, it took the round just over two seconds to reach the target.

United Nations FOB Boutros, Dragontooth Mountains

"And that, people, is why we're here! Freedom is a hard thing to define, and these 'freeholders' don't understand the freedom from worry, from burden, that life under the United Nations brings."

Weekly political bullshit meetings was what almost every officer—and enlisted too, truth be told—was thinking. Captain Sasha Zivcovic almost said it aloud but refrained. No need to get a bullet in the back of the head some night or assigned to some shithole. He watched her face and realized that she probably did believe it herself; she sounded like a true believer. In keeping with the modern way of things, one of the youngest enlisted had received the designation, for the week, and she was good at it, too. A smooth talker, the woman—girl really—was ridiculously beautiful, and had already been climbing the ranks the easy way. Her speech was directed at the base commander, her next target, and she aimed a flirtatious smile at him during pauses. Zivcovic grinned silently, thinking about how worthless she would be in the field.

"So, despite the tragic loss of Senior Private Imbuto last week to a cowardly sniper," she paused and spit on the ground for emphasis, while Zivcovic snorted, "we will continue onward in our efforts to bring peace and security to the colony of Grainne. There is nothing they can do to us that can stop us, because the majority is always the side of right!"

Senior Private Calhoon had replaced her normal winter fatigue cap with the Morale Officer baseball cap and, ten minutes into it, she suddenly seemed to realize that it was frigging cold as shit, despite her incessant smiling. She turned her head slightly and looked to where the actual political officer stood, a taller woman. The height was enough to make Calhoon tilt her head up as she looked at the PO.

She would make a perfect target, thought the Serb, who was head of the UN sniper section.

That slight movement of Calhoon's head to look up at the taller woman caused the round to enter the top of her neck just a tiny bit off target. The change didn't matter, really, in the end. The cavitation of the round, and the kinetic shock it generated upon impact, pretty much caused the base of her skull to shatter. The small pop of her eyes being blown out of her head was covered by the whip crack of a sonic boom generated by the round. The force of it pushed her body several feet to one side. Her feet twisted around in a macabre dance of death, arterial spray splattering crimson blood across the assembled command staff, and she fell like a sack of potatoes into the snow of the parade ground.

Apparently, someone agreed with him about her target potential.

Pandemonium erupted as UN troops scattering all over place, running for cover. Two men, junior privates, ran towards Senior Private Calhoon, or what was left of her. The cap had flown a few meters to the north, and a red pool spread on the snow, decorated with little chunks of bone and meat. Before they reached her Zivcovic shoved them aside, kicking one of them on the ass to do so.

"Hey!" yelled the teenager, "I'm going to file a Dignity Report, and you'll get written up, jackass!"

"Fuck your dignity," answered the officer, punching the private in the face and pushing a medic away from the scene. Kneeling in the snow, the man ignored the blood and the still-twitching body that had not realized yet that it was dead. He stayed there for a full minute, ignoring the whump of the artillery shots going out and the spooling up of two Guardians, looking at footprints and directions. He picked up her head, one eye dangling by the optic nerve, and looked at the ragged neck, tendons and ligaments still dripping blood, sticking his finger in the bullet entry hole to figure the caliber of the round.

He tossed the head aside, then stood and looked south, up into the mountains. One of the officers, the base commander, came out from under a concrete shelter, waving his nonlethal beamer around him as he duckwalked, aiming at everything and nothing. Not getting close to the body, he said hysterically, "I want your team out there, Captain Zivcovic, and put a stop to this! I can't have this in my command, it will look bad on my efficiency reports! TWO dead in a week!"

The Serb paid as little attention to the higher-ranking officer as he did the privates, who were now yelling at their leaders. It was a general clusterfuck, one that he had grown familiar with in his years with the UNPF. He stood, looking at the pattern of blood spray and measuring angles with his hands. Behind him, enlisted and officer started trading punches. Then he smiled a brutal grin. *Game on*, as the Americans said.

"Not sure . . . never mind," David corrected as he peered into the rangefinder. "She's headless now. Though that a strip of skin on the neck would hold the head on, but I was wrong. You were two millimeters high and four left. I blame that pocket of warm air that's about a thousand meters out."

"I hit her, she's dead," Ernesto proclaimed in a sulking voice. Truth be told, he was irritated that his shot had been slightly off on the impact point. He silently vowed to correct it for next time.

"So you warmed up now, you old coot?" David asked as the two began to slither backwards into the thick canopy provided by the brush palms.

"Warmed up?" Ernesto asked. "*Old coot?* You're only three weeks younger than me! Surprised you still can see anything, what with that glaucoma and all . . ."

"Then let's make it more of a challenge," David suggested as they quickly skedaddled, Ernesto in the front as David followed behind him, a fresh-cut bough dragging behind them to obscure any visible tracks. The walk back to the green machine was almost a kilometer away and the longer they lingered, the more likely it became that the UNPF would find the sniper nest. The hike back would also give them plenty of time to compare shooting notes. "I call a shot, you have to top it. Vice versa. Loser has to ... admit publicly that the other is a better shot. Oh, and buy a growler of Old Grainne Stout. Not that weak stuff, but the dark dregs."

"No cheating this time!" Ernesto declared in a hushed, angry tone. "I know that's how you won the sniper challenge back in '89!"

"Not my fault you fired when the breeze was kicking up." David shrugged his narrow shoulders as he tossed aside the branch as the snow began to thin out in the protected vale. The heavy canopy of trees overhead both obscured the green machine from anyone looking down as well as provided a break from the thick snow. It made the going a little easier for the two men. "I waited until it died down."

"You went over your allotted time!"

"Judges thought otherwise."

"Probably bribed one of them ..."

"Firing from the prone position only," David went on, ignoring Ernesto's accusation. "I doubt your knees can take anything else."

"You're the one with lumbar problems," Ernesto countered. "Maybe you'd like a pillow and a sleeping cap so you can be more comfortable while shooting?"

"Or fucking your sister."

"Asshole."

Dragontooth Mountains, Grainne
December 7, 210

Three days later found David with his own rifle, a slightly shorter but heavily customized M66, trained onto the long, winding road leading out of the UN FOB. Gnarled, arthritic hands gently traced the sleek rifle as he patiently waited for Ernesto to call the distance.

"Make up your damned mind already," Ernesto grumbled quietly as he checked the range finder again, looking for any obvious targets. He squinted as the sun was in their face today, which meant that they had to be careful with any reflections off their gear. Fortunately, aerosol hair spray was perfect for dulling reflective qualities of glass without disturbing the view too much. One of the many tricks he had picked up over the years, though this one came courtesy of his late wife and her love of theater. "Pick one."

The UN patrol had left the base thirty segs before, following the road as it skirted around the town of Rockcliff. The paved road eventually led out towards Mirror Lake, near the homesteads of the two men. Further out beyond that was the FMF Training facility, where all aspiring soldiers had once been sent. The rubbled area was now the location for the region's primary UN base. While a tempting target itself, they decided to stick with the UN FOB. These were the more experienced troops anyway, and their goal was to destroy the morale of the lower enlisted personnel. Privates, to be precise.

The remote eyes that they had installed on many of the game trails over the years were now trained onto the road, giving them a wide variety of angles to observe the UN patrol from. What both Ernesto and David saw did not really concern them. The MK-17 Infantry Light Armored Wheel Assault Vehicle, or Eel, was the best that the UN had to offer when it came to transport infantry through dangerous environments safely. The armor was thick and able to deflect incoming rounds during an attack, and the massive tires were hardened to protect against shrapnel and defeat disabling shots. However, all this extra weight meant that the Eel was very, very slow. UN infantry oftentimes found that in order for the vehicle to make it to the destination within a reasonable time frame, they would have to get out and walk in order to lighten the load. In short, the Eel was worthless in mountainous terrain, or anything with a hill grade steeper than three degrees.

It was that which the two snipers could not see that gave them pause.

Both men knew that there were two ways to hunt snipers. The first, and easiest, was to simply paste an area with artillery until the target was confirmed dead or they ran out of shells. Costly, but it did not risk the lives of soldiers who would otherwise be forced to wander around in unfamiliar grounds hunting those who call the woods their home. The second way was to run the gambit of a countersniper team, which had its own ups and downs.

Artillery was scary but typically ineffective. Countersniper teams were annoying and dangerous.

There were signs that they were being stalked by a counter-sniper team. They had located what looked like a potential sniper's nest while they searched for a new spot. They carefully avoided it after discovering that it was rigged to blow with an improvised explosive device. A clever ploy, and forty years ago might have gotten the duo while they were younger. Age and experience taught treachery and suspicion, however. Both men know that in war, if it appeared too good to be true, it was probably a trap.

"Does it matter which one I shoot?" David asked as he watched the feed of the remote eyes through his customized scope. The clarity was perfect and even came in color, and relay transmission was almost instantaneous. While they disagreed on almost everything else, both men could agree on one thing: AnthroLogic made fine trail cameras.

"Depends," Ernesto stated as he cast a sideways look at his in-law. "Those old hands of yours going to be able to pull the trigger a second time if you miss?"

"You don't hear your sister screaming for more, every night?" David snapped back.

"My walls are thick," Ernesto said in a quiet voice. "And I know for a fact that your old wrinkled ass can only go once a night. You really should close your kitchen curtains."

"Jackass."

"Moron."

"Range?"

"One-nine-three-six to the Eel," Ernesto reported. David grunted, causing Ernesto to grin a little. "Too close for you? If you like, you can slide back further, or wait until one of them is walking away."

"Fuck off."

"How about you make the shot, but the helmet stays on?"

A quiet exhale. "Bet."

"Range . . . one-nine-three-seven," Ernesto whispered as he peered through the range finder. He made note of the direction the snow was blowing between them and the FOB, as well as the lack of movement on the clothing of the soldiers at the base. "Found you a private. Scrawny guy, red sash tied around his neck. Very fashionable. You'd probably approve. Oh, he moved a little backwards two steps. You might get another meter out of this. No wind at target. Send it."

Crack!

"Target down," Ernesto confirmed. "Helmet's still on, head is...not. Well, shit. New target, range one-nine-three-three. Short soldier, big tits. Pointing a rifle directly at her CO. That poor bastard is oblivious. It's like they don't even teach basic firearm safety at the UN. Send it."

Crack!

"I think you got her blood all over her CO's face." Ernesto continued to scan the patrol as the UN soldiers tried to find somewhere safe from their invisible enemy. "He looks upset. Okay, two more targets. One on top of the turret of the main gun of the Eel. Armor protecting the body mass. Range one-nine-three-four. Second target, right three meters and down, same distance, driver of the vehicle. He's out in the open. What an idiot. Frozen like a lawyer caught by the headlights of a vehicle in the middle of the road. Make him croak."

Crack! A pause, then *crack!*

"Oh, look, more privates," Ernesto hissed. "Digging into positions on the side of the road. I think they figured out where they're getting hit from. No worries. They can't possibly imagine how far out we are. Three little ducklings, all lined up in a row. Range one-nine-two-eight. The lost looking ones?"

Crack! Crack! Crack!

"No more privates down there," David growled after consulting the feed from the trail cams. Ernesto checked and agreed.

"Want to drop an officer, just because?"

"That wasn't the plan, asshole. Junior enlisted only. Time to move," David muttered as he slowly slid backwards from their prepared position. A few loose rocks tumbled off to the side as he moved.

"Quietly, jackoff," Ernesto countered as he followed suit. This location had been one of his favorite hunting spots for years, though now he doubted anything other than a ripper would want to come through after the UN was through with it. He glanced skyward and frowned. "If they know we're up here, this entire area is going to get hit with arty any seg now."

"You're just upset that your favorite hunting spot is about to get pasted," David complained as they carefully began to pick their way back through the tall trees.

Ernesto grumbled. "Fine. Next time we use one of yours."

"Goddess, no. I like my spots."

"Pussy."

"You are what you eat."

Zivcovic lay at right angles to where the convoy proceeded up the road. He had left his team watching the rigged snipers' blind but didn't expect anything from that. This guy was too good of a shot to not be anything but a seasoned pro. Probably a retired instructor from the Grainne training facility who lived close to the base, for old times' sake.

He'd set up two acoustic sensors, a mile apart from each other. They would give them an origin of the shot, a second or two after it came, but he was also depending more on his own physical senses. The forest and mountains around would confuse the hell out anything if more than one shot was fired, and the UN troops leaving the base had finally been given live ammo to protect themselves. This spot was ideal because they had IDed the transponders of several active trail sensors. There were many scattered about the mountain range by hunters, still active, but only these lay along a convoy route.

Another hit on the FOB was unlikely, but they would go for a bigger target this time, and that meant a concentration of troops, out in the open. Zivcovic knew the propensity for the infantry troops to dismount from the underpowered Eel. He had seen it during the China Insurrection, when he was a senior lieutenant, leading a Serbian sniper platoon attached to a UN "peacekeeping" force. This terrain reminded him of home, the rugged mountains of eastern Europe where he learned to hunt.

The first shot actually caught him unaware, thinking back to his teenaged years, when he was involved in an unsanctioned war with those bastard Bosnians, snipers going out each night in a deadly game of cat and mouse. He just caught the man's helmet—*no, head*, he corrected—spinning through the air.

Zivcovic focused his binos on the next likely target, not far from the first. Less angle to move. The woman was knocked backwards, the spasm of the hit making her rifle fire, sparking off the APC next to her CO. The Serb grunted, seeing which way she fell. He kept watching as a gunner was hit, obviously they needed to knock out the heavy weapon. The driver in the open was just an easy shot.

"Going for the junior enlisted, not bad," he said out loud, as the patrol officer stood in the open, yelling orders and wasn't hit. The next three shots hit the troops trying to dig into the ditch, as he had shifted his scope upward. Shooting downhill was very difficult, but Zivociv had always admired the Grainne shooters when they came to matches. They were good and knew it and would use every advantage they had.

Got you! he almost spoke out loud, seeing movement more than two kilometers away, up the side of a hill. Several rooks tumbled downward, dislodging snow and causing a miniavalanche of snowballs to run down a slope.

He flipped the magnification and lased the area, waiting for more movement to give the insurgent sniper away. They would have to move, artillery was going to plaster the shit out of this place. He had already ticked the grid coordinate to the artillery battery on standby; in a minute a couple of volleys of variable time would shred the entire slope. But he wanted the kill himself.

There. Range was about two thousand meters, give or take a dozen. The figure was clad in white camo, fading in and out of the trees, but the long straight barrel of his rifle helped give him away. Or her maybe; women made good shots too.

He adjusted for distance, then took a long lead, to count for the steady movement of the man through the snow. Slowly taking up the slack of the trigger he exhaled gently, waiting for the kick. Then he stopped as more movement on the edge of his scope distracted him. He dialed down one click and saw another figure emerge, just behind the first.

It was a tough decision to make. Kill one, and then the Serb and the remaining man would play a dance all day. Zivcovic hadn't lived as long as he did by taking chances. Besides, he was beginning to enjoy this game. He realigned his rifle, breathed out again, and squeezed. The 12mm bullet took several heartbeats to destroy the bole of a tree fifteen centimeters in front of the second man, and both disappeared from sight.

The Serb laughed to himself and slowly worked his way back to his alternate site. He had been in a similar situation when he was younger, playing "tag" with a Bosnian sniper, caught totally by surprise. It was thrilling.

Behind him, he heard shells whine and explode.

✧   ✧   ✧

"I need new *chonies*," Ernesto groused as the duo set up camp on the south face of Capstone, the second tallest peak in the entire Dragontooth Mountains range. He picked at his pork and beans, still steaming in the small cup, and looked upwards at the heat deflector which protected them from infrared scanners. The graphene material did an excellent job of absorbing the heat as well as any excess light that might have come from the tiny camp stove. He looked back at David, his mood foul. "Why're you laughing? He almost shot me."

"We knew they'd send countersnipers eventually," David said as he scraped the last of his supper from his cup. "Just surprised at how quickly they figured out our position."

"It was the most obvious position we could take," Ernesto admitted in a quiet voice. He was silent for a moment as he considered the shot which had come so close to reuniting him with his wife. "But you know... I don't think he was trying to kill me."

"What makes you think that?"

"The shot was perfect," Ernesto said as he thought about the angle more. "He had us dead to rights. You were in front, so he probably spotted you first, then me. Wanted to let us know that he knew where we were... I wonder why he didn't just kill me then hunt you?"

"Because he's competitive, like us," David suggested, watching his breath steam into the crisp air. Ernesto nodded, seeing the logic in the argument. Invigorated, he quickly finished his dinner and tossed David his cup. A plan began to form in his mind.

"I got an idea for tomorrow," the older sniper said as he blew on his hands. The night was turning frigid and it was almost time for the two to crawl back into the green machine. "Tomorrow, we both hunt."

"You want to kill this sniper team, old man?"

"Hell no." Ernesto's grin was savage. "I want to torment them."

"You're getting more likeable." David nodded. "I like this side of you."

"Shut up. You're still the small spoon."

"We should flip that coin again."

"No way, crusty. You chose, you lose."

"Bastard. I know you used one of those double-eagle coins to cheat."

"Prove it... and for the record, unlike you, I knew both my mom *and* dad."

The next day Ernesto went to an old hunter perch he had used many years before while David moved up higher. As much as his brother-in-law bitched about it, Ernesto finally convinced David to let the older be the decoy. It was a ruse, one that might not work, but it should. Either way, they were sending a message back to the team that was hunting them.

The new patrol took a different path into the mountains. The two men moved out well in the predawn dark, using their familiarity of the area and their NVGs to make their way to their respective positions. Using the trail cams as guides they were able to find multiple receivers of their wifi setup. Determining which connectors were the UNPF and the countersniper team hunting them took a bit of detective work but finally they were able to narrow it down to the only signal that hadn't moved in two divs.

Trap set, it was time to go to work.

Ernesto sat in the gulch, idly following the opposing sniper with his scope as he moved from the perch where he had spent the night to a more advantageous position along the ridgeline. Ernesto had to admit that whoever the sniper was, he was both ballsy and good. No UNPF soldier wanted to be in these mountains, especially after dark. Rippers were dangerous, but there were other hazards to the wilds of Grainne that most UN soldiers were ill-equipped to handle.

It felt odd that he was allowing David to make all the kills for the day. He hated his brother-in-law with a passion born of many years of spite and anger, but over the past week he found that David didn't grate on him as much as before. Perhaps it was the mutual need for killing invaders which brought them together. Or it could be the fact that David understood not being able to sleep through the entire night without having to get up and piss at least three times. Whatever it was, for the first time ever Ernesto was glad for his company.

The opposing sniper finally settled into position and for a moment Ernesto thought that he had lost him. The sniper was better than good. It alarmed the elderly man that someone from the UN side could be so effective at hunting. As far as he understood it, the UN had neutered all their men long before in the name of equality and higher morals.

He focused his scope on the enemy sniper and saw precisely what he was going to shoot. Now all he needed to do was to wait for David to fire so he could use that to cover his own shot. That should throw off the sensors that the sniper was undoubtedly using.

Nice hat, asshole. A deep breath, exhale, relax the back. A second breath, shallower, even. *Would be a shame if something happened to it...*

The shot, when it came, wasn't what he expected. The "training manequin" he'd stolen from the medics lay prone in the snow, just behind some branches. Zivcovic expected the dummy's head to be blown straight off as he watched for the flash of his opponent's weapon. Instead, the hat, his favorite homemade Serbian army winter pattern camo cap, flew upwards, followed by the sound of the shot. The sniper himself lay two feet to the left, heavily camouflaged in a UN issue heat-dampening arctic suit. Occasionally, he had shoved on the stick that was duct taped to the dummy's torso, to elicit some movement and draw his enemies' attention.

He did see the flash, and a small bit of evaporation coming off the snow where the heat of the shot sublimated it. The hat actually spun up into the air and landed on the snow next to him, and he cursed as he lined up the shot. They had wrecked his hat on purpose, payback for scaring the shit out of them yesterday.

The rifle he used today was a Russian model, not UN issue, firing a sabot-jacketed 4mm tungsten bullet. Accuracy suffered past a thousand meters, but Zivcovic had worked his way inward toward where he thought they would be, favoring the lighter rifle over the ungainly 12mm. Going up against a skilled shooter, he knew that the time of flight of the thumb-sized rounds against an aware target actually gave a sniper, if he saw the shot, time to move. No, today would be close-in work, and he wanted to put an end to it. He could give a shit about the troopers who were killed by the enemy snipers, but he did have to go back to base eventually.

That second shooter might be a problem, but he was probably spotting through a broader angle scope and wouldn't have time to use his own weapon before Zivcovic took him, too. The scope behind the small puff of vapor was masked with cloth, and the face behind it almost completely obscured, but the Serb took up the slack in the trigger and fired. He was rewarded by a small splash of red, before the other man's face disappeared.

The return shot, coming from much higher up, shattered the Serb's rifle, sending pieces of metal into his face. Instead of jumping, or rolling away, despite the enormous pain he felt, Zivcovic, with iron discipline, lay atop his broken weapon, knowing that he was perfectly visible to the second sniper. He let the blood run out onto the snow, and held his breath to short, invisible sighs, directed down into his shirt to avoid creating any mist. He waited for the second shot, to make sure he was dead, and cursed himself for making a mistake. Well, at least he had gotten one of the bastards. When it didn't come, after more than an hour of bleeding onto the snow, he slowly slid himself backwards, deeper into the woods.

"Mother*fucker!*" David hissed as he moved quickly through the thickening trees of the forest. He dared not go back for his brother-in-law's body. Both men had known the risks they were taking when they had set out from the homestead the previous week, and now the Reaper had come to collect the overdue bill.

He had no idea what he was going to tell his wife. It would have been easy to let Ernesto walk away into the snow, freeze his ass off and watch him sulk back to his home divs later. Instead he had helped facilitate it. There was no good reason for it. David had wanted to prove, once and for all, that he was better than Ernesto.

Now Ernesto lay dead somewhere, an enemy sniper was down but possibly not out, and he potentially was on the run. He expected the UN to flood the area with more infantry over the next few days as they looked for him. Worst of all, he knew that Claudia was probably going to kill him over this. *Was it worth it, old man?* he asked himself for the umpteenth time. *Was it really worth it?*

It wasn't.

Reaching the green machine, he pushed the camouflage netting aside and tossed his rifle into the back. Angrily, David slammed shut the hatch. He moved around to the driver's side and paused, hand trembling as he reached for the door handle.

Trembles? Even at his age, his hand never trembled, his nerves were always calm. Three cups of coffee in the morning couldn't even cause this sort of reaction. What was wrong with him?

"Son of a . . ." his whisper trailed off. It shocked him to admit that he felt guilty about his brother-in-law's death. They never liked each other, with David going so far as to think that Ernesto actively hated his guts. He had always enjoyed tweaking the old bastard's nose, especially after he met and started dating Claudia. It had been the cherry on top when he had found out who she was related to. Damn. He actually *liked* Ernesto, in a strange and bizarre way.

Pulling his hand back from the door, he decided that he would continue the hunt. The sniper was definitely wounded—he had seen the blood, though he did not sit around to wait for confirmation—so he probably had a day or two before the next countersniper team was sent out. *Or they quit screwing off and carpet bomb the entire range.*

He checked the overhead cover and saw that it was still secure in place. Camo netting around the green machine in place, he opened the sleeping compartment and pushed his rifle aside. Knees aching, David grabbed the handle on the inside and pulled himself in before closing the hatch. He sighed and rolled onto his back, staring at the roof of the compartment in silent contemplation.

"There's gonna be a reckoning," he promised in a gentle yet firm tone as he drifted off to sleep.

A time of reckoning would have to wait. David needed to piss, and bad.

It was late, but the overhead moon lit the surrounding area nicely. His bladder had woken him up three segs before, and he wandered outside of his white camo netting around the green machine to use the bathroom. Freezing, he tried to make it quick but either the cold or his arthritis prevented that from happening. Annoyed, he waited a few long and cold segs before things remembered how to work properly.

In the distance he heard a hunting howl of a wild animal. Despite the cold winter air, the forest seemed unnaturally alive around him. Bird analogues, normally hibernating at this time of the year, were still out and calling into the darkness. For what, he wasn't sure. David had long experience hunting in these mountains and woods, but never in his life had he ever felt so alone. Perhaps the loss of Ernesto weighed more heavily on him than he realized?

Impossible, he thought as relief was finally had. The worst part was telling his wife that her brother was dead, not simpering over the loss of a rival like Ernesto.

Holding back a sigh of relief, David looked up at the clear sky above. Without cloud cover, the air was especially brisk, though he was thankful that there was no breeze. If there had been, it would have been a fifty/fifty chance of his piss freezing before it hit the ground. He had heard of soldiers on Earth suffering from this at some Goddess-forsaken place called Chosin.

Around him, the nighttime noises of the Grainne wilderness abruptly ceased as a thick tension filled the air. He had just a moment to wonder why before his noncaffeinated brain fully kicked in. There was a predator nearby and there was no way to know precisely what type until it wanted to be seen. The only weapon he had at his disposal was his junk in hand, and unfortunately—or fortunately for his wife—it did not spit lead out at fifteen hundred meters per seg.

A branch cracked somewhere behind him. David stilled his movements as his hands struggled to button his winter pants. *Idiot*, he cursed himself. He had stupidly left his compact subcarbine in the rear compartment, sleep and sadness causing him to make a sloppy mistake. He did have his Bowie knife on him. However, anything that hunted in these woods in the night would make short work of the foot-long blade. Besides, like many elderly men, he was not one for hand-to-hand combat.

"Hello." A soft voice carried on the still air. There was a decided accent in the speaker's voice which David recognized as one being from Earth. "I've been looking for you."

Well, fuck.

"Put your dick away before it freezes off. Even at your age, I expect that you still value it." Zivcovic smirked a bit at the look on the man's face but held his pistol rock steady as the old man buttoned up his coveralls, alert to any sudden movements.

"Can I put my hands down?" the Freeholder asked, having resumed his position of surrender.

"In a minute, maybe. We shall talk first." The Serb looked at the man closely, then said, "Yes, I know you! Archuleta!"

"What?" This revelation startled the retired FMF sniper.

"Yes! You are David Archuleta. I watched on holo as a boy, the matches. There is no such competition on Earth, and I wanted to come here to participate, eventually. Then I was too busy sniping those Muslim devils. Tell me, who was it that I killed?"

"My brother-in-law, Ernesto," said David, miserably. He knew he was about to die and was still worried more about informing his wife that her brother was dead.

"Ernesto Silang? Him who was always second best to you in the matches?"

"Only second best because I let him win all the time," a soft whisper floated across the frigid open space. The ripple down his spine to his fingertips was colder than the night air.

Zivcovic heard the flick of a safety being taken off, but didn't take his gun off his prisoner, merely said quietly, "I guess that gust of wind was stronger than I thought, I couldn't be sure. Always a problem with those light rounds, even with the sabot. How much did I miss by?"

"You took off my ear. I should shoot you just for that second-place comment, you son of a bitch. Never mind the ear." The voice came from the trees just past the small vehicle. The speaker continued, "If you call me One-eared Ernie I will shoot your balls off, David."

"You should shoot him now, Ernie," David called out into the darkness, ignoring the not-so-veiled threat. His eyes never left Zivcovic. "You've got him dead to rights."

"I should let him plug you once, just to even the score."

"You're the one who wanted to play bait. Well, guess what, old man? Sometimes the bait gets swallowed."

Zivcovic interrupted their banter. "I could have shot you the first time, either of you. We have learned that there is a difference between the range and the field. Who now is the winner?" The pistol in his hand never wavered, even when David slowly lowered his tired arms. "You can shoot me, but I will kill him before I die. Then you have to go home and explain this to his wife. I think you will be the biggest loser out of all of us! There are some things worse than death."

"What do you mean?" asked the voice.

"Hell is an angry woman. Ask me how I know."

David actually laughed, and said, "He's got you there, Ernesto. You know what Claudia is like. Go ahead, Captain . . ."

"Zivcovic."

"Captain Zivcovic. Shoot me, I'd rather die and watch him get a beatdown from the afterlife. That would just be me winning one more time."

"Kiss my ass, David," said the voice in the darkness.

Zivcovic actually smiled. He *liked* these two old bastards. It was going to be a pity to kill them both, though he doubted he would survive the shootout. Perhaps there was a better way. After all, what did he owe the UN? Nothing. Still holding the pistol at David's face, he said, "I have a proposition for you Freeholders."

"Put the gun down and we'll talk," said Ernesto from the woods.

"No, you come out and we will talk," said Zivcovic. "Keep your gun on me, if you want, I will kill your friend though if you try anything."

"Friend, my ass," came the steady and measured reply, but then he stepped into view, carrying a Merrill assault rifle. A bandage was wrapped around his head, and blood stained the front of his winter coveralls. The barrel was pointed at Zivcovic but the Serb remained unperturbed. Everyone knew how the next few moments would play out if someone took a shot. It was amazing how the accepted fact did not change any of their attitudes. "Talk, aardvark. What do you want?"

"Isn't it obvious?" Zivcovic asked, and smirked. "I am claiming asylum from political persecution."

"What?" David asked. There was confusion and disbelief in his tone. "Join . . . us?"

"That is what I said, no? You are both excellent snipers, even in your old age. I think, though, that I have a thing or two to teach you."

"Why would you kill your own people?" Ernesto asked in a cautious voice. He had heard of men switching allegiances during war for various reasons, but he wondered what drove this killer to do so. It wasn't remorse, that was for damn sure. One look into those cold eyes told him that regret and repentance was the last thing on this man's mind.

"My people? Those are not my people, those socialist shitheads," Zivcovic laughed and continued. "I am Serb, I am a free man, but that has caused me much trouble. I used to be lieutenant colonel, in charge of sniper school. I lost my rank beating shit out of a private for no respect."

"So just like that?" said Ernesto.

The man shrugged, still not lowering his pistol, "Yes. As I said, I am a free man. Plus, there is good hunting here, no? I have always wanted to try my knife against your Ripper animal."

David and Ernesto looked at each other, exchanging a silent message. In essence, this guy was a nut. And it was goddamned cold out, though that didn't seem to affect their enemy. The icy chill of the nighttime air made the decision rather easy.

"Fuck it." Ernesto shrugged after a pregnant pause. He lowered his rifle and gave his brother-in-law a look, nodding in acceptance.

Zivcovic holstered his pistol, then smiled in understanding when Ernesto raised the rifle again. "There's lots of ways to be the best, Captain Zivcovic," said the Freeholder. "Winner is always last man standing."

"Of course," the Serb agreed as he held up a flat palm, indicating for the man to not shoot him. He then slowly pulled a small device from his pocket. Both David and Ernesto could see the glowing red light on the top of it from where they each stood. Zivcovic waggled it in the air. "This is a remote detonator. It's tied in to my heartbeat. You shoot me, and it blows up, and will kill whoever survives because your vehicle will be in pieces. You take me as prisoner, let me kill UN dogs with you, we all live."

"Oh Goddess," David grumbled. "Fucking aardvark."

"Damn, you're a clever man," Ernesto allowed as he lowered his rifle slightly. "You brought a bomb to a gunfight."

"I try." Zivcovic shrugged.

"The only problem with your plan is we figured out you were a sneaky little fucker early on," Ernesto continued as he tossed a small device, no bigger than a grenade, onto the ground at Zivcovic's feet. "So of course, I checked the green machine over before I said anything."

"*Jebote,*" the Serb muttered under his breath. "I hid bomb well!"

"Not well enough." David chuckled. "Good job, Ernesto."

"What do we do with him now?" the old sniper asked his brother-in-law.

"No idea," David admitted. "Can't let him go. He'll get lucky and snipe one of us eventually. I have no problem killing him."

"Eh, what a waste of a good sniper though," Ernesto pointed out to him. "He could have killed you but wanted to talk. I think he's serious about joining our side."

"I am," Zivcovic proclaimed.

"Zip it, aardvark," David said. He turned his attention back to Ernesto. "What're you thinking? Three klicks?"

"Three and a half," Ernesto stated after a moment's contemplation. "That'll prove his mettle."

"What are you talking about?" Zivcovic asked as the two older men's grins became feral.

United Nations FOB Boutros, Dragontooth Mountains

The two-man guard duty at the forward operating base's front gate was something of a joke now, ever since the snipers stopped being a problem two days prior. It had taken almost an entire company of an armored convoy to put the sniper down but when the surviving officers returned, their operation was declared a success. Later scans had proven this claim, as reconnaissance drones flying overhead never picked up a sign of anything larger than small game animal heat signatures. It was mission accomplished for all involved.

Thus, it came as a bit of a surprise when the first guard's head was removed at precisely 1759 hours, exactly a minute away from the scheduled shift change. There was a brief moment of panic from the surviving gate guard before he managed to slap the base's general alarm, which stirred up the hornet's nest and activated the entire base into emergency lockdown.

It was later determined the shot came from a presumed-lost 12mm UN-issued sniper rifle, which caused some discomfort amongst the senior officers of the base. The officer in charge of the hunt for the snipers had *seen* Captain Zivcovic die on his scanners when the insurgent sniper took him out. How, then, had his weapon ended up in enemy hands? And who had taken the shot, which was determined to have been from roughly 3.5 kilometers away?

It would go down as one of the more mysterious moments of the war.

Fire in the Deep, Angel on the Wind

Christopher DiNote and Philip Wohlrab

1.

Go time.

Colonel Shaun "Mojo" Harvey took a breath, spoke into the mic, and his words were converted simultaneously into text and machine-to-machine instructions throughout the UN forces. "Three, two, one, time hack 0203 Terra-Zulu, time to go, push defensive counter aerospace."

Instantly, his screens showed a dozen Sentinel fighters flow from their racetrack-shaped holding patterns high above their home airfields and leap across the skies of Grainne. They looked high and low for any rebel air-to-air or space-to-atmosphere surprises. For the pilots, this mission seemed wasteful, and as procedural as a training sim. While doctrine called for constant air superiority sweeps, the UN had done a very thorough job of destroying Grainne's limited aerospace capabilities during the initial strike. Still, there were many colonial spacecraft unaccounted for, and the colonials had proven themselves to be obnoxiously resourceful. For all the UN's vaunted intelligence capabilities, the colonials could still have entire fighter squadrons stashed away underground somewhere, just waiting for the UN to get complacent. Hence, the very well-armed if also very underutilized aerospace superiority fighters converted millions of credits worth of fuel into noise.

Meanwhile, an equal dozen Avatar multirole fighters, loaded down with air-to-surface weapons and electronic warfare packages,

271

scoured the surface. They hunted the rare but still occasionally active rebel surface-to-air missiles, and the much less rare and always active anti-aircraft gun-trucks. If any pointy-nosed aircrew were going to get some action today, the Avatar drivers were it, and of course they would earn the glory as well. However, their success and survival belonged to Mojo.

He sat back in his chair at the MOB Unity Peacekeeping Combined Aerospace Operations Center, nicknamed the "Peacock," and watched his screens intently, waiting for first contact with the enemy. He listened to the latest orders update recording for the umpteenth time. He'd been briefed on Operation KESTREL HARVEST exhaustively. Repeatedly. In fact, he could quote the briefing in his sleep. KESTREL HARVEST, the UN's "midspring offensive," was a "sequel" of Operation MIDNIGHT KESTREL, the UN's overarching plan for the occupation and reintegration of Grainne colony.

He began his practiced scan technique across the sector sensor feeds. The depiction of each battlespace awash in various colors and alphanumeric data codes indicated smooth but slow going so far. The plan called for a massive sweep across the Plains District of Grainne, with the intent to flush out the insurgents, as well their official military special ops enablers, into open battle where the peacekeepers could defeat them in detail. At least that was the theory as of 0205 Terra-Zulu. After several months of trying, aerospace operations had given up on converting to local time standards and reverted back to Earth Universal Time. It didn't seem to help anyone's circadian rhythms, but they all enthusiastically ditched the locally procured timepieces which had proven susceptible to hacking.

Mojo cycled through the few sporadic fights that had already broken out, and synthetic audio recreated the sound, direction, and intensity of makeshift anti-aircraft weapons targeting "his" platforms. Thankfully, the demand for aerospace support was manageable. As the first night's Senior Aerospace Duty Officer, the "Aero," his job was to assess the need, assign a priority, re-task an asset if required, nod smartly for the debrief camera recording him, then "hmmm" into the mic, swipe "approved" or "disapproved," and keep his boss, Brigadier General Nigel "Adder" Blumly, appraised. Mojo welcomed the little bits of action; they kept him sharp and mentally engaged.

"LYNX 1-1, control released to your own discretion."

"One-one copies." The flight lead of an Avatar four-ship acknowledged Mojo's call, nonchalantly tipped his left wing in a steep, slicing bank and popped a dozen flares, defending against a probable man-portable missile that didn't even track on him or any of his flightmates. After the obligatory strafing run, the hubbub quieted quickly, so it was a good time for Mojo to catch a break. He'd really overdone it on coffee this morning, a bad habit he picked up years ago from the Americans, who apparently ran on the horrid stuff.

"OR-A-CLE." Mojo liked to drag out the syllables of his usual Senior Intelligence Duty Officer's callsign. It annoyed the hell out of the extremely twitchy Intel lead, NorthAm Lieutenant Colonel Ryan Fitzpatrick. Almost no one called him "Oracle." Instead they liked to use "Fizz," which Fitzpatrick hated with a passion.

"Mojo, Oracle here. What's up?"

"You have my station. I need a bio break."

"Roger, Oracle has it."

Mojo made a show of exiting the ops floor and made a beeline to the prefab gender-neutral facilities, whose basic design had not changed much over hundreds of years. He unzipped his flight suit but felt a slight vibration against his leg. *Oh, not now.* From a near-skintight inseam pocket, he withdrew a highly specialized, handcrafted data stick, one that required a thumb prick and blood sample to access and decrypt transmissions. Unlocking procedure complete, he pulled up the coded message displayed just for him.

"ORME OVERRUN. EMER CASEVAC SURVIVORS. EXFIL MI6-00 ASSET TO FOB WTRLOO."

Oh shit. There goes the planet. Mojo's day was about to get interesting after all. He hated "interesting."

2.

Specialist Molly Aujla went to ground beside a Badger that miraculously wasn't on fire, making it one of the few. Instead, the vehicle had been turned into Swiss cheese by an autocannon, and the engine compartment smoked. Beside her were two of the Irish soldiers she was tasked to support.

"Sergeant Owens, we have got to get out of here!" shouted Private Keene.

"I know that, Private, but you do see that we are under sustained artillery fire, correct?"

At least the private was asking to run, not like the others. I wonder what the sergeant's plan is, wondered Molly.

Sergeant First Class Owens grabbed the private and shoved him forcibly behind the smoking Badger. The cold, early spring damp that chilled her evaporated in the sudden heat of combat. He then motioned to Molly and two other privates near her to move to his location. She began to inch back to him, dragging her aid bag when Private First Class MacNulty was struck in the face by a bullet. MacNulty tried to scream, but half his face had been blown away. Molly got up briefly, for once thankful that the UN made her wear the bloody Red Cross brassard on her left arm and plastered it all over her helmet. So far, the insurgents had never directly targeted her, but artillery didn't discriminate.

She grabbed MacNulty's harness in one hand, and in her other she hauled her aid bag. At a hundred and fifty-eight centimeters tall, she didn't look large enough to pull the trooper, but looks were deceiving. She worked hard to be prepared for situations like this, which made her uncommon compared to many of her compatriots. She was in excellent shape; Owens went so far as to call her a "PT beast," and she had acclimated well to the higher local gravity. Molly was still winded by the time she got MacNulty back behind "her" Badger and began to work on stabilizing the wounded private. She carefully wrapped what was left of his jaw in place with some sterile gauze, applied clotting foam, and then cleared a lot of that away to ensure that his undamaged nasal airways were clear. She then inserted a nasal-pharyngeal airway to keep air flowing and then administered a mild painkiller via autoinjector. Not so much to sedate him, but to hopefully keep him from completely losing it to panic and shock. Somehow, over the din of combat, her instinct demanded that she look up.

A Grainnean rebel stared back. His mismatched uniform was drenched in blood, but his nametag remained readable, and proclaimed him as "Hanrahan."

Molly yelled in surprise. "Well fuck me, of all the . . . a fucking Irish."

The rebel Hanrahan's face was covered in dust and debris, his headgear lost, and his back propped up against the side of the Badger, legs splayed out in front of him. His eyes were unfocused, but his lips moved as he tried to speak, a bubble of foamy, bloody spittle popping on his lips. He held a pistol in his left hand, and his right, well, his right hand was missing, as was much of his right forearm. By Hanrahan's left leg, an autoinjector lay on the ground, the needle point bent.

Molly swore to herself, "Goddammit." Nevertheless, she checked MacNulty one more time, broke out one of her few remaining slap-tourniquets, and started to treat the Grainnean. Thankfully, the moist environment didn't affect the adhesive the way she feared it would.

Almost immediately, another wounded Irish soldier was dropped beside her, and then another. The battle raged around Molly Aujla but she couldn't care less; her battle was with death itself, and she worked furiously to save the lives of the soldiers under her care, friend and foe no matter.

"Specialist...DOC...DOC!"

"What?" asked Molly in an exasperated tone, only then she realized she was talking to S1C Owens.

"What is the situation on the wounded?"

Molly took a moment to compose her thoughts before responding, voice dry and steady.

"I have three urgent surgical cases, one urgent ambulatory, and three more priority ambulatory wounded. We need to get those two cases out of here now." She pointed to two of the Irish soldiers that were lying a little too quietly. MacNulty, thankfully, was breathing, but his breath came hard and wheezing. Molly spoke softly to him as she worked on him, to try and calm him, also to get him to relax the incredible grip he had on her arm. "And...one enemy urgent surgical, amputated right arm, tourniquet time stamp...shite, I don't know local time!"

"A rebel? Fuck him, let him bleed!"

"I can't do that."

"Worry about our people, Specialist!" Owens shouted at her, sounding incredulous that she'd waste valuable supplies on the enemy.

"He's my patient now, Sergeant! I *will not* abandon him to die out here!"

Molly stared at Owens, daring him to challenge her.

"Understood, I will get the call out," replied Owens.

3.

Things had gotten blissfully boring over the last couple of hours. The intel feeds were full of idle chatter, like "Hey is this really a 'sequel plan,' or a 'branch plan'?" Fizz finally had enough and reprimanded the talkative analysts, reminding them that *everything* in the chatrooms, over open voice, keystrokes, everything was recorded for debrief and disciplinary action. Not to mention the enemy hackers were sorcerers. Some of the most surprising intel leaked from the most secure channels.

Of course, Fizz's reverie, really his daydreaming, was then rudely interrupted by a nagging beeping sound. He tapped the icon, and a wall of block text visible only to him appeared smartly: "WARNING: SPECIAL PEACEKEEPING OPERATIONS" greeted him. *Lovely*, barely stopping himself from saying it out loud. If that had slipped out, he would never hear the end of it when it came time to debrief today's work. The icon sat on top of a blacked-out, irregularly shaped blob of surface-to-infinity-restricted air space. It was the Plains, around the otherwise useless and insignificant town of Orme. *There's a pretty big logistics base out there*, he reminded himself, *with a badly hidden, completely obvious Special Peacekeeping Operations Task Force compound right in the middle of the damn place.*

He knew nothing good could come from this, since the special ops task force was currently led officially by Earth Russian Spetsnaz. In actuality, they were mostly Novaya Rossiyan "contractors" with a shit-ton of attachments from all over Federal Europe and the British Union. Access to their area of operations, including the Orme Logistics Support Area, was restricted to certain briefed personnel and units only. No open feeds. No intel craft cleared to operate there. No satellite passes overhead. No conventional air or ground allowed in or out without special coordination first. Meaning, no one had the slightest idea what was going on in there and hadn't for weeks. Everyone knew, though, that if the Russkies were involved, you were better off *not* knowing what was going on in that chunk of Grainne roughly the size and shape of Belgium.

Scrolling text, video, and electro-optical stills filled Fizz's screens, showing mass carnage both in and around the logistics base. The stay-behind TOC-roaches and REMFs were getting slaughtered. *I don't think I'm supposed to see this*, again thankful he didn't say that out loud. Fizz realized that Mojo had been in such a hurry, that when he transferred control to him, the fool hadn't set the retinal scan "for your eyes only" screen security lock.

"Fizz, Mojo is back, and I have the stick," Harvey sounded off as he marched back to his command chair. He didn't even bother with the polite pretense of saying "Oracle."

Oh shit. "Mojo, all yours." Fizz backed out of Mojo's shared screen, but not quite fast enough.

Mojo slid into his screen and realized his mistake very quickly. "What were you doing..." *FUCK! I didn't put my retinal lock on the damn feed!* "Fizz, what did you see?"

The North American gave Mojo a hard look, and Mojo shook his head to say, *You don't want any part of this, trust me.*

Before, the conversation progressed further, Adder broke in abruptly. "Major Kournikov, Mojo, in my office, now please," Adder boomed across the main Ops Floor channel. This caught everyone on the floor's attention, the desired effect. Idle chatter ceased; headsets came off, and faces turned. Screens collapsed as technician eyes turned towards the trim, dark-haired British officer, and then towards an obviously peeved Russian "liaison."

Harvey and the lithe special operations major silently stood up from their chairs and walked purposefully toward Adder's office.

When securely inside, Adder loudly greeted them while still inside his private bathroom and asked them to sit down in front of his desk while he finished up, but the Russian continued to stand. Kournikov had his arms folded, and made his displeasure known. "What do you want?" No customs or courtesies. Mojo was appalled by the Russian's uncouthness.

Mojo wasn't about to let him get away with that. "Your little outpost buried inside the Orme base isn't doing so well, is it?" He stifled a smirk but let a little posh sneak through.

"Fuck you." The Russian turned to leave.

"Your whole contingent out there is dead. There are some Irish and British survivors, support troops mainly. There isn't one Spetsnaz survivor. The insurgents are very thorough. Sword thrusts; you've seen some of the imagery of course? You kept us all in the dark while you've been off killing civilians for fun, in addition to occasionally killing guerillas and running a nasty little black market with some of the quartermasters. Very bad form."

"That's enough, Mojo!" barked Adder, now in view but still buttoning himself up. "You." He pointed at the Russian, "Out. I already heard everything I need to hear from you. Get out of my Ops Center, and off my planet within twenty-four hours."

Without so much as a word or acknowledgement, the Russian left.

Adder turned to Mojo. "Now, I received an encrypted message, directed my eyes only, to call you in here and discuss a new tasking, let's get on with it!"

Mojo said, "We need to put an immediate aero casualty evacuation mission into Orme, sir."

"What in the fucking hell do you mean, I'm going to direct a CASEVAC into the middle of that ass-fucked AO?" Adder finished buckling his belt, and in a practiced pinch, singlehandedly buttoned his entire blouse without missing a button, his beret now neatly tucked under the right epaulet in a croissant roll.

"Home Office directs, sir. There are survivors in the base, and a special asset near the Russian compound. We are to recover them, forthwith, and move the asset to FOB Waterloo in the Hinterlands."

"Forthwith? Why not reinforce Orme, repulse the attack?"

"Well, Home Office seems to feel that the Russkies can 'get fucked,' as the saying goes."

Adder slumped. "Not that I'm particularly bothered. Right, then. I saw the codes. I saw the messages. Maddie Kornberg confirmed them."

Mojo smiled at that last bit. When Adder retired to his office behind the Battle Cab after the morning commander's update briefing, everyone on the ops floor pretended not to notice that his only company was a rather lovely officer known to be from the inspector general's office. *Gives a whole new meaning to the phrase "you may not love the fucking IG, but the IG sure loves fucking you,"* Mojo thought, not at all in line with the latest human relations training standards.

His poker face dropped into a sullen frown for the remainder of the conversation. The Irish were still steaming over the Russian "hostile takeover," but they had doubled-down on maintaining their troops and operational control of Orme. They couldn't endure the loss of standing (and funding), in both MilBu and GenAssem that a full withdrawal would spark. The political cost for Sinn Fein's fragile coalition government was too steep for them to walk away.

What Mojo really didn't like though, was how this mess also sucked in a contingent of British advisors, mostly medical but also a very deeply, quietly, and exquisitely concealed intelligence asset. This part of his mission briefing took place in Adder's office three nights ago. Adder made it clear, that while the British Union maintained a close relationship with the European Federal Union, in practice this fell well short of full integration. The Protectorate kept the continent in the dark when it came to certain intelligence activities, mainly British "incidental" spying on their European "partners," only because it couldn't be really helped you know, old boy? Absolutely unavoidable, of course.

Mojo laid out his plan, it wasn't much of one, given the paucity of assets nearby due to all the restrictions on the Spetsnaz area. "There's one Werewolf gunship out on the hunt, and a lifter well within earshot of him. The last of the insurgent anti-air gunners seem to be accounted for."

"Seem? Seem? Mojo, you'd better be right about this. Our little Home Office asset boosted a signal that the Russkies don't know is compromised, and I guarantee you Kournikov suspects something."

"Nothing's certain, sir. Orme, if you'll excuse the North American patois, is a 'shit show.' We need to pull certain assets home, because this fight is lost, we're conclusively fucked and far from home, and we're better off planning for the cleanup than trying to stop it."

Neither officer looked at each other, and both fell silent, but they didn't get much chance for contemplation.

"Adder, Sir," Fizz's voice broke up the conversation, "we have a CASEVAC request in-vicinity-of a spec ops compound, Plains."

"Bollocks."

4.

"Bad news, Specialist! We don't have a CASEVAC asset close by. We have to move to an alternative site for evac." Sergeant Owen's voice was brittle as he relayed the news to Molly.

Molly was more focused on doing what she could for Private Second-Class Oliver, one of her fellow Brits, than on what Sergeant

Owens was saying for it to register at first. She finished getting an artery to stop bleeding out before she bothered to look up at Sergeant Owens. Her face was splashed with Oliver's blood, so she did not notice that when she wiped her brow, her sleeve deposited another smear of it just under the brow of her helmet. The misty air caused the blood to bead and drip down her face, but she ignored that too. If she could just get a little more time, she was sure Oliver and MacNulty were savable.

"What's that, Sergeant?" she enquired.

"We have to move the wounded out on foot. The Badgers are all shot to hell and none of the Eels survived. It seems like the insurgents are leaving us alone for now, and from what I can tell they are pushing their final assault in on the Spetsnaz compound. We need to move now before they turn their attention back to us!"

Molly looked down at Private Oliver assessing whether he would survive being moved. Then she looked around at the others. Sergeant Owens had managed to rally a total of twelve Irish Peacekeepers, not including the seven wounded soldiers at her makeshift casualty collection point. Her supplies were running low, and she only had two-fold-out litters scavenged from the Badgers that were not burning.

"We don't have enough litters for all the wounded, we will need to make two improvised litters for those that can't walk. We are going to be moving slowly, Sergeant. Do you think the rebels will leave us alone for that long? Should we not see if they will let us surrender?"

Sergeant Owens looked for a long moment at one of the burning farmhouses, and his gaze found the smoldering remains of burned bodies. Then he looked back at Molly and gestured in the direction he had been gazing.

"Look Spec, given what the Russians have done out here, I doubt the rebels will take prisoners, and given the screaming going on back there, they are butchering the Spetsnaz where they find them."

"You're right," Hanrahan croaked from his spot behind the Badger. He coughed, cleared his throat, and tried again. "You're right, we won't take prisoners. If they see you, they'll kill you where you stand."

Molly spoke. "What do you mean 'if'?"

"I mean I know a path out to your clearing that's not typically monitored. I can lead you through."

Owens sounded skeptical. "Why would you help us? Why should we trust you? You could have an ambush waiting to finish us off just inside the treeline."

Hanrahan shrugged painfully. "Because she helped me. She could have let me bleed out, but she didn't." He winced and gritted through his teeth. "What choice do you have, Sergeant? Besides, we're all Irish here, most of us? I think that should count for something."

Owens's voice had a tinge of disgust. "I'm from fucking Birmingham, me and Oliver there." He put on his command voice. "We will move out. Alright, Troopers, get those litters rigged, follow Hanrahan here's directions, we will exfil this area through the bush and run parallel to the river. There is a clearing between here and there, about seven klicks away that we will use for a Dustoff flight once a resource is freed up."

Molly and the surviving Peacekeepers hurried to implement Sergeant Owens's orders, thankful to not be under missile fire. The rebels absolutely loved fire-and-forget missiles with self-guiding terminal seekers, as well as good-ol' fashioned unguided rockets fired by simple count-down timers. The peacekeepers moved cautiously to gather supplies for improvised litters. It took them a few minutes to rig up a pair out of uniform jackets and nearby branches that had been brought down by the barrage. Their clothing as well as the wood were made slippery in the soft and quiet rain that had come upon them unannounced. In the distance they heard a snarling cry from one of Grainne's many predators, but none of the troops paid it much mind.

5.

Mojo was in Adder's office for a long time. He saw that Fizz tagged the CASEVAC request and sent it direct to Adder's station. The sheer complexity of the whole operation turned his stomach into a giant knot, and he wondered how they would execute their new miniature "war inside of a war."

There was a lot at stake here. All over the Plains, UN forces advanced: clearing, fixing, tracking, engaging, and destroying. About three-quarters of all available UN aerospace in the Iota Persei system focused on an expanse the size of the Canadian Shield, and about as hospitable and underpopulated. The freshly rebuilt MOB Unity Operations Center was the primary command and control node, but the operation required forces scattered all throughout the system. It required technicians onboard Skywheel 2, the Combat Information Center of the cruiser *Montevideo,* and three gigantic, hypersonic, near-orbit command aerospacecraft whose sensor and transmitter footprint covered the whole of Grainne. However, the very real fear that the colonials had successfully compromised at least some part of the UN's secured networks meant that things ran slower in reality than in doctrine and exercises. Not a little bit slower, but much, much slower, as manual checking and live two-person integrity were the norm once again.

Mojo finally convinced Adder to concur with his plan, really the best course of action they could manage, and pinged Fizz on the Ops Floor.

"Fizz. FIZZ!"

"Go for Intel!" Fizz stuttered, as Mojo caught him completely off guard and distracted.

Mojo went into full business mode, his usual sardonic wit completely absent. "I'm coming back down, standby for words."

Adder boomed in both their headsets. "Aero, Intel. Execute the CASEVAC, and they'll need overwatch. All special ops protocols around Orme have been removed, you'll have full access to everything. Prepare to receive the databurst with the info and get them some intel top cover overhead."

Sliding into his chair, Mojo pinged his enlisted data technician, "Get me a freq and something resembling a command element somewhere on the ground. Who called in the CASEVAC request?"

A headshot and bio file appeared right in front of him of an Irish peacekeeper NCO named Owens. *Well, hopefully it's actually him,* Mojo prayed, as this data was coming straight from "body beacon" files which were supposed to be refreshed every ten seconds, when the rebels weren't fucking with every data source they could touch. *Let's give it a try.* Owens came up on the radio as "GEESE 1-7," indicating that he was a platoon sergeant. *Wow, the whole chain of command down there must be dead and gone already.*

Mojo kept his voice steady. "GEESE 1-7, GEESE 1-7, copy CASEVAC request. We're working something up now." And very quickly, Mojo pinged the closest vertol with passenger capacity.

Ah, here we go, TROIKA 1-1, conventional forces Russian trash hauler. God, I hope she's up to this.

"TROIKA 1-1, TROIKA 1-1, this is Aero, standby to copy priority CASEVAC request." Mojo's transmission automatically "grabbed" TROIKA's cockpit videofeed, and greeted him with the sight of an expressionless, combat-sealed helmet and oxygen mask combination. The visor slid up and revealed an ice-blue set of eyes and blonde eyebrows. She briefly looked at the camera before her visor closed again, and she acknowledged Mojo's comms.

Lieutenant First Class Lyudmila "Wyvern" Vladimirovna shook her head and gave control to her copilot. "Aero, this is TROIKA 1-1, say again?"

"TROIKA 1-1, this is Aero, you are now DUSTOFF 3-1, prepare to receive databurst."

Oh shit, this is real. "DUSTOFF 3-1 is ready to copy." Wyvern acknowledged the request and clicked on her electronic kneeboard, which translated the databurst and displayed it on her heads-up display:

LINE 1: Landing Zone grid location: 10SGJ0683244683 (accompanied by a small map)

LINE 2: Comms: 106.3 MHz, Darjeeling, GEESE 1-7 (authenticated)

LINE 3: Number of patients by precedence: 5 Urgent Surgical, 3 Priority (AMPUTATION)

LINE 4: Special equipment: Ventilator, Resupply, 2 Litters

LINE 5: Number of patients: 3 Litter, 5 Ambulatories

LINE 6: Security at pick-up site; enemy infantry in area, escort required

LINE 7: Method of marking: Infrared panels

LINE 8: Patient nationality and status: 7 military, UN; 1 lawful combatant, colonial

LINE 9: Negative CBRN-E contamination: chems, bios, radiologicals, nukes, or EMP.

Wait. This is odd. Orme? Her trash runs never took her by there, but Unity had another surprise for her.

"Your escort is DRAKUN 2-6, also now mission commander, check-in when able." Wyvern's datalink was suddenly awash in icons and intelligence pings she'd never seen before.

DRAKUN? A Werewolf? This can't be good. The databurst made it clear things were bad inside the special ops "container" as she and all the other conventional aircrew called it, but now her instincts screamed at her, *get out*, which she couldn't, and in fact, wouldn't have, even if she could.

"Aero, DUSTOFF 3-1 copies all." She clicked over to inter-plane direct comms. "DRAKUN, what do you have for me?"

6.

Fizz swallowed hard as the new DUSTOFF ended her radio call. Something really bothered him. He and the other intel geeks had started to suspect that something was seriously wrong with UN sensor data and automated analysis algorithms weeks ago, but, lacking any hard evidence, that assessment received an official cold shoulder from the chain of command. Most of it. Mojo seemed more willing than most to consider it, but he wasn't high enough in the food chain to make much difference.

Ah goddamn fucking stupid fucking piece of junk! Fizz ripped his headset off, clasped his whole left hand over the minicam bud on his collar, spun around, and dug his right hand's fingertips into his temple.

"Alright, alright, alright. Let's think here." The relevant point, right now, was that the lockdown protocols were removed and special ops was actually sharing something useful, so he could see the IR signatures of the mobile survivors and also the wounded. The ever-present spring rain caused tons of problems with IR, but today was better than most. There were precious few survivors overall, from all sides of the fight, but he could also...maybe... just make out some "shadows" in other sensor bands, maybe they were false hits, but they seemed to be moving across the main engagement area, and...

"Oh no. Oh, dear God no." Fizz smashed the comm button. "MOJO! INTEL!"

"Go?"

"You need to look at this, NOW." Fizz shared his live feed to Mojo's station.

"What the hell...what's happening?" Mojo stared, then flipped his screen from false color to black-on-white infrared. Incredibly, the huddled and prone black-white silhouettes fidgeted, spasmed, and splashes of liquid white exploded and washed out his screen. He flipped back to color, briefly saw a "shimmer," and heard Fizz cry out.

"It's the wildlife!"

Mojo hammered down his switch and overrode every other transmission on the net. "GEESE 1-7, you need to get moving, immediately!"

7.

The screams changed in tenor behind them. Molly was pretty sure she heard two different screams, one an animal's, the other, human. She quickly put that aside when Private Oliver rolled his head to one side and threw up a great gout of blood. Molly moved from MacNulty's litter to Oliver's improvised one, almost slipping on the slick ground, and instructed the two peacekeepers carrying him to put him down. She was pretty sure she had found all of Oliver's injuries but throwing up blood was a very bad sign and so she double-checked her interventions. Sergeant Owens moved up beside her.

"We have to keep moving!"

"I understand that, Sergeant, but if we keep moving, Oliver is going to die. Let me try to stabilize him," Molly hissed through gritted teeth.

"We don't have time. Higher is telling us there are things out here that will eat us. We have to get to the clearing for DUSTOFF."

"I can't let him die," Molly replied exasperatedly.

Owens's voice was cold and hard as he said, "Specialist Aujla, if we are to make rendezvous and survive, we have to keep moving. Do what you can for him but do it on the move. Let's go, people."

Hanrahan weakly grabbed a litter pole with his remaining hand. He met Molly's gaze before scanning the forest again.

"He's right," he said urgently. "We have to keep moving. If we stop now, we all die."

Sergeant Owens motioned to the two peacekeepers on the ends of the improvised litter to pick him up and keep moving. Molly fumed, but even through her anger she realized there wasn't much more she could do for Oliver; he was just too badly injured for what supplies she had on hand. *Maybe if those bastards had sent me to Sergeant's Q-Course, I could do more.* Molly sighed. She theoretically knew how to do a chest tube, but had never been taught, as that level of care was deemed to be beyond that of a junior NCO. *The Americans probably trust their field medics to do this,* she seethed. She knew the rebel military did.

That's when she heard the human scream again.

The ragtag group of Irish and British peacekeepers pressed on, while Sergeant Owens kept radio contact with a flyer. The light rain finally stopped. After an hour, the band came upon the clearing and Owens directed three of the Irish to set up an impromptu landing zone. No sooner had the panels been set, they heard the unmistakable howl of an inbound vertol.

Molly looked up as the craft banked over the clearing. She thought she could make out the pilot looking down at them, but it passed out of sight. She heard the machine's engines change pitch, and it reappeared. The big buglike machine was a Russian job, its distinctive paint job and a red star edged in yellow proclaiming such. It hovered another moment over the clearing before the engines changed tone and the machine touched down. The engines ran while the side doors opened, and a man motioned for the soldiers to stay put. He spoke into his comms before disconnecting his helmet from a line to the aircraft and jumped down to the ground. The flight engineer walked over to Sergeant Owens to deliver what Molly assumed were instructions. Nodding, Sergeant Owens ran to stage his people.

"Okay listen up! We're loading the litters first with Specialist Aujla, then the other wounded. The rest of us will cover overlapping sectors of fire as we load up behind them. I will board last. Everyone understand?"

"YES, SERGEANT," the group chorused.

"Good, let's move out! And you!" he said, pointing at Hanrahan, "you're sticking right next to me where I can see you!"

The team picked up the litters while the flight engineer directed them to load and in what order. The vertol engines were deafening, and Molly was sure she was going to have hearing loss, but she could deal with that later. She moved out with the last litter team, the one carrying Oliver. The man was somehow still breathing, but Molly wasn't sure he would be for much longer. As the team approached the bird, she could feel the thrum of the engines in her chest, but then she was inside the vertol and donning a headset. She caught the pilot's instructions to her mid-stream.

"... And medic, this is not a MEDEVAC ship, but I do have a large first-aid kit beside the flight engineer's station. If you need more supplies feel free to use them," the female pilot said over the internal comms.

"Thank you, Ma'am," replied Molly.

Molly was grateful as she had used up most of the supplies in her aid bag. She moved forward and expected to see a small kit. Instead, it was a rather large bag that looked similar to an Army folding litter kit. She wasn't sure though, as she couldn't make out the Cyrillic letters on the bag. Molly opened pouches at random on the outside of the bag and found various types of field dressings and airway kits. Opening the main compartment, she found the suspected folding litter. She motioned to a pair of soldiers nearby to help her unfold the litter, then transferred Oliver to it from the improvised one they were using. After doing that, she finished securing him to the deck of the vertol with the assistance of the flight engineer. After finishing with Oliver, she helped secure MacNulty's litter as well. Molly and the flight engineer then jury-rigged an inner seat harness such that Hanrahan could sit up securely but without much weight on his wounded arm. It still couldn't be comfortable for him, not by a mile.

"Pilot, everyone's loaded," called out the flight engineer.

Molly felt her stomach lurch as the vertol lifted straight up at speed, and viffed right. Looking around at the group it suddenly hit her that there were fewer than twenty peacekeepers left out of the company that had started the day, not counting the reinforced company of Spetsnaz. She wanted to be ill, and she could see the same shock dawning on the faces of the others. Everyone except for Sergeant Owens, who just looked grim. The aircraft banked slightly, and Molly settled in for the trip towards FOB Waterloo, the main Irish base on Grainne.

8.

:: BIGTOP, Hey Fizz, recommend you tell Aero to reroute that DUSTOFF on a different flightpath ::

Fizz squinted at the chat ID—*BIGTOP? That's a cyber analysis shop, on the* Montevideo. *Really hot lieutenant running it.*

:: INTEL: Say again? ::

:: BIGTOP: Indications of possible suicide drones and auto-jumper mines stashed in the trees in that area, pretty reliable signatures, so better safe than...Crap! Look out!! ::

9.

Molly was checking the respirations on one of her patients when she heard the flight engineer scream something in Russian. Before any of the peacekeepers could react, the right side of the vertol's troop compartment blew out, and several of them were torn to shreds or thrown out of the stricken bird.

"OH MY GO—" she started to scream.

There was a loud bang from outside the aircraft and Molly was nearly thrown out the gaping hole in the side. She was saved by a cargo strap that had somehow wrapped itself around her leg and by the motion of the deck as the pilot fought to save the doomed vertol. She guessed the source of the bang as their escort craft tumbled past the exposed gouge. Some type of explosion had completely sheared away its cockpit.

"HOLD ON, WE ARE GOING IN," screamed the pilot.

A second loud bang, and a screeching noise filled Specialist Molly Aujla's world, overpowering all her other senses. She managed to grab hold of another strap and pin herself down to the deck. She saw Sergeant Owens looking up at the roof of the cabin and muttering something, while the remaining troops tried to brace for impact. A third bang sounded from outside the aircraft, and to Molly's horror she could see one of the craft's two engines shear off, causing the ship to spin before Wyvern somehow managed to stop it. Molly looked toward the front of the cabin, but all she could see was sparks and smoke.

The vertol hit the ground nose up and slid. "Am I alive?"

asked a dazed voice. It took Molly a minute to realize that she was the one who had spoken.

"Da, you are alive," replied the shaken flight engineer.

A groan from Sergeant Owen indicated that he was also still alive, but there were precious few others. Molly looked over at her litter patients and could tell instantly that only MacNulty survived the crash. Looking at Private Oliver, she could feel her gorge rise at the sight of a metal splinter that had nearly gouged the man in half. Molly flexed her limbs cautiously, worried she might have a break or fracture. Feeling nothing amiss, she scrambled over to one of the few peacekeepers left and helped the woman unbuckle from a jump seat. The pilot emerged from the ruin of the cockpit, somehow miraculously intact although she had a nasty gash on her left upper arm. Molly pulled an emergency dressing from one of her pockets and bandaged the Russian pilot, who nodded her thanks.

The survivors exited the broken ship, gathering what supplies they could. Molly cut Hanrahan loose from his seat, noting that the improvised secure harness that she and the flight engineer concocted had probably saved the rebel's life. Sergeant Owens pulled a datapad from his pocket and attempted to divine their location relative to Orme and Waterloo, while Molly did what she could for the survivors, including a thoroughly disoriented Hanrahan.

She could finally see the damage to the vertol. The craft had skidded along the ground through a clearing that the pilot somehow maneuvered the aircraft into. It had hit a patch of trees and come to rest on the stub of its left wing. Everything else had ripped off the fuselage.

"Where are we?" Molly could barely croak.

"We are about a hundred klicks from Orme, but about forty or so offset from Waterloo. Seems we covered some distance in the wrong direction," replied Owens. "Any idea where our escort went?"

Molly spoke up, "I think I saw him go down. Cockpit looked like it was completely gone."

The Russian pilot sighed. Molly got a good look at her for the first time, and the first thought that sprung to mind was tall, leggy, and blonde. Her nametape said "Wyvern," and she looked feral, with a steady flow of blood from a jagged gash on her chin.

The pilot gazed at Molly for a moment before continuing with Sergeant Owens.

"*Gavno!* Well, the ship's completely dead so I don't have a radio anymore. What about you, did yours survive?" Wyvern asked in clipped Standard English.

"Yeah, ah, yes, ma'am. I have one long range comm left with Private First-Class Elgin there, but right now all comms are out. Something is playing merry hell with all modes, and we can't get a signal out." Sergeant Owens sighed.

"*Zadnitze.* We know the rebels have been doing stuff to the comms, but command still hasn't acknowledged it." The pilot looked over at Hanrahan, now leaning unsteadily on Molly's shoulder. "What do you have to say, *bratan*?"

Hanrahan said nothing, and merely grunted.

"Private Elgin see if..."

A scream cut Sergeant Owens off and everyone turned to face its source. The flight engineer's high-pitched scream turned to a mewling as he crumpled over. Molly now felt completely distant, removed as if watching the nightmare through someone else's eyes. Her first impression was that something had splashed red paint all over the man, but then she realized that what she saw was blood. She perceived a blur in her peripheral vision and something big and sleek came out of the brush and grabbed the Flight Engineer, pulling him into the treeline.

"WHAT THE HELL WAS THAT?" screamed the Russian pilot, in nearly accent-free English. Fear seemed to do that, but she slipped back into her native tongue just as quickly. "*Chërt poberi!*"

"I...I don't know," stammered Owens.

"Sarge, there is something over..."

Private Keene did not get a chance to finish his statement as another creature bounded into the clearing. It was all slashing claws and gnashing teeth, and yet moved with the sleekness of a hunting wolf. It grabbed Keene's throat in its jaws and shook its head violently. The young man's head flew free from his body and the creature bounded back into the tree line with its meal. Molly threw up violently.

Sergeant Owens opened up with his rifle, blasting away into the trees where the creature had disappeared. When he had exhausted his magazine, he dropped it and inserted a second, but before he could pull the trigger the Russian pilot grabbed the end of his rifle and pushed it up into the air.

Hanrahan rasped, "Save your ammo, Sergeant. You aren't doing any good and we have no idea how many are out there. That's what we call a 'dire yote.'"

Owens stared at Hanrahan, blinking several times, his grip on the rifle turning his knuckles white. "A fucking what?"

"A dire yote. They hunt a bit like Earth coyotes, but they're much bigger, meaner and much, much harder to kill. Best to avoid them."

Owens looked at Wyvern for a moment and then over to Hanrahan before nodding.

Molly moved closer to the others, looking around her fearfully. She was not armed, per the Geneva Convention, and was acutely aware that she had no way to defend herself from a wild animal.

"Sergeant Owens, I don't have a gun."

He turned toward Molly considering her for a moment.

"Have you ever used one of these?" Owens held up one of the bullpup-style carbines that the Irish favored.

"No, I came into the Forces as a medic, so I never went through weapons familiarization."

"Stupid rule," Owens muttered. "Okay, here is how it works. The magazine goes into the well here, the safety for the weapon is here, and you pull this to make it shoot. To aim it you put the red dot on what you want to kill and squeeze the trigger. Always face it forward."

Owens went through the motions, pointing to various things on the rifle for Molly. For her part she was a little queasy at the idea of holding a gun but was violently opposed to becoming a snack for some forest predator. Owens picked up Keene's fallen weapon and handed it to Molly.

"The round counter indicates that there are twenty-five rounds left in the magazine. Here is one more magazine of fifty rounds. Do not waste them, got it?"

"Yes, Sergeant."

"Okay, we need to keep moving. Corporal Walsh, you take point. Then you, LT and our medic carry MacNulty's litter. Elgin will help Mr. Hanrahan, and then I will take up rear security. Hopefully, whatever those things were have been satisfied for now and will leave us alone." Owens looked disgusted at the thought.

Hanrahan coughed and spat. "Satisfied. You'd better hope so. My folks don't even operate out here if they can help it. Certainly not overnight. Not without leopards."

Owens laughed coldly, "Heh, what is it with you fucking people and your fucking leopards?"

Hanrahan's voice was gravel as he replied, "They're smart and vicious enough to keep the local beasts under control. Somewhat."

10.

Adder was apoplectic. "The *fuck* happened out there, Intel! Mines? Drones? How could it all be 'completely automated'? What do you mean something's jamming their comms?"

Mojo froze, *Home Office's asset should still be able to get something through. His gear is exquisite and specially made for that type of interference.*

One of Fizz's high-altitude drones, well above the altitude rebel drones and other threats could reach, collected just enough background infrared and other spectral bands on the crash site to issue a warning. "ALCON, multiple unknown contacts heading towards the survivors."

Mojo sighed. *Well, no time like the present to call in a favor.*

11.

Molly swallowed her fear. She didn't relish the thought of going into the trees. The ever-shrinking party left the clearing and blazed a trail southeast back toward Waterloo. It was rough going with Walsh having to frequently stop to cut through some particularly dense piece of foliage. Every fifteen minutes, Elgin attempted voice radio calls, beacon captures, and satellite uplinks. On the move, their odds of getting a good link were low, and worse, Elgin thought there was active rebel jamming in play as well. Elgin finally convinced Sergeant Owens to let them halt for ten minutes, so he could attempt to "burn through" the jamming.

Wow, he's a brainy one, isn't he? Molly thought. *Seems a bit old for his rank. Gear is a lot nicer than the usual crap I've seen; must be nice to spend your life inside the wire.*

"I think I got a couple of packets through the noise." Elgin seemed pretty proud of himself. "When they hit one or more receivers, doesn't matter what kind, they all have a little self-replicating instruction that will look for traces of the rest and reconstitute the message. Someone *will* hear that. It might take a while though. It's not quick."

Hours passed, but Molly wasn't sure they had gone all that far when there was a scream from in front of her. She watched helplessly as Corporal Walsh was speared through the chest by something she couldn't see, and the woman was lifted up into the air. Walsh continued to scream what air was left in her lungs out and then her attacker dropped her into a gurgling, moaning heap. Her reprieve lasted only for a moment before whatever it was came back and lifted the dying woman up into the trees. *Canines shouldn't climb trees*, was all Molly could think upon actually seeing it. *Is that a barbed tail?*

Wyvern fired her wicked-looking submachine gun at the creature, and it dropped Corporal Walsh to the forest floor. Molly tried to move to the woman, but Wyvern held her back until Sergeant Owens was right beside her. Only then did the three of them move to Walsh's side. Molly could see the wound was fatal and couldn't believe she'd survived even that long. Walsh looked up at her pleadingly as if asking Molly to do something, but Molly knew there was nothing that she could do for the woman that was in the regs.

Fuck the regs, she thought as she pulled out three morphine autoinjectors. She jabbed Corporal Walsh with all three in rapid succession and watched as the other woman's eyes closed for the last time. A moment later, Walsh's labored gurgling and breathing stopped. Tears ran down Molly's face and she angrily scrubbed at them.

"It was all you could do." Wyvern laid a gentle hand on Molly's shoulder. The medic looked up at the pilot, who was a head taller than she, and nodded silently.

"Dammit." Owens sighed. "Okay we have got to kee—"

Molly gasped and stared in horror. Sergeant Owens was ripped in half. The look of shock on his face was the last thing Molly saw of him as two creatures dragged the halves of him into the underbrush. They didn't go far, and she could hear the things cracking bones and eating the dead man. Thank God he was dead. She didn't think the predators cared.

They were down to Molly, Wyvern, MacNulty, Elgin, and

Hanrahan, who, missing limb or not, was plenty motivated by adrenaline and fear to keep moving under his own power. The three uninjured UN personnel took turns assisting MacNulty. With great effort he was able to walk, albeit slowly and leaning heavily on one of them at a time for support. It was slow going.

"Fuck this, I want to go home," said Molly out loud. Wyvern chastised her for the noise, but with a hint of care in her voice. It had fallen to the young pilot officer to keep the group together, regardless of whatever side of the fight they'd started the morning on, and thus far she seemed up to the task.

Hours passed and the survivors struggled through the forest. The creatures that had decimated their party so abruptly seemed to have been sated by their carnage and left them alone. Wyvern navigated via her handheld comp, which now worked perfectly. Apparently, the jamming ceased during their battle with the dire yotes, and now she kept them heading generally in the right direction.

It was just one more nightmare for Molly, who had grown up in a prefab suburb of Winchester. She had thought the forest preserves of Britain were wild and magical places when she was a girl, but compared to the forests of Grainne, those were mere parks for playing in. *I didn't have to worry about being eaten back home*, she thought.

"How far have we left to go, Leftenant?"

"According to my comp we have some thirty klicks. Wait."

A low and menacing growl from the undergrowth just to the right of the two women interrupted Wyvern. The sound differed from the dire yotes. This sounded bigger, madder, *hungrier* than the horrors they'd already faced. Molly felt an overwhelming need to piss herself and then the creature burst forth from the bushes. It streaked between the two women, knocking them both down. Wyvern reacted first, trying to shoot the creature with her submachine gun, but missed. The monstrosity effortlessly swatted her aside and then lunged for Molly. Molly brought up her rifle and pointed it desperately at the charging horror, and had just enough time to wonder if this was one of those "ripper" things that intel was always going on about, and pull the trigger. Nothing happened.

"Nooo," Molly began to scream, but the ripper was thrown violently sideways.

Molly's ears rang, and to her surprise a boy, no, teenager, stepped out of the bushes from where the ripper had come, holding a rifle. A *really big* rifle. She could tell he spoke, but through the ringing she could only hear some faint mumbling, as though he was speaking underwater. She thought he said, "You really shouldn't be out here, Miss. This forest is dangerous enough for us, but you Earthers have no chance out here."

"Who the hell are you?" asked Wyvern, nursing a gash near her hip.

Molly saw the injury and rushed to her side.

"How bad is it?" she asked as she probed the wound. Wyvern let out a hiss but allowed Molly to do her job. The boy made no move to interfere and actually averted his eyes as Molly bound the lieutenant's wound.

"My name is Max. Max Goldbach. And as I said before, I really think you should come with me. Unless, that is, you have a better, and hopefully immediate way out of here, because right now the rippers are mating and that has driven them into fits of the old ultraviolence." The boy wore a look of both amusement and fear.

12.

Adder sat behind Mojo in the front of the battle cab and watched as anger, confusion, and fear unfolded on his operations floor.

"WE'LL HAVE NONE OF THAT! Mojo, play that audio again!"

Mojo replayed a clipped, static-laden transmission for Adder's ears once more: "REQU...IMMED...EVAC...EMER...FOUR UN SURVI...ONE COLONIAL...44KM sou—est...WATERLOO..."

Still alive, and our asset doesn't disappoint. The rebel we saved is someone they'll parley for. Wait. Over forty klicks from Waterloo? And the fix has aged out, shit. Mojo was amazed they'd made it that far. *This transmission is old too, they could be even further along now. Still, it's worth a shot.*

"Sir, I recommend you authorize a rescue mission," he said in a private channel in Adder's headset.

Adder scoffed, "Into that mess, Mojo? It's almost as bad as Orme."

"It might be time to try and bargain with the rebels. We've saved one of theirs, and Fizz is about to tell us with his usual sources that they've saved our people as well."

"What do you mean?"

Mojo then realized that he had to choose his next words very carefully. "I think we should ask for a ceasefire to retrieve the survivors and make an exchange. Fizz has some additional intel."

"Go on." Adder scowled at Mojo, but against his better judgement, decided to listen.

Mojo allowed Fizz into the channel, who spoke quickly. "Sir, the rebel survivor that our forces retrieved at Orme is someone the insurgents will want back. I'm positive of this."

"I don't trust this. How important can he be?"

Mojo reinforced Fizz, knowing that Adder needed the reassurance. "Sir, apparently, our medic saved a local civic leader. Family head of some sort. The rebels went so far as to send an operator out to assist our people a short time ago, and he was able to intervene and save the survivors."

Adder shook his head, "And how did they find our people? I'm not fucking doing this. Do you know how much time and resources it's going to take to build a rescue package? There's only one assault strip long enough for it to land in that AO, I know you've seen it! That place is unacknowledged, and also under constant attack."

"What do you suggest, sir?"

"Start writing posthumous medals for your survivors, I'll be damned if I—"

A booming chime interrupted all communications on the floor.

"Adder, stand by for words from Kestrel Six Actual, prepare to copy."

The clipped accent and impeccable diction sounded familiar to both Adder and Mojo, and the callsign "Kestrel Six Actual" belonged only to one individual in the entire system. Mojo remembered from the briefing that the *London* had redeployed to a high orbit, in order to transmit intelligence to General Huff and his senior staff.

"Actual sends, 'Execute. With all speed.'" On a channel only open to Adder, Mojo, and Oracle, General Huff's aide conveyed further instructions. "Tell them you want a truce, they're listening."

Mojo smiled slightly. *Fucking well-timed, Sandeep. Huff's been listening the entire time. Even he realizes this needs to happen. Maybe there is a God.*

"Acknowledged." Adder sighed. "All right, people, get to it.

Mojo, Fizz, we'll broadcast this over the open 'Guard' freq: 'To the commanding officer, rebel forces in vicinity of FOB Waterloo, UN command requests temporary cease-fire to retrieve isolated UN and opposition forces personnel.'"

Fizz cut in, "Adder, sir, and Mojo, I have something you need, audio only."

Without waiting for his superior, Mojo cleared Fizz's response. "Roger. Go ahead."

In a private channel, Fizz relayed his latest intel. "I just received a message force-fed through my terminal. I don't want to risk forwarding it to you or anyone else, because whoever it is, they can do some scary shit. This tool is amazing, and I'm stunned the rebels would just burn it like this." Fizz paused for effect, but Mojo wasn't interested in the ins-and-outs of rebel cyber expertise at that particular moment.

"Fizz, get to the point." Mojo pushed the brilliant but often scatterbrained intel officer, knowing that their boss was about out of patience, and that if Mojo didn't move this situation along, Adder could unintentionally explode the entire situation, and no one would survive.

Fizz verbally relayed the enemy's transmission, as fast as it came in. "Sir, they're willing to trade safe passage to our designated MEDEVAC LZ, and they're willing to cease artillery and rocket fires, stand down jamming, deactivate mines and drone kill zones. Break. So long as we care for their wounded and release him as soon as medically possible along with the individual guiding the survivors. Break. 'The Freehold partisans are not to be detained.' Break. They're also willing to hold a POW exchange, as a sign of good faith. Break. There's a warning too; 'There are local forces in that area *not* under Freehold Forces command and control, conducting unsanctioned operations.'"

Adder laughed, dryly, and without humor. "Well this day just keeps getting more and more entertaining by the moment, doesn't it?"

13.

"...And that's the honest truth, Ma'am."

Lyudmila, by now Molly had finally heard Wyvern's actual name, looked at the young man, her face a mask of skepticism.

Molly, for her part, remained silent. Grainne's predators had whittled down the group of survivors, leaving Wyvern in impromptu command of Molly, MacNulty, and Elgin. They were locked tight in a strange truce with the rebel Hanrahan and this boy dressed in khaki shirt and trousers, with what looked like hand-painted camo splotches and a patch bearing the words "KIBBUTZ DEGANIA ALEF." Enemies, but not so different in that all wanted to get through this night alive.

According to Max, the group had to now cover only about seven kilometers due west, albeit away from Waterloo, until they hit a small UN firebase, one that wasn't on the books as far as Molly knew. A rebel contingent, recognized by the UN as lawful combatants, would help retrieve Hanrahan, and then Lyudmila, Molly, and their survivors would get their ticket home.

Molly shook her head. *This war gets crazier by the minute.*

"How can we trust you?" Lyudmila's face was a stone mask to Molly, but her voice hinted at tiny cracks forming in the ice-cold façade.

"The way I see it, ma'am, you're just going to have to take a leap of faith. I've killed an Aardvark or two in my time, I ain't going to lie. But we respect honorable enemies when we see them, particularly the medic here, and well, our leadership decided that you all deserve a chance at not dying today, especially for keeping our mate Mr. Hanrahan alive also. You could have easily let him die, or killed him yourself, but you didn't. That makes you worthy."

Molly wanted to kill him. She had no idea what to say, if she could say anything. *Worthy? WORTHY?*

Max glanced at a buzz on his wrist comm. He continued. "We're going to your obscure Firebase Cobra. All recognized Freehold Forces have been ordered to stand down and clear us a path."

Lyudmila looked at Molly and frowned, then drilled Hanrahan with her eyes. "Hold there, what do you mean, 'recognized'?"

Hanrahan sighed and spoke with a gravelly voice. "Ma'am, you bunch have pissed off a lot of people since you arrived here, and not all of them were exactly 'model citizens' before all this started. They didn't play ball with the Freehold before this war, but they like you even less than they like our government in Jefferson."

Max nodded vigorously in agreement. "They're even more fucked-up and violent now, and they would very much like to overrun that firebase. In fact, they might just pull it off, so I suggest we get moving now, just in case."

Hanrahan strained, exhausted, and desperate to finish this parley. "Their actions are *not* sanctioned by Freehold Combined Forces, either Regular or Provisional. My Provos will meet us there and will do their best to maintain the integrity of the truce."

"Do their best? Do their fucking *best*? You fucking tosser, fuck you and your whole fucking planet. I've lost all me mates trying to fucking help you, you fuck!" Molly's tears flowed, and she couldn't stop them.

To her shock, Lyudmila took her into a full bear hug that lasted several seconds, and then took back control of the group.

"Again, from the top."

14.

The team rehearsed their approach on the firebase one last time with sticks and dirt in a makeshift sand table, going over commands and signals, ensuring that everyone who could move under their own power was on the same page. Each member took their positions. Molly caught the final signal, a nod from Lyudmila to Max, and they moved out.

Max took point through the trees, with his rifle that was the size of a heavy machine gun at ready carry. Molly and Lyudmila carried MacNulty's makeshift litter between them. Elgin supported Hanrahan, who seemed to be in the throes of infection finally. Infection, plus the wear and tear of shock, blood loss, the side effects of combat stims, and the moist, humid, shitty Grainnean "spring" conspired to break him at last. While traveling, they had wrapped him in as many field blankets as they could salvage from the dead, but their only ally now was speed. Elgin, ever ready to carry the wounded or haul extra gear, certainly didn't seem much like a command post weenie and remained silent the entire time.

True to Max's word, their trek towards the firebase went unmolested, at least by insurgent forces. Max deftly steered them clear of the damn-near invisible dire yotes, only once having to put one down with his giant game rifle before it could pounce.

They were less than a klick away now, close enough to smell

and hear an active flight line, when the report of rockets and guns, really big ones, blasted the air and shook the ground.

Lyudmila motioned to Molly to lower the improvised litter. "I thought your people agreed to a damn truce!" She grabbed the boy by his collar, towering over him a by a full foot.

Max shook her loose. "Be quiet!" He squatted down and motioned for them all to follow suit. "These aren't Hanrahan's people, or mine," he whispered. "I told you, we have a lot of 'contingents,' but not all of them listen to us. Some of them are really well armed."

Starburst shells flashed overhead, and Molly could see not only the base, which had thankfully cut its lighting off, but also just how alive the woods were with animals and weapons, and presumably, crazed colonials, hopped up for a total assault.

Elgin spoke up, "Leftenant, I think you'd better send the code, see if your ride is ready."

Wyvern clicked three times on the datapad she'd recovered from Sergeant Owens's body and checked the screen.

"Inbound. Ten mikes. We'd better move, now! On three. One." She and Molly grabbed the makeshift litter's poles, MacNulty swaying gently between them.

"Two." Max had slung his big rifle and brought up a small carbine, easy to handle while running.

"Three!" Elgin and Max flanked Hanrahan and made a run for it. With barely fifty meters left to the perimeter, two mortar shell explosions dropped haphazardly to Elgin's left, then his right, and he slowed but kept going. The base's impeccably aimed defenses lit up a swath of destruction, covering everything but a narrow strip. About thirty meters from the base, a patrol met them and took over carrying MacNulty's litter while a pair of soldiers hand-carried Hanrahan the final distance. Then, mortar rounds impacted the base and all around it, and a rocket took down one of the guard towers.

Molly's ears rang. She picked herself up and prepared to stagger-sprint her way inside to relative safety, when she saw Mac-Nulty's litter on the ground, his bearers either dead or otherwise absent. She crawled over to him and checked for new injuries. There was a lot of blood, but he was breathing. The laborious sound assured her that MacNulty had blast injuries. Molly saw where one of the bandages had been shredded on his chest, and frantically searched her pockets for an occlusive dressing, but all she found was a wrapper for a ration cookie. "Improvise, adapt, overcome," Molly said to herself. She tore the wrapper to flatten it out and slapped it over the shredded bandage, taping it down on all sides. "Alright, Colm, let's get you through that gate." Although she never would have believed it possible, she managed to pick up and fireman's carry MacNulty's hefty frame step by painful step, until a UNPF ILAWAV with a light cannon gun mount pulled up alongside. Hands ensconced both her and Colm MacNulty away. Molly barely registered that her rescuers were mixed company; she saw both UN camo and rebel ersatz uniforms.

She finally had a few moments to relax slightly, when the Eel rolled up on the beautiful sight of a dropship, which had somehow survived a combat descent and come to a hover stop on the firebase's frighteningly short runway, with an open ramp and a loadmaster waving them all aboard.

The last to board was Max. He said nothing but proceeded through the cargo bay and up into the cockpit. They didn't see him for the rest of the journey that followed.

Projectiles and fragments pinged, and as the ramp raised up Molly caught the sights and sounds of both flame and death. Like a robot, she rattled off the condition of MacNulty, Elgin, Hanrahan, Lyudmila, and lastly, almost as an afterthought, herself to the flight engineer, assisted where she could while they stabilized the wounded, then strapped in and braced for the combat ascent.

They landed uneventfully at FOB Waterloo. The ramp lowered once again, and they were met by a trauma team from the base hospital, known to be some of the best on the planet. MacNulty and Hanrahan were taken away separately, and within minutes, MacNulty was in receipt of a planeside transfusion.

Max Goldbach walked down the ramp as if nothing had happened. When he reached the bottom, Molly saw him turn to face both Lyudmila and her. He smiled and touched the corner of his eyebrow in a lazy, casual salute.

15.

Waterloo's lead surgeon wasn't taking no for an answer. Certainly not from a pompous windbag like Brigadier "Adder" Blumly. "We've started a walking blood bank, or rather, the troops did.

I've got one hundred soldiers lined up, and I've even got POWs who want to donate blood to save this guy. It won't be enough, we need an urgent aeromedical evac, and the Level Three trauma team onboard Skywheel Two. My en-route Patient Staging System team is ready to build this mission whenever you are, Brigadier."

Adder shook his head at the doc on screen. "Do you know what it takes to get a mission like that built? It's never been done before. There's nothing available in theater and won't be for two full days!"

"He doesn't have two more days."

"There's nothing we can do." Adder was about to cut the discussion short, when his private channel popped open on his leftmost screen.

:: KESTREL SIX ACTUAL: I DON'T CARE HOW YOU DO IT, BUT YOU WILL MAKE THIS HAPPEN. ::

Well fuck me.

:: YOU WILL ALSO BE ONBOARD THAT SHIP TO PICK ELGIN UP AT WATERLOO. AND YOU WILL TAKE PART IN A REPATRIATION CEREMONY FOR SUBJECT HANRAHAN, AND SUBSEQUENT PRISONER EXCHANGE. SANDEEP IS SENDING YOU THE PROMOTION ORDERS AND MEDALS FOR LT VLADIMIROVNA, SPEC AUJLA, AND PFC MACNULTY. ::

Well, okay then. He sent a short text to Mojo. "Mojo, just make it happen, whatever magic it takes, just fucking do it."

Mojo smiled behind his screen, "Right, let's get to work! We are building a new critical care aerospace transport mission here. Break. From Waterloo, pick up urgent patient, fly him to MOB Unity for an orbital ascent to Skywheel Two, and no one has ever done this before. What's that I see before me? An empty gray-tail coming home from the Delph'? Perfect! They're now REACH 979, and they have a new job. Also, find us two extra crews and two refuelers."

"Wonderful," said the surgeon over the net. "Now here's what *I'm* going to need: one each, critical care nurse, ultrasound tech, a physician, respiratory therapist, at least one extracorporeal membrane oxygenation specialist, that's an 'EMOC,' and a lot of money for regen therapy."

16.

Molly stood straight as a rod, uncomfortable as hell in a set of dress greens that someone had found, and that almost fit. She stood next to the bald, bulky, and extraordinarily black Brigadier General Blumly. He could barely keep a sneer off his face. He did not want to be here, that much was certain. Truthfully though, Molly didn't want to be here either. Her skin itched where she knew she would be picking out bits of rock and shrapnel for years to come. Her joints were stiff with exhaustion; she felt dazed, relieved, guilty, and worn. Soul-worn. *This is probably PTS,* she realized, and rather than dwell on that, she tried to focus on what was now the most awkward event she'd ever attended. *Who the hell thought this was a good idea?*

She almost missed the call to step forward, though whether due to the tinnitus or just plain boredom, she couldn't say. First, they tacked a new stripe on her sleeves, the adhesive making far too much noise in the otherwise silent room. Then, Molly performed the classic "shake, take, salute," and even forced herself to smile as they pinned the medal on her. As she stepped back, with her peripheral vision, she caught a barely noticeable hint of satisfaction on Lyudmila's face, and a slight nod of approval from the colonel aerospace controller who had accompanied the Brig to Waterloo.

Now all Molly really wanted to do was to check in on Mac-Nulty. Instead, Molly watched now-Captain Second Class Lyudmila Aleksandrovna Vladimirovna step forward to receive her medal. Molly, like mostly everyone else in the room, couldn't help but stare at the statuesque beauty. She figured that poor Lyudmila had probably dealt with that her entire life. It often accompanied the experience of being grossly underestimated in intelligence and ability. Now, Molly thought, they saw something different. The new scar on Lyudmila's face, just below her lip and across her chin, burned red across her pale skin. The one visible mar seemed to suck all the air out of the room. Molly could almost see the controlled rage and contempt beneath Lyudmila's façade, her body language just screamed *"Fuck you all."* Nonetheless, Lyudmila was the picture of professionalism, did the shake-take-salute, and stepped back into the small formation.

✧   ✧   ✧

Mojo couldn't help himself and stared at the Russian ice queen. *She's beautiful, but terrifying,* he thought. As proffer, Mojo narrated the entire event, and managed the proceeding as if it were nothing more than a boring end-of-tour ceremony back in garrison. General Huff himself, apparently, had conceived the brilliant idea of combining the awards ceremony with the POW exchange. The ceremony celebrated and applauded human bravery under extreme conditions. It demonstrated that both sides in this conflict could be humane and civilized. The Grainne remnants received a chance to demonstrate legitimacy. The UN got to save face. Mojo relaxed as Adder finally turned on the charm, the way he always did when pressed, as he presented an excellent, and thankfully short, set of remarks. Adder managed to keep any negative observations about the somewhat ragtag, but obviously dangerous group of colonials in front of them to himself. Instead, he, and the rest of the UN personnel focused on the nameless Freehold Special Warfare soldier flanking a relieved-looking UN command colonel wearing an obviously brand spanking new flight suit.

In front of the UN personnel stood Peter Hanrahan, all cleaned up, with his right arm stub in a regen cast. He wore a brand-new camouflage shirt, khaki trousers, and sported a surplus UNPF beret, but with a Freehold Provisional Forces flash. Behind him stood three of his kinsmen, dressed in hunting gear with the barest military accoutrements and a unit patch indicating their status as legitimate combatants. Mojo had seen their pictures before, in some of the very exquisite intel reports from Elgin that went only to a very small group of people, including himself and Adder. These three, the two men and one woman, were from large family homesteads around Orme, leaders of their own resistance cells, and they terrified him. All three carried the look that old war literature called the "thousand-yard stare." Mojo would remember those three sets of blue eyes for a long time, and how they looked beyond him, beyond everything in that makeshift auditorium, and saw something else entirely. Behind them stood Max Goldbach and an elder from his kibbutz, their field-expedient uniforms capped off by yarmulkes. Max's eyes scanned for any sign of threat, while the old man prayed, hands upraised, eyes closed, and rocked slowly back and forth.

Hanrahan saluted the UN delegation with his left hand, with the clenched raised fist the colonials used, and took one step

back. The very thin and fragile-looking NorthAm officer stepped
forward to the UN side, made an about-face, and saluted Brevet
Colonel Hanrahan and the small group of Provos. He didn't even
attempt to look at the Special Warfare officer. No one exchanged
words. Hanrahan, however, stepped forward, and pressed something small into the hands first of Molly, and then Lyudmila,
giving them both a small smile. His rebels came to orders and
marched out under flag of truce. As they exited the makeshift
auditorium, one of Hanrahan's people suddenly began to sing,
"The minstrel boy to the war is gone" and joined by his fellows,
bellowed, *"in the ranks of death you will find him..."* Still sing-
ing, they boarded an armed aircar, and slowly lifted away. Max
and his elder boarded a second car, and quickly did the same.

Mojo ended the proceedings with complete professionalism,
announcing, "Please remain standing for the departure of the
official party."

Adder simply said "Dis-missed!" The peacekeepers about-faced
and fell out.

As they were dismissed, Molly finally looked at the coin
Hanrahan had given her. One side showed a harp superimposed
on the old Irish tricolor. The other depicted the Jolly Roger. She
couldn't decide whether to keep it or throw it away.

Not long after the rebel "guests" departed, the truce officially
ended and the intermittent but everpresent indirect fire started
back up. Against that backdrop, she finagled her way to stay by
MacNulty's bedside before he went into Waterloo's main surgical
suite. The UN brass awarded him his medal and promotion at his
bedside. Brig Blumly made it through that, but only just barely,
before disappearing into a bathroom for several minutes. The
smell in the burn ward on the second floor above them perme-
ated the entire hospital, despite the staff's best efforts.

Assuming he survived the first round of surgeries, MacNulty
would get a very expensive brand-new face, mostly grown from
his own cells, but with a good solid frame of ceramic underneath to help it form properly. With that peculiar mix of love
and crassness that only soldiers can really master, some of the
other patients called out "Jaws!" as Molly and the nurses prepped
him for surgery. All poor Colm could do, barely conscious, was
knit his eyebrows in disapproval, flip a defiant, obscene gesture

with both hands, and scribble "these still work," barely legible, on Molly's hand. The nurses had to pry his fingers loose.

MacNulty spent almost twenty-four hours in surgery. The operation was still underway when the transfer team rushed purposefully into the surgical ward, just as MacNulty's procedure started to wrap up. The AeroMed Evac team lead approached the head nurse.

"ETA to transfer?" asked the young blonde captain 2nd. Her name tag read "McFarland."

"They're still working on him."

"Well, plug him up and get him on the bird. We're taking fire out there!"

The nurse relayed the message to the surgical team who finished their current sutures and packed his other injuries with as much sterile gauze as they could. There wasn't much more they could do, anyway. The surgeons were exhausted, and supplies were running dangerously low. They covered the site with a sterile vacuum seal for movement onto the plane. Molly pushed herself up out of chair she had slumped over in, close to the surgical theater. She was exhausted but determined to see this through to the end.

A second nurse accompanied the team, verbally relaying all the information she could. "Jaw severed. Blunt force trauma injuries to upper chest. Over fifteen separate perforating injuries to both the large and small intestines, spleen completely severed and removed, lost seventy-five percent of the liver, and a large aortic aneurysm. Transfused with ten units of whole blood, five units of plasma, BP 98/45, pulse ox ninety percent."

The FOB Waterloo medical team continued rattling off numbers and details, and followed the REACH team onboard, with Molly quietly tagging along at the rear. They maintained respiration and medication flow until the whole entourage reached the hard-interior door to the clean ICU compartment deep within the aircraft. Captain Sue McFarland stopped the Waterloo doctors at the door. "We'll take it from here."

Molly tried to push her way in, "That's my patient."

"Not anymore he's not."

"You don't understand!"

"Look, Corporal. You've done a great job. He wouldn't be alive right now without you, but we've got this. There's nothing else you can do for him. Thank you very much and get off my plane." Captain McFarland didn't wait for a response. She physically turned Molly toward the ramp and gave her a gentle push. Molly resisted, and turned again, enough to get the attention of both the loadmaster and the security forces fly-away team who now seemed to take an alarmed interest in her.

"Wait, take this!" Molly cried and held out a small item to Captain McFarland.

McFarland waved off the security forces NCO, who was about to cold-cock Molly, and took the tiny item into her hand. It was a note, in what looked like Hebrew.

"That boy Max said to give it to him. He said it's called 'Mi Shebeirach.'"

McFarland nodded, and disappeared into the ICU to assist her team.

The loadmaster yelled at Molly to exit the plane immediately, or she'd eat duracrete. She complied but stayed as close as she could to the flightline to watch.

REACH performed a combat ascent under fire, and Molly feared MacNulty wouldn't make it. The Waterloo medical team had been thorough in briefing his injuries, and they were just as severe as everyone had feared. It would be a miracle if he survived liftoff, let alone long enough to get him to a proper surgical theater.

17.

Aboard *London*, General Huff put down his journal, checked his watch, and pinged his aide-de-camp. "Sandeep, are they in orbit yet?"

"Yes, sir! It took two refuelings, one in high stratosphere, and one near-orbit. The plane was so heavy they had to top off as soon as they got airborne, and they had to take a circuitous route to avoid some of the recent hotspots. We were really concerned about computer systems security onboard. Sir, I'm sure you understand just how unbelievable this mission truly was. In addition to the eighteen medical folks, Adder's people built a team of maintainers to install a highly sophisticated prototype airborne intensive care suite. This thing was sitting all wrapped up and forgotten about in one of Waterloo's hardened aircraft shelters. Well, forgotten about by everyone except your command surgeon, sir. It was intended for all sorts of tests here planetside but lost its funding in GenAssem. Bloody amazing."

"How about the orbital ascent? How did the patient fare?"

"Swimmingly, sir. They packed him into a cryo-couch, gyro-stabilized, covered in oxygenated ballistic gel. Really cutting-edge trauma care stuff. They stabilized him on the ground and he actually improved in low-g. So, he's almost ready to come off the ventilator, but they kept him on it from launch through rendezvous with the Skywheel."

"Excellent. Whatever else happens in this war, Sandeep, I hope both sides remember this. It's something worth holding on to. Our humanity."

The Price

Michael Z. Williamson

Four Jemma Two Three, Freehold of Grainne Military Forces, (J Frame Craft, Reconnaissance, Stealth), was a tired boat with a tired crew.

After two local years—three Earth years—of war with the United Nations of Earth and Space, that was no small accomplishment. Most of her sister vessels had been destroyed. That *4J23* was intact, functional, and only slightly ragged with a few "character traits" spoke well of her remarkable crew.

"I have a message, and I can't decode it with my comm," Warrant Leader Derek Costlow announced. The crew turned to him. This could be a welcome break from the monotony of maintenance. Jan Marsich and his sister Meka, both from Special Warfare and passengers stuck aboard since the war started, paid particular attention. Any chance of finding a real mission or transport back to Grainne proper was of interest to them.

"Want me to have a whack at it, Warrant?" asked Sergeant Melanie Sarendy, head of the intelligence mission crew.

"If you would, Mel," he nodded. "I'll forward the data to your system."

Sarendy dropped her game control, which was hardwired and shielded rather than wireless. Intel boats radiated almost no signature. The handheld floated where it was until disturbed by the eddies of her passage.

Jan asked, "Why do we have a message when we're tethered to the Rock? From who?"

Meka wrinkled her brow.

"That's an interesting series of questions," she commented.

"The Rock" was a field-expedient facility with no official name other than a catalog number of use only for communication logs. The engineers who carved and blasted it from a planetoid, the boat crews who used it, the worn and chronically short-handed maintenance personnel aboard had had little time to waste on trivialities such as names. There were other such facilities throughout the system, but few of the surviving vessels strayed far enough from their own bases to consort with other stations. "The Rock" sufficed.

They were both attentive again as Sarendy returned. She looked around at the eyes on her, and said, "Sorry. Whatever it is, I don't have a key for it."

Meka quivered alert. "Mind if I try?" she asked.

"Sure," Costlow replied.

She grabbed her comm and plugged it into a port as everyone waited silently. She identified herself through several layers of security and the machine conceded that perhaps it might have heard of that code. A few more jumped hoops and it flashed a translation on her screen.

The silence grew even more palpable when she looked up, her eyes blurred with tears. "Warrant," she said, voice cracking, and locked eyes with him.

Costlow glanced around the cabin, and in seconds everyone departed for their duty stations or favorite hideyholes, leaving the two of them and Jan in relative privacy. Jan was family, and Costlow let him stay. In response to the worried looks from the two of them, Meka turned her screen to face them.

The message was brief and said simply, "you are ordered to destroy as many of the following prioritized targets as possible. any and all assets and resources are to be utilized to accomplish this mission. signed, naumann, colonel commanding provisional freehold military forces. Verification x247." Attached was a list of targets and a timeframe. All the targets were in a radius around Jump Point Three, within about a day of their current location.

"I don't understand," Jan said. "Intel boats don't carry heavy weapons. How do they expect us to do this?"

"It was addressed to me, not the boat," Meka replied. "He wants me to take out these targets, using any means necessary."

That didn't need translating. There was a silence, broken by Costlow asking, "Are you sure that's a legit order? It looks pointless. Why would they have you attack stuff way out here in the Halo?"

Meka replied, "We know what the enemy has insystem. We know where most of their infrastructure is. If Naumann wants it taken out, it means he's preparing an offensive."

"But this is insane!" Jan protested. "The Aardvarks will have any target replaced in days!"

"No," Meka replied, shaking her head. "It's a legit order. All those targets are intel or command and control."

Costlow said, "So he wants the command infrastructure taken out to prevent them from responding quickly. Then he hits them with physical force."

"Okay, but why not just bomb them or use rocks in fast trajectories?" Jan asked.

Costlow said, "It would take too long to set that many rocks in orbit. Nor could we get them moving fast enough. Maneuvering thrusters and standard meteor watch would take care of them. As to bombing them, they all have defensive grids, and we're a recon boat."

Jan paused and nodded. "Yeah, I know. And there aren't many real gunboats left. I'd just like a safer method." He asked Meka, "So how could you get in?"

"UN stations have sensor holes to ignore vacsuits and toolkits. Ships can't get in, but a single person can."

Costlow looked confused. "Why'd they leave a hole like that?" he asked.

"Partly to prevent accidents with EVA and rescue, partly laziness. They lost a couple of people, and that's just not socially acceptable on Earth," she said. "It's the Blazers' greatest asset to penetrating security. Systems only work if they are used. Backdoors and human stupidity are some of our best tools."

"Didn't they think anyone would do what you're discussing?" Jan asked. That was dangerous. It would push EVA gear to the edge.

"No," she said, shaking her head. "They would never give such an order. The political bureaucracy of the UNPF requires all missions be planned with no loss of life. Not minimal, but zero. Yes, it's ridiculous, but that's how they do things."

Jan asked, "So you EVA in, and then back out?"

"How would I find a stealthed boat from a suit? How would you find me? It's not as if there's enough power to just loiter, and doing so would show on any scan." Her expression was flushed, nauseous and half grinning. It was creepy.

"...But even if you get through, they can still get new forces here in short order," Jan said. He didn't want his sister to die, because that's what this was: a literal suicide mission. His own guts churned.

"No," Meka replied. "Or, not fast enough to matter, I should say." She tapped tactical calculus algorithms into her comm while mumbling, "Minimum twenty hours to get a message relayed to Sol...flight time through Jump Point Two..."

Jan had forgotten that. Jump Point One came straight from Sol, but it no longer existed. Professor Meacham and his wife had taken their hyperdrive research ship into it, then activated phase drive. The result of two intersecting stardrive fields was hard to describe mathematically, but the practical, strategic result was that the point collapsed. No jump drive vessel could transit directly from Sol to Grainne anymore, and the UN didn't yet have any phase drive vessels that they knew of.

Meka finished mumbling, looked up, and said, "Median estimate of forty-three days to get sufficient force here. They could have command and control back theoretically in forty hours, median two eighty-six, but that doesn't help them if they are overrun. It's risky, but we don't have any other option."

Costlow said, "That may be true, but they *can* send more force. It's a short-term tactical gain, but not a strategic win."

"I know Naumann," Meka replied firmly. "He has something planned."

"Unless it's desperation," Costlow said.

Shaking her head, her body unconsciously twisting to compensate, she said, "No. He never throws his people away, and he has very low casualty counts. If he wants me to do this, then he has a valid plan."

"Trusting him with your life is dangerous, especially since you don't even know that's him," Jan said. They'd almost died three times now. She'd almost died a couple more. This one was for real.

"We're trusting him with more than that," she said. "And that's definitely him. Security protocols aside, no one else would have the balls to give an order like that and just assume it would be followed. Besides, it authenticates."

"Okay," Costlow reluctantly agreed. "Which target are you taking?"

She pointed as she spoke, "Well, the command ship *London* is the first choice, but I don't think I can get near a ship. This crewed platform is second, but I'd have to blast or fight my way in. If I fail, I still die, and accomplish nothing. I suppose I have to chicken out and take the automatic commo station."

"Odd way to chicken out," Jan commented in a murmur.

"Are you sure of these priorities?" Costlow asked. His teeth were grinding and he looked very bothered.

"Yes," she replied. "If I had more resources, I'd take *London*, too. We don't have any offensive missiles, though."

"We have one," the older man softly replied. They looked at him silently. "If you're sure that's a good order," he said. His face turned from tan to ashen as he spoke.

"I am," she said.

"Then I'll drop you on the way. Just think of this as an intelligent stealth missile," he said, and tried to smile. It looked like a rictus.

"Are you sure?" she asked.

"No," he admitted. "But if it's what we have to do to win . . ."

There was silence for a few moments. Hating himself for not speaking already, hating the others even though it wasn't their fault, Jan said, "I'll take the automatic station." Saying it was more concrete than thinking it. His guts began twisting and roiling, and cold sweat burst from his body. He felt shock and adrenaline course through him. "That takes it out of the equation, and you can fight your way into the crewed one."

Costlow said, "It's appreciated, Jan, but you're tech branch. I think you'd be of more help here."

It was a perfect escape, and Meka's expression said she wasn't going to tell his secret if he wanted to stop there. He was a Special Projects technician, who built custom gear for others, usually in close support, but too valuable to be directly combatant save in emergencies. The act of volunteering was more than enough for most people, and he could gracefully bow out. He felt himself talking, brain whirling as he did. "I do EVA as a hobby. I'm not as good as Meka, but I can manage, given the gear." There. *Now* he was committed.

"You don't have to, Jan," Meka said. "There are other Blazers. We'll get enough targets."

"Meka, I'm not doing this out of inadequacy or false bravery." Actually, he was. There was another factor, too. When she looked at him, he continued, "I *can't* face Mom and Dad and tell them you did this. No way. I'm doing this so I don't have to face them. And because I guess it has to be done."

After a long wait, staring at each other, conversation resumed. The three made a basic schedule, hid all data and undogged the cabin. They each sought their own private spaces to think and come to grips, and the rest of the crew were left to speculate. The normal schedule resumed and would remain in force until the planned zero time, five days away.

The three were reserved in manner during the PT sparring match that evening. The crew each picked a corner or a hatch to watch from in the day cabin, a five-meter cylinder ten meters long, and cheered and critiqued as they took turns tying each other in knots. Sarendy was small but vicious, her lithe and slender limbs striking like those of a praying mantis. Jan and Meka were tall and rangy. Costlow was older and stubborn. Each one had his or her own method of fighting. They were all about as effective.

Jan was strong, determined, and made a point of staying current on unarmed combat, partly due to a lack of demand for his services. He and Costlow twirled and kicked and grappled for several minutes, sweating and gasping from exertion, until Jan finally pinned the older man in a corner with a forearm wedged against his throat. "Yours," Costlow acknowledged.

Jan and Meka faced off from opposite ends, both lean and pantherlike. They studied each other carefully for seconds, then flew at each other, twisting and reaching, and met in a flurry of long limbs. Meka slapped him into a spin, twisted his ankles around, locked a foot under his jaw and let her momentum carry them against the aft hatch, where her other knee settled in the small of his back, pinning him helplessly as she grabbed the edge. Her kinesthetic sense and coordination never ceased to amaze the rest of them.

Passive Sensor Specialist Riechard gamely threw himself into the bout. He advanced and made a feint with one hand, orienting to keep a foot where he could get leverage off the bulkhead. He moved in fast and hard and scored a strike against Meka's shoulder, gripped her arm, and began to apply leverage. She countered by pivoting and kicking for his head.

Riechard spun and flinched. "Shoot, Meka, watch it!" he snapped.

"Sorry," she replied. Nerves had her frazzled, and she'd over-reacted, her kick almost tearing his ear off. "I better take a break. Default yours."

The crew knew something was up. Costlow and the Marsichs were on edge, irritable, and terse. The session broke down without comment, and everyone drifted in separate directions.

Jan signed out and headed into The Rock the next morning. The scenery was no more exciting, being carved stone walls with sealed hatches, but at least it wasn't the boat. The air seemed somehow fresher, and it was good not to see the same faces. It wasn't his choice for a last liberty, but there wasn't any alternative. It was either the ship or The Rock.

Throughout the station, soldiers and spacers moved around in sullen quiet. The reserved faces made it obvious that other boats and ships had similar instructions. Jan had to smile at the irony that everyone had the same orders, and no one could talk about it. Then he remembered what was to happen and became more withdrawn himself.

He'd wanted Mel Sarendy for two years, but crew were off-limits, and it grew more frustrating as time went on. Their society had no taboos against casual nudity, and the spartan supplies and close quarters aboard boat encouraged it. He'd spent hours staring at her toned body, surreally shaped in microgravity. Her ancestry, like her name, was Earth Cambodian, diluted perhaps with a trace of Russian. That he occasionally caught what he though was a hint of reciprocation in her speech and actions made it almost torture.

He didn't want to drink, in case he crawled into the bottle. He settled for a small cubicle where he could just sit in silence and alone, a luxury unavailable aboard the boat.

Costlow was excited when he returned. Jan recognized cheerfulness when he saw it and was impatient to find out what had changed.

Some time later, the three gathered on the command deck and sealed it off. "Talk to me, Warrant," Meka demanded.

"There's enough guidance systems to set a dozen charges. We can do this by remote," he said.

"No, we can't," Meka stated flatly.

"Shut up and wait," he snapped. "We program them to loiter outside sensor range, then do a high-velocity approach on schedule."

"Thereby running into sensor range and right into a defensive battery. I suppose you could hide a charge in a suit, but I doubt it would maneuver properly, and you couldn't program it to steer itself. We aren't using us to deliver from lack of resources, it's because we can get through and a drone can't. If you want to try to program them for a fourth target, do so. It can't hurt, unless of course you need them as decoys later."

Jan breathed deeply and slowly, feeling sick to his stomach. Crap, this was the worst experience of his life. Were they going to do this or not?

Costlow looked sheepish. "I thought I had it there. Sorry," he said.

"Don't apologize, sir," she replied. "The fact that you missed that means the Earthies think they are solid and can't be taken. This will work."

A depressed silence settled over them, but then Jan had a different thought. He cleared his throat.

"There's another factor," he said. "The crewed station might have viable oxy or escape pods. After Meka takes it out, she can hunker down and await rescue . . . there's a chance you could survive, Sis."

"Well, good!" Costlow said.

Meka flushed red. "Yes, but that's hardly fair to you two."

He shrugged. "What's fair? We do what we have to. After that, who can say?"

She looked at Jan. He smiled, of course, because he was glad of the possibility. He was also furious, nauseated, frightened, and there was nothing to say, except, "Good luck, then."

It was wholly inadequate. They were all lying, they all knew it, and it was just one more cold lump in the guts.

Two tediously painful days later, the two soldiers and the pilot gathered in the crew cabin once more. They checked off lists of essentials that had been requisitioned or borrowed, finalized the schedule, and prepared to start. The equipment made it fairly obvious what they planned.

"First order of business, clear the ship," Costlow said. He sounded the intercom for all hands, and everyone boiled in.

When they were clumped around him, he said, "We have a mission for which we must reduce mass and resources, so the rest of you are being temporarily put on The Rock. Grab what you need, but you need to be off by morning."

The crew and techs looked around at each other, at the three who would remain, and it was seconds only before Pilot Sereno said, "How much mass are you stripping?"

Costlow replied, "None yet. We'll be doing that later in the mission."

More looks crossed the cabin, thoughts being telegraphed. After an interminable time, Sereno said, "Yes, Warrant," and headed away. The others silently followed his lead.

Yeah, he knows, Jan thought.

Over the rest of the day, they returned, one by one, to make their cases. Every single member of the crew was determined to accompany the boat on its last mission. Death was to be feared, but staying behind was unbearable.

Sereno spent some time arguing with his superior that he was more expendable. While true, Costlow was the better pilot. He left dejected and angry.

Boat Engineer Jacqueline Jemayel had more success. She simply handed over a comm with her checklist, and said, "No one else has the years of training and familiarity to handle your hardware in combat. If you think you can handle that while flying, I'll leave." Costlow twitched and stalled, but relented to her logic and determination. They'd been friends and crew for a long time, and he was glad to have her along.

Engine Specialist Kurashima and Analyst Corporal Jackson got nowhere. Neither was needed for this. They might be needed on another vessel. Costlow wasn't taking anyone except Jemayel, and only because she did have a valid case. A good boat engineer was essential generally, and for this especially. He listened briefly to each of the others, wished them well and sent them packing. He was proud that his crew were so dedicated and determined, and he left recommendations for decorations in his final log file.

It was mere hours before departure time when the hatch beeped an authorized entry. They looked over as Melanie Sarendy swam in, followed by Sergeant Frank Otte, the equipment technician for the intelligence crew.

Costlow was annoyed, and snapped, "Sarendy, Otte, I ordered you to—"

She interrupted with a stern face, "Warrant, the *London* has Mod Six upgrades to its sensor suite. If you want to get close, then you need offensive systems as well as sensors. This is a recon boat, not a gunboat. I'm the best tech you're going to get, I can get you in there, and I'm coming along. Sergeant Otte is here to build a station for me on the flight deck, and modifications for offensive transmissions, then he's leaving." She moved to swim past them toward her station. How she'd found out the details was a mystery. No one had told her. Costlow blocked her. She looked determined and exasperated, until he held a hand out. "Welcome aboard, Sergeant," he acknowledged.

It took Otte, Jemayel, and Jan to build the devices necessary. Sarendy's requested station wasn't a standard item for a recon boat, and there were few spare parts aboard The Rock. Judicious cannibalization and improvisation yielded an effective, albeit ugly setup. Additional gear was used to build an offensive electronic suite, and some of it had obviously been stolen from other ships. As promised, Otte left, but not before trying desperately to convince them he was as necessary as Jemayel. He failed, but not for lack of determination.

4J23 departed immediately. The time left was useful for rehearsal and training, and those were best done without distractions. The short crew strapped in as Costlow cleared with Station Control, detached the umbilical, thereby cutting them off from communication, the boat being under transmission silence, and powered away.

It would avoid awkward goodbyes, also.

Meka began laying out gear for herself and Jan. They each would take their duty weapons. Jan had a demolition charge large enough for the structure in question. She took extra explosives and ammo. Both would carry their short swords, not so much from need but because it was traditional. They both required oxy bottles. He'd wear her maneuvering harness, she had a sled designed for clandestine missions. They had enough oxy mix, barely, to last them two days. That was tantalizingly close to enough oxy for a pickup, but still short. A boat might conceivably get into the vicinity in time, but rescue operations took time. If they could run this mission in the open...but of course, they couldn't.

Costlow spent the time getting trajectories from the navigation system. He needed to pass by two stations whose locations were approximate, get near the *London,* which was in a powered station orbit around the jump point, observe, plan an approach, execute the approach to stay unseen, and arrive at a precise point at an exact time with sufficient fuel for terminal maneuvers. Very terminal. He consulted with Sarendy as to detection equipment ranges and apertures to help plot his path. Jemayel tended the engines, life support, and astronautics. None of them spoke much.

Jan had little to do until his departure. He spent it moping, getting angry, and finally beating on the combat practice dummy for hours, twisting in microgravity. When Meka called him over to explain the gear, he was more than eager to just get things over with.

She showed him the mass of gear and began to go through it. He checked everything off with her. Weapons and gear needed little explanation. He was familiar with the technical details of her maneuvering harness and the munitions fuzes even though he'd never used them. The briefing would be far too short a distraction.

"We'll synch our chronos," Meka said.

"Goddess, don't give me a clock," Jan begged, shaking his head. "If I have to watch it count down, I'll be a basket case. Just put me there with some stuff to read and let me go." He spoke loudly, eyes wide, because the stress was getting to him.

"You need one in case the auto system fails," Meka said. "You're getting a triple load of ammo. It seems unlikely, but if anyone shows up to stop you—"

"Then I hold them off as long as I can."

"Right," Meka agreed.

Costlow showed the plotted course in a 3D, and asked, "We let you off here. Are you sure you can maneuver well enough for that distance?"

Shrugging, Jan replied, "End result is the same for me either way, but I'm sure. I do a lot of EVA. Unlike some people, I like it."

"Bite me, Bro," Meka replied and laughed, too loud from stress. She had always *hated* long EVA, and that's what this was.

She was assembling a pile of gear including her powered sled, two oxy bottles, the basic demolition blocks from everyone's standard gear plus her own larger pack, weapons and stuff the others wouldn't recognize. Her actions were trained, expert, and only a little shaky from tension. She'd done long trips in the dark before, and survived, but that didn't make it fun. She had her sled for this one, Jan was making a far shorter infiltration, and the boat wasn't her concern. She prepped everything, had Jan and Jemayel double check, and went through exercises to calm herself. Those didn't work for Jan.

With less than four hours until his departure, Jan sat staring at the bulkhead of the day cabin. His bunk was folded, and his few effects sealed in a locker. He'd recorded a message and written instructions, all of which made things rather final. He didn't feel thoroughly terrified yet, but did feel rather numb. Rest was impossible. He nodded briefly to Sarendy as she swam in, and tried not to dwell on her. It was all too easy to think of justifications to break the fraternization ban. He didn't need rejection or complications now, and the sympathy ploy was the only approach he could think of. It wouldn't work, as she was in the same boat as he, quite literally.

"Come back here," she said, gesturing with a hand. She turned and swam for her intel bay.

As he followed her in, she closed the hatch and dogged it. The bay was dimly lit by one emergency lamp, there being no need for its use at this time, and there was just enough room for the two of them inside the radius of couches and terminals set against the shell. While his brain tried to shift gears, she grabbed him by the shoulders and mashed her mouth against his while reaching to open her shipsuit. Both their hands fumbled for a few seconds, then his stopped and drew back while hers continued questing.

"Mehlnee," he muttered around her kiss. She drew her full lips back a bare few millimeters, and he continued, "I appreciate this . . . but it won't help me deal with . . . this."

"It helps me," she replied, voice breathy, and wrapped herself more tightly around him. Her lips danced over his throat and he decided not to argue with her logic. His hands were on the sinuous curves of her golden-skinned hips, and long-held fantasies solidified into reality. Frantic, unrequited lust made thought impossible, and that was a good thing right then.

Jan was first out. He doffed his shipsuit and donned his hard vacsuit, intended for short duration EVA maintenance and not the best for this mission. It was what he had, though. Meka's assault harness fit snugly over it and would provide thrust. Three bottles rode his back, two oxy-helium, one nitrogen for the harness. His rifle and clips were along the right bottle, and his comm on his wrist, programmed with everything he needed. Strapped to his chest was a large, bulky pack with over twenty kilos of modern military hyper-explosive. It would be more than enough for the station in question.

Melanie and Meka checked him over and helped him into the bay. The other two were busy on the flight deck. Ignoring his sister's presence, Melanie kissed him hard and deeply. He kissed back, shaking, wanting to leave before the whole situation caused him to go insane. Meka waited until Sarendy was done, then clutched him briefly. "Good luck," she said.

"Good hunting," he replied.

Behind him he heard, "Oh, I will," as the hatch closed.

Jan stared out the open bay into cold black space with cold, bright pinpoints of light. "God and Goddess, I don't want to do this," he muttered. His stomach boiled and churned, and he wished he'd filled his water bottle with straight alcohol. Even the double dose of tranquilizers was not enough to keep him calm.

A light winked once, twice, then a third time, and he jumped out briskly, feeling the harness shove him in a braking maneuver. He was immediately thankful for the suit's plumbing, and his brain went numb. *I'm dead now*, was all he could think.

The station Jan was attacking would note the passage of the anomaly that was the boat as well as it could, and report later. Meka's target was more complicated. It was crewed, and they would react if they saw her. She'd have to ride her sled for some distance and most of a day, and try to time it for a covert approach. That might be the hardest part of this mission.

In the maintenance bay, she strapped herself to her sled and had Jemayel check her over. With a final thumbs up and a lingering hug, she turned to her controls and counted seconds down to her launch.

The boat passed through the volume as stealthed as possible, oriented so the bay opened away from the station's sensors. There were no emissions, only the operating radiation and a bare hint of the powerplant. Her braking thrust was hidden by the mass of the boat and should be almost invisible at this distance. That should put her right on top of the station at Earth clock 1130 the next day, when the crew would hopefully be at lunch.

Once the vibration and heavy gees tapered off, she checked her instruments and took a trank. It would be a long wait, and very eerie in complete silence and blackness.

And now I'm dead, she thought.

Sarendy reported when they were outside the known range of the station, and Costlow waited a planned extra hour before bringing up the plant and engines. He wanted to be lost in background noise.

The thrust built steadily in a rumbling hiss through the frame. Most of the impulse would be used now, with only enough left for margin and maneuvers. That would simplify the approach by minimizing emissions then. The velocity increased to a level the boat had rarely used, and he nodded to his remaining crew as they completed the maneuver. Now they had to wait.

"Anyone for a game of Chess?" he asked.

Jan watched for the station. It was a black mass against black space, and he was glad to see it occult stars. He'd been afraid the intel was wrong and he was sailing off into space for nothing. Odd to feel relieved to see the approaching cause of one's death, he thought. It had been a three-hour trip, and he was hungry. He would stay that way for the next day and a half because his suit was intended for maintenance EVAs only, not infiltration, and had no way to supply food. So much for the condemned's last meal. Then, there was the irony that his boat had IDed this particular piece of equipment, which is why it was on the list, and why he was here.

The occultation grew, and he got ready to maneuver for docking, landing, whatever it was called in this case. He switched on the astrogation controls, adjusted his flight toward it, then braked relative. He was tense, lest the reports be inaccurate and the station blast him with a defense array, but nothing happened. He

didn't overshoot, but did approach obliquely and had to correct
for touchdown.

There was no one and nothing nearby, which was as expected.
He snapped a contact patch out, slapped it to the surface, and
attached his line. There were no regular padeyes on the unit.

A short orientation revealed where the power cell was. He
planted the standoff over it and slapped it down with another
contact patch. When it triggered, the blast would turn a plate of
metal beneath it into plasma and punch it through the shell into
the power cell. He armed it, and all he had left to do was defend
it against what appeared to be nothing, wait until it detonated
and die with it. Simple on file. Doing it didn't seem quite that
by the numbers.

At first, he was terrified of being near the charge. He realized it
was silly, as it would kill him anyway, and if it didn't, suffocation
would. He compromised between fear and practicality by hiding
over the horizon of the small, angled object. It was a bare three
meters across, five meters long, and almost featureless except for a
docking clamp inset at one end. Its signals were all burst through a
translucent one-way window. He longed to tear into it for the sheer
joy of discovering if the intel briefs were correct about this model,
but that might give him away. He'd sit and wait.

He did have emgee, and a suit, and a tether. He decided to
rest floating free. The technique had helped him before when
stressed. He stared out at the stars and the distant pointy glare
of Iota Persei, their star, and fell into a deep sleep, disturbed by
odd dreams.

Meka approached the station gradually. She'd have to leave
her sled behind and finish the trip in just her suit to avoid
detection. While a bedecked suit would register as maintenance
or a refugee with the sensors, the sled would trigger alarms as
an approaching threat even if the enemy didn't have knowledge
of the precise design. She made one last correction to her orbit,
set the autopilot, pulled the releases, and drifted loose from the
frame. Her minuscule lateral velocity should be of negligible effect.

The sled burped gently away on gas jets rather than engines
and would hopefully never be detectable to the station. It was
near 0800 by Earth clock, and another three hours should bring
her quite close. That's when it would become tricky.

First, she'd have to maneuver with an improvised thruster. Jan had her harness, she had only a nitrogen bottle and a momentary valve. He'd—hopefully—made his approach with power but no navigation. She had the navigation gear in her helmet, but improvised power. The risks they were taking would cause a safety officer to run gibbering in insanity. On the other hand, they were dead either way.

There was also the substantial risk of the station noting her approach to its crew. They might await her, or send someone to investigate, or shoot her outright. She was betting against the last, but it was just that—a bet. If they met her, it meant a fight. She would win one on one against anybody she faced, but the station might have up to twenty crew. It was effectively a large recon boat with maneuvering engines, and she didn't relish a fight within.

Unlike her previous long EVAs, she was relaxed and calm. Perhaps it was experience. Maybe it was the complexity of the task and the associated thought that kept her too busy to worry. Perhaps it was fatalism. As she neared her target, more issues interfered and she dropped all those thoughts.

There were no obvious signs of disturbance as she approached. That meant that if they did see her for what she was, they were at least holding their fire. She checked her weapon again by touch and began readying her muscles for a fight. If someone met her, she'd go along peacefully to the airlock, then start smashing things and killing on her way inside.

Nothing happened. Either the station's sensors didn't see her, or they assumed she was performing maintenance and ignored her. It was good to see the intel was accurate, but it still felt odd that her presence wasn't even reported. Perhaps it was and they were waiting for her. Dammit, no second guessing.

She was close enough to think about maneuvering now, and there were still no signs of enemy notice. The nitrogen bottle beside her breathing bottle was plumbed into a veritable snakepit of piping Jan had built for her, that ended front and back at shoulders and hips, much like a proper emgee harness. She hoped the improvised controls worked so she wouldn't have to attempt it by hand. Her record on manual approaches was less than perfect.

She vented a pulse of gas and the harness worked as planned. Two more short ones brought her to a bare drift. She sent more thoughts of thanks after her brother, who had turned out to be essential to almost every mission she'd fought in this war. His technical skill in every field was simply genius.

She managed a gentle touchdown on the station hull, letting her legs bend and soak up momentum. She caught her breath, got her bearings, and went straight to work. She had no idea how long she could go unnoticed.

She placed the prebuilt charges with a rapidity born of years of practice. Each charge was designed to punch a hole into a compartment, hopefully voiding them all and killing the occupants instantly. She danced softly across the hull to avoid noise inside that might give her away, swapping tethers as she went, and planted them precisely with the aid of thoughtfully provided frame numbers. Magnetic boots would have made it easier... if the shell had been an iron alloy and if clanking noises didn't matter.

She caught movement out of the corner of her eye. She pivoted to see a UN spacer in gear, staring at her in surprise.

Her combat reflexes took over. He was unarmed, meaning he was conducting routine maintenance or inspections. It was possible he wore a camera that was observable inside on a monitor, and he would definitely report her as soon as he recovered from the oddity of the situation. She twisted her right arm to unsling, then pointed her rifle and shot him through the faceplate.

The eruption of atmosphere and vaporized blood indicated he was dead. She put two more bullets through him to make sure, the effect eerie in the silence. The recoil of the weapon was mild, but with no gravity or atmosphere it started her tumbling. She steadied out with a grasp of her tether and brought herself back the half meter to the shell. Now what?

Her pulse hammered and her breath rasped. Despite the massive damage and casualties she'd caused in her career, it was only the second time she'd killed someone directly and up close. She forced her emotions into quiescence and considered the situation. If he'd reported her, she had seconds to deal with it. If not, she had a little longer before he was missed. If she killed the crew early, they might miss a scheduled report and the secrecy of her mission would be compromised. If she waited, they could report her presence. She didn't see much of a choice.

Her fingers activated the system through her comm, she paused a second to confirm the readings, and then detonated the charges.

If the atmosphere gushing from her enemy's helmet had been

impressive, this was awe-inspiring. Brilliant bursts of white were swallowed by fountains of spewing air and debris. The station shook beneath her feet as the hull adjusted to lost pressure. Anyone not in a suit should be dead. Now to hope no report was expected before her mission zero time. It was a long shot, but all she had. And it was unlikely that the omission would be considered more than a minor problem at first.

Costlow was a first-class pilot, but this would strain even his capabilities. The astronautics would take over for evasive maneuvers only. The approach would be manual.

While there was a timed window for attacks, the closer together they were the better. Any hint of action would alert the enemy and reduce the odds of success for others. He wanted to time this to the second, as much as possible. To avoid detection, he had to rely on passive sensors operated by Sarendy across from him. Passive sensors didn't give as accurate a picture as active ones, which meant he'd have to correct the timing in flight. As he would approach at a velocity near the maximum physics and Jemayel's bypassed safeties would allow, that left little time for corrections. He wanted to get inside their weapons' envelope and right against the skin before they deduced what he was. That also increased the risk of their particle watch picking him up, assuming him to be an incoming passive threat, and shooting preemptively.

They were only a few hours from target, and he'd already brought them around in a long loop behind the *London*'s engines. The emissions from them would mask their approach in ionized scatter. He wondered again just how hard this would have been without Sarendy, Jan and Otte. Sarendy was pulling all her intel from the sensors up to the flight deck and using it to assist in astrogation, and was preparing a counterintel system for use when they were detected, and would utilize the active sensor antennas as offensive transmitters. He hadn't realized that was even possible, but Sarendy was a witch with sensors, Jan an expert on improvising hardware, and Otte had kept up with both of their orders and put the system together. Amazing. If a crew had ever earned its decorations, this one had.

"Your turn, Warrant," Sarendy reminded him.

Right. Chess. "Um..." He moved his queen, looked at the

board with satisfaction, and leaned back. Her rook's capture of his queen and declaration of checkmate stunned him.

"Perhaps we should stop now," he suggested. "I didn't see that coming and I have no idea what you did. And both my bishops are on white."

"They are?" she asked. "So they are. Let's call it a game."

Meka swam through the main corridor, counting bodies with faces reminiscent of dead fish, and checked that every compartment was open to vacuum. Nodding to herself, ignoring the grisly scenes, she made her way to the powerplant and unlimbered the large charge on her chest. In seconds it was armed, placed, and she swam back out to face the outer hatch. Little to do now but wait.

She wondered how other troops and units had done. Was anyone trying to retake the captured Freehold facilities? Or to destroy them outright? Would the attacks be successful, and allow the presumed counter to work? Would they win?

She'd never know. She could only wish them luck.

Jan awoke with a start. Guilt flooded over the adrenaline, as he realized he'd slept past when he was supposed to be on guard. He shrugged and decided it didn't matter, as the chance of anyone interfering was incredibly remote. It still bothered him.

It was close to deadline, and he realized he didn't even know what this operation was called, only that it probably involved the entire system, aimed for infrastructure, and was suicidal. That was probably enough.

He still had a couple of hours of oxy.

Hypoxia/anoxia would be pretty painless. A little struggle for breath...he could take those two hours. It wasn't impossible a rescue vessel might show up. It just took a hell of a lot of zeros to make the odds. Two extra hours of life, though.

He decided he didn't have whatever it took to let himself die slowly. He was already shivering in shock; the tranks were wearing off.

He snagged the tether and dragged himself hand over hand to the station. He hooked to the contact patch near the charge. The only thing worse than being blown to dust, he thought, would be to be injured by it and linger for hours in pain. He wished Meka luck, aching to know if she'd make it. That hurt as much as anything else. There were fewer zeros on her odds, but they were still ludicrously remote. Their mission was to smash enemy infrastructure, not occupy and set up housekeeping.

There was nothing left. He settled down to read, gave up because he couldn't focus, and turned on music to break the eerie silence. If he had to die, he wanted it to be painless and instantaneous.

When the charge underneath him detonated, he got his final wish.

Costlow sweated, with aching joints and gritty eyeballs from sitting far too long at the controls. He watched the display in his helmet, trying to ignore the way the helmet abraded behind his left ear, and made another minute flight correction. He had minutes left to live.

4J23 was close behind the *London*, and undiscovered as far as they knew. Sarendy screwed with their emissions, inverted incoming scans, sent out bursts low enough in energy to pass as typical, powerful enough to keep them hidden and the gods only knew what else. He wished there were some way to record her competence. She was a fifteen-year-old kid, and likely knew more about her job than all her instructors combined. Add in her bravery, and she deserved ten medals.

No, he thought, she deserved to live. Rage filled him again.

He forced the thoughts back to his mission. He was hungry and thirsty, but he daren't pause to do either. This could all come down to a fractional second's attention. Especially now that they were so close.

He brought *4J23* in in a tight, twisting curve from the blind spot behind the drives, and aimed along the approaching superstructure. *London*'s defenses found him, and a launch warning flashed in his visor. It missed because Sarendy switched to active jamming and burned its sensors out with a beam that should have been impossible from a recon boat and would almost fry an asteroid to vapor. The brute force approach was an indication that all her tricks were exhausted, and it was doubtful they could avoid another attack. He flinched as the missile flashed past, even though it was detectable only as an icon in his visor, and heard a cry of sheer terror start quietly and build. He realized it was his voice. He'd wet himself, and was embarrassed, even though he understood the process. He could hear Sarendy panting for breath, hyperventilating behind him, and wondered what Jemayel was doing in the stern. His eyes flicked to the count in his visor—

Now.

Alongside the *London*, within meters of her hull and at closest approach to her command center, a small powerplant overloaded and detonated. It was enough to overwhelm her forcescreens, vaporize her forward half, and shatter the rest in a moment so brief as to be incomprehensible. One hundred UN spacers were turned into incandescent plasma by the blast, along with the three Freeholders.

Meka watched the seconds tick away in her visor. She dropped her left hand and grasped the manual trigger, set it, and held on. It would blow if she let go, or on schedule, and her work was almost done. The count worked down, and she closed her eyes, faced "up" and took a deep breath to steady herself. She opened them again to see it count 3 . . . 2 . . . 1—

Whether her thumb released or the timer acted first was irrelevant. The blast damaged the station's fusion plant, which shut down automatically, even as it vented to space. She felt the cracking and rumbling of the structure through her body, fading away to nothing. It would take a dockyard to repair that, and they'd have to remove the wreckage first. She moved back toward the powerplant, navigating by touch in the dust, and dragged herself around several supports twisted by the blast. She entered the engineering module and waited. The particles cleared very slowly, as there was neither airflow nor gravity. It all depended on static charges and surface tension to draw things out of vacuum, and Meka stayed stock still until she could get a good look through her faceplate, cycling through visible, enhanced and IR to build a good picture. She nodded in approval of the damage. The blast and fusion bottle failure had slagged half the module.

Her task was now done, but she had no desire to die immediately. She could have embraced the charge on the reactor and gone with it. Her rationale had been that she should be certain, although the charge had been three times larger than she'd calculated as necessary. The truth was, she couldn't bring herself to do it. Death might be inevitable, but she still feared it.

She studied the life support system whimsically. Without a

proper deckplan, she'd just vented every compartment from outside to be sure. Her charge over this one had punched into the makeup tank. There was a functional air recycling plant, but no oxygen. A meter in any direction...

There were no escape bubbles. This was a station, not a ship. If damaged, the crew would seal as needed and call for help. She'd fixed that when she vented atmosphere. There were extra suit oxy bottles, but the fittings didn't match. Even if they did, there was no heat, and her suit powerpack was nearing depletion. Jan would easily have cobbled something together or tacked a patch over the hole in life support and used the suit bottles, but even if she could do so before her own gas ran out, it still meant waiting and hoping for a rescue that would likely never come. There was no commo capability, of course. That had been her prime target. No one knew to look for her. The remote possibility of rescue they'd discussed had been for Jan's benefit, to let him hope she might survive. He'd probably figured out the lie by now.

With time and nothing better to do, she planted charges on every hatch, every port, every system. She fired bullets liberally to smash controls and equipment; wedged the airlocks with grenades to shatter the seals and render them useless. Even the spare parts inventory was either destroyed or blown into space.

Finally, she sat outside on the ruined shell, watching her oxy gauge trickle toward empty. Her weapons were scattered around her, some lazily drifting free in the emgee, each rendered inoperable and unsalvageable, all save one. She really had harbored an unrealistic hope that there'd be some way out of this and cried in loneliness. There was no one to see her, and it wasn't the first time she'd cried on a mission. Blazers didn't look down on tears and fear, only on failure. She had not failed.

The stillness and silence was palpable and eerie. She brought up her system and cycled through her music choices. Yes, that would do nicely. *La Villa Strangiato*. The coordination and sheer skill impressed her, and the energy in the performance was powerful and moving. It filled the last five-hundred seconds and faded out. Silence returned.

A warning flashed in her visor and sounded in her ears, becoming more and more tinny as oxygen was depleted. She'd black out in about a hundred seconds.

One thing she'd always wondered was how far her courage went. People died all the time. Soldiers died when ordered to fight and the odds ran out. Sick people died because life was not worth living.

But, could she die by choice? Her courage had been tested throughout her career, and this last year to an extreme. But did she have the strength to pull that switch herself?

After prolonging the inevitable this long, it was rather moot, but her life wouldn't be complete without the experiment. She armed the grenade, stared at it as her body burned from hypoxia, and tried to force her hand to open. Lungs empty now, she gritted her teeth, pursed her lips, and threw every nerve into the effort. Her wrist shook, thumb moving bit by bit. Willpower or self-preservation?

She was still conscious, though groggy, as her thumb came free and the fuse caught. Three seconds. Hypoxia segued to anoxia and her thoughts began to fade. The last one caused a triumphant smile to cross her face, even as tears pooled in her eyes.

Willpower.

On slabs of green and black marble in Freedom Park are the names of two hundred and sixteen soldiers who accepted orders they could not understand and knew meant their deaths. Words were said, prayers offered, and torches and guards of honor stand eternal watch over them. Their families received pensions, salutes and bright metal decorations on plain green ribbons, presented in inlaid wooden boxes.

One family received two.

ABOUT THE AUTHORS

Jamie Ibson is from the frozen wastelands of Canuckistan, where moose, bears, and geese battle for domination among the hockey rinks, igloos, and Tim Hortons. After joining the Canadian army reserves in high school, he spent half of 2001 in Bosnia as a peacekeeper and came home shortly after 9/11 with a deep sense of foreboding. After graduating college, he landed a job in law enforcement and has been posted to the left coast since 2007. He published a number of short stories in 2018 and 2019, and he released his first novel in January 2020. He's pretty much been making it up as he goes along, although he has numerous writer friends who serve as excellent role models, mentors, and, occasionally, cautionary tales. His website can be found at ibsonwrites.ca. He is married to the lovely Michelle, and they have cats.

Jonathon D. Green is an IT professional as well as a part time machinist, crafter, knitter, martial artist and leather worker. Other than the story in this anthology, he has written a short adventure for *Spider-Woman* for Marvel and co-scripted *The First Death*, the Anita Blake Vampire Hunter comic, with his wife. He currently resides in St. Louis, and dreams of the Ocean.

Kevin J. Anderson has published more than 170 books, 56 of which have been national or international bestsellers. He has written numerous novels in the *Star Wars*, *X-Files*, and *Dune* universes, as well as unique steampunk fantasy novels *Clockwork Angels* and *Clockwork Lives*, written with legendary rock drummer Neil Peart, based on the concept album by the band Rush.

His original works include the Saga of Seven Suns series, the Terra Incognita fantasy trilogy, the Saga of Shadows trilogy, and his humorous horror series featuring Dan Shamble, Zombie PI. He has edited numerous anthologies, written comics and games, and the lyrics to two rock CDs. Anderson and his wife Rebecca Moesta are the publishers of WordFire Press. His most recent novels are *Stake*, *Kill Zone*, and *Spine of the Dragon*.

Kevin Ikenberry is a lifelong space geek and retired Army officer. As an adult, he managed the U.S. Space Camp program and served as a space operations officer before the Space Force was a thing. He's an international bestselling author, award finalist, and a core author in the wildly successful Four Horsemen Universe. His eleven novels include *Sleeper Protocol*, *Vendetta Protocol*, *Runs In The Family*, *Peacemaker*, *Honor The Threat*, *Stand or Fall*, *Deathangel* and *Fields Of Fire*. He's co-written several novels with amazing authors. He is an Active Member of SIGMA—the science fiction think tank.

Jessica Schlenker holds an M.S. in Information Security and Assurance, a bevy of industry certifications, and a B.S. in biology. She works as a professional nerd in the field of IT Security. Sadly, she is too much of a white hat to actually combine these specialties into creating her own cyborg army. But she's thought about it.

Jaime DiNote is a veteran of the Florida Army National Guard and US Army Reserves and has mobilized for Operation Noble Eagle, providing air defense over the National Capitol Region. She holds a BA in Criminal Justice from Seattle University. She is currently residing in the Florida Panhandle as a full-time Air Force spouse to husband, and usual co-author, Chris, and as stay-at-home-mom to their daughter Remy. This is her first solo publication.

William McCaskey is a veteran of the United States Army, with an MS in Homeland Security and Emergency Management, who traded in the hot and sandy for the hot and humid of central Florida with his family, dogs, and a very demanding feline overlord. In his free time, he enjoys honing his martial arts skills while imparting a few of them, traveling, and scuba diving. William made his debut with the science fiction novel *Dragon Two-Zero* and is co-editor of the bestselling anthology *Fantastic Hope*.

Justin Watson grew up an Army brat, living in Germany, Alabama, Texas, Korea, Colorado and Alaska, and fed on a steady diet of *X-Men, Star Trek*, Robert Heinlein, DragonLance, and *Babylon 5*. While attending West Point, he met his future wife, Michele, on an airplane, and soon began writing in earnest with her encouragement. In 2005 he graduated from West Point and served as a field artillery officer, completing combat tours in Iraq and Afghanistan, and earning the Bronze Star, Purple Heart and the Combat Action Badge.

Medically retired from the Army in 2015, Justin settled in Houston with Michele, their four children and an excessively friendly Old English Sheepdog.

J.F. Holmes is a retired Army Senior Noncommissioned Officer, having served for twenty-two years in both the Regular Army and Army National Guard. During that time, he served as everything from an artillery section leader to a member of a Division level planning staff, with tours in Cuba and Iraq, as well as responding to the terrorist attacks in NYC on 9/11.

From 2010 to 2014 he wrote the immensely popular military cartoon strip, "Power Point Ranger," poking fun at military life in the tradition of Beetle Bailey and Willy & Joe.

His books range from Military Sci-Fi to Space Opera to Detective to Fantasy, with a lot in between, and in 2017 two were finalists for the prestigious Dragon Awards. As of August 2020, Mr. Holmes has nineteen books and two novellas published.

In 2018, he launched Cannon Publishing, specializing in science fiction and military science fiction.

Jason Cordova is a 2015 John W. Campbell Award finalist and a 2019 Dragon Award finalist. Author of the popular "Kin Wars Saga," he has been featured in previous Freehold anthologies. A US Navy veteran, Jason currently lives in Virginia.

Christopher "MOGS" DiNote, has served over twenty-one years in the United States Air Force and Air National Guard (Pennsylvania and Ohio). He has deployed for Operations Enduring Freedom, Iraqi Freedom, and Noble Eagle. Chris is a graduate of the US Air Force Academy and the USAF Weapons School. He holds an M.A. in Military History from Norwich University, and a Master's in Strategic Studies from the Air War College. Chris also plays saxophone and bass guitar and has performed in several bands. He was born in Philadelphia PA, raised in South Jersey, and currently resides in the Florida Panhandle with his wife and usual co-author Jaime, and their daughter Remy. This is his second work of fiction.

Philip Wohlrab has spent time in the United States Coast Guard and has served for more than fourteen years in the Virginia Army National Guard. Serving as a medic attached to an infantry company, he earned the title "Doc" the hard way while serving across two tours in Iraq. He came home and continued his education, earning a Master of Public Health degree in 2016. He currently works as a DoD contractor designing wargames for the United States Air Force and with occasional work for the United States Space Force. He also does game design work for the civilian market.

ABOUT THE EDITOR:

Michael Z. Williamson is variously an immigrant from the UK and Canada; a retired veteran of the US Army and US Air Force with service in the Middle East; a consultant on disaster preparedness and military matters to private clients, manufacturers, TV and movie productions and occasionally DoD elements; bladesmith; award-winning and best-selling editor and author. His hobby of collecting weapons has led him into an arms race in which he outguns Barbados and Iceland, so far.